AF425435

Praise For

Anyone But Her

"A psychological, edge-of-your-seat thriller set in Denver with a twist you won't see coming!" — Colorado Humanities, Thriller Selection Committee for 2025 Colorado Book Awards (Winner: Thriller)

"If you're going to write a novel that uses Denver as its setting, here's how you do it...Not only is it a treat to turn these pages on the merits of their own suspenseful mystery, it's also a blast to feel the atmosphere of old Denver drift out of each scene." — *Westword*, 2025 Best of Denver, "Best Nationally Published Novel"

2025 Finalist, Mystery/Thriller — WILLA Award, Women Writing the West

2024 Best Mystery/Thriller — Indie Author Project

"Great psychological mystery...Just a bit spooky, too." — Colorado Public Radio "Books We Love," 2024

"Suzanne's story, both past and present, is an unflinching portrayal of a family gone haywire, when, in the face of tragedy, communication lacks and secrecy builds." — *BookLife*

"Cynthia Swanson excels in creating evocative, compelling scenarios...highly recommended for novel readers seeking disparate characters and twists and turns that are not easily predictable." — *Midwest Book Review*

"Masterfully crafted, distinctly Denver, and a must-read for anyone who loves a gripping, edge-of-your-seat mystery." — *Denver Life*

"Drop the needle on *Anyone But Her* and you won't want to stop until the last fade-out. Like any great album—and I'm talking vinyl—there are two great sides to this smoothly-written story, and they come together, past and present, to tell a gripping tale. Cynthia Swanson's latest is top of the charts." — Mark Stevens, author of *The Fireballer* and The Allison Coil Mystery Series

"*Anyone But Her* crackles with suspense and shines a light on how far we will go to protect the people we love. Swanson tackles the elusive search for identity and the many faces of motherhood. Sometimes the ghosts from our past can illuminate the way forward and ultimately reveal how little we know about our families and ourselves. This is a brilliant, beautifully crafted novel that will give readers complex characters to root for and book clubs plenty to discuss." — Nancy Johnson, author of *The Kindest Lie*

"*Anyone But Her* is psychological suspense at its finest—taut and tender, with characters who feel so real we care deeply about every twist. Swanson's latest is a moving and brilliantly crafted mother-daughter mystery about love, loyalty, and making peace with the past. A beautiful, unforgettable novel." — Amy Mason Doan, bestselling author of *Lady Sunshine* and *The California Dreamers*

"Conflicted emotions leap from the page in Swanson's remarkable new novel, *Anyone But Her*. Skilled storytelling coupled with vibrant characters enchant and entertain in this dual timeline narrative that follows a determined daughter and a loving mother as they seek the truth and understanding in the aftermath of tragedy." — Eldonna Edwards, bestselling author of *This I Know* and *Clover Blue*

"A frightening and gripping path to the truth...a tale that is enriched with details on the music of the time and the feeling of enduring love. For all who love a solid mystery." — *firstClue Reviews*

Anyone But Her

Cynthia Swanson

Columbine York

First edition September 2024
LCCN: 2024913022
ISBN 979-8-9908074-2-6
ISBN 979-8-9908074-1-9 (ebook)

For Sammy

There's no one but you.

Rocky Mountain News

Friday, August 27, 2004

DENVER WOMAN MISSING

Denver police are asking for the public's help in locating 18-year-old Darcy Powles, who has been missing since Tuesday. Powles was last seen getting into a red Honda Accord, license plate 321-HTH, owned by Robert Shelton Jr., 25, whom Powles reportedly was dating.

Shelton has several past convictions, including burglary, forgery, and disorderly conduct. Police ask that anyone with information about his or Powles's whereabouts contact the police hotline.

1

1979

My mother first spoke to me from the grave on an August night shortly after my father began dating Peggy. Mom arrived on a whisper, laden with intention.

"Suzanne." Her voice broke through the stillness in my room. "It's me."

Reflexively, I opened my eyes—but it wasn't with them that I saw her. I simply *knew* she was there—and for a moment, it felt like time before. Like she was just checking on me before turning in for the night. I was fourteen years old, and until February twenty-second, my mother had checked on me every night of my life. Leaning close, whispering that she loved me, that I was her everything.

A smile broke across my face. "You're *here*!"

"Shh." I felt rather than saw her press a finger to her lips. "You'll wake him."

Her attention turned to my six-year-old brother, Chris, who was tangled in a crimson-colored sleeping bag on the floor. Chris had his own room, next door to mine, but ever since we lost Mom, he often wandered into my room like a sleepwalker and collapsed on my floor. He slept fitfully and woke up crying, crawling into my bed and letting me hold him as he talked about nightmare demons, trolls, dragons—all of whom, Chris explained, waved firearms but never actually shot anything. "They just *look* like they will," he said.

Chris rolled over, his breath ragged, but didn't awaken. "But you finally came," I whispered to Mom. "I *knew* you would."

"I expect you did, my little seer."

Mom had always called me her "little seer." Our Queen Anne Victorian house in Denver's Capitol Hill neighborhood was built in 1888, and inside its walls spirits regularly appeared to me like decades flowing through the ancient rooms. Not far from home was Cheesman Park, which had been built on a desecrated paupers' graveyard; rumors of ghosts abounded. When I was small, Mom would take me on twilight walks in the park. "Tell me what you see, Suze," she'd implore.

Toddling after her, using my limited vocabulary, I'd attempt to explain that I didn't actually *see* ghosts with my eyes. Rather, I envisioned some essence of them—something more than light but less than human. Energy, you might call it, an energy that manifested in impressions, whispers, shadows cast on floor or field.

"I believe you, my little seer," Mom would reply. "I wish it happened for me, too."

Since her death, I'd been expecting Mom to show up. Not alive, but more real than she'd been since the night six months ago when a lowlife junkie named Robert Shelton entered Zoe's Records, Mom's hole-in-the-wall record store on Colfax Avenue, demanded all her cash, and wound up shooting her three times in the chest.

One, two, three.

I felt those three bullets—a lot. Felt their searing heat. Since Mom's death, I always slept on my side. I couldn't be chest up—too vulnerable. And I couldn't be chest down. Too painful.

I closed my eyes, knowing I could better focus on Mom's ghost that way. She spoke more distinctly than any spirit I'd ever sensed, using Mom's warm, round voice—like the sun speaking. I felt the presence of her long, honey-brown hair and amber eyes, her narrow shoulders and wide hips. Three scarlet blossoms, like red anemones, burst across the front of her faded flannel shirt. Knowing she sensed *me* sensing *them*, I heard her say, "I'm sorry about those. I can't seem to make them go away."

Opening my eyes, swallowing the lump in my throat, I said, "It's okay."

I felt her hand brush across my forehead. "You're beautiful as ever, Suzie Blue."

"I've been waiting," I said. "Why didn't you come sooner?"

"I couldn't." She paused. "You know, when I was alive, I was uncertain what the afterlife would bring, but somehow I didn't think it would be this. On this side, nothing's in your control."

"That must be a hardship for you," I said, and she laughed.

I pressed a hand to my chest. "I miss you so much, Mom. It's not the same without you."

"I think that's why I'm here. Because of tonight."

"What about tonight?"

Mom paused again. "I saw your dad with that woman. That Peggy Hicks."

"Oh," I replied.

Dad and Peggy had been dating for a few weeks. It seemed hasty, but it wasn't as if Dad and Peggy had just met. He'd introduced Chris and me to Peggy back in December, when our parents temporarily split up—a "trial separation," Mom had called it. Over dinner the week before Christmas break, he'd told us Peggy had been his girlfriend in high school and they'd reconnected at their twentieth reunion in the fall.

"Are you seeing her now?" I'd asked.

"No." Wiping his mouth, letting his napkin flutter onto his plate, Dad stood. "I'm disinterested in dating. I want your mother back. You know that, Suze."

Yeah. I knew that.

But then Mom died.

For several months after my mother's funeral, Peggy appeared every week or two, bearing food. If I answered the door, I thanked her but said little else. When Dad was home, he'd invite her to chat. Sometimes

I overheard him throwing out one of his obscure little facts, like telling Peggy when she brought a blueberry pie that he was glad it wasn't cherry because Zachary Taylor, the twelfth U.S. president, had died from eating too many cherries in one sitting. When he talked like that, Peggy's laughter was hearty, echoing through the halls of my mother's house.

As spring crackled into summer, there might have been an uptick in Peggy's visits; it wasn't something I'd paid attention to. I was too busy stumbling through each day, feeling like my head and heart were on fire, to notice who brought us covered dishes of meatloaf or macaroni and cheese.

Then one July night, Dad told me he was having dinner with Peggy. He whistled as he high-stepped toward the garage. From the back door, I called out, "Dad? Is this a date?"

He turned, his eyes meeting mine. "If it is, then Clotho, the spinner of fates, will decide its outcome," he said.

Now, in my room, my mother said, "Honeypie, I don't want your dad to be lonely. Despite everything we went through, I'd never want that. But this woman...there's something about her." After a beat, she asked, "What do *you* think of her, Suzie Blue?"

I shrugged. "She's okay."

"Actually..." Mom's voice lowered. "She's not."

I felt her rise, step over Chris's sleeping form, and touch his forehead the way she'd touched mine. He didn't stir. Her energy moved toward the window, and it seemed she was looking out on the street.

"Peggy is not okay," she repeated. "And I think I'm here because I need your help fixing it."

"Fixing it? What do you mean?"

I felt her turn to face me. "Last year, after their high school reunion," she said. "After I met Peggy, I told your father—and it was a joke then, Suze, a joke—I told him that if I died, I wanted him to remarry. I said he could marry anyone he wanted, anyone at all, except..."

I waited.

"I told him that he could *not* marry Peggy." In an instant, she was across the room; I sensed her heat beside me and I leaned toward it.

"Do you understand what I'm saying, Suzie Blue?" Mom asked. "I told him he could marry anyone but her."

2

2004

The footsteps I heard were light, as if they belonged to a house cat or a stealthy fox. Stevie heard them, too; she whined and strained against her leash. Our new house's deadbolt had been locked when we arrived; I'd opened it with the key we received at closing. The rooms were empty, the August air inside close. Despite the house's age, I sensed no spiritual presence; what I heard was earthly. Had to be an animal, I thought, bending down to stroke the soft fur behind Stevie's ears.

Turning to my husband, Brett, as he stepped inside the house, I asked, "Did you hear those footsteps?"

He shook his head. "Footsteps?"

I glanced at our blue merle Australian Shepherd. "Stevie heard them, too."

"I'll look around, Suze," Brett said.

As he went down the hall, Stevie and I stepped forward, her toenails clicking and my footfalls echoing on the hardwoods. I pressed a hand against my collarbone—an ancient, ritualistic practice of mine. The house, a Denver Square, was about two miles east of my childhood home. With its square shape and simple layout, the Denver Square was unlike my family's ornate Victorian, yet its character reminded me of my childhood home. The original woodwork and built-ins. The stained glass. The front porch running the width of the house.

Stevie tugged on her leash. In the kitchen, I opened the back door to let her into the fenced yard. But when she put her nose to the threshold, I pulled her leash back.

On our doorstep was something lumpy and gray. Appearing behind me, Brett said, "I didn't see anything." His gaze followed mine toward the floor. "Ugh, what's *that*?"

I crouched, examining what was before me. Then I looked up.

"It's a rat," I said. "A dead rat."

I last lived in Denver in 1982. That fall I began my freshman year at the University of California, Berkeley. Not once did I look back.

I visited, of course. Spent brief vacations with my family. Assured myself that my baby brother was thriving, robust as a favorite houseplant. But every year I scoured the Bay Area for summer jobs and internships so I could stay in California, with no retreat to Colorado.

At Berkeley, I resolved to embrace the intellectual, the pragmatic. I joined student government and majored in business administration. I met a boy with kind eyes and strong shoulders, the type of boy that girls call on when it's raining and they need a ride, when some other guy dumps them and they need someone to tell them what a loser that guy is. After graduation, I married the boy. Brett and I had two kids and bought a house in Mountain View. He was a software project lead; I managed the call center for a midsize hardware firm that specialized in printers and scanners. I organized playdates and coordinated the neighborhood block party. I volunteered at a food bank and served as PTA president for my kids' school.

I patted myself on the back until the Dot Com crash and ensuing proliferation of tech outsourcing cost Brett his job. We hobbled along on my modest salary until I, too, was laid off. Then we began using credit cards to pay our bills. We were barely hanging on when Brett was thrown a lifeline—a job at a Denver-based internet securities company. A prior colleague of his, Nicole, had recently made the move and recommended him. He flew out to interview and they extended an offer on the spot. He told them he needed to discuss it with his wife.

Back home, Brett told me it was an incredible opportunity and there was no reason not to go. "I know it's Denver," he said. "But enough time has passed to soften...everything."

I didn't reply.

"Your dad's not getting any younger," Brett said, and I rolled my eyes. "Wouldn't you like being near your brother?" he asked. "And Donna?"

I agreed that I would.

"You'd find work there," Brett continued.

Would I? I had no vision of being employed in Denver, but I reminded myself that I lacked skills to see into the future. I didn't have that kind of clairvoyance, not when I was a kid and certainly not now.

"Caitlin needs a fresh start," Brett said. "And The Children's Hospital there is supposed to be excellent. A great resource for Austin."

I thought of our children. Caitlin, our fourteen-year-old—the same age I'd been when my mother died. Caitlin, with her hooded, overly made-up eyes, blood-red lipstick, and penchant for black clothing. Her hostility and detachment.

Then there was nine-year-old Austin, with his inability to sit still, constant interrupting of conversations, overblown meltdowns—things most children outgrew by his age, but not our son. Austin had been diagnosed with ADHD and put on Ritalin, but he still struggled. His behavior, combined with his small stature—he'd been held back in kindergarten but was still the shortest in his class—meant he was frequently picked on. When it happened, he flew off the handle, which only exacerbated things. Just that afternoon, I'd been called to school because Austin clawed another child's cheeks when the kid called him a dweeb.

Convinced there was more to it than ADHD, I'd been researching other mental health conditions. Austin didn't meet the qualifying criteria for autism, but there were other, rarer disorders. If we knew what it was, could it be treated?

The more I dug, the more intrigued I became by the genetic aspects of mental health. Sometimes, I learned, certain family members only have genetic markers for a condition, while in other relatives the condition manifests. I couldn't deny my own oddness, particularly when I was younger. Had I passed something on to Austin? Once, hesitantly, I'd asked him if he ever saw ghosts. He laughed and said ghosts were stupid and not real.

When I learned that some conditions are more prevalent in males than females, it got me thinking about my father. Like Austin, Dad had weird speech patterns and trouble reading situations. He'd never received a diagnosis—hardly surprising, given the times, as well as the life of privilege he'd been raised in. Surrendered to an orphanage as an infant and adopted shortly thereafter by my well-heeled grandparents, Dad had everything handed to him on a silver platter. His idiosyncrasies were simply excused.

But what caused his eccentricity? Where did it originate? Dad had no interest in finding his birth family, saying his upbringing was unbelievable and there was no reason to probe the past.

I had reason. And living in Denver, where Dad had been adopted, meant proximity to information that might provide a clue—one that could lead to a diagnosis for Austin.

For me, Denver meant the past would encroach. But we were a family; it wasn't only about me. So I wrapped my arms around Brett and said, "You're right. There's no reason not to make the move." I kissed him. "We should go."

Palm on Stevie's chest, keeping her away from the rat's corpse, I felt a twisting knot in my stomach. Did this rat randomly die on our back stoop? Or did it choose this location for its last breath?

Or did someone place it here?

"That's disgusting," Brett said. "I'll find something to get rid of it."

Our kids came through the kitchen then—Caitlin clomping in combat boots, Austin sprinting in tennies. He dropped to his knees, reaching toward the rat. "Ooh, cool!"

I pulled him back. "Don't touch it, honey. It could carry disease."

Caitlin regarded the furry carcass. "Lovely," she said. "What an auspicious start to our new lives in Denver."

Biting my tongue, I said, "Cait, go out on the front porch and watch for the moving van. Take Austin with you."

Later, I directed movers as they carried in our possessions. The yellow-bricked Denver Square—so ubiquitous in Denver, they were referred to as such, though I knew they were called Four Squares in other cities—sat on a tree-lined street in the Congress Park neighborhood. There was a detached two-car garage with deep bays, one of them providentially equipped with an L-shaped hobby space. In my mind's eye I had the space organized: my belt sander and buffer to one side, my bandsaw and drill press to the other, with my knife sharpener alongside them.

After the movers left, Caitlin retreated to her new bedroom. While Austin zoomed from room to room, Brett and I flopped onto the plastic-wrapped couch.

"Should we start unpacking?" I asked.

"We have all weekend," Brett replied. "But maybe we should call an exterminator. What if that rat had friends?"

There was a high-pitched screech from the hallway. *"Mommy!"* Austin yelled. "I *need* you!"

Brett and I rushed to the staircase. Austin was on the second-floor landing, dangling over the railing, feet flailing behind him. His torso hung so low, I thought he might plunge headfirst onto the hardwood floor below.

"Jesus!" I took the stairs two at a time, Brett on my heels. Grabbing the back of Austin's shirt, I sat him down on the landing and wrapped my arms around him.

"Don't do that again, honeypie." My voice shook. "You could fall."

Austin wouldn't have known this. Our single-story home in California didn't have an open staircase. He'd seen objects fall from heights, of course, but our nine-year-old was unable to make associations when faced with brand-new experiences. A leads to B leads to C didn't add up for him.

Austin whimpered. I ran my hand over his hair. "It's okay, bud. Thanks for calling for me when you did."

He nodded. "But that's not it, that's not it, that's not what I wanted to tell you."

"What did you want to tell me?"

"The toilet seat is blue. It's *blue*."

My lips twitched into a smile. "Okay. Go play now."

Austin scampered toward his bedroom. Heading down the stairs, I asked Brett, "Should we put up baby gates?"

Brett shook his head. "He just needs it spelled out. I'll explain the physics to him."

I put a hand on his arm. "Are you okay with me getting out of here for a while? Can you watch Austin? I need a walk."

When he nodded, I grabbed my phone and called my mother's best friend, Donna. Not long before Mom died, Donna had moved from Denver to San Francisco. It was one of the reasons I'd ended up there for college; I fell in love with the Bay Area on my numerous visits to Donna during high school. Recently she'd resettled in Denver, where Evan, her only child, lived with his wife and son.

"So glad you made it, kiddo," Donna said. "It's fab to hear your voice."

"Yours, too. Want to go for a walk?"

"Sure. Come to my place and we'll stroll Cheesman."

"I'll be there in fifteen minutes," I said.

Upstairs in our new bedroom, I unlocked a case I'd directed the movers to place there. Inside, I located the leather sheath holding my favorite knife. It had a desert ironwood handle with plum-colored spacer, a brass finger guard, and a four-inch, drop-point blade with a through tang. It wasn't the first knife I'd ever made, but I was proud of the craftsmanship, and its small size made it convenient to carry. I knew the likelihood of defending myself with this or any knife was slim. Assuming a face-to-face encounter, a knife wielder has to be up close, personal, and prepared to do serious damage—not to mention facing an adversary who is unarmed and doesn't overpower the wielder in size.

Still, I felt safer when I had a knife on me. I slipped it into my shorts pocket and headed out.

Clipping Stevie's leash to her collar, I led her through the back gate, into the alley. Brett had placed the dead rat, loosely wrapped in a plastic grocery bag, on top of the debris in the dumpster behind our house.

Reaching forward, I tugged at a corner of the bag. It opened and the rat's body rolled out. I leaned in to examine it. I'd sensed something earlier but didn't want to say anything to Brett or the kids. Plastic bag over my fingers, I parted the animal's neck fur, unsurprised to see an angry red slash from ear to ear. My fingers twitched, and I gripped Stevie's leash.

That rat didn't die from a predator attack, natural causes, or even poison. It was killed by a person, and it was killed with a knife.

3

— · —

1979

The day after my mother's first spectral visit, I heard her voice in my head repeatedly—a scratched, lacerated record. *Please help me, Suze. Help me.* All I could do in response was whisper that I'd try.

That night, I made TV dinners for Chris and me. Afterward, he wanted to return to his Atari, which he'd sat in front of all day. But I challenged him to Trouble, knowing he'd accept; he was crazy about the plastic bubble imprisoning the dice. He won three rounds, then I put him to bed. I sat beside him, rubbing his back like he was a baby until he fell asleep.

Stepping outside onto our front porch, I spied a cigarette glowing from the porch next door—my neighbor, Laurie. "Come over," she called.

Laurie was beautiful in that effortless way of some girls. She had perfectly feathered hair, generous boobs, and long legs that she liked to show off in Daisy Duke cutoffs. A year ahead of me in school, she was already at Denver East High, where I'd start tenth grade in a few days—kids in Denver were in middle school until ninth grade, then high school for tenth through twelfth. I liked thinking that Laurie and I were friends but I knew that rationally, our connection was based primarily upon long years of adjacency, not unlike two sweaters folded side by side in a dresser drawer.

Still, she was kind to me when other kids weren't. I'd never been popular anyway, but in the final months of ninth grade I might as well have had a tattoo across my forehead: *Girl Whose Mom Was Killed*. Everyone made a wide circle around me.

But Laurie sometimes took me cruising in her yellow Ford Pinto. She'd taught me how to mix drops of food coloring with water to create amber, which could be used to top off a parental liquor bottle when you took the occasional nip. Once in a while she gave me castoff clothes.

On her porch, Laurie lit another Virginia Slim, handing it to me. I rarely made it through an entire cigarette, mostly just holding it and tapping the ashes into my palm before flicking them into the juniper bushes. In the near-darkness, I peeked sideways toward her tight t-shirt. At nearly fifteen, I had nothing happening on top and rarely wore a bra. What would it be like to have a body like Laurie's?

She asked if I wanted to go for a drive. "I can get Bruce to babysit," she said.

Bruce was Laurie's brother, a year younger than me. He liked playing on Chris's Atari and would sometimes do so in exchange for being a body in our house when I went out. I knew I shouldn't leave Chris, but he never came into my room before midnight. And Dad—working late, as he often did—wouldn't know the difference.

When I nodded, Laurie asked, "Got any money? I'm almost out of gas. And if we want beer, forget it. I'm broke."

"Let me go check," I said.

I had no money but didn't want to say so. But I knew where Dad kept his extra cash—in the file cabinet in his study, lowest drawer, in a manila envelope. I grabbed ten bucks and headed back to Laurie's. On the way I nodded at Bruce, slumped on our library's couch. The soft bleeps and bloops of the Atari were the only response.

Laurie and I drove east on Colfax and parked off Havana, where we could sit on the Pinto's hood and watch planes landing at and taking off from the airport. She opened two cans of Coors, handing one to me. "Cheers," she said.

The beer, cold and watery, slid down my throat. Laurie put a hand on my shoulder. "How're you doing?" She shook her head. "I still can't believe what happened to your mom."

I gazed at the scrub grass beside the road. Whenever someone mentioned Mom's death, the words felt as powerful as an avalanche, as indelible as a subdermal scar.

Here are the facts.

The night of February twenty-second, Mom kept Zoe's Records open late, as was her custom on Thursdays and Fridays. She was alone in the store, counting money on the counter, when a guy walked in, pointed a gun at her, and demanded she hand over her cash.

We later learned that Mom's killer, Robert Shelton, had a miles-long rap sheet of drug convictions, both possession and dealing. Months later, I still couldn't get his mug shot—pale blue eyes, greasy, rat-brown hair, pasty skin covered in oozing sores—out of my mind.

What I don't understand, am unable to envision, is what happened next. Perhaps Mom made a sudden move and Shelton thought she was going for a weapon. Or maybe she froze, too stunned to respond. Whatever the reason, he shot her three times, point-blank in the chest. Then he swiped the cash—about eighty-five dollars—and ran.

Shelton didn't make it far. It was East Colfax, a street with plenty of traffic and always the possibility of cops driving by. Two officers, Powles and Coleman, heard the shots as they cruised Colfax in their cherry-top. When they pulled over and began chasing Shelton on foot, he turned his gun on them. After Shelton shot Officer Coleman (not lethally, that lucky cop), Officer Powles returned fire. Shelton ran into the street, where he was struck by a bus and launched into oncoming traffic. He was rushed to Denver General. He did not survive the night.

Leaning back on Laurie's windshield, I looked up at the sky. It was a clear night, the stars appearing one by one. The North Star twinkled, bright as a gemstone.

"I'm okay," I said, answering Laurie's question. "As okay as anyone in my situation could be."

In truth, the encounter with my mother's spirit the night before had left me feeling better than I'd felt since she died. But the idea of mentioning it to Laurie, or anyone else my age, was absurd. I was socially awkward enough; I didn't need to make it worse. Once, when we were small and I'd told Laurie that I see ghosts, she said, "You mean Casper? Everybody sees Casper...he's on every Saturday morning." Discerning it was best to simply agree, I'd nodded. Later, when I told my mother about it, she said, "That was probably wise, my little seer."

As for my dad, he'd never made much of my claims—a lifelong Lutheran, he believed, if anything, in the straightforward nature of a Biblical heaven and hell. Mom once told me she'd mentioned it to Donna, who said kids have remarkable imaginations and I'd outgrow it.

"What will happen to your mom's store?" Laurie asked.

I sipped beer. "Don't know."

Soon after hiring cleaners to take care of the crime scene, Dad had closed Zoe's, securing the deadlocks on the front and rear doors. None of us had been there since. Dad wrote a check to the landlord, covering rent for the remainder of the year. He didn't say so, but I knew the reason: throwing money around was my father's preferred technique for banishing disturbing subjects from his mind.

"All those records, and that mannequin she named the store after." Laurie lit a cigarette. "That was cool."

Zoe was not a real person. She was a mannequin in the corner of the shop. Mom had adorned Zoe with a shaggy blond wig, a newsboy cap, a flowing, floral-print dress, and four strands of colored beads around her neck. "One for each person in the family," Mom said. My beads were purple.

Mom positioned and wired Zoe's arms to hold a beat-up electric guitar she'd scored at a thrift shop. She named her Zoe to put her at the other end of the alphabet from her own name, Alexandra. "We're yin and yang, this old girl and me," Mom said, patting Zoe's butt.

In the late 1970s, Denver was flooded with record stores. You couldn't walk two blocks in any commercial district—South Broadway, West Colfax, Colorado Boulevard, not to mention suburban thoroughfares and malls—without running into an independent or chain record store. Record Town, Musicland, Peaches—the chains were a dime a dozen. But there were also indies, like Twist & Shout, Wax Trax, and Mom's Place. (Not *my* mom's place; that was the name of another store.)

Zoe's Records was a small indie with, as my mother put it, "a focus on the female artist." The stereo spun records by women, ranging from Sarah Vaughan to Joni Mitchell to Sister Sledge. Because of Zoe's inventory, most of our shoppers were female. Women appreciated that Mom didn't blast music too loud for conversation. They were happy to have someone knowledgeable on hand, someone like Alex Parry, to point them toward what they wanted. Even when they didn't yet know what it was.

Alex knew. Alex always knew.

A car pulled up behind Laurie's, and three guys got out. "Hey, ladies," one of them said. "Mind if we join you?"

I didn't recognize them, and Laurie didn't seem to, either. They were big, hulking guys with no necks—probably football players, probably from some other school, not East. I sensed a fourth dude hovering near them, bullet holes in his abdomen—accidentally killed, I knew, on a hunting trip with his dad last fall.

"We'd rather be alone." Laurie flung her hand backward. "Park somewhere else."

He leaned on the Pinto's hood. "What if I want to park next to you?"

"Get lost," Laurie growled.

Beers in hand, the other guys came around the car—one beside his buddy and Laurie, the dead one and another on my side. "Let's just party," the live one beside me said. "What's wrong with a little party?"

I felt fury emanating from the dead guy—but whether directed at his buddies for hanging out without him, his father for allowing the hunting accident to occur, or Laurie and me, I couldn't tell. Clutching my beer can in both hands, I glanced at Laurie.

"Come with me," she said, scooting off the hood. I followed. She opened her hatchback and pulled out two baseball bats, handing one to me. "Don't be afraid to use it, if you have to," she said. "But you probably won't have to."

Then she swung her bat toward the guys. "I *said* get lost."

"Jesus, bitch." The first guy's face paled. "All we want is to have some fun. Bitches!"

They backed off and drove away. Laurie hopped back onto the Pinto's hood.

"Hang onto that," she said, nodding at the bat in my hands. "You never know."

4

—·—

2004

I walked to Donna's under a canopy of leafed-out oaks and cotton-woods, interspersed with the occasional thin stand of aspens. As I walked, I admired the houses. I'd always loved this old-time Denver architecture. The tall brick homes, wrought iron gates, and curious details—gargoyles, turrets, colorful gingerbread trim. There were houses like this in San Francisco but few in Silicon Valley, where I'd lived for over a decade.

On a telephone pole I spotted a poster about a missing woman—a teenager, really. I examined her photo. She had dark, glossy hair, much like Caitlin's, and a pretty smile.

Scanning the text identifying the man she was last seen with, I froze. Could it be? It *had* to be. Robert Shelton Jr. wasn't exactly the most common name around.

I'd wanted better things for Shelton Jr. That poor girl. I hoped she'd be all right.

Rereading her name—Darcy Powles—I furrowed my brow. Where had I heard the name Powles before?

Donna lived in the guest cottage on the grounds of her son Evan's house, which overlooked Cheesman Park. When Stevie and I arrived, she was waiting on the sidewalk, cigarette dangling from her fingertips. With her wild hair, now gone mostly gray, her wide grin and huge, rounded sunglasses, Donna reminded me of Janis Joplin—or what Janis might have looked like if she'd aged, instead of OD'ing when she was twenty-seven.

As Donna said my name in her familiar, raspy voice and enfolded me in a smoke-scented hug, the feelings that always overtook me in her presence upended themselves inside me. Donna had known me my entire life. She'd seen me grow from quirky kid to grieving teenager to the pragmatic adult I'd worked so hard to become.

More importantly, Donna had known my mother—better than anyone else, really. Donna was like a living, breathing family heirloom, a link to a past that most people had forgotten.

I'd never forgotten.

Others jogged past us on the path around Cheesman Park, but Donna, Stevie, and I took our time. In my mother's day, Cheesman had been a cruising spot for gay men. When Mom and I walked the lawns seeking spirits, we were often the only two females there. Now, like much of Denver, the park had become trendy. On a warm, sunny Friday afternoon, dog walkers, picnickers, and runners proliferated. My eyes darted around the bright grass and lifted toward the tall cottonwoods. Intuiting nothing unusual, I sighed with relief. It was a good sign.

I listened as Donna talked about her preschooler grandson's latest exploits, then I caught her up on our cross-country drive and the new house—omitting mention of the rat. When we reached the west side of the park, she stopped, placing a hand on my arm.

"How does it feel, being here?" she asked.

"So far, it feels…" I took a breath. "Like Mom would approve."

Donna laughed. "You've got that right—Alex would be glad you're here." She paused. "But that's not a *feeling*, Suzanne."

I squinted at the sun. "I feel like I can handle it. As long as I keep moving forward with intention, everything will be fine."

"Honey." Donna withdrew a pack of Salems from her pocket. "You know I adored and admired your mom. But I'll tell you something I used to say to her." She lit up. "I'd say, 'Alex, old girl, quit goddamn trying to control everything.' And your mom would hold up her hands and say, 'I can't *help* it, Don!'"

I smiled. "I can envision such a conversation."

Donna blew smoke upward. "I'll say the same to you, Suzanne. Let go." She gazed at me. "Trust in the process, okay?"

Walking home, I considered what Donna had said. Was I trying to control things that were out of my control? I didn't believe that. And yet I wasn't ready to tell her—or Brett, or anybody, least of all my father—why I'd agreed to the move. No one knew about my hope to discover information that might help Austin.

In California, Austin had seen specialist after specialist. Driving home from an appointment last spring, I'd thought if I heard the words, "It's normal childhood behavior, Mrs. Archer," one more time, I'd push a few doctors out a window, just to wipe those condescending expressions off their faces.

Maybe, like Brett said, The Children's Hospital, or some other miracle facility here, would have answers...*maybe*. But maybe a genetic link was the key—and it was up to me to find it.

Over the years, Dad had rarely mentioned his adoption. All he knew was what his mother told him: he'd been surrendered as a baby to the Little Denver Home for Children. His original last name was Lewis.

"Did you have siblings?" I'd once asked. Dad said he had nary a notion.

According to their website, the Little Denver Home for Children was no longer an orphanage; these days, it provided services to kids in the foster system or juvenile detention who were experiencing trauma. But I hoped they'd have old records from when the facility served a different purpose.

I zigzagged north, then east, then north again. Hearing footsteps behind me, I turned. The sidewalk was empty.

As soon as I pivoted and started walking, I heard them again. I whirled, but no one was there.

Ensuring my knife was still in my pocket, I waited—but I saw and heard nothing else. Resuming my walk, I willed myself to relax and count my blessings one by one, like coins in a pocket. Stevie trotted by my side. We had a beautiful new house, and Donna lived nearby. Brett had landed a good job. I'd find answers that would help Austin. Caitlin would go to high school and make new friends.

Spying the poster again, I even decided that missing girl *would* turn up. And if her parents were smart, they'd make sure she never saw Robert Shelton Jr. again.

Everything would be okay.

At home, I walked into silence. Where was everyone? If Brett had had time to set up Austin's Wii gaming system, that's where I'd find him; he was as enamored with the Wii as Chris had been with his first-generation Atari, back in the day. I checked the basement TV room but the Wii was still packed.

I found Austin in the back yard. One hand was clenched around a three-inch plastic version of Pikachu, his favorite Pokémon character. With his other hand, he was pulling so hard on the garage's doorknob, I thought he might rip it off.

"What are you doing?" I called out.

Austin turned. "Maybe there's something to do in there."

There *wasn't* anything to do in there—not for him. Austin owned a scooter and a bike but rarely rode either. His balance wasn't great, and falling frustrated him.

My tools and supplies were in the garage, waiting for me to set up my new workshop. But I'd never give Austin access to those.

"Where's Daddy?" I asked.

"He left. He told Caitlin to watch me."

Brett hadn't said anything about going out. I called him and when he answered, I heard laughter, music, and clinking glassware. "Where are you?" I asked.

"I asked Caitlin to watch Austin, and I ran out to meet Nicole for a quick drink. She wanted to give me some inside info before I start on Monday."

"On a Friday afternoon? At a bar? Sounds more like happy hour than business."

Immediately, I regretted my words. The new job was everything to Brett. If meeting with his colleague today was vital, so be it. "I'm sorry," I said.

"It's all right. But where's Caitlin?"

"She's supposed to be watching Austin."

"Hold on." I turned to Austin. "Where's your sister?"

"She told me to find something to do. Then she left."

My mouth fell open. She *left*? Austin was nine years old. And Austin was…Austin. He couldn't be unsupervised.

"Honey?" Brett asked. "Is Austin okay? Are you okay?"

My hand shook. "We're fine. But I need to call Caitlin."

With jellylike fingers, I dialed Caitlin's number. It went to voicemail. Wrapping my arms around Austin, I relished his grubby scent—dirt, combined with a hint of bubble gum from the sugar-free stuff we let him chew.

"Let's go inside," I said. "Let's get you a snack. Then we'll go look for your sister."

"How *could* you?" I cried. "How could you leave him alone?"

She'd come in as Austin and I were heading for my car. She straightened, her height nearing mine. "You always make a big deal out of everything."

"Because it *is* a big deal! You do not—under *any* circumstances—leave your brother alone!"

"Oh, for freak's sake. It was like twenty minutes. He was fine."

"He was not fine. He cannot control his actions. Besides…"

My eyes darted around the room. I wanted to warn her about—what, specifically? I thought about the rat, the footsteps. About Shelton Jr. and that girl. About what else might lurk in these streets.

How could I explain all that? I couldn't. "Your brother needs to be *watched*, Caitlin."

"Could you *be* any more dramatic?" She grabbed a Gatorade from the fridge. "What did you think he'd get into? A little sugar?" She smirked. "Or was it your precious knives?"

I felt the familiar twist in my gut that hit me whenever Caitlin and I clashed. But all I said was, "Besides not leaving Austin alone, I don't want *you* walking around by yourself."

"Why not? Why shouldn't I see more of this place you and Dad decided would be so *good* for us?" Her eye roll was so histrionic, I thought her eyeballs might disappear inside her head.

I pressed a hand to my clavicle. "I know it looks safe, but you can wander into some dangerous neighborhoods around here, Caitlin."

"Jesus, you're paranoid." She crossed her arms over her chest. "And clueless. You have no idea some of the stuff I used to do back home."

My stomach flip-flopped. "As I said—this is different. You don't know your way around."

"I'm not five. I can find my way around in broad daylight. And I have a phone."

"Which you failed to answer when I called!"

"Sorry. I was talking to someone." Her gaze softened. "Mom, please stop worrying so much."

I hesitated. Told myself I'd imagined noises in the house, footfalls on my walk. As for the rat…well, that had to be neighborhood kids playing pranks.

And Caitlin was a smart girl. She knew to stay away from boys—men—like Shelton Jr.

"You've had your walk," I said. "Please stay inside now. I'll get pizza for dinner."

Backing out of the garage, I tuned the radio to the "Adult Contemporary" station—a mix of newer pop music and classic rock. In the back seat, Austin fiddled with his seat belt. "Leave it alone, honeypie," I told him.

I could've had the pizza delivered but I felt like taking a drive. On Colfax Avenue, I rolled down the windows and inhaled the scents of my hometown. Many of them—gas fumes, trash, cooking oil—invoked familiar sensations. And some, like construction dust, were new.

The pizza place was east on Colfax, but I'd turned west, deciding to cruise the avenue. When I was growing up, the businesses along Colfax ranged from the ordinary—drugstores, car washes, restaurants—to more questionable establishments like strip clubs and pay-by-the-hour motels. Now the landscape was dotted with boutiques, niche bakeries, and adorable little flower shops. Donna had told me the city was trying to clean up Colfax. I could see hipness seeping in, like fog beneath a doorway.

Austin kicked my seat so hard, the force jabbed into my lower back. "Mommy, this is a long, long, long way for pizza."

"Don't kick," I said. "Why don't you play the Sentence Game?"

"Only if you play with me."

I glanced at the license plate on the car in front of mine. TSC-478. "Talented singers croon," I said.

The Sentence Game was invented by my father—or, if not invented by him, I'd never heard of anyone else playing it. Using the letters on a license plate, you figure out, in order, words that comprise a sentence. First real sentence wins the round.

Dad always came up with wild—and wildly accurate—ones. "Fraud introduces investigation!" he'd shout. "Diaries manufacture sagas!"

Austin did several. He tended to talk a lot, but his speech patterns were unlike my dad's—rather than developing an extraordinary vocabulary, Austin struggled to remember the meaning of any new word he encountered and often repeated words for emphasis. His Sentence Game offerings were always basic. *I eat oranges. Cartoons have cats.*

"I'm bored," he said, kicking my seat again. "This is stupid, stupid, *stupid.*"

"Stop kicking, please. We'll be there soon." Making a U-turn in a parking lot, I headed east.

Life claws people. Records reveal truths.

As I passed Denver East High—my alma mater, the school where Caitlin would go—Joni Mitchell's voice came through the speakers, singing "Both Sides, Now." It was a song I rarely heard on the radio. Too folksy, I guess.

"Both Sides, Now" was the final song on Joni Mitchell's second album, *Clouds.* Judy Collins, a favorite of Mom's and mine, had recorded the song first. But Joni's version, according to Mom, "showed the world that Joni wasn't only a songwriter—she was a hell of a singer, too."

I can still see my mother's shining eyes when she said this. "Can you imagine, Suzie Blue? Joni not only wrote every song, she also did the album cover artwork. A self-portrait." Mom's voice lowered, as if she were speaking of a deity. "Imagine the talent. Imagine what it takes to cut a record of that brilliance."

The song was a message—telling me to drive past my mother's old shop, make sure the building hadn't been torn down like so much else on Colfax. Note what sort of business was in the space. After Zoe's Records closed, it frequently changed hands. It had been an accountant's office, an appliance repair place, a head shop, and many others.

As I approached a red light at the intersection, I glanced over. The building that once housed Zoe's Records hadn't changed. Single story, red tile roof. Home to three businesses. In the 1970s there'd been a lawyer's office in the west space, but you rarely saw anyone there; my mother claimed it was a front of some sort. Back then and still today, Frederick's Tailoring occupied the middle space.

Zoe's Records had been on the east end. My eyes widened as I took in the darkened shop windows—and the For Rent sign taped on the door.

When the light changed, I maneuvered into a parking space along the avenue.

Holding Austin's hand, I peered into the dusty windows. The space seemed mostly empty, just scattered cardboard boxes and some shelving inside. And my mother's ancient checkout counter, apparently used by those who took over the space in ensuing years.

I glanced at Frederick's shop. Mr. Frederick had been a sweet man who gave Chris and me cans of soda pop and pennies for his gumball machine. He'd have to be in his eighties by now, likely retired and turned the business over to his children. Or maybe someone else took it over but kept the name.

Austin tugged my hand. "What is this place, Mommy? And isn't our pizza getting cold?" He wrapped his other arm around himself. "Cold, cold, cold."

"They keep it warm in an oven," I said. "But you're right. Let's go."

I turned away—and then I turned back. Fishing in my purse for a pen and a scrap of paper, I jotted down the For Rent sign's phone number. In my car, I took one final look before heading out.

5

—·—

1979

Around ten o'clock the following night, too early for Chris's wanderings, I again sensed my mother in my room. I felt her spirit, whom I'd nicknamed Mom-not-Mom, sitting on a throw pillow in my circular space. Like many Queen Annes, our house had a turret, and the second story of it was in my bedroom. Five narrow, creaky windows encircled the space. Mom had let me string mini Christmas lights, and over the years I'd filled the space with cushions and stuffed animals.

I rose from bed, crossed the room, and sat beside her, trying to ignore the scarlet anemones on her chest. "I'm glad you're back," I said.

"Me, too. But I really need your help, Suzie Blue," she pleaded. "You didn't do anything about your dad and Peggy."

"Can we talk about something else? I want to talk like we used to, Mom."

"Me, too, but I don't think I can. When we start talking about other things, I feel myself fading away."

It was true; I felt it, too. How frustrating, to have her here and yet not here. Connecting with me, but only about Dad and Peggy. It felt unfair.

Not as unfair, however, as being shot to death.

"What am I supposed to do?" I asked. "I didn't even see Dad tonight. He was working late."

My father was CEO of the Parry Auto Group, three car dealerships established decades ago by my grandfather. Two years before Mom's death, Grandpa Parry had a fatal heart attack. The year before that, Nana, Mom's mother, had died. At the time, those events had felt like emotional tsunamis. I hadn't been able to fathom anything worse.

Grandma Parry, who used to be doting and sweet, was now senile. She had a live-in attendant and barely remembered our names. Dad's only sibling, Aunt Sadie, had no interest in selling cars. So everything at the Parry Auto Group was on Dad.

"Dad wasn't working tonight," Mom-not-Mom said. "He was with *her*."

"How do you know?"

"No idea."

I recalled a documentary Mom and I had once watched about ghosts. Some expert said spirits only come around if they have unfinished business. Otherwise, the dead rest peacefully.

"Do you think the spirits you see have unfinished business?" Mom had asked me.

I'd shrugged. "I guess so. They do seem kind of sad."

We'd both fallen silent. Finally, Mom said, "How tragic, being denied eternal rest. To only come back because you have unfinished business."

Now, I asked Mom-not-Mom, "Are you here because you have unfinished business?"

"I think so. Now, anyway." I felt her rise from the cushions. "Before this Peggy thing turned serious, I didn't feel...anything. But now..." She paused. "Listen, they're making some major plans."

"Dad won't marry Peggy. No matter what you think, it's not serious." My face contorted. "You don't know what it's like around here. We miss you. For Dad, Peggy's a distraction."

Just like last winter—when Mom had kicked him out.

There was a flutter as Mom-not-Mom reseated herself on the pillows. "That may be all he intends, but men are stupid. You haven't had the experience yet, but men follow…" She paused again. "Well, you're not dumb, Suze. Men follow their dicks through the world. Even your dad."

"Oh, my God." I laughed. She'd always talked like that. "Even if that's true, it could be a passing thing. Right?"

"It could," Mom-not-Mom said. "If Peggy didn't want more than that." Her voice lowered. "Listen, I saw them tonight. Their conversation kept dancing around the topic of marriage. Your dad was asking her things like, 'What would you want in a permanent partner?' 'What would you want that's different from your ex-husbands?'"

I shrugged. "That's just Dad."

My father collected quirky facts and unusual vocabulary. He was prone to alliterative speech and comments only marginally related to a current conversation. We'd be at dinner, everyone talking about their day, and he'd ask if we knew that the first person to discover a dinosaur bone was a nineteenth-century English scientist named Richard Owen. Asked what prompted the comment, he'd point to the pork chop bone on his plate.

"Discussing marriage isn't like that," Mom-not-Mom said. "Men don't say that sort of thing randomly."

"So go haunt *him*. If he's the one whose mind you have to change, why not visit him in the middle of the night?"

"I tried talking to him. He didn't respond. Same with Chris…I can tell he doesn't sense me." I felt her gaze on Chris's empty sleeping bag. "I'm worried about him, Suze. He's so young. He's vulnerable. If no one prevents it, Chris is likely to fall prey to…to…"

"To what?" I asked.

"To individuals who do not have his best interests at heart." Her voice shook. "And I'm powerless to do *anything* about it."

I recalled the night last winter when Dad introduced Peggy to Chris and me. We were at Grandma Parry's spacious home, where Dad had stayed during the trial separation. There was plenty of room for him to come and go, have Chris and me over, and not inconvenience Grandma or her caretaker.

The night we met Peggy, Dad's plan was to decorate the Christmas tree he'd set up in the living room. He'd lugged out boxes of antique ornaments and lit a fire in the fireplace, adding so many logs I thought he might burn the house down.

Initially, Peggy was friendly. She smiled widely, showing off a mouthful of straight white teeth. But for the rest of the evening, while I huddled on the couch tapping the face of my watch as if doing so would pass the time faster, she shot me occasional glances. I sensed that Peggy saw in me someone whose company she'd have preferred over mine.

Mostly, though, her attention was on Chris as the two of them decorated the tree. Chris wanted to use all the silly ornaments, glass renditions of cartoon characters from Dad's childhood—Mickey Mouse, Popeye, Felix the Cat, plus a legion of Santa Clauses. With manicured fingers, Peggy guided his hand as he reached toward the higher branches. She didn't seem like someone who did not have Chris's best interests at heart.

"I understand you're upset," I said to Mom-not-Mom. I stood, leaning out the window toward a breeze that didn't come. "But I don't think Dad will just up and marry Peggy."

"No?" Mom-not-Mom said. "If you don't believe me, Suzie Blue, listen to the tape."

I turned. "What tape?"

There was no answer. She'd vanished.

6

2004

On Saturday morning, needing a break from unpacking, I went outside. Crossing the sunny back yard, I watched Stevie doze in a warm patch of grass. We'd had her since she was a puppy, and she was unequivocally my dog. I knew she'd follow me to the ends of the earth—whither thou goest, I will go, as Leonard Cohen sang. As much as I'd worried about how the kids would handle the move, I'd worried about Stevie, too. Twelve years old is an advanced age for a dog to make a major move, but Stevie was settling in.

In the garage's hobby space, I arranged my power tools, organized supplies, and hung my collection of blades, sorted by size and type, on the wall. Donning gloves and safety glasses, I turned on my buffer.

I got into knifemaking long ago. The reasons for that were obvious to me but I chose not to dwell on them. Instead, I relished the craft's precision. Knifemaking required patience, time, and strict adherence to safety. It was also expensive as hell, due to its addictive nature. Over the years I'd acquired tools as I could afford them. As for supplies, I was continually adding to my stash; I had a treasure trove of blades, handle materials, and hardware.

I'd fashioned numerous blades myself, using the sheet stock removal method—scribing the outline of the blade on a precut piece of tool steel, then using my belt sander to shape the blade and grind the bevel. It took weeks to make a single blade, and early on I messed up plenty of them, but eventually my skills improved. The blades had to be sent out for heat-treating—proper equipment to do that at home would've been cost prohibitive—but everything else I managed on my own. More often than making blades, however, I refurbished old knives I bought at flea markets and thrift stores—cleaning, sharpening, and polishing the blades, then fashioning new handles from hardwood, stacked leather, or Micarta.

Amid the whirl of the buffer, I put a finishing polish on what had been a scratched, dull Santoku knife from the 1970s that I'd begun to clean up before we left California. Years ago, my mother had owned a knife like this. Originating in Japan, the Santoku was similar to a chef's knife but had a different blade shape. Mom said "Santoku" meant "three virtues."

"By virtues, they mean 'three uses,'" she explained. "Chopping, dicing, and slicing." In our quirky old kitchen, she'd pressed my fingers—I couldn't have been more than seven—around the handle, showing me a proper grip. "It's an effective tool. Use it wisely, Suzie Blue."

When the blade was clean, I wrapped painter's tape around it, ensuring safety while I worked on the handle. One time, another knifemaker I knew did a real number on himself—an unwrapped knife fell off his workbench and severed his tibialis anterior tendon, requiring surgery, the wearing of an ortho boot, and months of physical therapy.

I marked pinhole locations on the scales—the wooden blocks from which I'd fashion the handle—lined up with the pinholes in the knife tang. With my drill press, I drilled pinholes into the scales. I was using a gorgeous, honey-brown Hawaiian Koa hardwood, one of my last purchases before I packed up my workshop in Mountain View.

After inserting dummy pins, I outlined the handle shape with a Sharpie and used the bandsaw to cut the scales. Attaching a belt to my sander, I sanded both pieces to the desired shape. Then I inserted new pins and used epoxy to glue the scales to the tang. I put four clamps on the knife to secure it while the epoxy dried. Tomorrow I'd sand the handle, rounding the finish, then buff and polish the hardwood to a sheen.

The process took several hours. As I worked, I felt my mind and body relax. Surrounded by tools and knives, I was among friends.

That evening I was cleaning out my purse when my fingers detected a scrap of paper. For the rest of the weekend I couldn't get it out of my mind.

I called on Monday, after dropping Austin for his first day of third grade. It took a while—by the time I registered him, spoke with the principal and his teacher, and did my best, as he clung to me with his little plastic Pikachu pressed to his chest, to assure him that he'd make friends and have fun—it was almost noon.

I scheduled an appointment with the Zoe's building manager for the following day. Who was I kidding, I thought as I hung up. I had no idea how to run a retail business. True, I'd been raised at my mother's knee in Zoe's Records, but decades had passed since the store was shuttered. I didn't even work retail in high school or college.

I should call the building manager back and cancel the appointment. I had plenty of work to do on my secret project—tracing Dad's history—but just as importantly, I needed to find a job. Before leaving California, I'd sent my resume to the HR managers of a dozen Denver companies in various fields. None were advertising jobs for which I was qualified, but you never know. I hadn't heard anything, but those dozen companies were hardly the only employers here. If I focused, I could whip off emails to five more HR heads before fetching Austin from school.

But I was drawn to the notion of a new Zoe's. Perhaps not a store that exclusively sold records and tapes, or even CDs. It was no longer the 1970s; most people didn't spin records like my mother once had.

But what about a store that supported all kinds of female artists? Could the new Zoe's be a place that carried creative works of all sorts, musically and otherwise, made by women?

I had no idea how to turn this chrysalis of an idea into a butterfly of reality. But something about it made my heart flicker. Perhaps the flicker was knowing there was one person who, if she were here, would enthusiastically approve.

Before leaving home to fetch Austin, I went upstairs for a knife. Reaching for my knife case, I frowned to discover that it was unlocked. I *never* left it unlocked. Shuffling through it, I assured myself that everything was there. Telling myself to be more careful, I slipped the drop-point into my pocket and firmly turned the case's key.

As Stevie and I stepped outside, the mail carrier arrived. Welcoming me to the neighborhood, she handed over a stack of mail. "Popular already, I see," she said.

I locked and double-checked the front door, then inspected the mail as I walked. A notice from the post office confirming our move. A thank-you note from our realtor. Two fliers for grocery stores and several takeout menus.

And a postcard. On the front, it showed a palace-like structure with gold-plated walls, situated on a body of water. The words "Greetings from India's Golden Temple" were scripted across the top of the card.

I turned it over and read.

Salutations, Suzanne, Brett, Caitlin, and Austin. I trust you're settling in. This adventure is astonishing. Did you know the kitchen of Sri Harmandir Sahib in Amritsar, also known as the Golden Temple, is the largest free kitchen in the world? A battalion of believers serves gratis grub each day. I avidly anticipate seeing the Archers in due time.

Love,
Dad/Grandpa

I read it again. Logically, I should bring it home to share with my family. They'd enjoy the picture and my dad's update.

Instead, at the next alley, I tossed the card in a dumpster. Then I resumed my walk—taking long strides, ears half-cocked for footsteps behind me.

7

1979

The Saturday before school started, Dad invited Peggy to dinner. Turned out that meant she'd cook at our house. When she showed up laden with grocery bags, I was sprawled on the front porch swing re-reading the dirty parts in *Scruples*. I'd taught myself to read at age four—I just picked it up, according to Mom—and never looked back. Books were reliable companions, better than most people. I'd torn through the summer reading list by the first week in June, and earlier that day I'd read the second half of Octavia E. Butler's *Kindred*, engrossed in main character Dana's terrifying time travels to the antebellum South. *Scruples* was one-eighty from *Kindred*, but I'd wanted to lighten up.

Peggy loomed over me, her shadow darkening the swing. "Hi, Suzanne. Whatcha reading?"

I held up the novel.

Peggy frowned. "That's inappropriate for a young girl."

I eyeballed her. Peggy had a good figure for someone her age, and she seemed to enjoy showing it off. She wasn't slutty, but her top and pants were fitted, accentuating her flat stomach, her curvy boobs and ass. An image of her engaged in acts like those described in *Scruples* flashed through my mind, and I dry-heaved.

"My mother never censored my reading," I said. "Dad doesn't, either."

"Well, he should. Trash like that is more dangerous than you realize, Suzanne."

When I didn't reply, Peggy went inside. A short while later, I followed her into the kitchen and opened the refrigerator, selecting a Tab. Mom always said it was poison, but Laurie got me hooked on it.

Peggy was shucking corn into a grocery bag. Silk strands littered the floor, and as she crouched to pluck them off the faded linoleum, she said, "Ugh, this house. Everything is so *old*. I don't know how all of you put up with it."

I scowled. Mom had loved this house and our neighborhood. In 1888, when the house was built, Cap Hill was *the* neighborhood for fashionable Denverites. By the 1930s, the neighborhood had turned seedy and the house became, as my mother adored calling it, a "House of Ill Repute." It changed hands a few more times before my parents bought it in 1965, the year after my birth.

"The realtor was the first to use that term. 'House of Ill Repute,'" Mom would say, giggling. "Then her face turned red. Guess she thought we wouldn't buy the house, given its past."

Dad would chime in, "That real estate lady had an inaccurate impression of you, Alex."

Indeed, this was exactly the sort of thing that charmed my mother: living in a once genteel, later dilapidated Queen Anne Victorian that had also done time as a whorehouse. The house, its history, and its ghosts—like the frowning pair I sensed hovering behind Peggy, one in a maid's uniform, on her chest a single anemone like my mother's three; the other a young woman with a long, horsey face and the oddest, splayed-every-which-way hair I'd ever seen, dressed in finery from some decade I couldn't identify and sporting a single bullet hole in her temple—these aspects of our home were exactly what drew my mother to it.

Dinner was steaks on the grill, corn, and salad. Wine for Peggy and Dad, lemonade for Chris, and Tab for me. Peggy began the meal with a prayer, something about Jesus being our guest. Dad joined her—he knew all the words—while Chris fidgeted and I stared into my lap.

After we'd eaten, Dad patted his belly. "Peggy, you know how to feed the flock. Thank you."

She beamed. "Thank *you*, Jimmy." She leaned toward Chris. "Do you want more lemonade, sweetie?" As she refilled his cup, Dad topped off his wine and Peggy's. I crunched the ice in my glass.

"Peggy and I have an announcement," Dad said. "That's why I asked her to dine with us tonight."

My stomach, filled with Peggy's cooking, flip-flopped. Was Mom right? Had Dad *proposed*?

He looked at me. "Suzanne, assuming responsibility for Chris these past few months has placed a behemoth burden on you. With school starting, it's indeed infeasible. Therefore, I'm elated to announce that Peggy has offered assistance. She'll pick up Chris from school daily, bring him here, and make dinner." Dad's smile widened. "This will make things easier on you, Suze. You can frolic in your first year at East."

I pursed my lips. "You're hiring her to babysit Chris?"

"No!" Peggy cut in. "I wouldn't dream of taking money for this. I just want to help."

My queasiness transformed into tension. I thought about the roly-poly bugs Laurie and I used to look for on the sidewalk when we were kids, remembered how we'd poke them to make them curl into themselves. My insides felt like one of those bugs.

On the surface, Peggy's offer seemed generous. But I knew it would set off alarm bells for my mother.

Peggy's presence transformed our home life. She did all the household stuff Mom used to do, and then some. She completely took over Chris's care. She even took him on little expeditions—the library, the toy store, the zoo. She ran errands, cleaned, and cooked, setting grandiose platters on our table nearly every night. By mid-September we'd been served honey-roasted duck, Beef Wellington, spinach-stuffed salmon, and pork vindaloo (meat in a spicy curry sauce, we were told; Peggy had learned to make it when she was a missionary in India). Peggy ate dinner with us, seated in Mom's chair. She didn't stay overnight, but she left our kitchen spotless and tucked Chris in before going home to her apartment.

I waited for my mother to come around again. Finally, deep into one black, starless night, she whispered my name.

"You're back!" I said, opening my eyes.

"I'm back. But where's your brother?" I sensed her moving toward Chris's empty sleeping bag.

"In his room," I replied. "He doesn't sleep here as much as he used to."

We were both silent. I missed my brother coming into my room at night, his small form nearby, his shallow, little-boy breath. While I was glad his nightmares seemed to have ceased, I hated the implication: Chris slept better now because someone was mothering him.

I could tell Mom-not-Mom felt it, too. "What can I do?" I asked her.

"I told you. Listen to the tape." I felt her heat beside me. "You remember, don't you?"

Suddenly I did. A week or two after Mom died, I'd found a mix tape in the parlor beside the hi-fi. The label said, For Suzie Blue. Happy Valentine's Day. Love, Mom.

Valentine's Day was eight days before Mom's death. She'd given me a card and a chocolate heart wrapped in red foil. Why didn't she give me this tape? Upon discovering it, I'd taken it upstairs to my room, inserted it in my cassette player, and pressed Play. Rickie Lee Jones's mournful voice filled the room. Her first album had released the week Mom died—at Zoe's

Records, we'd had a promo copy—followed by the release of the single "Chuck E's in Love." Mom had said I looked like Rickie Lee Jones.

The song Mom chose for my mix tape was "Company," a melancholy tune about missing someone. Rickie Lee Jones probably meant a lover, but I couldn't stop thinking about Mom. I'd snapped the tape out of the player, burying it in the plastic bin of cassettes next to my stereo. I hadn't listened to it since.

Now I got out of bed, turning on a lamp and pawing through my jumbled cassette collection. From the bed, Mom-not-Mom watched me. In the lamplight, I felt the glow of her honey hair.

When I hit Play, the music started exactly where I'd stopped it seven months ago, in the middle of that sad Rickie Lee Jones song. "This is weirdly prophetic." I blinked. "And it's making me cry."

"Fast forward." Mom-not-Mom's voice was gentle.

I flipped between the Fast Forward and Play buttons until I reached the next song: "If I Can't Have You," by Yvonne Elliman. It was a disco-y tune about unrequited love.

I arched an eyebrow. "Really?"

"I had a feeling you were interested in someone, even if you didn't provide details," Mom-not-Mom said.

My face reddened. "There was nothing to tell."

The disco sound gave way to Joni Mitchell's luminous voice singing "Both Sides, Now." I felt Mom-not-Mom's eyes on me. "I had to include it. You know I love this song."

I nodded. "Me, too."

"Next one, as well," she whispered.

The next track was "Suzanne," sung by Judy Collins. The song was based on a poem by Leonard Cohen. It was about a dancer he'd known in Montreal, a woman with whom Cohen purportedly had a deeply spiritual yet platonic relationship. He later set it to music and eventually recorded it himself—as did numerous other musicians over the years. But Judy Collins recorded it first.

"Suzanne" was my namesake song. My mother had heard Judy—a Denver native and East High grad—sing it in a little club on Colfax when she was pregnant with me. The song gave Mom shivers. She said she knew I'd be a girl and that Suzanne was the perfect name for me. Besides calling me her little seer, Mom also called me Suzie Blue, because my eyes were as blue as Judy's.

"Oh, Mom," I breathed.

"The music gets livelier after this." Her voice was thick.

The opening notes of "We Are Family" by Sister Sledge came through the speakers. It was another song we both adored. Last winter when the album released, Mom played it incessantly. "We Are Family" was the first track on Side Two, and after it finished playing, Mom would lift the turntable needle and begin the song again. We'd both sing and dance around Zoe's Records. Corny, I know, but Mom had a way of making corny things cool.

The single of "We Are Family" released in April. It wasn't long before the song hit the Number Two slot on the Billboard chart. But by then, Mom was dead.

There was rustling, the jangle of the bell signifying Zoe's door opening. Over the next song on the album, I heard Mom say, "Can I help you?"

Mom-not-Mom explained, "I made your tape using the boombox. Remember how the tape deck in the stereo at Zoe's was on the fritz?"

I nodded. The music continued, but the voices were louder. Mom—her tone stiff—said, "Oh. Hello."

"Well, hello there, Alex!" The customer's voice was artificially upbeat.

Pressing Pause, I looked at Mom-not-Mom. "You're kidding, right?"

I felt her cross the room and sit beside me. "Just listen."

I hit Play. The conversation went like this:

Peggy: "Do you remember me? It's Peggy...from Jimmy's reunion."

Mom: "I remember you." The sound of a zipper closing. "Is there something I can help you find?"

Peggy: "I stopped in...to..." A high-pitched laugh. "I don't know why, actually. In any case, it appears you're closing soon."

Mom: "At nine. Thursday and Friday nights, I'm open late."

Peggy: "But not the past few Fridays. You've been seeing Jimmy on those nights, haven't you?"

Mom: "Is that what you came to speak with me about? Do you have a problem with James and me getting back together?"

Peggy—sharply: "No!" Then, lower, "I just...wanted to make sure..."

Mom: "Make sure what?"

Peggy: "That he's happy." Her voice dropped again. "He called today to let me know he was moving back to your house. He seemed pleased." A beat. "Which, perhaps, is a good thing. Jimmy's too nice a guy to be alone. He shouldn't be lonely."

Mom: "He's not lonely. We had some things to work out, and we're doing that."

Peggy: "Your son must be glad to have the family back together."

Mom: "My son? Not my daughter?"

That high-pitched laugh. Then, Peggy: "I meant both children, of course. It's just that for the wee ones, two parents in the home, parents who are truly devoted to the child...every young child needs that."

Mom: "Both my kids have that." A lull. Then, "Look, Peggy. I appreciate your concern about James. About our family. But we're fine."

Peggy: "Alex, here's the thing."

A drawn-out silence. Then, from Peggy: "I don't believe that. Not for a second."

That was it. The tape was at the end of its reel. "You see, Suzie Blue?" Mom-not-Mom asked. "Do you see now?"

"Did she say more?" I whispered.

"No. She changed the subject, asking for recommendations. She bought an album. Then she left."

"Did she come in other times?"

I felt Mom-not-Mom's level gaze at me. "Well, what do you think?"

I hugged my knees to my chest. "She was harassing you." Dropping my chin onto my kneecaps, I closed my eyes. "Why didn't you tell anyone?"

"What could I say? She'd claim she was simply a customer. She bought something every time she came in." I felt Mom-not-Mom nodding toward the tape. "Turn it over."

I flipped the tape and pressed Play. Donna Summer's voice filled my room, with her Number One hit, "Bad Girls." It was about hookers—and it *was* bad and sad, the idea of making a living turning tricks.

"I'm not bad, Mom," I said. "Not in *that* way."

"Of course not," she replied. "But there are as many ways to be bad as there are to be good." I felt a feathery touch on my shoulder. "And sometimes, Suzie Blue, when someone is bad to us, we need to be bad in return. Only then can we find the good."

8

— • —

2004

The manager of the building that once housed Zoe's Records was a goateed young hipster named Cameron. He'd likely been in preschool when my mother died, so it was unsurprising that he knew nothing of Zoe's history. I told him about the shop but not about Mom's death.

"And you'd do the same thing?" he asked. "Run a record store?"

"Not just music and records," I clarified. "Other forms of art, too. All created by women."

He rubbed a hand along his scruffy chin. "Hmm, well, if you think it would work."

Not exactly a vote of confidence. We went inside.

When Cameron flipped on the overheard lights, I felt blinded—due not to the lighting but to my frame of mind.

My memory banks brought it all back. Mom had rarely used the overheads; instead, there'd been floor lamps and spotlights for reading album titles and playlists. The wooden floors had been covered with area rugs and runners. There were plants in multicolored pots. There were posters on the walls, which Mom had painted cerulean blue.

I could hear the music. I remembered Mom and me dancing to "We Are Family" playing from the speakers in the upper corners. I could envision the customers browsing record bins. Some humming along, some swaying to the music. All smiling at our mother-daughter dance.

Approaching the counter, I ran my hand along it. The wood was dusty, in need of polish. I pictured myself ringing up new customers, today's customers. Imagined myself interacting with clientele, helping them make selections. Like Alex had.

My gaze fell on a spray of tiny, dark dots on the surface of the wood. I traced a fingernail along them.

Bloodstains. Had they been there all this time? It seemed impossible. They must be dark paint, something that looked red—to my eyes, anyway.

Maybe. Or maybe not.

I looked up at Cameron. "I'm very interested," I said.

I spent the next week composing a business plan. The lessons I'd learned in Entrepreneurship 101 at Berkeley came back to me, and I supplemented them with online and library resources. After reading everything I could on the subject, I put together a thorough plan for a small, independent retail business.

When I projected startup expenses, the calculations resulted in a number that overwhelmed me—well into five figures. I ran and re-ran it, whittling where I could, but the numbers came out relatively the same.

"I need to show you this," I said to Brett, setting the plan in front of him.

He glanced over it, then looked at me. "How did I not know this was something you were considering?" His tone, usually so affectionate, bordered on accusatory.

I looked away. I'd been afraid to share my idea with him—which seemed ludicrous; Brett had always supported me. But now I felt like a little girl asking for a raise in her allowance.

Turning to him, lifting my chin, I said, "You're making a good salary now. We're starting to pay off the credit cards. We have a little savings in the bank."

He pointed at the bottom figure. "Not like this, we don't."

"So I could take out a loan."

"*If* you could get a loan...which, let's be honest, is questionable." His brow furrowed. "And even if you could, this idea scares the crap out of me. The failure rate for small businesses is astronomical. Borrow this much money, and you—or better said, *we*— are pretty much guaranteed to be flushing it down the drain."

My face burned. What did *he* know? My mother had succeeded. Why shouldn't I?

"Fine." I swept the pages into a pile and walked to the window. My back to Brett, I listened to the sounds of the city—traffic on Twelfth Avenue, cicadas singing. The screech of a neighbor's back gate opening, then the sound of something being tossed into the dumpster. Shoulders tensed, I listened for the tread of footsteps out of the alley, back into the neighbor's yard. Away from my house.

I faced Brett. "Fine," I repeated. "You have zero faith in me. Good to know."

"Suze, I have faith in *you*. But taking a financial risk like this is reckless." He ran his fingers through my hair. "Look, babe, I know you're disappointed that no interviews have come through. But don't let a slow start shake you."

I pressed my lips together. "That's *not* what this is about."

"Don't be that way, honey." Brett took a step back. "Look, I get it. Just this afternoon, Nicole and I were talking about how hard it is to find a good job these days. She said she sympathizes with you—"

I inhaled. "You were talking with Nicole about me? Why?"

He raised his hands. "It just came up. She wanted you to know she understands."

My cheeks burned. "I'm sure your coworker understands exactly zero about me or what I want," I said. Then I turned and left the room.

"That sucks," Donna said when I stopped by her cottage to say hello. I'd told her about my plan for the store—and what Brett said.

"It does," I replied. "I could try to get a loan anyway...it's not like I need his permission. But I hesitate to move forward without Brett on board."

We were seated on the side terrace, with a view across the lawn toward Cheesman Park. The main house, where Evan lived with his family, was old-school Denver swank—marble floors, three stories, and a widow's walk boasting a magazine-worthy view of the Denver skyline, the Front Range, and the Rockies. It had been in the family of Donna's ex-husband, Vern, for generations. After Vern died, it passed to Evan. When Donna returned to Denver, Evan and his wife had invited her to stay in the guest cottage. She'd only intended to live there short-term but they all became accustomed to the situation. It gave her vindictive pleasure, Donna said, to live on the premises. "Vern wouldn't just roll over in his grave," she'd said. "He'd be doing goddamn somersaults."

I thought about the ghosts I used to sense in Cheesman when I was a kid—laborers or criminals, most of them. I knew that ghosts generally didn't care about their earthly bodies, but my sense of the Cheesman ghosts was that many were missing body parts—or, like a cubist painting, the pieces were out of place. This, I later learned, was valid: in 1893, when bodies were exhumed so a park could be built, little care had been taken to keep skeletons intact.

Today, mid-morning on a weekday, I sensed no spirits. All I saw were dog walkers, runners, and some guys playing Frisbee. High clouds drifted across the sky, causing the ancient trees to cast long, fingerlike shadows on the grass. A solitary bird watcher, wearing dark, shapeless clothes and a ball cap, used binoculars to scan the horizon, stopping to focus on Donna and me. When Donna waved, the bird watcher sprinted away.

Donna squeezed my hand. "Suzanne, I'd help if I could. But I'm my own charity case these days." She tapped her cigarette on an ashtray. "You know, I had a hell of a time in San Francisco. Best of times, best of friends. But I never saved a dime. Never would I have expected, at age sixty-one, to be the recipient of my son's largess."

Her words gave me pause. After my dad paid for Berkeley, I never accepted another dime from him. Brett had taken out loans for college; we were still paying them off. I'd always attempted maintaining a household budget but was hopeless at it. And everything in the Bay Area had been so expensive—it was no wonder we couldn't get ahead. Our months of unemployment had only exacerbated things.

Last year Brett turned forty. Next month I'd join that club. We needed to save for retirement. Caitlin would leave for college in several years, a major expense.

It was unknown what Austin needed, because Austin's situation was unclear. He'd seen a pediatrician and we received a referral to the outpatient behavioral health clinic at Children's Hospital. When I called, they said he needed to be re-evaluated there before they'd treat him. They put his name on the waiting list. I'd contacted several private practitioners but when I described the situation, they'd all referred me to Children's.

"Hey." Donna ground out her cigarette. "I know your dad is on his big trip right now. But if anyone has money, it's James. He fronted your mom when she started up—and wow, was she excited. Perhaps you don't remember that. You were little."

"I remember," I murmured.

"Maybe he'd do the same for you. Why don't you ask him?"

I stared at her. "You have got to be kidding," I said, stacking the words one by one, like cards in a deck. "There is no way in hell I'd ask my father for money. Or anything else, for that matter."

9

1979

The night after Mom-not-Mom and I listened to the mix tape, I retrieved a thick volume from a lower shelf in our library. Clutching the book, I sank onto the couch.

Like me, Dad had attended East High. He graduated in 1958, the year after Judy Collins. His yearbook cover was red, with a checkerboard-type graphic, a big '58, and the title *Angelus.* The words *East High School, Denver, Colorado* appeared below the title.

Paging through, I found numerous handwritten remarks and quips.

James, it was swell being on swim team with ya! See you in the funnies! - Edwin Stone

To a nice guy and Peggy's sweetheart—you <u>are</u> a sweetheart! Good luck! - Betsy Warner

To James, the Walking Encyclopedia of the Class of '58, loads of luck in the future! - Francis R.

Beside his senior picture, I read, "James L. Parry: A Capella, Swim, Sq. dancing, D club, Ski."

I found Peggy's listing: "Margaret Hicks: A Capella, Seraph Sis., Sq. dancing, Bible research, Girls' rifle."

I examined Peggy's picture. Her hair was rolled the way girls used to wear it; these days, her auburn hair was cut in a short wedge like the figure skater

Dorothy Hamill. Other than a different hairstyle, the Peggy I knew looked about the same as in high school.

Near the back, I found her inscription to my dad.

Jimmy,

What can I say? (Not much, since this is public, ha ha.) THANK YOU for everything. For singing "Peggy Sue" with Buddy Holly and me. (Is this our song? I think it is!!) For the rides in your Bel Air with the top down, the milkshakes at the Chat & Chew, and for every corsage. Although we'll be apart next year, you'll never be far from my heart.

Love,

Peggy

It seemed like standard boyfriend-girlfriend stuff. I could picture Dad and Peggy spiffied up for a dance, her in a satin dress and those crinoline petticoats girls wore, him in a suit and white buck shoes. The corsages. She thanked him for the fucking *corsages*. Well, likely they were fancy, expensive ones.

Footsteps echoed in the hallway. His nightly glass of scotch in hand, Dad peered in. "Hey, Suzanne. It's getting late."

"I'm heading up soon." I considered sliding the yearbook off my lap, to the side away from Dad, but there was no way to do that without being obvious. "I was looking at your yearbook. To see if East back then was like East now."

He laughed. "The two are indisputably incomparable. Did you know the first bound yearbook in the United States was for Yale, Class of 1806?"

I shook my head. Dad sat beside me. "Let me see that." I handed him the book. "Eons ago," he mused, flipping through.

I cleared my throat. "I saw Peggy's picture."

Dad smiled. "She and I had entertaining episodes in those days."

Plan carefully what you say next, I heard Mom-not-Mom say in my head.

"Well, life was easier then," I replied. "Much less responsibility than now."

He finished his drink, setting the empty glass on an end table. "Infinitely less. Indeed."

"I'd guess being in a relationship now is more challenging," I said. "It's not just the two of you anymore."

His look seemed far away. "In many ways, it was more than just the two of us then, too. Peggy and I had known each other for years—we ran with the same crowd—but we only became steadies senior year. After graduation, we shared a splendid summer of adventures. But in the fall, Peggy went to college out of state. She broke up with me in October." He stared at his hands. "We saw each other over winter break, but that was it." Clearing his throat, he repeated, "That was it."

"I'm sorry." I patted his arm. "Still, it was a high school romance. Mostly, those don't last, do they?"

Dad shook his head.

"And it's different now," I said. "It's not just proms and corsages. Riding around in a convertible. Having 'a song.'" When he glanced at me, I said, "I saw what Peggy wrote to you."

"If I recall correctly, her inscription was innocuous," Dad replied. "If memory serves, Peggy went so far as to be careful what she wrote since it was 'public.'" He stood, replacing the yearbook on the bookshelf. "Indeed, on a shelf in a man's family library is a suitable site when there's...nothing to hide."

Was there something to hide?

Dad reseated himself. "I comprehend that you're not crazy about Peggy's presence in our lives. Nonetheless, she's doing us a favor."

"Understood." I paused. "But Peggy isn't Mom. She'll never be Mom."

My eyes and his—identically indigo blue—met one another's.

He nodded. "You're correct, Suzanne."

We stood and he switched off the lamp. In the dim light from the hallway, Dad said, "Peggy is nothing like your mom."

When school let out the next day, it was raining in sheets. I ran home; I'd forgotten to bring a jacket. Peggy was in the kitchen, and Chris and his pal, Jeff, were in the library, watching TV and eating ants on a log.

Rubbing my wet hair with a towel, I observed Chris and Jeff from the doorway. I was glad he had a friend over. There weren't many kids in our neighborhood anymore—not since Denver Public Schools started busing students all over town, and families moved to the suburbs in droves.

"These are yummy," Jeff said, biting into his celery, peanut butter, and raisin snack. "Your mom's a good cook."

"She's not his mom," I said.

They both stared at me. "She just helps out around here," I explained to Jeff.

"I thought she was your mom," Jeff said to Chris.

"She's like a mom. She does mom stuff." Chris flipped the switch that turned the TV from broadcast to Atari, then handed a joystick to Jeff. "Wanna play *Street Racer?*"

With the force of an angry bear, I banged my hands against the sides of the doorway. But Chris and Jeff ignored me, already engrossed in their game.

Upstairs, I peeled off my wet shirt and took out a dry one.

"Honeypie," I heard. Closing my eyes, I sensed Mom-not-Mom in my circular space. Behind her, buckets of rain poured off the gutters and streamed down the wavy, ancient glass of the windowpanes.

"I don't want you catching a cold," she said. "Don't go out again without a jacket."

This sounded so much like the Mom I missed, I almost burst into tears. I wanted so badly to feel her hold me. But I knew that couldn't happen. So I just whispered, "Okay, Mommy."

The next morning, I paged through the phone book to a listing for Hicks, Margaret E., with an address a few miles south off Colorado Boulevard. After school, I boarded a Colfax bus. At Colorado Boulevard, I transferred to a southbound bus.

I stood on the sidewalk inspecting Peggy's three-story brick apartment building. Stepping into the entryway, I read names on the mailboxes. Peggy's apartment was on the second floor.

The glass door separating the entryway from the rest of the building was locked. A woman appeared on the other side with a toy poodle on an orange leash. As she opened the door, I smiled, making eye contact—Mom always said eye contact is key in every interaction, large or small. The woman smiled back, and as she exited the building, I slipped inside.

Peggy's apartment door had a thin silver cross on it. There was a welcome mat that said, "God Bless All Who Enter."

Even those who break-and-enter?

Remember what I told you, Mom-not-Mom said. *Sometimes, you have to be bad to find the good.*

"But what am I looking for?" I whispered aloud in the empty hallway.

I don't know. But you'll figure it out, my little seer.

I turned the knob and was surprised it gave. Did Mom-not-Mom facilitate that, or did Peggy figure that since the building was secure, she didn't need to lock her apartment?

In front of me was the living room, with a small dining area beyond. Across a half-wall from the dining area was a spotless kitchen. There were about a dozen potholders stuck to the refrigerator with magnetized hooks. Who needs a dozen potholders? Stepping closer, I saw they had sayings on them.

Happiness is Homemade.

Count the Memories, Not the Calories.

Honey, Bee Yourself—with an image of a smiling bee, of course.

I began inspecting every drawer and closet. I didn't know what I was looking for...anything that might tell me more about Peggy. Anything I could use against her.

It was unsurprising to find that Peggy, former Girls' Rifle club member, had a small handgun tucked into her nightstand drawer. The only guns I'd ever seen before were on TV. When I picked it up, it felt cold. Was it loaded? Probably.

My fingers light on the trigger, I held the gun aloft and looked in the mirror over the dresser. I imagined a gun like this aimed at my body. Imagined the gun firing so rapidly, there was no time to do anything except, in stunned silence, accept the bullets entering my flesh.

One, two, three.

I barreled across the room, replacing the gun in Peggy's nightstand drawer and slamming it shut. Then I closed my eyes and concentrated. Opening them, I walked directly to Peggy's desk.

It was a compact wooden desk with a matching chair. Its surface held an IBM Selectric typewriter, a pen holder, and a vase of silk tulips. I opened desk drawers, finding folders labeled in block letters: BILLS, CHURCH, MISSION WORK, TAX RECORDS. There was one called LITERACY WORK that contained brochures about a charity for helping adults learn to read. In the bottom drawer was a folder marked MOM: HEALTH AND INS. Flipping through it, I saw medical and insurance records for a Mrs. Mabel Hicks. Behind that was one labeled Photos. I rifled through them; most seemed to be pictures of Peggy's missionary days. There was also a black-and-white studio portrait of a chubby baby, with no name or date on the back.

Then I came across a folder that stopped me in my tracks. Printed in the same block letters was the name BOBBY SHELTON.

Fingers trembling, I paged through. Peggy had clipped every article about Mom's death from the *Rocky Mountain News* and *The Denver Post*. The story made the front page of both papers—"Local Record Store Owner Shot in Armed Robbery" was the *Post*'s headline—and there were several follow-up articles mentioning that Shelton was tied to the crime by fingerprints at the scene, his footprints in the snow, and an eyewitness who, upon hearing gunshots, saw him run out of Zoe's Records. Officer Powles was described as a hero, and neither he nor the bus driver was penalized for Shelton's death. There was a picture of Powles, a burly young man with a cleft chin.

Peggy had also clipped Mom's and Bobby Shelton's obituaries. I could've recited my mother's obituary by heart, but I'd never seen her killer's. "Shelton, Robert 'Bobby,' age 19, of Denver. Passed away on February 22, 1979. Born March 20, 1959. Survived by his father Mark Shelton of Aurora and sister Tammy of Santa Fe, NM. Preceded in death by his grandparents and mother Doris Shelton. Burial at Riverside Cemetery."

That was it. Mom's obituary was five times longer. It listed Dad, Chris, and me. It talked about Mom's education and about Zoe's Records. It alluded to the tragedy of her being the victim of an armed robber. My eyes became misty when I read the quote from Denver bluegrass artist Aspen Ferraro: "Alexandra Parry embodied everything brilliant about the Colorado music scene, especially for female musicians. Her enthusiasm and advocacy have helped countless artists, myself included, build their followings. Alex was universally loved and will be greatly missed."

I sifted through the folder's items. Besides the articles and obituaries, there was a single sheet of paper with several short, typed sentences: "The flowers in the garden are pretty." "My house is on Sixth Street." "The cat sleeps on the window sill."

Under that was a scrap of paper that made me gasp aloud. In neat cursive was Shelton's first name, followed by a phone number.

I grabbed a ballpoint pen, copying the number onto my other hand. I searched the rest of the desk but there was nothing else about Shelton or Mom.

Not a thing, besides that folder, connected either of them with Peggy.

"What the hell does Peggy know about Bobby Shelton?" I asked Mom-not-Mom that night. "Why does she have those articles? And his obituary and yours? And his *phone number?*"

"No idea," Mom-not-Mom said.

"How can you have no idea? You're the one who sent me there in the first place."

"Not really," she replied. "You figured out on your own to go there, Suzie Blue."

I expelled a long breath. "Did Peggy actually *know* Bobby Shelton? She must have. But how? Why?"

"I wish I could tell you, but I have no clue."

Climbing out of bed, I went to the window. "This is *so* crazy—that Peggy knew Shelton. Please tell me that's crazy, Mom."

I waited for a response.

"Mom?" I turned around.

She'd vanished. I sank to the floor, my back against the cracked plaster wall beneath my open window. A light breeze came in, and the muslin curtains grazed my hair. I closed my eyes, relishing the feeling. Knowing it was my mother's hand.

10

— · —

2004

I called Cameron to ask if a lower rent could be negotiated for the Zoe's space. After speaking to the building's owner, he told me they could go down fifty dollars a month. "We've had other interest, so you should decide soon," he said.

That was probably bullshit; nonetheless, ending the call felt like re-wrapping a present I'd only half-opened. I slipped my business plan's file folder into the "Low Priority" bin on my desk. I sent out a few resumes, then consoled myself by curling up to read Anita Diamant's *The Red Tent*. Maybe that was all I was good for—reading, and dreaming about things that couldn't be.

Oh, stop it, Suzanne, I chided myself. Self-pity is *not* a good look.

Putting the novel aside, I got in my car and drove to the Little Denver Home for Children. I didn't have an appointment but I hoped to find someone who would speak with me, perhaps even show me Dad's records.

The license plates of cars I passed bore positive signs. LFC: *Looking for clues*. IWO: *Information will open*.

The Little Home consisted of several squat, brick buildings on a side street off University Boulevard. A chain-link fence enclosed the buildings and a yard that featured a rusted swing set and a basketball court in need of repaving and new nets. Locating the only unfenced building, marked Administration, I stepped inside.

"I'm sorry," a bespectacled women told me when I gave her my father's name and birth date. Her sunshine-yellow name tag read BECKY in bright blue letters. On her sweatshirt was an image of a kitten curled up in a basket. "We have records but they're sealed. We can only release information to adoptees themselves. And then only with a court order."

"He doesn't want the information. But I do." I swallowed rawness in my throat. "It's health related, Becky. It's for my son."

Behind her glasses, Becky's eyes were sympathetic. "I wish I could help. But our hands are tied by the system. Your best bet is to ask your father to put in a court order."

"I know his original name." My voice became desperate. "He was James Lewis before he was adopted."

She tilted her head. "Who told you this?"

"He did."

Becky frowned. "And you say he was adopted as an infant?"

"That's my understanding."

She paged through some materials on her desk. "I'll tell you this. At any orphanage during those times—including here at the Little Home—it would be highly unusual for someone adopted that young to know his birth name. If he was an infant, his original birth certificate, if he even had one, would've been sealed. His adoptive parents would have received a new certificate with their names on it. They wouldn't have known his birth name, and neither would he."

I shook my head. "But he *told* me his name."

"If he knew that, my guess is he wasn't an infant. He was likely old enough to know something of his past. Probably at least five or six years old." Becky leveled her gaze at me. "Again, if I were you, I'd ask your father about this."

The next morning after dropping Austin at school, Stevie and I walked up to Colfax. The leaves were turning—brilliant reds on the maples, exquisite yellows on the aspens. We crossed Colfax and walked west.

I was still thinking about Becky's words. Had Dad been older when he was adopted? If so, why claim to be an infant? Did my grandparents sell him that narrative for such a long time, he eventually believed it? Or—and, knowing Dad, I had to consider this possibility—was he well aware of his past but lied because he didn't want to talk about it?

There was no way to know—except, as Becky said, to ask him. But that would do no good. I'd left my number with Becky, asking her to call if she thought of anything else. I doubted I'd hear from her.

Reaching Zoe's, I peered in the window. I could see it in my mind's eye, could visualize my store's layout. Could see the bright colors, the artwork on walls and shelves. The diversities of design, the textures and patterns. I could hear the music—a mixture of old stuff and contemporary, up-and-coming, local and national artists. Jazz and classical and funk. Everything.

Wiping the dusty windowpane with a tissue, cupping my hands around my eyes for a better view, I mentally arranged a display of my knives. It had been years since I'd entertained the idea of selling a handmade knife, but now I longed for the opportunity.

My phone rang. It was Donna. "I might have a solution for you," she said. "Can you meet me in fifteen minutes?" She named a coffee shop about a mile west on Colfax.

"I'm out now," I said. "I'll head that way."

The route I strolled was my well-worn teenage path—from Zoe's, past the Bluebird Theater, which in my mother's time had been an X-rated movie house but now was a trendy music hall she'd have loved. I entered the zone of one ambrosial eatery after another, some of them around for decades, others new. Passing East High, looking up at the classic, Jacobethan Revival-styled building with its iconic clock tower, I wondered how Caitlin's day was going. Whenever I asked her about school, she said little.

Most mornings, she slept in and was the last to leave the house, so I hadn't seen her today.

On lampposts and the sides of buildings, I spied additional posters about Darcy Powles and Robert Shelton Jr. Poor girl, I thought. I hoped she'd soon be found, or she'd come home on her own.

If I continued walking, eventually I'd reach my childhood street. But I had zero intention of going that far. The coffee shop was a few blocks east of our old street, and I was glad of it. Walking part of the familiar route was enough to make my legs shake, not from exertion but from raw recollection. Especially when I passed a particular phone booth—now dirty and nonfunctional, the receiver missing, the metal cord hanging like a severed noose.

I felt a lump in my throat. After passing the booth, I turned to stare, marveling that the sight of this simple, archaic device still held such sway.

Outside the coffee shop, Donna and another woman were seated at a bistro table. Donna hugged me, then said, "This is my daughter-in-law, Renee. Renee, this is Suzanne."

It was my first time meeting Renee. Several years ago, Brett and I had been invited to Colorado for Renee and Evan's wedding, but we'd had a conflict and couldn't make it. Now they had a young son—and sadly, over the summer Renee had miscarried twins at sixteen weeks' gestation.

Evan was five years younger than me, and Renee looked about the same age as him. She was short and curvy, with volumes of dark, billowing hair. The blouse she wore was extraordinary. It was jade-colored cotton, sewn all over with patches of fabric shaped like every type of tree imaginable, in dozens of hues and textures. It was like a wearable painting. Scripted across the right shoulder were the words "Tree Love."

"Great top," I said. "Where'd you get it?"

Donna and Renee both smiled. "She made it," Donna told me.

I recalled Donna once telling me that Renee was an artist who did fabric work. "It's beautiful," I said.

"Thank you." Renee set down her espresso. "Can I get you something, Suzanne?"

Donna stood. "On me." She took my order and went inside.

Renee turned to me. "I hear you're looking to open a gallery."

"Not really a gallery." Images of stark white walls, a sparse collection of paintings and photographs, perhaps a few dramatically lit sculptures on sleek stands, filled my mind. I envisioned openings with expensive wine and cheese, witty conversation—the type of event that left me tongue-tied, only hours later coming up with amusing remarks I *could* have made. "More of a shop. The space I have in mind isn't big. My idea is to sell commissioned pieces by local artists. All women."

"A solid idea, and much needed," Renee said. "Female artists rarely get the recognition they should."

Tiny, starburst-shaped scars dotted Renee's fingers. Catching my gaze at them, she said, "Pinprick and needle scars. Occupational hazard, I'm afraid." She nodded toward my hands. "Yours look rather careworn, too."

I nodded. "I have some hobbies. My hands get beat up."

Donna returned. "Did you tell her?" she asked Renee, setting a cup in front of me and a plastic bowl of water on the sidewalk for Stevie.

I added sugar to my coffee. "Tell me what?"

Renee leaned forward. "Suzanne, I'd love to see your business plan. I've recently begun to think about investing in a business, and this might be the investment I'm looking for. My work is selling well, and besides that, I've had a bit of inheritance from my mother. She, too, was an artist, and when she died…" Renee stared at the midmorning traffic on Colfax. "I inherited her collection. I kept my favorites, donated a number of pieces to museums, and sold the remainder." Her eyelids fluttered. "It's netted me a sum that I'd like to put into something that she…"

Donna put her hand on Renee's. "That she'd support," Donna finished for Renee.

Something flashed through me then, causing my skin to redden, my face to feel flushed. Envy, perhaps, at the sight of Donna's hand on top of another woman's? At the idea of Donna mothering another motherless daughter?

Other emotions erupted, too. Excitement—maybe the new Zoe's really *could* happen. And fear. I had no idea what it was like to have a business partner. What if we didn't get along? What if the business failed and Renee blamed me? I reached down, entwining my fingers in Stevie's ear fur.

"It's just an idea," Renee said. "But if you're interested in exploring it, so am I."

I emailed Renee my business plan and she responded the next day. I set up an appointment with Cameron so we could tour the space together. Renee inspected every inch, taking in the lighting and dimensions. "You're right that we'd have to be modest in our inventory," she said. "This space would be best for those working on smaller scales. Jewelers, perhaps, and those creating moderately sized paintings and photographs. Definitely fiber and textile arts."

I nodded, furiously taking notes. If nothing else, I could benefit from Renee's expertise.

As for actually partnering with her, I had hesitations. The fear and anxiety that had gripped me at the coffee shop remained, clinging to my gut and winding through my body into my hand, sweaty and slippery on the pen as I wrote.

My mother used to say that what we feared most was what we most needed to confront. I knew what I feared now: trying something new and having it turn into a sinking ship. And when that happened, people mocking me, finding me ridiculous. The Peggys of the world calling me a failure.

I strode toward Renee. "What do you think? Could we make this work?"

11

1979

The next day after school, I stepped into a phone booth on Colfax and dialed the number I'd found in Peggy's apartment. There was no answer. The rest of the week, I called daily. Once, I got a busy signal and hung out in the phone booth for another half hour. I tried over and over, but I kept getting a busy. Most days the phone just rang.

The following Sunday, Dad informed Chris and me that we'd be having a "special supper." All afternoon, Peggy was a hurricane in our kitchen. Roasted chicken with dried fruit stuffing. Duchess potatoes. Green bean casserole and homemade rolls. It was like a mini Thanksgiving.

Peggy called us to dinner with a clap of her hands. "Come and get it, everyone!"

The dining room table was adorned with a burgundy tablecloth I'd never seen before, matching napkins, and white tapers in silver candlesticks. Peggy had dimmed the chandelier, and the room glowed.

"Holy shit," I said. "You went all out, Peggy."

She stared at me. "A simple 'wow' would suffice...but thank you, Suzanne."

After Peggy murmured her Come-Lord-Jesus prayer, Dad poured Cabernet Sauvignon for everyone except Chris—full glasses for Peggy and himself, half a glass for me. "Some occasions," Dad said, "are cause for colossal celebration."

I sipped. The wine wasn't bad, although I preferred beer or Tab-with-whiskey, which Laurie sometimes served me. Dad looked at me, then at Chris. "Do you know what's coming? Have Peggy and I been blatantly barefaced?"

I drained my wineglass. It tasted like eating too much fruit in one sitting.

"You're getting married, right?" Chris asked, and I imagined a light bulb, like in a cartoon, over the top of his bowl-haircut head.

I was too late. I'd failed my mother. I reached for the wine bottle but instead almost knocked it over. Peggy jumped up, grabbing it before it toppled. Her eyes—dark green, serpentine—met mine.

Looking away, I mumbled, "Excuse me," and dashed to the bathroom. Kneeling in front of the toilet, I let the wine—and my remorse—find its way out.

I splashed water on my face, then regarded myself in the bathroom mirror. Yes, I'd failed. But I wasn't going to hide in my room crying.

When I entered the dining room, everyone stared at me. "You okay, Suze?" Dad asked.

I took my seat. "Just needed the restroom."

Peggy smiled in my general direction. Dad once told us that someone who fakes a smile is called an eccedentesiast—and that's exactly what Peggy was. "Do you feel all right to eat?" she said. "I can fix you something else, if you prefer."

I stabbed the serving fork into a slice of chicken on the platter. I filled my plate with sides and began eating. "Have you set a wedding date?" I asked, my mouth full of food. With satisfaction, I noticed Peggy making a face.

Dad poured himself more wine. "Not yet. We're thinking March." He set down the bottle. "Did you know ravioli was first consumed in the U.S. in the late 1800s?"

I frowned. "And you're telling us this because..."

"National Ravioli Day is March twentieth," Dad explained.

Peggy laughed, then said, "The wedding won't be huge. A church wedding followed by an intimate reception with family and a few friends."

We were not a churchgoing family. Back in Brooklyn, Mom had been raised Catholic by a single mother—her father died in World War II—but she'd long ago given up the religion of her childhood and identified as agnostic. She said you didn't need church if you were essentially a good person and not an asshole. Dad clung to the Lutheran beliefs of his childhood but only occasionally went to church. We never went with him, and for whatever reason, I don't think he'd ever pressed the issue when Mom was alive.

When I asked which church, Peggy named the Lutheran church that Dad sometimes attended. "Is that your church, too?" I stared her down. "Mom wasn't religious, and neither are Chris or me. You *do* know that, right?"

"Your dad and I were raised in the same church." Peggy spoke to me but smiled at Dad. "Years and years of youth group together. Now I belong to a much larger Lutheran church. It's a lovely place, but for nostalgia's sake, we want to marry in our home church."

"Does Grandma know?" I asked Dad.

His mouth was in a flat line. "Not yet. I'll tell her, although I don't know…"

No one replied. Would the news register with senile Grandma Parry? Probably not.

"Will I be in the wedding?" Chris asked.

Peggy squeezed his arm. "Would you like to be?"

Get your fucking hand off him, I wanted to scream. Do not *touch* him!

Chris ducked away from her grasp. Good for you, bud, I thought.

"Not really," he said. "People would be looking at me."

"It won't be many people," Peggy promised. "But we'll work out the details later. Don't worry about it, sweetheart."

He held his cup toward her. "Can I have more milk?"

"Can I have more milk *what*?"

"Please," Chris said.

Peggy rose, scurrying to the kitchen with his cup. From the doorway, I heard her humming. It sounded like that 1960s song about going to the chapel.

Holy freakin' hell.

"Do you have anything to articulate?" Dad asked me. "Any inquiries?"

"None that can be answered in the time it takes to pour Chris a cup of milk." I refilled my wineglass. "This seems awfully fast, Dad. What's the rush?"

He nodded toward my glass. "You were only meant to have a minuscule amount, miss. Just for jollification."

Could he *never* talk like a regular person? "You didn't answer my question," I said.

"Peggy suggested that since we were getting serious, we should make a commitment."

"Mom's only been gone for seven months," I replied. "If Peggy really loved you, she could wait."

As I spoke, Peggy appeared in the doorway. Taking her seat, she looked at me. "Listen, Suzanne, I understand," she said. "I lost a parent, too, when I was young." Her eyes met Dad's. "After my father passed, my mom dated but never remarried. I wasn't crazy about the idea of her remarrying—and I made sure she knew it." She glanced at the dripping wax on the candlesticks. "Here's the thing, though: she dated truly decent men, and one of them might've made my mother very happy. And probably would've been a wonderful stepfather to me." Her look was far away. "So many things might have been different if I'd had the support of another parent." She pressed her lips together. "But I missed out—and my mother missed out—because I was unwilling to give it a chance."

A *chance*? Who the hell did she think she was?

As I opened my mouth to respond, Peggy held up her hand. "Don't make the same mistake." She picked up her fork, pointing it toward me. "Have an open mind, Suzanne."

That night in bed, I tossed and turned. Waiting for Mom-not-Mom. Waiting for sleep—and hoping it would be a solid, black one. Wanting to wake up and discover it was all a bad dream, that things were how they'd been before February twenty-second.

Finally I got out of bed, creeping downstairs and into Dad's study. Fumbling in the top desk drawer, I found the flashlight he kept there. Flashlight in hand, I located the item I sought, although it was shoved far back in the drawer. Had Dad pushed it as far back as possible, believing that removing this visual reminder from daily viewing would also delete its implications from his mind?

I switched off the flashlight, throwing it back in the drawer. I slipped what I'd taken into my pajama pants pocket. In bed, I turned onto my side, feeling the small, ridged item pressed against my body as I willed myself to sleep.

The next afternoon I walked east on Colfax. I passed the gyros place and, a few blocks down, inhaled the overpowering aroma of the Pick-a-Rib barbecue joint. I scurried past the Bluebird Theater, which reeked of piss and stale alcohol.

Soon afterward, I faced Zoe's Records.

A summer's worth of thunderstorms had collected grime and dead leaves in the corners of the storefront. I peered in through the filthy window. Mom and I used to give the windows a weekly Windexing—and this time of day, with the sun stretching to the west, they'd gleam in refracted sunlight. Now I could barely see inside through the dirt.

I pulled from inside my shirt collar a long leather cord holding a keyring—the item I'd taken from my father's desk drawer. With the key on the ring I unlocked the deadbolt, opened the creaking door, and stepped inside.

A faint smell of bleach—used by the cleaning people after Bobby Shelton murdered my mother—hung in the air. Dad must have instructed the cleaners to toss out the bloodstained items on the counter, because it was cleared of the assortment Mom had kept there. The cash register was gone. So was the small bucket—a sign taped to it reading "TAKE ONE!"—full of plastic-tabbed keyrings shaped like an LP with the words "ZOE'S RECORDS" scripted across it; the keyring on my leather cord was one of these. A ceramic dish holding record centerpieces, ten cents each or free with purchase of a 45, was also missing—as were the stacks of fliers for upcoming shows around town. The shows were at venues like the Denver Folklore Center, Tulagi's up in Boulder, and Ebbets Field—which Mom had especially liked because it was named after a ballpark in Brooklyn that she remembered from childhood. Promoters or sometimes band members themselves would stop in, asking if they could leave fliers. Mom always obliged, whether she'd heard of the band or not. She said everyone had to start somewhere.

In the darkness—the electricity had long ago been shut off—I looked around, wondering what would happen to the items remaining in the store. In a business like Zoe's Records, stock rotated all the time. My mother ordered new records weekly and returned unsold ones that had held promise but didn't take off with the buying public. We carried consistent top sellers but Mom also kept her stock up to date with new releases.

All of it should probably go back, if the distributors would take it. If not, it should be donated.

What made me consider a practicality like that? Who gave a flying fuck? Some other junkie, someone like Bobby Shelton, could break in, steal everything, and attempt to sell it on the street. But that wouldn't bring my mother back.

I imagined Zoe's Records as it had been—the lighting soft, music playing, a rainbow of colors. I could see all of us—the customers, Mom and me, and Chris hanging out in a corner, building a house of cards.

Taking four long steps across the room, I came face to face with Zoe the mannequin. I took in her shaggy hair, beads, and guitar. She gazed at me sympathetically, knowingly.

I put my arms around her, leaning my head onto her plastic shoulder and closing my eyes.

12

2004

Renee and I signed a partnership contract and a twelve-month lease on the space. I contributed only a modest amount of startup money, which meant Renee was the controlling partner. That was risky but I didn't care. It was better than not being able to do it at all.

Truly, Renee was a godsend. She mentioned connections I couldn't have fathomed. She discussed the publicity we could get for our launch. She knew a graphic artist who could create our logo and branding. She loved my suggestion of calling the store Zoe's—omitting "Records," since we'd sell much more than that—and using the tagline "A focus on the female artist." Ideas for the space came to both of us like waterfalls; sometimes we'd say the same thing simultaneously, then laugh aloud as I added it to our growing wish list.

To get a jump start on the holiday shopping season, we set an opening date of Friday, November fifth, just days after the presidential election. "Either people will be in the mood to celebrate, or they'll seek a distraction and find it in supporting a local business and artists," Renee said. "Either way, it's a win for us."

The plan to open that soon was ambitious, but I was determined to make it work. Daily, I was at Zoe's from the time I dropped off Austin until school pickup. Renee came by when she could, but due to her creative work, she had limited availability. Mostly, she left me to my own devices.

The arrangement was a dream come true. I couldn't believe my luck—but I told myself that maybe I deserved some luck coming my way.

One afternoon in mid-September after fetching Austin, I went into the kitchen and poured myself iced tea. Paging through *The Denver Post*, I came across an article about Darcy Powles.

SEARCH CONTINUES FOR MISSING WOMAN

Police continue to search for 18-year-old Darcy Powles, last seen with her boyfriend, Robert Shelton Jr., 25, on August 24. Shelton was driving a 1992 red Honda Accord, license plate 321-HTH. There have been no sightings of the vehicle.

"RJ seemed like a nice guy, and Darcy trusted him," said Elaine Thomas, Powles's aunt, speaking for the family. "The night she disappeared, they were planning to celebrate his birthday. We can't understand it. Darcy would never go this long without contacting family."

According to Thomas, the couple had been together since July. "RJ was too old for her," Thomas said. "But she's an adult and in charge of her own decisions."

Police ask that anyone with information about the case contact the police hotline.

The article included photos of both Darcy Powles and Robert Shelton Jr. His photo looked like a better-kept version of his father's mug shot from 1979. Cleaner hair and no oozing sores on his face, but the pale blue eyes were identical.

My stomach twisted. Stuffing the newspaper in the recycling bin, I went out to the garage. Wedging the door open to let in warm autumn breezes, I began rehandling a butcher knife I'd picked up at a thrift store. As I worked, I paused periodically to run my finger over the blade's sharpened surface, feeling myself grow calmer with each stroke.

"It's really shaping up in here," Renee said, stopping by Zoe's a few days later. "I'm impressed."

I looked up from pulling painter's tape off the baseboards. That morning I'd finished painting the walls pale blue—lighter than they'd been at Zoe's Records, but pastel would better showcase the artwork. The color gave the space an inviting, personal mood.

Renee began helping me pull tape. "I'm trying to envision this space when it was your mother's shop." Her eyes met mine. "I'm sorry. Perhaps that brings up difficult memories."

"Not at all." Some time ago, explaining to Renee the vibe I wanted in the new shop, I'd told her about Zoe's Records. Now, pausing from my task, I added as many details about the old shop as I recalled.

"How inventive," Renee said. "I've never been in a record store like that."

"There was nothing else like it."

"Donna says Alex was quite a go-getter," Renee said. "Did she have a background in business?"

"Not really," I replied. "She was a poor but brainy girl from Brooklyn. The University of Denver offered her a full scholarship—that's how she ended up here. She started undergrad as a history major, but she dropped out junior year to have me."

"And she met your dad in college?"

"No, he was a few years older, already done with school. One day, he strolled into the record department of the downtown Denver Woolworth's, where Mom was clerking to earn extra cash. He asked her out and they began to date. Within a few months she became pregnant, so they got married." I twisted the full trash bag closed. "When I went to kindergarten, Mom returned to school and got a business degree. She took unpaid internships at three different companies and minimum-wage gigs in record stores. When she felt ready to open Zoe's Records, and my dad agreed to back her—" I grimaced, recalling Brett's lack of enthusiasm for my business venture "—she was in business."

"And it all worked out," Renee said.

"It all worked out," I echoed.

I left it at that. I assumed Renee knew, through Donna, what happened to Mom. But Renee had recently lost a mother herself. She wasn't a teen when her mom died, but the death of a beloved mother is enormous. I knew that all too well.

As much time as I spent at Zoe's, I also spent considerable hours at Austin's school—whenever he landed in the principal's office. The first time, it was because he became flustered during an assignment and took it out on the classroom teacher's aide by slapping her face. In another incident, he wrangled with a kid on the playground who teased him about carrying his plastic Pikachu everywhere. Austin, tiny as he was, managed to push the kid off his feet, and the kid's head slammed into the asphalt.

"Austin needs to learn healthy ways to channel his frustration," the principal said when I arrived another day, this time because he'd grabbed the papers from every student's cubby and begun ripping them to shreds. His reason? I'd inadvertently sent peanut butter crackers for his snack, and nuts were prohibited in the classroom.

The principal glanced at her computer monitor. "I see that Austin has an ADHD diagnosis. Have you looked into comorbidities? Does he see a therapist?"

I pressed my lips together. "We're working on it." We'd tried a private-practice child psychologist, but Austin refused to speak to her, instead resorting to infantile babbling and cat meows. Thinking he might connect better with a male therapist, she referred us to a colleague. But that was worse—Austin threatened to slug the man "if you ask me one more stupid question."

My heart ached for my child. I wanted someone to tell me something miraculous, something to unlock the mystery that was Austin. I needed a key that, much as I loved him, eluded me.

Later that afternoon, I called Children's to check on the wait list but was told only that we were still on it. I asked if they had suggestions for other resources, and they said to contact our pediatrician.

Circles and circles and circles. I hung up, feeling defeated.

Then an idea came to me. I called Becky at the Little Home. She listened as I explained Austin's situation. When I finished, she said, "And you're asking if he could be seen here? Unfortunately, we don't do that. We're government-funded, and all our clients are referred via the county. Have you tried Children's Hospital?"

I sighed. "We're on their wait list."

Becky paused. "Suzanne, I didn't know if I should tell you this, but since you called...here goes. I might have some helpful information. It's at my home." I heard other voices, then she returned to the line. "Can you come to my house? Tonight?"

That evening, I asked Caitlin to keep an eye on Austin while I ran a quick errand. "He can play on the Wii," I told her. I knew there'd be a price to pay for that; Austin didn't sleep well if we allowed gaming after dinner, so we rarely did so. "Just sit down there with him, Cait. And keep the doors locked."

"Such bullshit," she muttered. "But whatever."

Refusing to take her bait, I ran upstairs for my drop-point. The knife case was locked. When I opened it, my knives were neatly arranged, as expected.

But the drop-point was missing.

I sorted through the two dozen knives in the case. I checked my purse and the pockets of jackets I'd worn recently. The drop-point was nowhere to be found.

Closing my eyes, I tried to see it, which sometimes works when I misplace something. But the knife's location failed to manifest. I selected a small tactical knife with a rosewood handle, then headed out.

Becky lived in the suburb of Lakewood, in a well-lit, modest ranch on a cul-de-sac. She and her tabby, Gladys, greeted me at the door. "Only one cat," she said. "Which means I'm not a crazy cat lady."

Seated beside me on the plaid couch, Becky handed over a scrapbook. "It's sort of a hobby," she said. "I collect stories about orphaned children." Gladys jumped into her lap. "I don't know why I'm drawn to them. Maybe from a childhood love of orphan stories. *The Boxcar Children. A Little Princess.*" Becky ran her hand over Gladys's fur. "I like happy endings. I don't know if these children had happy endings, but I hope they did."

I paged through the scrapbook. Some of the stories were original yellowed newsprint, but there were also photocopies and printouts of website pages. Tales of infants left at church doorsteps. Depression-era mothers knocking on orphanage doors, begging the homes to take in their starving children. Parents dying from disease, accidents, food poisoning.

What an unusual thing to collect. I said nothing.

"That one." Becky pointed as I turned the page. "That's the story I wanted you to see."

I scanned the article, then reread it slowly.

It was about a Denver woman named Claranna Lewis. In August 1946, Claranna committed suicide by burning down her house. Claranna had two young children who, according to the article, "had been trapped inside but narrowly escaped the hellish inferno." The next paragraph mentioned that "following the tragedy, the older child, a girl aged 12, remains with her father to comfort him."

There was one more line: "The younger, a boy aged 6, has been surrendered to the Little Denver Home for Children."

13

— • —

1979

After my first time there, I regularly visited Zoe's after school. I began squirreling supplies at the shop. A flashlight, pencils, and Bic pens, so I could do my homework while sitting at Zoe's feet. Pillows for my butt, because even with area rugs, the hardwood floor got uncomfortable. Batteries for the flashlight and boombox Mom had kept at the store for use during power outages—the same one she'd used to create my mix tape, recording songs from albums she played on the stereo to a blank tape in the boombox nearby.

I listened to cassettes, which I took from the bins, breaking their plastic seals. I played all the music Mom had loved. Billie Holiday, Carly Simon, Dolly Parton. Emmylou Harris, Donna Summer. Joni Mitchell and Judy Collins.

I longed for Mom-not-Mom but felt her neither at home nor at Zoe's. I knew she must be heartbroken about Dad and Peggy's engagement. I took the knowing, sympathetic eyes of Zoe the mannequin as Mom's attempt to be present.

One day the tailor next door, Mr. Frederick, came out of his shop as I was going into Zoe's. When he asked what I was doing. I told him my father said I could go to the shop any time I wanted, as long as I locked up afterward.

Mr. Frederick tsk-tsked. "Your mama was such a nice lady. Tragic, a thing like that happening. The world is crazy, you know?"

I nodded.

"You need anything, you come over." He laughed a big, Santa Claus laugh. "But getting your pants hemmed probably wouldn't help much, right?"

I managed a smile. "No. But thanks, anyway."

"Well, I got soda pop in a fridge out back. I got the gumball machine. Anything you want, I'll give you, honey."

One warm afternoon, I was at Zoe's, studying for a geometry exam with the door wedged open. An Aretha Franklin cassette was in the boombox. Feeling someone watching me, I glanced up and saw a shadowed figure in the doorway. I let out a small scream.

"Sorry." The male voice was vaguely familiar. "I noticed the open door and I wondered if the store was open again."

I shook my head. "No, sorry. We're closed. I was just letting in sunshine and fresh air."

He stepped inside. I aimed my flashlight, trying not to zap him in the eyes. He wore jeans, a Levi's jacket, and work boots. His features came into view and again I stifled a cry. Standing there was a slightly older version of Scott Eames, a guy who'd been new in my middle school last December—and who was, briefly, my obsession. Mom's suspicion that I'd had a crush was correct, but it dissolved upon her death. After I lost Mom, chasing a boy around seemed as frivolous as fretting about the dust accumulating in our house.

Like me, Scott had been bussed across town for middle school—we'd ridden the same bus—and was now a sophomore at East. "You look exactly like someone I know from East High," I said to the guy standing before me.

"You mean Scott?"

I lowered the flashlight. "How'd you know that?"

"He's my brother. I'm Carey."

"Like the Joni Mitchell song." I stood. "When she's in Greece. And Carey has a cane and steals her camera."

Carey raised an eyebrow. "How do you know that song? You're too young for it."

I smiled. "Come on, man. This is a record store."

He laughed. "Still, it's a pretty obscure song."

I shrugged. "You go to East?"

"Nah. Dropped out of school a couple years ago." He sidled past me, taking in Zoe from head to toe. I watched her face; she seemed to stare back at him but I sensed she was okay with him being there. "I used to come in here sometimes," he said. "The owner, Alex, was a nice lady. I heard what happened to her. It sucks."

"Yeah." I put a hand on my collarbone. "She was my mom."

"Oh, wow." From the corner of my eye I saw Carey giving me a good look—as good as possible in the semi-darkness. "Now I...I see..." he stammered. "There's quite a family resemblance."

"Everyone says that," I replied. "My eyes are the same color as my dad's but otherwise I look like my mom. My baby brother is the spitting image of our dad. But because of my eye color, I'm more a combination of my parents."

I didn't know why I was babbling. I shut my mouth.

Carey took a step toward me. "I'm really sorry...um..."

"Suzanne."

"Suzanne. Like the Leonard Cohen song?" When I nodded, Carey said, "Alex used to play that song a lot. All the versions. Judy Collins, Noel Harrison, Nina Simone, and of course Cohen's version." He rubbed his forehead. "I never asked her why she played 'Suzanne' so much. Now I know."

I gazed at the floorboards. "Now you know."

"Hey," he said, and I looked up. "You okay, Suzanne?"

"Yeah." I blinked, trying not to cry. Stupid.

He moved toward the door. "Listen, I shouldn't bother you. I'll be on my way."

"Wait!"

He turned.

"If there's something you wanted, you might as well take it." I glanced around. "I don't know what we'll do with all this stock. You can have a record, if you like."

"I couldn't do that, Suzanne. These records belong to your family."

"But you remember my mom." I blinked again. "She'd *want* me to give you something."

Carey seemed rooted to the floor. Finally he said, "I was thinking about grabbing a bite to eat. Can I bring you a burger? Some fries, or something to drink? If you let me bring you something, I won't feel bad about taking a record."

"Fries sound good."

He broke into a smile that reminded me of Scott's—just slightly cuter. "I'll be right back."

I didn't expect him to return. He had to be twenty, or even older. What guy his age would choose to hang out in a darkened, defunct record store with a fourteen-year-old? Almost fifteen-year-old...but still.

Twenty minutes later, he showed up laden with fries, milkshakes, and burgers. "I thought you might change your mind, want something more." He opened the bag of food. "I know I did."

"You can keep the burgers. I'll still take the fries," I said. "And a shake, if you have vanilla."

"They're both vanilla." Sitting beside me on the floor, he handed over a cup. "Vanilla gets a bad rap. People say it's flavorless but that's crazy. Anyone who thinks that has never tasted pure vanilla."

"I'm not sure *I've* tasted pure vanilla."

"You can make extract at home with vanilla beans and cheap vodka."

"No shit?" I ate a handful of fries. "So a person can get drunk on a vanilla shake?"

"A little pure vanilla extract goes a long way, so I don't think so. Not unless you drank a hell of a lot of shakes in one sitting. You'd get sick before you'd get drunk."

I raised my cup. "Cheers to that."

Carey pressed his cup against mine, then scooched over, leaning against the checkout counter. "Can I ask you something?"

I nodded.

"Why are you hanging out in your mom's store?" He took a bite of burger. "Scott's doing all this extracurricular stuff at school. School newspaper layout. Photography for the yearbook. And he and Ken Wilson are helping design sets for the school play."

"That doesn't surprise me," I said. "They'd both be great at that."

Scott was a fantastic artist; everyone said so. He drew caricatures like something you'd see in *The New York Times* Arts section. At lunch, kids asked him to create their likeness. He had a best friend, Ken Wilson, who was also an artist and kind of a crack-up. Ken was super-smart but not in a bookish way. He just knew quirky stuff that other people didn't. He reminded me of my dad in that way.

"Yeah, they're really getting into it. They're doing *Heaven Can Wait*." Carey shifted his weight to his other hip. "So, like, there's no shortage of stuff to do at school, right?"

"Right." I changed the subject. "Did you go to East?"

"Nope. I went to school in Grand Junction, where we lived before the car crash."

"Car crash?"

"You don't know about that?" Carey asked. "I figured everyone who knows Scott probably knew."

I hadn't known, couldn't decipher details, but as soon as he spoke, I understood that someone important to Carey had been hurt. Not killed, but definitely hurt. I waited for him to go on.

He swallowed, his Adam's apple bobbing. "My sister and I had a little run-in with the side of a concrete overpass. I was driving. I was fine, but Joanne almost died. We moved here so she could go to rehab. She lives at the rehab center, but we're hoping she can come home soon."

"I'm sorry," I said. "That's horrible."

"Yeah." He brushed his long, straight blond hair across his forehead, out of his eyes—exactly the way Scott did. "By the time of the accident, I'd dropped out of school. My parents said I could stay in Grand Junction—or, if I wanted to come with them to Denver, I could get a fresh start and be near Joanne." He grimaced. "It was the least I could do after almost killing her."

I nibbled a French fry. "She's getting better now, right?"

"She is. She's in a wheelchair, but she can do stuff with her hands. Her mind isn't in the best shape; otherwise she'd probably be in school. She should be a senior now." He sighed. "I wish Joanne could go back to school. Of everything, that's what I feel most guilty about."

I studied his face. "You seem too nice to be a high school dropout."

Carey laughed. "I hated school. Maybe I'd like it now, except I'm too old. I might get my GED someday."

"Do you work?"

"Yeah, I work nights as a security guard in a bank downtown. Downtown is dead at night, which I guess is why they need a security guard."

"It sounds like a boring job."

"It is, but they pay pretty good. And I get to pack heat." He made a face. "That was rude. I'm sorry."

His words made me tremble, imagining Bobby Shelton's gun. But I only said, "As long as you're not a junkie, I guess I'm safe with you."

"I wish I'd been here that night. And had my gun on me," Carey said. "That loser wouldn't have stood a chance."

My throat felt raw. "Well, shoebox-sized record stores generally don't have security guards. Too bad."

"Too bad," Carey echoed. Then he asked, "So, are you friends with Scott?"

I hesitated. The truth was, I hardly knew Scott. What had prompted me to develop an interest in him anyway, when we'd rarely spoken? In one afternoon, I'd exchanged more words with his brother than I'd ever exchanged with Scott.

"We went to the same middle school, but we didn't talk much." I felt my cheeks flush. "I'm kind of shy. Maybe that's why I haven't joined a ton of clubs at East."

"You'll find your place, Suzanne." Carey stood. "I should get going."

I rose, too. "Thanks for the snacks. I still owe you a record." I swept my hand around the store. "Take anything you want. Here—use my flashlight to browse."

He selected a Joan Baez album. Tucking it under his arm, he placed a hand on my shoulder.

"Take care of yourself, Suzanne, okay?"

"Yeah." I'd never been touched by a guy so much older than me. But I didn't flinch.

His hand lingered a moment. Then he removed it, turning to leave.

"Hey, Carey!" I called.

In the doorway, he paused. Zoe and I both studied him.

"I'm here just about every afternoon," I said. "Stop by anytime."

14

— · —

2004

I couldn't stop thinking about Claranna Lewis. Was it truly arson? Had she intended to murder her children while also taking her own life? And was she my grandmother? I tried conjuring details about her, but none came.

The next morning, Caitlin, Austin, and I were headed out the door at the same time. As always, Caitlin's makeup was meticulous—eyes ringed with thick eyeliner, brows heavily accented, lips as wine-hued as Marilyn Manson's. It was too much for a fourteen-year-old, but I'd long ago decided Caitlin's makeup was not a hill I was willing to die on.

She wore a top I'd never seen before—silky black material with long, fitted sleeves. "Where'd you get the top?" I asked. "It's cute."

"I, um, borrowed it," she said. "From a friend."

We began walking up the street. We only had a block together before she'd continue north toward the high school, while Austin and I took a right. It was the first of October, a bright, warm day. Slipping off my jacket, I said to Caitlin, "I'm glad you're making friends."

"A few." She heaved her backpack higher. "Kids here suck, for the most part. What a bunch of fucking snobs."

"My school, too," Austin put in. "They're all fucking snobs."

"Language," I said. "Both of you."

"I know what that word means, Mommy," Austin said.

"I'm sure you do. But that doesn't mean we use it." I turned to Caitlin. "There are some nice people, right?"

She shrugged. "There's girl, Alli, who's okay. Her sister is that girl who went missing."

My fingers twitched. "With the older guy?"

"Yeah." Caitlin pushed her hair back from her face. "But Alli says her sister *chose* to go off with him. Besides, I heard the guy isn't so bad."

I felt bile rise in my throat. "Where did you hear that?"

"From Alli."

"Cait." I stopped walking, and so did she. "You need to be careful," I said. "There are lots of creeps out there. Like that guy."

She raised her eyebrows. "How do you know? No one's heard *his* side of the story."

"If he has a side and that girl is safe, they both should come forward."

"Right. If he tried to come forward, the cops would probably gun him down before he could speak."

"I doubt that." I placed a hand on her arm. She flinched but I didn't let go. "Until that girl is home safe," I went on, "I don't want you going anywhere alone."

Her raccoon eyes widened and she jerked away from my grasp. Stomping a combat boot against the pavement, she yelled, "Will you fucking lay off? Let me live my life!"

She strode away, her steps so swift, Austin and I would've had to run to catch up with her. I watched her go, my heart in pieces inside my chest.

For her first eleven years, Caitlin had been a delight. She'd been an easy baby, a friendly toddler, and a versatile, outgoing preschooler. Brett and I expressed sympathy when other parents complained of sleepless nights, when other kids had meltdowns in store aisles. But privately, we congratulated ourselves. Clearly, we were doing *something* right.

Austin, arriving fussy and screaming when Caitlin was five, provided a harsh reality check. But Caitlin took to him naturally. "*My* baby," she'd say, swaying him to calm his incessant crying. As he grew, when a tantrum threatened she diverted him with silly games she made up on the spot. If other kids picked on him, she defended him with the gallantry of a knight.

In the years when Austin was small and required so much of my energy, I made sure to reserve some exclusively for Caitlin. She and I did girlie things—shopping, pedicures, weekend lunches at breezy oceanside restaurants. She was a talented artist, and I enrolled her in every art program I could find, exclaiming over each piece she produced.

She basked in my praise. "Hang it here, Mommy," she'd say, pointing to the wall above my nightstand. "Where you can see it every day." Eyes shining, hands clasped, she added, "I used lots of purple—your favorite."

"How do you know purple is my favorite?" I'd asked.

She wrapped her arms around my waist. "I *know* you, Mommy."

Looking back on those times, I felt melancholic at how sweet, how fleeting they were. Did I appreciate them enough? Or did my anxiety about Austin eclipse my gratitude for his sister? Was that why she began to distance herself?

Maybe it was simply growing pains. Puberty had hit Caitlin early and hit her hard, and as her body changed, so did her attitude. Her previously balanced moods oscillated between ridiculous highs and horrifying lows. She gave up art, proclaiming it "boring." She abandoned her childhood friends, instead choosing to run with a questionable crowd of middle schoolers—rowdy, rude kids, both boys and girls. She was often caught cutting classes.

After we'd told the kids about the move to Denver, there'd been shouting, slammed doors, tears, and melted mascara staining Caitlin's face. Nights when she ran off, and I called everyone we knew while Brett scoured the neighborhood. I'd wondered if we'd have to forcibly stuff Caitlin into the car when we made the drive to Colorado.

But this fresh start *would* be good for her. Notwithstanding Caitlin's comment that East kids were snobs and the fact that she had a slender connection with Shelton Jr., things weren't *all* bad. At back-to-school night a few weeks ago, as the teachers gushed about how curious and insightful Caitlin was, I'd felt my face glow. Surely, once she had a chance to adjust, she'd develop a strong group of friends. Maybe start dating some nice boy.

She'll be fine, I told myself—willing it to be true.

"It's typical behavior," Brett said, when I told him about the incident on the walk to school—omitting mention of Shelton Jr. "She's fourteen, Suzanne."

"Fifteen next week," I reminded him.

"Fifteen next week," he echoed. "She's just like my sisters at that age. Crappy attitude at home but excellent everywhere else." He settled into his lawn chair. "She's acting like a normal teenage girl."

I heard the edge in my abrupt laugh. "I guess I have no compass. I was anything *but* a normal teenage girl."

Brett squeezed my hand. "I wish I could change things for you. You know that, right?"

I nodded. Throughout our relationship, after I'd told him about my mother's death—which I did within our first few months of dating, explaining enough of the story to give him a sense of what happened—he'd been nothing but sympathetic. But there were things I'd never told him. Aspects of the story, and of myself, that I wasn't sure Brett would understand. So I'd censored them from my narrative.

Now that we lived in Denver, the waspy buzz of worry nagged me. Donna wouldn't say anything, but would my brother tell Brett what he knew? Dad was traveling, but he'd be home by Thanksgiving. What might he say to Brett then?

I adored Brett, and I did trust him. But how could he understand? Brett's childhood was so traditional, he made Norman Rockwell look like an anarchist. He had two sisters, one older, one younger. His family didn't have much money, but he'd grown up in a modest, comfortable Cincinnati neighborhood. His parents were still married, still living in Brett's childhood home.

We were in our back yard, enjoying what was likely one of the last warm evenings of the year. Austin was inside, playing on the Wii.

As for Caitlin, at dinner she'd asked to go to a movie with friends. "What movie?" Brett had asked.

"*The Bourne Supremacy*," Caitlin replied. When I pointed out that she'd already seen that film, back in California, she rolled her eyes. "Jesus, I can't see it again? Not everyone has seen it."

"We need to meet your new friends," I said. "Dad and I would like you to invite them over."

She set down her fork. "Are you saying I can't go to a movie until you've met my friends and approved?" She nodded toward Austin. "What am I, a toddler?"

"I'm not a toddler," Austin protested, shoving spaghetti in his mouth. His face was covered in tomato sauce.

Caitlin made a face. "Uh huh."

"How are you getting there?" I asked.

"The bus," she replied. "I'm meeting Claudia on the corner."

I gave her a long look. "Claudia? Not Alli?"

"Alli's not going. Claudia lives a few blocks away." She stood. "Can I go?"

"Yes," Brett said. "But I agree with Mom. Please arrange a time to have your friends over. You can get pizza, play on the Wii."

"The Wii is stupid," she said.

Austin rose from his seat. "It's not stupid, but it's mine, mine, *mine*—and you can't use it!"

He shoved his plate, and it clattered to the floor. We always gave him plastic, so it didn't break, but his meal went everywhere. Tears ran down his cheeks.

I leaned over, smoothing his hair and glaring at Caitlin.

"Sure. Take his side, as usual." She slammed her dinner things into the sink. "I'm outta here."

"Wait!" I called to her.

Caitlin turned. My eyes met hers. "You recall the conversation we had this morning," I said. "If you want to go, I'll walk with you to the corner and meet Claudia. And when you get back, you call us. Dad or I will walk up and meet you."

She shook out her gorgeous mane of dark hair. "Seriously?"

"Seriously."

"Fine," she sighed.

But when it was time to go, she found me in the kitchen and said, "Movie plans are off. I'm staying in tonight." She strode from the room, clomping up the stairs. I watched her go, wondering if I'd ever again understand her.

In the yard, I sipped wine. "It's wonderful to have you home in the evening, for a change," I said to Brett.

"Wonderful to be here." He clinked his glass against mine. "A rare break."

Brett's new job was more than either of us had bargained for. Despite my years in tech, I didn't understand what Brett's new company did, exactly—something to do with internet security, which he said was going to be an increasing issue as more and more websites cropped up. His company was a startup and their products were, apparently, cutting edge. But they needed to get the product to market as quickly as possible, and they were relying on Brett and Nicole, his colleague who'd also relocated from the Bay Area, to spearhead the work.

It meant long days, recurrent evenings at the office, and many missed dinners. It reminded me of the way my father had worked constantly while my mother both ran Zoe's Records and managed our household. But Brett had told me it was temporary and things would settle down soon.

"So you think in a few weeks, work will slow down?" I asked.

"Oh." He twirled his wineglass stem, contemplating the twilit sky. "I forgot to tell you. We went over the project plan yesterday and there's no way we can be done as soon as we'd thought. But the pressure's still on." He looked at me. "I'm sorry, babe."

"Just like my dad," I murmured.

"No! *Not* just like your dad."

His vehemence startled me. I stared at him.

"I mean it," Brett said. "This is just an intense patch. It won't last forever. Not like your dad." He drained his glass. "Or your brother."

"Okay," I replied. "I didn't mean anything by that."

I *didn't*, I told myself.

Brett shifted in his seat. "Speaking of your brother, isn't your lunch with him tomorrow?"

I poured more wine for both of us. "Indeed, it is."

15

1979

After meeting Carey, whenever I saw Scott Eames at school I thought differently about him. Scott was such a kid, goofing around. Drawing pictures of hands, then slicing off the fingers using the paper cutter in the art room. Hanging around with Ken Wilson, oblivious to girls, the big stupid jock guys, and pretty much everything besides themselves and the other artsy kids.

It wasn't my world. I wasn't sure why I'd ever thought it could be.

I remembered what Carey said—that I'd find my place. I wasn't convinced. At East, there were hundreds of people I'd never met before, but I didn't know where I fit in. Most of the time I felt anonymous. But in my head, I remained *Girl Whose Mom Was Killed*.

The first Tuesday in October, I took my seat in biology beside my lab partner, Kara Schrock, a stoner girl who smelled like pot and frosted donuts and wore wrinkled, hippie-dippie shirts in a rainbow of colors. "*Not* looking forward to this," Kara said.

It was piglet dissection day. We'd been warned about this day, informed that squeamishness was *not* an excuse, that those with delicate constitutions should prepare themselves accordingly.

"I swear," Kara continued. "I've felt like puking since Mr. Walter told us about it. I'm a vegetarian. I don't eat animals, much less chop them up." Her donut/dope smell wafted in my direction. "Walter is an asshole."

I laughed. Kara stared at me. "That wasn't a joke, Suzanne. This is against everything I believe in."

"Oh," I said. "Sorry."

"You're gonna have to do it," she said. "I'll sit here but I am *not* cutting into an animal."

"Even though it's already dead?"

"Even though," she insisted. "You'll have to do it."

It would've been nice if she *asked*, instead of *telling* me. But whatever.

As I examined the instrument kit on our lab table, Mr. Walter passed out stainless steel trays with little dead pigs on them. "Please remember that these fetuses were harvested from sows on their way to slaughter." His was flat, like the narrator on *Nova*. "They wouldn't have been born under any circumstances."

"In other words," Louie Trabini called out. "This ain't no *Charlotte's Web*."

"*Isn't any*, Mr. Trabini, but yes. Your point is well taken." The teacher glanced at Louie. "Have you read the classic children's novel by E.B. White?"

"Hell, no," Louie said. "But my kid sister loves the movie."

Everyone laughed, including me. Chris was crazy about that movie, too.

Kara's and my pig was placed on our table. It looked like a girl pig. "Should we name her?" I asked Kara.

Kara's hands were over her eyes. Through her fingers, she peered at the piglet, shaking her head.

I donned surgical gloves, secretly naming the piglet Beth after the tragically dead sister in *Little Women*. "Put your gloves on," I told Kara. "You have to make a show of it. Otherwise Walter will give us both an F."

As instructed by Mr. Walter, I wrapped rubber bands around Beth's front and hind legs. Wincing, Kara positioned the bands around the tray's bottom as I stretched Beth's legs apart, exposing her middle.

"Take the scalpel and make two angled incisions, shoulder to sternum," Mr. Walter said. "Use a light touch. You only want to go through the skin." He reminded me of Julia Child explaining how to butterfly a chicken.

My hand, clenching the scalpel, hovered over Beth. I pierced the corner of her collarbone. There was no blood.

It's just a pig that was never born, I told myself. Animals have spirits; I knew that—but Beth hadn't been given the opportunity. She never felt the pain of losing her life. She didn't breathe farm air, warm with hay and manure. She never experienced sunshine crossing her face when she walked into the barnyard in the morning. She didn't nudge her way toward her mother's teats, finding her place among her litter mates. She didn't grow up and wean, mature enough to eat her daily slop, licking her chops when the trough was empty.

She was not—as Louie had so eloquently pointed out—Wilbur from *Charlotte's Web*.

After my mother died, a detective informed Dad that a blood spatter analyst wanted to examine the scene in more depth. The analyst had been there immediately following "the incident," the detective said. He'd examined the scene; he'd taken photos and samples. The authorities determined it was an open-and-shut case. Robert Shelton killed Alexandra Parry; then, as Shelton attempted to escape Officer Powles's gunfire, he sustained deadly injuries by hurling himself into Colfax traffic. But because the blood spatter analyst was working with some new techniques and technologies, he wanted to spend extra time on the case. So Zoe's remained taped off, a crime scene although the crime was solved.

One day about a week after my mother's funeral, I walked by. From the sidewalk I saw the blood spatter analyst inside, taking measurements, writing things down, using complicated-looking instruments.

I stepped inside and the analyst looked up. "I'm sorry," he said. "This is a crime scene. I have to ask you to leave, miss."

I didn't move. "The thing is," I told him, "This was my mother's store. My mom was the lady who died here."

He gave me a long look. "Okay. I understand."

In the end, he provided an overview of his work. He said that because the case was so clear-cut, they could use evidence that was already known—the type of gun, where the shooter likely stood and where the victim (as he referred to my mother; he never once called her by name or said "your mother") stood in relation to the shooter—to help solve more complex crimes in the future. He explained that because he already knew so many details, he could determine the "bullet trajectory"—he actually used those words—which, if the shooter were unknown, would narrow down a suspect list.

"So many crimes are difficult to decipher," he'd said. "This situation provides a rare opportunity. We can use this evidence to create models for future scenarios."

I nodded, knowing he believed he was giving me a gift. A small shred of worth in my mother's death.

But the thing is—I didn't feel gratitude about that. It was shitty, the way she died. It was shitty that Shelton had killed her.

And it was shitty of *me*, I decided, staring at Beth's chest, to chop up this piglet. So what if I could learn something? So what if Kara could, or Louie, or anybody in a tenth-grade biology class in Denver, Colorado? Who cared?

Suze, Mom-not-Mom said. *You must understand the difference.*

She was back! My grip on the scalpel lightened, relief surging river-like into my fingertips.

There's knowledge to gain here, Mom-not-Mom went on. *Shelton learned nothing when he killed me. But this isn't like that. Don't be afraid of discovering something new, honeypie.*

Was that why I could hear her, even if it wasn't specifically about Peggy? Because she wanted me to be brave when it came to discoveries—of any kind?

Yes, Suzie Blue. That's exactly why.

"Make an incision from your piglet's sternum to its pubis," Walter said, producing titters from the class. "Avoid the umbilicus."

Kara glanced at Beth. "You're falling behind," she hissed. "If you don't keep up, we're both screwed."

She's right, Suze. Get on with it.

I began to cut. Beth's skin was firm yet yielding under the knife.

We went on to remove the flaps created by our incisions, then scrape away the tissue and lift off the breast plate to expose the organ block. As we moved through the motions, I heard others, Kara included, gag and whine. But after Mom-not-Mom helped me get over my hesitation, I began to appreciate the precision required. It *was* a process of discovery. Where would the world be if no one had ever risked discomfort to gain knowledge?

Exactly, Mom-not-Mom said. *Exactly, Suzie Blue.*

16

2004

Chris's and my adult relationship was complicated and inexplicable, evoking an avant-garde painting of emotions inside me. Whenever he got on my nerves, I tried to think of him as the little boy he'd been when our mother died, the boy who'd loved Atari and *Charlotte's Web*. And I reminded myself what an enormous loss Chris had suffered, without truly understanding what he'd lost at all.

But it was difficult. He liked expensive, big-boy toys—boats, motorcycles, any car that caught his eye. He could be standoffish like our father, but he had none of Dad's quirkiness. Nor did he seem to have much of Mom in him. Nothing of that combination so uniquely hers—acumen, receptiveness, a tender spirit.

Like Dad, Chris worked at PAG, and he worked crazy hours. That was the reason, I told myself, that until now we hadn't arranged a time to get together, although I'd been living in Denver for almost two months.

I met him at Racine's, a longtime Denver favorite with a new location on Sherman Street. As always when I saw him, I was struck by how much Chris resembled our father. Same lean build, same dark hair, same indigo eyes. Chris was beginning to thin on top, as Dad did in his thirties, but he was still handsome.

And as always, I wondered why Chris wasn't married or at least in a long-term relationship. He had no shortage of girlfriends; a revolving door of women made their way through his penthouse apartment. It wasn't lack of opportunity that prevented a wedding ring from finding its way onto my brother's finger. Perhaps Chris was simply reluctant to throw himself into married life.

Look where it got our father, after all.

I almost expected Chris to shake my hand, as any good car salesman will. Instead, he enfolded me in a brief hug. As he released me, images flashed through my mind of the sweltering summer of 1979, when Chris clung to me nightly, his little body, heart, and mind wracked with confusion and hurt.

After we ordered, I told him about Zoe's. "Mom would be so into it," I said, hearing the lift in my voice.

He sipped iced tea. "I'm sure she would."

Chris's tone was neutral—typical of him whenever Mom came up. He'd been six when she died; surely that was old enough to have memories of one's own mother, but he never talked about her. I wished Chris and I could speak freely about Mom, share memories and stories. But whenever I gave him an opening—like this—he didn't take the bait. His impassive replies left me unsure how to keep conversation about our mother going.

My mind jolted to Claranna Lewis and her son. If that little boy was Dad, he'd also been six when his mother died. Perhaps when they grow up, six-year-old boys *don't*, in truth, talk about their dead mothers.

"Tell me about the kids," Chris said as our meals arrived. The server set a steak knife beside his plate, and he used it to drench his baked potato in butter. He always could put food away without gaining an ounce.

I topped my Thai peanut salad with dressing. "They're adjusting. But Austin is a handful." I didn't mention the Caitlin drama; he wouldn't understand. "I'm getting a lot of calls from school."

Chris looked up from his plate. I told him about my visits to the principal's office, my struggles to find services for Austin.

"That stinks. I'm sorry." He ate a piece of potato. "I could take him sometime," he offered. "For an afternoon. We could do something together, Austin and me."

I stared at him. "You'd do that?"

"Sure."

I smiled. "Well, I'd...I would love that, Chris." I scooped a forkful of salad. "Thank you."

"My pleasure." Chris signaled for more iced tea. "So, have you heard from Dad?"

I stiffened, my eyes on the server's hands as she refilled Chris's tea. The ice cubes jangled like pieces of broken glass. "Look, there's not much to say about that—right?"

"Suze," Chris said as the server walked away. "Dad is recently widowed. Have some compassion."

"Widowed for the second time," I replied.

"Widowed for the...second time," he repeated. "On his own...again."

Did I detect wistfulness in his voice? Was he thinking about *her*?

As I had a million times since we were kids, I wondered if I'd ever decide the time was right to tell Chris everything that had happened back then. The marrow of our family story, the things he didn't remember. And the things he'd never known in the first place.

Was it time? Was today the day? I opened my mouth to speak.

Then I closed it. What would be the point? Chris knowing wouldn't change the past.

Instead I nodded toward his plate. "Don't let that get cold."

He picked up his knife and began slicing his sirloin steak. Wordlessly, I watched the knife slide back and forth. I stared as the tender, rare flesh came apart, piece by piece.

17

1979

On my way home from school, I was still thinking about Beth the piglet. In the kitchen, I chuckled to see Peggy butterflying a chicken.

"What are you laughing about, miss?" Peggy asked. A big, fake smile spread across her face. Eccedentesiast.

"Nothing." I stepped toward the refrigerator for my afternoon Tab.

"Ouch!" Peggy yelled.

I whirled to see her holding a bloody hand. "Are you okay?" I asked.

Peggy grabbed a kitchen towel, wrapping it around her hand. "Cut my finger," she breathed. "Whew. That knocked the wind out of me." She sagged against the counter.

I inspected the half-butterflied chicken on the cutting board. "I could finish that for you," I offered. "I'm pretty good with a knife."

"No!" Peggy rose to her full height, grabbing the knife in her uncut hand and pointing it toward me. "I've got this, Suzanne."

The veins on the back of her hand popped like stark, inverted fault lines during an earthquake. To my right, I sensed the shadowy forms of the maid and the wild-haired woman, both with hands clamped over their mouths. Behind Peggy, the cutting board with the chicken on it began just the slightest dance across the counter, as if it wanted to sashay out of the room—clever, but Peggy didn't notice, and while I appreciated the ghosts' alliance with me, I knew they lacked sufficient power to remove the knife from her hand.

"Get out of my kitchen," Peggy commanded.

Holy crap. I scuttled to the library—wanting to find Chris and assure myself that he and I were together, and we were safe.

"She's crazy," I told my father that night in his study. "She pointed a *knife* at me, Dad."

There was no small irony in the fact that if I told him about the kitchen ghosts, he'd call me the crazy one. Or no—he'd never use a word as basic as *crazy*. More like *maniacal* or *nonsensical*.

"Suzanne." He sipped scotch. "Peggy was wounded. She was decidedly disconcerted. I'm sure she didn't mean anything by it."

"She absolutely meant something by it. She is *dangerous*."

"You're being histrionic." Dad set down his glass. "Let's go straighten this out."

Peggy was in the kitchen, humming as she dried dishes. "Jimmy, I swear," she said when he walked in ahead of me. "This kitchen will be the death of me. Ancient stove, ancient refrigerator, no dishwasher. My hands are suffering." She held up the uninjured one, presumably to illustrate how dry it looked, how her otherwise perfect manicure was chipped.

Then she saw me behind him. "Oh. Suzanne."

Dad took the dish towel from her hand, setting it on the counter. "Suzanne tells me you had quite an afternoon. I'd like to hear about it—from you."

She wiggled her bandaged fingers. "You saw this at dinner. The knife slipped while I was cutting chicken. Not enough to require stitches, but it gave me a fright."

"Suzanne says she offered to take over, and you...refused."

"Oh, I was fine!" Peggy said, smiling. "I had everything under control. A few Band-Aids, and I was good as new."

"You pointed a knife at me," I said. "You told me to get out of *your* kitchen."

"Pointed a knife?" Her look was quizzical. "I did nothing of the sort, Suzanne. I *picked* up the knife, yes—to get it out of the way until I could resume cutting. And I asked you to run along and check on your brother. But what you're describing..." She shook her head, looking at my father. "That simply didn't happen, Jimmy."

"She's lying!" I slammed my fist on the counter.

I expected Peggy to jump, to recoil. But she only smiled again at Dad. "Teenagers...so *dramatic*." She turned to me. "Suzanne, I was a teen once, too—and drama was the name of my game." Her eyes met my dad's. "Right, Jimmy?"

Dad chuckled. "That's absolutely accurate."

"Teen girls..." Peggy murmured. "I know what teen girls can be like."

"This sounds like a mild misunderstanding." Dad squeezed her uncut hand. "I believe we're finished here."

"I agree, Jimmy." She wrapped her arms around his neck. "Let me get these dishes dried, then I'll be on my way for the night."

"Okay, Pegs." Dad's hand slid toward her ass.

I felt bile rise in my throat. Were they going to get it on right here in the kitchen? I didn't stick around to find out.

October fifth, my fifteenth birthday, went unnoticed at home. Mom had always made a big deal out of birthdays, but Dad seemed to have forgotten the date, and Chris was too little to know something like that. It was a Friday, and that morning Laurie drove me to school, as she occasionally did. When I mentioned my birthday, she invited me to go cruising that night. I drank a couple beers, and the ensuing buzz made it easier to slip into the house, dash up to my room, and fall into bed, where the solitary, silent witness to my desolation was my pillow.

Hoping my birthday might bring Mom-not-Mom around, I stayed awake waiting for her. I felt a faint presence, but she was silent. I knew it was because I had no new information to offer about the situation with Peggy.

I'd never felt lonelier.

The next night, there was a knock on my door. "Suzanne, can we chat?" Dad asked, seating himself on my bed. I shrugged.

"I'll come right to the point," he said. "I feel like Sisyphus, pushing the boulder of your Peggy-fueled fury up an endless hill."

I shook my head at my dad's idea of "coming right to the point."

"Might you explain?" Dad asked.

"Why?" I asked. "It wouldn't change anything."

"Suze." Dad met my gaze. "Peggy is a positive part of our family. She's superb with Chris." His eyes glistened. "Kids his age need a mother. If not their own..." He stared at his hands. "...then a marvelous mother figure, like Peggy."

I rolled my eyes. "Whatever."

"I'd like to understand your specific objection."

Would he really? I took a breath. "Peggy wanted Mom dead. From the moment you started hanging out with her last winter, she wanted Mom out of the picture."

"Suzanne. Goodness." Dad's face crumpled. I'd never before understood that expression. It seemed ridiculous, a face scrunching up like a piece of paper. But that's exactly what Dad's face resembled—a picture of his face smashed into a ball, then spread out.

"How can you *say* that?" He blinked. "Yes, Peggy was a congenial companion for me last winter. But she was merely being a friend."

"She was not. She *always* wanted more from you."

"Suzanne—"

"No," I told him. "Listen to this." I slipped Mom's mix tape into my tape deck, winding it to the conversation between Peggy and Mom.

When it was over, I said, "You see?"

"That proves nothing," Dad replied. "Peggy told me she visited Mom's store. She was concerned about me—worried I wasn't adequately convinced that getting back together with your mom was appropriate. And Peggy was correct about that, Suzanne. When your mom died, she and I were still working things out."

"But Peggy went to Zoe's other times," I protested. "She was harassing Mom."

"What makes you think that?"

His question caught me off guard. Why did I think that? Because Mom-not-Mom claimed it happened.

He'll never believe you, I heard her say. *You need more than the tape. You have to find proof, my little seer.*

"Fine." Snapping the tape out of the deck, I stood. "Is there anything else? Because if not, I have homework to do."

Dad hesitated, then rose. "Nothing else. Sleep well, Suzanne."

18

2004

On October fifth, I turned forty. Before leaving California, we'd hosted a combination going away/early birthday party, so I hadn't expected much for the actual day. But Brett surprised me by knocking off work early and taking me up to Red Rocks. There was no show that night; the concert season was winding down and the park was open to visitors. We settled on a bench in the amphitheater, using cushioned stadium seats Brett brought along.

Red Rocks' dramatic setting—the open-air theater, built in the 1930s by WPA laborers, with rock cliffs on either side of the seating, the stage below, and the Denver skyline in the distance—was like no other concert venue anywhere. During high school I'd spent countless evenings at Red Rocks, seeing The Blues Brothers, U2, Elvis Costello, and others. Any time anyone was going, if I could come up with the ticket price and approval from my dad, I went.

That was long ago. And it was after 1979.

Brett opened the picnic dinner he'd purchased from an upscale deli in the Tech Center, along with a pricey Cabernet. A velvety sunset illuminated our meal before stars began appearing overhead. The lights of the city twinkled below.

"Everyone should see this place at least once, especially when there's a show," I said. "Let's come up for a concert next year."

Brett smiled. "Do they have concerts that old fogies like us would en-joy?"

I slapped his leather-jacket clad arm. "Hey, I'm forty—not *that* old." I bit into my smoked salmon salad sandwich. "We'll check the schedule when it comes out next spring." I glanced at my watch. "Speaking of schedules, do we have a time limit?"

"Nope. We can get home whenever we want."

Brett had topped off his plans by arranging a babysitter for Austin. We could've made Caitlin do it, but since such requests generally resulted in opposition, I was grateful to bypass it on my birthday.

The babysitter Brett hired came through a nanny service. When I asked how he'd found the service, he said Nicole helped him research.

"I thought Nicole didn't have kids," I said.

Brett opened a container of pasta salad. "She doesn't, but she's great with them. For Take Your Kid to Work Day, she always organized the ac-tivities. She said she'd have babysat Austin herself if she didn't have plans."

I gave him a quizzical look. "Your *colleague* would have babysat for us?"

He shrugged. "Like I said, she loves kids." His eyes took on a shimmer that matched the brightness of the emerging stars. "Nicole is a marvel. She can do anything."

"Right." I decided to let it go. It was my birthday, after all. I set aside my sandwich and reached for the salad, watching the sky deepen to violet.

Rapid fluttering made us turn our heads. A large black-and-white bird, its wingspan looming, landed beside my sandwich, grabbed the top crust, and flew off.

Brett shielded his face with his hands. "Jesus, what *was* that?"

"Camp robber," I told him. "Also known as a magpie. They make off with your food if you're not careful." I wrapped the remnants of my sandwich, adding it to our trash. "They're bold but I've never seen one *that* bold."

Brett laughed. "Guess you have to watch your back, here in Colorado."

I nodded. "Guess you do."

Caitlin's birthday was on the seventh, two days after mine. I always said she was the best birthday present I'd ever received. When she was little, she relished sharing our "birthday season," as we called it. I'd get us coordinating outfits for the occasion, and while she always wanted a typical kid birthday party, we also did something special, just us.

Those events were only memories now. Two years ago, turning thirteen, Caitlin had been glum during our birthday lunch, and last year she declined altogether to celebrate with me. I'd wanted to insist but Brett said I shouldn't push.

"It's a phase," he'd said then. "It'll pass, Suzanne." Understanding my hurt, he'd held me tightly. "I saw this pattern with my sisters and mom. Sylvie and Lisa had to exert their independence, but it didn't last. Caitlin will come around and be your buddy again. I promise."

This year, I begged her. "Please, Cait, will you do something with me? It's a big birthday for me."

She finally agreed to an hour-long "Haunted Cheesman Park" tour that I'd found an advertisement for. Purportedly, there were thousands of bodies still buried in the park, and many people believed their spirits remained. Hoping the tour would appeal to Caitlin's goth sensibilities, I had high hopes—and I personally discovered some gruesome tidbits, such as speculation that the first two men buried there, in the 1870s, had been the victim *and* the perpetrator of the same crime, buried together in a single grave.

The tour guide said something I hadn't known but that didn't surprise me: many in the paranormal community believe that not all ghosts who haunt Cheesman Park are among those buried there when it was a nineteenth-century graveyard. "Close your eyes and take a moment to be silent," the guide said. "Feel the energy. See if you can feel how *any* restless soul connected to this area—to Capitol Hill, even simply to Denver—might be drawn to this place."

I kept my eyes open. The days when I'd walked Cheesman with my mother, prattling about the spirits I sensed, were in the past. Still, the spirits were present; of this I was certain. The air around me buzzed and the tree branches rustled, though there was little breeze.

Who was doing that? The half-buried dead here, certainly. But I dared myself to hope for more. Dared myself to hope that the spirit who'd loved our old house, loved Cap Hill, might be here, too.

Glancing at Caitlin, I wondered what she felt. Her expression was neutral. I wanted to ask her if she sensed anything, but her impassive look prevented me from speaking. Maybe, I thought, I'll bring it up on the way home.

But as soon as we began the walk back to our house, she took out her phone and made a call. I walked behind her—watching and longing.

The following Tuesday, I headed downtown to the central Denver Public Library. In the Western History section, I located microfiche cartridges for the *Rocky Mountain News* from August 1946. Seated at a microfiche machine, I began with the date for the article Becky had shown me.

On page 3, I found the story about Claranna Lewis's suicide. After re-reading it, I advanced the microfiche, looking for more. In the edition dated several days after the suicide, in the corner of page 12, there it was.

DETAILS EMERGE REGARDING ARSON – SUICIDE – ATTEMPTED MURDER

Police have concluded their investigation regarding the death via suicide by Claranna Lewis, 32, of Fox St., Denver. On the afternoon of the sixth, the Lewis home was lit afire from within. John Lewis was not home, but his wife, Claranna, and their two children were inside. Police suspect Claranna Lewis intended to trap the children inside with her, but they escaped the blaze.

The Lewises' daughter, age 12, told authorities she witnessed her mother douse the living room furniture with kerosene, then proclaim, "This wretched world warrants none of us!" before flinging a lighted match onto the sofa. As the room erupted in flames, the girl took her brother, age 6, by the hand and ran outside. She reported turning back to see her mother in the window, making no attempt to escape. The girl called for her mother, who, according to the girl, appeared deaf to her pleas.

The girl remains with her father in temporary housing. John Lewis has relinquished his young son to the Little Denver Home for Children, where, this reporter hopes, a loving family will soon be found to help the child forget the anguish of his past.

Relinquished him. Why? His sister was old enough to help care for him. Surely he'd have been better able to process the trauma by remaining with his family, rather than going to an orphans' home.

If the boy was my father, then my grandparents adopting him made sense. It was exactly like do-gooder Grandma Parry to read an article like this and decide to take in the poor, dear urchin. But his original family relinquishing him? That, I could not understand.

Beside the article was a studio portrait. *Lewis Family, 1942,* read the caption. I zoomed in for a better look. The photo was ragged at the edges, as if copied from one carried in a wallet. John Lewis and the daughter stood on either side of Claranna, who was seated on a stool and grasping the waist of a toddler on her lap.

John was a portly man; the chubby daughter seemed to take after him, while Claranna was slim. Mother and daughter both had dark, smooth hair—the daughter's in braids, Claranna's pulled into a bun. Typical of long-ago formal photos, John and his daughter wore earnest expressions. But Claranna's was downright grim. Her face was narrow and deeply lined.

Doing the math, she was only twenty-eight when the photo was taken, but she looked much older.

The child on her lap seemed frightened. His limbs were outstretched, making him look like a starfish. His feet kicked to either side and his hands were clenched into tiny fists.

My throat closed, imagining this child. What had his life been like?

The boy had large, deer-in-the-headlights eyes. The father's eyes were narrow and light in color, but Claranna and her daughter had the same shape and eye color as the boy's. In the monochrome photo, all three appeared to have eyes that were deep gray.

But I knew better. In our home growing up, there had been black-and-white photos of my father after his adoption, and plenty of me before color photography became commonplace. In those monochrome photos, our indigo eye color was represented by gray as dark as a thunderous sky.

Eyes that looked exactly like the eyes in this photo. Exactly.

Leaving the library, I tucked printouts of the articles about Claranna Lewis into my purse. I'd scanned the microfiche for an obituary, to no avail. I'd also asked the research librarian for a Denver telephone directory from the early- to mid-1940s. They had 1945, and in it I found a listing for John Lewis, with an address on Fox Street in the Baker neighborhood.

I couldn't stop thinking about it. And I couldn't avoid the nagging question: would chasing this trail lead to anything that might help Austin? I'd begun this quest because of learning about DNA possibly showing propensity for particular conditions—but that science was in its infancy. If Claranna Lewis—who likely had mental health issues—was Dad's biological mother, would that information provide clues into how Austin's mind worked?

I had no idea, but I was determined to keep searching until I found out.

The next day on the way home from school with Austin, I spotted yet another poster about the still-at-large Shelton Jr. and Darcy Powles. A ten-thousand-dollar reward was being offered for information leading to their whereabouts. I studied Darcy's sweet, dimpled face. How had this girl gotten tangled up with Robert Shelton Jr.?

Along with the reward, this poster included additional information I hadn't seen before: "Darcy Powles is the daughter of Diane Powles and DPD Officer Grant Powles."

As we walked and Austin prattled about Pokémon, I half-listened, interjecting the boilerplate questions I'd learned to ask. *Why is Ash considered the main character, instead of Pikachu? Who is the strongest Pokémon? Which was the first Pokémon?*

But my mind remained on the name I'd seen on the poster: *Officer* Grant Powles.

At home, I ran to my computer. An internet search revealed a recent photo of Officer Powles receiving an award from the mayor.

Darcy's father, in DPD dress blues, brought me back to 1979. He'd been younger then, a rookie. I remembered his deep-cleft chin. Now his hair was silver at the temples, but his jawline was the same.

And now I knew why the name Powles had seemed familiar.

19

1979

It was clear: my father would only take me seriously if I told him Peggy knew Bobby Shelton. But unless I confessed that I'd broken into Peggy's apartment, I couldn't tell him about the folder labeled with Shelton's name.

I still had Shelton's number. Was it worth trying again? I'd given up because most of the time it just rang and rang. But I *did* get a busy signal once.

After school I walked to the phone booth on Colfax. Stepping inside, I inserted a quarter and dialed. This time, some chick answered on the first ring. "Yeah?"

I couldn't tell how old she was. She didn't sound like a little kid and she didn't sound grown up. Somewhere in between. "Um..." I said. Then, with resolve, I asked, "Is this where Bobby Shelton lives?"

Smart, Suzie Blue—talking about him in the present, as if you don't know he's dead.

"Who's this?" the chick asked. "Who wants to know?"

"Um...I'm an old friend of his. From...sleepaway camp."

Nice one, Suze.

"It was a long time ago," I went on. "I'm in town, and I thought, why not call Bobby and catch up?"

"I'm pretty sure Bobby wasn't the sleepaway camp type," she said. "Dirt poor kids generally don't go to camp."

"This was a scholarship thing," I replied. "You know, where they send underprivileged kids to camp. I was one of those kids, too."

When we were kids, Laurie went to an overnight camp in the mountains every summer, and she'd write me letters. She told me about horseback riding. She described the wood-paneled cabins, the campfires and s'mores. There were always a few scholarship kids. Laurie said you knew them because they never had the right gear. They had to borrow stuff from the lost-and-found to get through the week.

The chick didn't say anything. I began to panic, unsure what to say next.

You're doing a good job, Mom-not-Mom said. *Make it up as you go, Suzie Blue.*

"Anyway," I continued. "I thought it'd be cool to catch up with my old camp friend."

"Well, maybe that makes sense," the chick said. "Bobby came from a tough scene. He told me about it when we met in Texas, before we moved here. His dad's a real sonuvabitch, you know? Bobby didn't talk to the guy. Didn't even like talking *about* the guy."

"Oh, sure." I nodded, alone in my phone booth. "Bobby said it was a stormy situation."

"That sonuvabitch blames me for the whole thing," she said. "Because we needed money and all."

"What whole thing?" I asked—knowing, of course, to which "whole thing" she was referring.

She sniffled. "Let's just say you missed Bobby by eight months. He was gunned down by a cop last spring."

Really? *That's* her interpretation of what happened?

"Wow." I forced myself to add, "I'm sorry."

"Yeah, it blows. Whatever happened to innocent until proven guilty?"

"Did he...did they think he'd done something to warrant it?"

"They said he shot some store clerk. But there was no proof."

Sure there was. A witness saw him leaving Zoe's Records immediately after the shots were fired. And he was shooting *at* Officers Coleman and Powles, for God's sake—before throwing his *own* stupid self into traffic.

Take a breath, Suze.

"Man." I let out what I hoped was an authentic-sounding sigh.

"What's your name?" the chick said. "I'm Rosalie. I was Bobby's girl-friend."

"I'm...Laurie."

"What camp did you and Bobby go to, Laurie?"

"Mountain Meadow," I said, retrieving the name of Laurie's camp from somewhere in the back of my memory. "It's near Grand Lake."

"Never heard of it."

"It was pretty. Being in nature was good for us, you know?"

"Sure," she said. "You live in Denver, Laurie?"

"Not anymore. Just passing through," I said. "Listen...did Bobby ever mention a woman named Peggy?"

"Peggy?" There was a lengthy pause. "Why?"

"She was...she was..." Think, Suzanne. "She donated to the scholarship thing. He told me about her. Like, she was someone he knew or something. I wondered if he still knew her."

Rosalie was silent. I tried to sense what she was thinking, but I had no idea. I might have been Mom's little seer who could sense ghosts and sometimes knew things I had no business knowing—but I'd never been good at that mind-reader stuff.

"Are you there?" I asked. "Did Bobby know somebody named Peggy?"

After a beat, Rosalie said, "Bobby knew lots of people. He did business wherever he went."

"What kind of business?"

She laughed. "Listen, I have no idea who you are. I'm just talking to you because I'm bored. Sitting here day after day, starving because I don't have money for food, and God knows how I'm going to pay next month's rent."

"And take care of a baby," I said. "That must be so hard."

She paused. "How'd you know I have a baby, Laurie?"

I swallowed. The words had just come out—I sensed the baby and spoke about him. Dammit, Suzanne, I chided myself, you know better.

It's okay. Just keep going, my little seer.

"I thought I heard a baby in the background," I told Rosalie. "I'm sorry if I was mistaken."

"No, you're right—he's just waking up. I didn't think you could hear him." She sighed. "Most of the time, you'd hear him fine, because mostly he just screams his head off. That's why I answered the phone so fast—he was sleeping and I didn't want him to wake up. I swear, this kid *never* sleeps."

As if on cue, the baby began to wail. I heard Rosalie attending to him, then she was back. In a low voice, she said, "Honestly...and why I'm telling this to a stranger, I have no idea, but honestly, I'd have had an abortion long ago. But Bobby wanted me to have the baby. And then, it wasn't long after I told him I was pregnant, that he...was gone." Rosalie sniffled. "After that, I don't know...I felt like I couldn't do that to him. Like maybe if I had an abortion, Bobby'd come back and haunt me, you know?"

"I can see that," I said. "I believe in ghosts."

"Do you? I didn't used to, but now that someone I loved is...gone...I'm not sure." I heard her blowing her nose. "Bobby and I were gonna get married. But now, who the hell knows what I should do? I'm from Dallas; I might go back. But if I can scrape together November rent, I might stay."

"How much is your rent?" I asked.

"One-fifty a month. Where am I gonna come up with that?"

"That's tough," I said. "Maybe I can loan you the money."

What are you talking about, Suze?

"Wow," Rosalie said. "That's real generous of you, Laurie. You must be doing okay for yourself."

"Well, camp helped," I told her. "Like I said, all that nature. It made me not want to be a dirt-poor kid anymore."

She laughed. "Who *wants* to be a dirt-poor kid? What kid *wants* that?"

"Right," I said. "Listen, Rosalie, let me see what I can do about the money. I'll call you back when I have more info."

"Well, that would be hunky-dory of you, Laurie."

"What's your address?" I asked. "In case I can't get you on the phone."

"I'm not giving my address to a total stranger," she said. "Call me when you have the money, then maybe I will."

"Fair enough." I didn't blame her. I mean, I could be anybody.

That night, I took out my bank book. Mom had set up accounts for Chris and me, somewhere to deposit birthday checks from our grandparents and that sort of thing. Mom said managing money was a skill we should learn from an early age.

But I liked spending money. I'd beg my mother to let me cash my birthday checks to buy toys I coveted, books I wanted to read, colorful socks I thought were cool. Mom reluctantly obliged, making sure I reserved a few dollars from each check in my account.

"You need to build *something*," she'd say. "Everybody should have a nest egg."

Why did I need a nest egg? *I* didn't pay the bills. I didn't know if we had a mortgage, or if my parents put money aside for our college educations and their retirement. All I knew was that Mom was thrifty, and Dad made lots of money but didn't talk about it. And I liked spending it. My sad little bank book showed a balance well short of what Rosalie needed for rent.

From behind me in my circular space, I heard Mom-not-Mom speak. "This is why I told you to save, Suzanne." She paused. "You really think if you pay that girl's rent, she'll give you information?"

I shrugged. "Only one way to find out."

That night I dreamed about Carey. We were nude, bodies pressed together, somewhere I couldn't identify—it wasn't Zoe's and it wasn't my room. There were white walls and modern furniture, including a soft, dove-gray couch that felt warm beneath my naked body.

Carey was on top of me. I felt the heat of his skin, saw the radiating flush on his face and neck. His blond locks fell forward, tickling my brow. There was soft, fine hair on his chest, and I combed my fingers through it.

He ground himself against me. Eagerly, I parted my legs.

I awoke, gasping and sitting up. Thankfully, Chris wasn't there.

Never before had I dreamed anything like that. I closed my eyes, trying to put myself back in that space, ready and willing to experience what came next.

I couldn't get Carey out of my mind. Seated at a lunch table with kids I half-knew, kids who didn't say much to me but at least didn't tell me to get lost, I relived the dream in my head.

After school, I went to Zoe's, but Carey didn't show. I locked up and began walking home. I inhaled the familiar scents of Colfax—every kind of food, from pizza to donuts to burritos, combined with traffic fumes and the musky smell of fallen leaves.

I imagined Carey and me in a restaurant. Having a real date, something adults did. Dinner, a movie. Followed by being alone together in that room...wherever it was.

Ahead of me on the sidewalk, I saw Scott Eames and Ken Wilson. I kept my distance, trailing them at a pace of about ten yards. When they turned and headed south, I followed, watching them enter a house that long ago—back when I had a crush on Scott—I'd identified as belonging to the Eameses.

Stepping behind a tree, I scoped it out. Could I slip Carey a note? The mailbox was affixed to the house, beside the front door. No way I could sneak onto the porch and stick a note inside.

As I was about to walk away, a mailman approached. He climbed the Eameses' porch, stuffing letters and fliers into their mailbox.

Of course. I didn't need to deliver a letter personally. For the mere fifteen-cent price of a stamp, the U.S. Postal Service would do it for me.

The letter I sent to Carey went like this:

Hi. Remember me? I've been thinking about that record you chose. There are others you can have if you want. Stop by if you're interested.
Hope to see you soon,
You-know-who

Short, sweet, and anonymous, in case it was intercepted by someone else in his family. And no hint of throwing myself at him. Now all I could do was wait and see if he showed up at Zoe's.

And in the meantime, figure out my much more urgent problem—connecting with Rosalie again to see if I could acquire proof that Peggy was linked to my mother's death.

20

2004

I couldn't stop thinking about the Powles and Shelton families. I remembered Rosalie's rather loose interpretation of the events of February 22, 1979. Had Shelton Jr. abducted Darcy because his mother told him that Darcy's father had killed *his* father?

I called the police anonymous tip line, explaining what I knew. Likely they'd already made the connection—if not, maybe it would help. But I had nothing else to offer. Going in to talk with the cops would only inflame my own wounds—and potentially subject me to questions about the past that I preferred not answering.

For the first time in years, I wished for more acute psychic powers, something beyond my childhood ability to sense ghosts, a lifelong strong intuition, and the occasional parlor trick like locating a lost item by conjuring it in my mind. I'd read about clairvoyants assisting in police investigations, but that had never been me. Now, I longed for something more specific from the spirit world, some clue about Darcy's whereabouts. But I didn't have that type of power.

I sank onto the kitchen floor beside Stevie's bed and scratched her ears. Her solid warmth and kind eyes comforted me. It'll be all right, Mom, she seemed to say.

Burying my face in her fur, I whispered, "Stevie baby—it will."

The next morning, a story in *The Denver Post* made me gasp—this time with relief.

MOTHER OF AT-LARGE MAN QUESTIONED

Following an anonymous tip, Dallas, Texas police have questioned Rosalie Singer, mother of Robert Shelton Jr., who is wanted for questioning in connection with the disappearance of Denver woman Darcy Powles. Following Powles's disappearance on August 27, sources report that there is speculation Shelton has returned to the Dallas area where he was raised, possibly with Powles accompanying him.

Police continue to ask for the public's assistance in the case. Any tips should be reported to the police hotline.

Setting the paper aside, I drew Austin to me, enveloping him in a hug. Across the kitchen, Caitlin watched us, arms crossed over her chest.

I beckoned her. "Come here and I'll hug you, too."

Caitlin snorted. "Yeah, right." She strode from the room and stomped up the stairs.

I kissed the top of Austin's head. "Go brush your teeth, honeypie. It's almost time for school."

Upstairs, I knocked on Caitlin's door. When I heard a muffled groan, I opened the door.

"I'm dressing in here!" she shrieked, tugging on black leggings. "Why can't you leave me *alone*?"

"Cait." I held up my hands. "Why are you so angry? Whatever's going on, I can help."

"You'd never understand. You know nothing about what it's like to be happy, like I was back home..." Her chin trembled. "And then not be happy anymore. All because of circumstances beyond your control."

I opened my mouth to protest. I knew *nothing* about that?

But how could Caitlin understand this? She had no clue what had happened when I was her age.

Brett's mother had always been affectionate with Caitlin, as she was with all her grandchildren. But when Caitlin, at age five, had asked where her "grandma on the other side" was, I'd only said she died in an accident. Pressed for details, I outright lied, saying it was a car accident. I asked Brett to maintain my "white lie," saying it would scare Caitlin to know otherwise. I promised him I'd tell her the truth eventually—and Austin, too. But eventually never came.

Maybe it was time. Would the story teach her a lesson?

My mind jolted to Peggy all those years ago, talking about her teenage years. About how I could learn from her example. So I only said, "I'm sorry you feel as if I couldn't understand, Cait."

She gave me a pointed look. "Would you go now?"

I blinked. "Have a good day. Don't forget to lock the house when you leave."

She didn't answer. I about-faced, went to help Austin finish getting ready, and headed out.

"That's rough," Donna said when I told her I was having a hell of a time with Caitlin. We'd met for a quick midday walk in Washington Park—not our neighborhood but she'd suggested a change of scenery. Wash Park featured a picturesque two-mile loop that provided an opportunity to talk.

I nodded. "I'm at a loss."

"Invite her to Zoe's," Donna suggested. "She's into art, right? Maybe she'd like to see what you and Renee have going on."

"She wouldn't be interested."

"Bullshit. Give it a try. What do you have to lose?"

Passing us on the path, a group of women pushed double strollers—all moms of twins, I surmised. They laughed and chatted, stopped to tend their children. When I admired a duo of baby boys in coordinated, blue-and-green fleece outfits, their mother thanked me, the creases on her face deepening when she smiled.

Donna and I watched the group walk away. Likely, her thoughts were on the twins Renee had miscarried. As for me, I was thinking about Caitlin and Austin. Despite them being a handful, they were *here*. And they were safe.

When Caitlin asked for permission to go to the mall on Saturday, I told her she could under the condition that she spend Friday afternoon at Zoe's with me. I had Austin on the wait list for daily after-care at school, but until a slot opened, Friday was my "long day" at Zoe's because he was enrolled in a movement-based enrichment program until five.

"I have zero interest," Caitlin said. "This is *your* thing, Mom."

"Just come for a bit." I gave her a feeble smile, like a chef offering a food critic a particularly humble dish. "I think you'll like my store, Caitlin."

On Friday, as three-thirty approached, I put Sheryl Crow on the stereo—her greatest hits album, which had released the year before. Caitlin had always liked Crow's music. Then I resumed my earlier task—painting display shelves a bright, glistening white.

Paintbrush in hand, I noted how sweaty my palms had become. How was it possible that a fifteen-year-old girl could rattle me so much?

Had *I* rattled anyone, at that age? If I did, I could think of only one possibility. One person.

My hand shook and I dropped the brush onto the tarp I'd spread on the floor. White speckles appeared against the blue of the tarp.

"Nice move, Mom."

Caitlin had slipped in silently. I planned to install a jangling bell like the one my mother had used, but I hadn't gotten to it. "You're here!" I said. Feeling the overeager look on my face, I scaled back, pulling my mouth straight.

She scowled. "I'm here."

Sweeping a hand around, I asked, "What do you think of my store?"

"It's...uh...something," Caitlin replied.

Her phone buzzed. Whispering, she explained where she was. "I'll call you back. This won't take long."

"You want a soda?" I asked as she closed her flip-phone. "There are some in the mini fridge in the back room."

She returned with a Coke. "There's a guy back there," she announced.

"Yeah." I admired the smoothness of my brush strokes on the shelves. "He's installing the security system."

"Well, he said he's almost done."

"Yep, I am," the alarm-company guy said, appearing in the doorway to the back room. "Can you come back here, ma'am, so I can show you how to set your code?"

Caitlin trailed after us, drinking her Coke and leaning on the back room's counter as the guy and I talked. Good, I thought. It's beneficial for her to understand the ins and outs of running a business. I was doing right by her. The same way my mother had by me.

After he left, Caitlin and I returned out front. "You want to help me paint?" I asked. "I have another brush."

She picked a hangnail. "No, thanks."

"Suit yourself." I returned to my project. Sheryl Crow started singing "The First Cut is the Deepest."

"Got any better music than this?" Caitlin asked.

"I thought you liked Sheryl Crow. You used to, anyway."

"*Used to* being the key phrase." She twirled the Coke can in her hands. "Do you have anything by The Mission? Or Love and Rockets?"

"We focus on female artists," I explained. "The way my mother...your grandmother...once did." I steadied my painting wrist with my other hand.

"Well, Lacuna Coil, maybe? Or Concrete Blonde? They're both fronted by women."

I took a breath. "I don't have anything by either of those, but I'll look for them. Thanks for the recommendations." When she didn't reply, I went on, "Why don't you browse those sample prints on the counter? An artist dropped them off for me to check out. I'd love your opinion."

Caitlin sighed, stepping over to the counter. Earlier, I'd skimmed the prints, which were by an artist named Tori Flynn. Tori's work featured abstracts in bright colors, but when you studied them closely, images began to appear: a couple dancing, a pen and paper, and in one of them a building with a clock tower, like East High. Their style seemed like something Caitlin might appreciate.

I concentrated on painting and deep breathing. The year I turned twelve, Mom had taken an eight-week meditation course. "I tried so hard," she'd told me when the course was over. "But my mind kept wandering." At home while working on sewing projects, Mom would take long breaths like she'd learned in class. She said the hum of the sewing machine was more soothing than her attempts at meditation had been. "The instructor said it takes time, but honestly, Suzie Blue—I don't think I'd ever have gotten it." She paused. "I thought if I meditated, maybe I could connect with the spirit world...like you do." Tilting her head, she'd asked, "Is that how it works for you?"

"I don't think so," I said. "They just come to me."

"Lucky you," Mom had replied. "I wish I had that talent."

Caitlin's phone rang again. She began to chat, absently flipping through the samples. Her Coke was on the counter next to her, and as she chugged, drops fell onto the plastic-encased prints.

"Caitlin," I said. "I gave you a task. Please hang up and give it your attention."

She ignored me.

"Caitlin," I repeated.

"I'll call you back." She closed her phone and faced me, tigress-like in her stance.

I stood. "I'm not asking for much. An hour of your time." I held out my arms. "Look around you. Isn't it pretty? Isn't it bright? Can you envision the paintings, the photographs? You're an artist, Cait—at least, you used to be. Can't you see my vision?"

She shook her head. "I'm sorry, Mom, but what I see is... kinda dumpy." She shrugged. "I really am sorry, but you asked for my opinion." She nodded toward the half-painted shelves. "I mean, where did you get those—a thrift store?"

"Yeah," I said. "Actually, that *is* where I got them. They just need a little paint to brighten them up."

"You couldn't buy new ones?"

I pressed my lips together. "Stuff costs money, Caitlin. I'm being frugal. That's a good lesson for you, too."

"But are you the best person to teach it? *Frugal* has never been your strong suit." She smirked. "All those knifemaking supplies add up, don't they?"

And your art lessons, I wanted to retort. And living in one of the most expensive areas of the country. And your father and me losing our jobs. It hadn't been just one thing. Besides, I was truly trying. Couldn't she see that?

Feeling my gut twist, I bent forward. "I'm doing my best, Caitlin," I said quietly.

"Fine, but..." She crushed her empty Coke can. "Think about it. What artists will want to sell their stuff here? Who'd want their stuff in a dump like this?"

Fuck you, I wanted to scream. *Fuck you*, Caitlin.

The words were there, balanced on my tongue like venom. One of these days, would I completely lose it on her?

I took another deep breath. "You don't like it, you can go."

"Oh, thank God." Grabbing her backpack, she slipped out the door.

I sank onto the tarp. Sheryl Crow sang about how nowhere was far enough.

"You said it, girlfriend," I murmured. My hands spattered with paint, I rested my cheeks in my palms and closed my eyes.

Late that afternoon when I arrived home with Austin, I could tell immediately that something was wrong—although on the surface, everything seemed fine. The back door was locked. The house was quiet.

That was the problem. The house was quiet.

Where was Stevie? She usually came running to the door when she heard my key in the lock. I called her name, then enjoined Austin to help me search. We looked everywhere, from the top of the house to the bottom and back again.

"Mommy," Austin called from the front hallway. "Is the door supposed to be like this?"

I rushed to the hall. The front door was ajar—a gap of about eight inches, enough for Stevie to get out.

She got out. I ran outside, yelling up and down the street for her, Austin following me. Sensing my fear, he clung to me and slowed me down as I zigzagged the blocks and alleys adjoining ours.

"Lost dog!" I cried to everyone I passed. "Please, a little Australian Shepherd with a black and white coat. If you see her..."

Austin whimpered, plopping onto the sidewalk. "Mommy, I'm tired. Can we go home?"

I swallowed the lump in my throat and helped him up. "Of course, bud," I said, my voice hoarse from shouting.

"You left the door open!" I said an hour later, when Caitlin came home.

I screamed it, really—as loudly as she'd ever screamed at me. I'd been on the phone with every animal shelter in the city. I'd called Brett, who promised to come home as soon as he could get away. I was desperate to go out and look again, but I couldn't leave Austin alone.

Caitlin glared. "What are you talking about?"

I pointed to the front door. "You left it open and Stevie got out. And she's gone!"

Tears streamed down my cheeks, but Caitlin appeared not to notice. "That is complete bullshit. I closed and locked the door this morning when I left."

"Then how did she get *out*?"

"How should I know? But it wasn't me. Jesus, you blame me for every-thing."

Caitlin stomped up the stairs. I watched her go, my hands balled into fists.

Brett and I put up posters everywhere. I visited every shelter in Denver and the nearby suburbs, although all of them had assured me on the phone that no dog matching Stevie's description had been turned in. Each day for a week, I made the rounds to the shelters. I offered a reward of five hundred dollars, then increased it to a thousand. I had no idea where we'd get the money if Stevie was returned, but I didn't care.

I tried to see her in my mind's eye. Tried to sense where she was. But like Darcy Powles, Stevie failed to materialize for me.

Without her, the house was desolate. I could barely look at her food and water bowls, at her bed in the kitchen where she slept during the day. Brett went out each evening to search, then came home and held me, silently shaking his head. In bed, my feet reached for Stevie's warm belly in the spot near the footboard where she liked to spend the night. Brett wrapped his arms around me as I cried myself to sleep.

"You can get another dog, Mommy," Austin proposed. "That would make you feel better. You'd be better, better, better."

Caitlin nodded. "He's right, Mom. It's only a dog. Just get another one."

Should I replace *you* if you go missing? I wanted to snap at her. I couldn't get mad at Austin—he had no filter and understood so little—but Caitlin should've been more sympathetic.

Especially because it was her fault.

21

1979

On Sunday we acquired and carved pumpkins—four of them like every year, but this year the fourth pumpkin was Peggy's. She carved a skeleton face, elaborately sculpted and spooky, with curved lines for the bone structure and delicately chiseled teeth.

A respectable pumpkin carver myself, I decided to memorialize Mama Cass, who died a few years ago. Throughout that July day, Mom had played music by The Mamas and The Papas at Zoe's Records. On my pumpkin's surface, I recreated Mama Cass in happy times—grinning, eyes wide, signature double chin. It wasn't a half-bad job, I decided, taking a few final swipes with the paring knife. All she needed was a wig of long brown hair.

Chris and Dad went simple, as always. Pumpkins were the lesser element in Chris's Halloween—his favorite holiday, even more so than Christmas. For him, the costume was everything. Every year, he decided what to wear long before the big day. This year, he was dressing as a wizard, a costume he'd begun talking about before Mom died. She'd scored a wand from a thrift store toy bin. She bought yards of purple silk and tucked it away in her sewing cabinet in the parlor, presumably planning to make Chris's costume closer to Halloween.

One summer day, I'd glanced into the parlor. I hadn't entered it since I found the mix tape Mom had made me. The shades were drawn, Mom's houseplants were dead, and the furniture was dusty. It had come with the house—stiff-backed Victorian sofas and horsehair chairs that, considering our house's history, I'd always been reluctant to sit on. You didn't have to be anyone's little seer to envision the activities that probably took place there at one time.

Standing in the doorway that hot afternoon, my ears rang with the memory of the sewing machine's reassuring whirl. I considered teaching myself to sew, so I could tackle Chris's costume—I'd never be as proficient as my mother, but maybe I could get the job done. But the idea overwhelmed me, and instead I slid the oak pocket doors closed.

After that, I doubted Chris's wizard costume would come to fruition. But it turned out Peggy knew her way around a sewing machine. When Chris told her about the costume, she opened the parlor doors, cleared out the dead plants, dusted everything, and investigated Mom's sewing station. Peggy bought a pattern and used Mom's machine and the purple silk to fashion Chris's wizard robe. She spread the robe on the parlor floor and, applying glue and glitter, created swirling patterns across it. She bought a witch's hat from the Halloween section at Kmart and fitted it with additional purple silk, then repeated the glue-and-glitter effect.

The costume was magnificent. It was every bit as beautiful as something Mom would've made.

That night, all of us—Chris in his wizard costume—set our pumpkins on the front porch and lit their candles. Dad, Peggy, and Chris oohed and aahed—and I thought about how screwed up my family had become.

Later, after Peggy had gone home and Chris was in bed, I stepped back onto the porch. My pumpkin looked enough like Mama Cass that *I* could tell who it was, even if no one else could. But Peggy's carved skeleton was the indisputable star of our collection.

I went inside, grabbing Mom's Santoku from the butcher block knife holder in the kitchen. On the porch, I began slicing Peggy's pumpkin to shreds.

No one would know it was me. Peggy was miles away, Chris was asleep, and Dad was in his study. When the damage was discovered, everyone would assume it was vandals.

"Suzanne? What're you doing?"

I jerked my head to the left. Laurie was on her front porch.

"Jesus," I whispered. "You scared the crap out of me."

Laurie crossed to our yard. "That's quite the slash job, Suzanne."

"Please," I said. "Please, Laurie—don't tell anyone."

She blew smoke to the side. "Why would I do that?"

"Thanks," I said. "Really, I mean it...thank you."

"Come over." She nodded toward her house. "My mom's not home."

I wiped the Santoku on my jeans. "I'll be right over."

In her kitchen Laurie split a can of Tab into two glasses, then spiked them with Jack Daniels. She held her drink up to mine. "Cheers, kiddo."

"Cheers." I sipped.

She leaned on the counter. "So I'm not going to tell anyone what you did. But I have to know—what the hell is going on over there?"

My fingers prickled and I pressed them around my glass. I'd known Laurie forever, since we were little kids fighting over Barbies and hopscotch. If I couldn't trust Laurie, who *could* I trust?

"You've seen the addition to our household, right?" I asked.

Laurie nodded. "She's come over a few times. Brought banana bread and stuff. Chris follows her around like a puppy dog."

I winced at this. "She's up to no good. She was involved in my mom's death. She *knew* the guy who killed Mom."

Laurie's eyes widened. "You're joking, right?"

"Completely serious. But I have no proof—only a theory that she want-ed my mom out of the picture so she could..." I winced again. "...hook up with my dad."

"Oh, Jesus, this is *good*." Laurie drained her glass and opened another Tab. "It's like an episode of *Kojak*."

"Except this is real," I replied.

Bruce came in, making a beeline for the fridge. We were silent as he rummaged around. "Hurry up, loser," Laurie said. "We're talking in here."

He turned. "You're *drinking* in here."

"What are you gonna do about it?" She grinned. "Tell Mom, and I'll tell Suzanne what I hear from your bedroom at night."

Bruce's face turned ripe tomato red. Grabbing a Coke, then a bag of potato chips from the cabinet, he scurried out. Laurie said, "He has the hugest crush on you."

"Gross." I finished my drink, pushing my glass toward her.

She refilled both of us. "How'd you come up with this theory about Peggy?"

I told her about breaking into Peggy's place. "Problem is, I can't go back and just *take* the evidence, you know?" I said. "Besides, it proves nothing except that Peggy knew Shelton. I have no idea what their relationship was. I'm trying to track that down, too." Omitting details about appropriating her name and camp experiences, I told Laurie about Rosalie and the ques-tions I'd asked her.

"I like this side of you, kiddo." Laurie's eyes glowed. "Good for you, having the balls to take this on."

I wrinkled my nose. "I hate that expression. Can't a person have the ovaries to take something on?"

Laurie snorted.

I finished my second drink. "I should go. But I'll keep you posted."

Laurie held up a hand. "Suzanne? You know what I overheard Peggy telling my mom?" She dropped empty soda cans into the trash. "Mom and Peggy got cozy one day, over coffee and slices of banana bread. Peggy said that she and her ex-husband had a son but he was stillborn. She said it's tragic that she never had the chance to be a mother. Then she told my mom that Chris reminds her of her child."

"Holy cow," I said. "That confirms my suspicions. It's sad she lost a baby, but what she said about Chris—that's creepy."

Laurie's expression was thoughtful. "You're right. It *is* creepy."

I blinked, turning away so Laurie wouldn't see me cry. Then she did something unexpected. Reaching forward, she wrapped her arms around me. "I'm so sorry about your mom. She was the best."

Tears hurricaned in my eyes and ran in rivers down my cheeks. "I hate that she's gone," I blubbered. "And I hate that Peggy is closing in on Mom's territory. She's going to *move into* our house. She's going to sleep every night in my parents' bed. She's going to be right down the hall—having *sex* with my father."

Laurie released me. "I wish I could change it all for you." Her half-drunken voice brimmed with sincerity. "Is there anything I can do for you, Suzanne?"

Wiping my eyes with a paper towel, I gazed at her. She couldn't help solve my biggest problem. But maybe there *was* something Laurie could do.

"Not about Peggy," I said. "But maybe something else."

"What?"

"There's this guy." I felt myself blushing. "I kinda like him."

She smiled. "Cool. Who is it? Maybe I can put in a good word for you."

"I'll never tell. But you might be able to help in another way."

I crossed the room, examining myself in the darkened kitchen window. The image was blurry, and I felt woozy from the whiskey, but I took stock of what I saw. My long, straight, do-nothing hair, pulled into braids. My makeup-less face. My humdrum navy-blue sweater.

I faced Laurie. "You can make me over." I waved my arms wide. "Go ahead. I'm putty in your hands."

Within the hour she'd transformed me. After drinking two glasses of water each in an attempt to sober up, we went to her room. Laurie explained the mascara, the liquid eyeliner, and how to select the most flattering shade of lipstick. She used her curling iron to create feathered curls along the sides of my head.

Spraying my finished 'do with Aqua Net, Laurie said, "This came out okay, but you need a decent, layered haircut to make it work properly. I can give you my stylist's number if you like."

I tilted my sticky head at her. "Maybe."

She raided her closet, finding a colorful sweater—rainbow-striped and form-fitting. She loaned me a black lace, padded push-up bra.

I nodded toward her boobs. "I thought they were perky all on their own."

She shrugged. "They *mostly* are...but a little help never hurt anybody."

"Here's the question, though." I looked at myself in the mirror, stunned to see what resembled an actual female chest. "Won't he be disappointed, if and when he sees the real, braless deal?"

Laurie laughed. "You go that far, and I guarantee, no guy is going to ditch you based on your tits not being exactly what he'd expected." Standing behind me, she put a hand on each shoulder. "Look at you," she said. "You're gorgeous. You look just like..."

She trailed off. In the mirror, our eyes met.

"Just like your mom," Laurie murmured.

I stared into the mirror. She was right. Standing tall, shoulders back, I looked like Mom.

But it wasn't the hairstyle and makeup that made the difference. It was how I held myself. Proudly, confidently. The way Alex used to.

Were things different at school the next day? Maybe a couple of heads turned. Girls are mean; if they noticed, it was with disdain. As for boys, I don't know. I didn't care about Scott Eames, nor any other boy at school.

At Zoe's I combed through the inventory, trying to recall artists who'd recorded "Suzanne." I found the Judy Collins album *In My Life*, which I knew included the song. Nina Simone's *To Love Somebody*. Roberta Flack's *Killing Me Softly*.

That was enough of that. Remembering the album Carey had selected, attempting to conjure Mom-not-Mom, I asked her—if someone liked Joan Baez, who else would they like? She didn't reply, but artists' names flowed to me. Odetta. Buffy Sainte-Marie. Holly Near.

Maybe he'd like something more rocking. Linda Ronstadt. Fleetwood Mac, featuring Stevie Nicks. Should I take things in a different direction? What about someone bluesy or jazzy? Bonnie Raitt. Etta James.

I set the records on the counter and propped open the door. I put a Carly Simon tape in the boombox, fluffed my hair, and reapplied lipstick. Laurie would be proud.

Twenty minutes later he strolled in. I was in my usual spot at Zoe's feet, a textbook on my knees. Carey came over, standing in front of me. "Hey, you-know-who." His hands were in the front pockets of his jeans—but I tried not to look there. "I got your note."

I nodded at the counter. "I put aside a few records for you. Take what you like."

He didn't move, staring at me. "You look nice today."

Our eyes met. Suddenly, he seemed uneasy. "Listen, maybe I should go."

I waved my hand toward the counter. "Pick out some records first."

"You don't have to do this," he said. "I can buy my own records."

"Sure, you can. But these need a good home. And when you listen to them…" I paused, hoping to sound dramatic. "…you can think about me."

He began sorting the records. "I like that sweater on you," he said. "Love all the colors."

"Thanks."

He leaned on the counter. "You look like…" He shook his head. "Never mind."

I stood. "I look like…?"

He didn't reply. "You wanna get out of here? Grab a bite to eat? My treat."

Fantasy into reality. Was this a date? I wasn't about to ask…just in case he said no.

We went to the same lunch counter from which Carey had brought me takeout. Over cheeseburgers and shakes, we discussed music, school, and siblings. If my crush on Scott Eames was still a thing, I'd have gleaned much knowledge that afternoon. But by then, nothing Carey said was likely to reinstate my prior esteem for his brother.

Afterward, we walked back to Zoe's. I unlocked the door and we went inside. "Thanks for the bite," I said.

"Anytime. I like hanging out with you, Suzanne. You're different from most girls." He faced me. "I can tell you don't play games."

I shrugged. "I'm just me. I'm not trying to be anyone else." This wasn't entirely accurate; my clothes, hair, and makeup were all evidence to the contrary. But he didn't know that.

He looked at me for a long minute, then asked, "Do you have a hairbrush?"

What an odd question. "Sure, but why?"

"Can I borrow it?"

I retrieved the brush from my backpack and handed it over. "Turn around," he said.

My back to Carey, I felt the brush tug gently through my hair. "I love your hair this way," he said, his voice low. "Loose, not in braids. But it's too stiff with all this crap in it. My sister says the only way to get out hair spray is to brush with an easy, soft stroke."

I held my breath.

He worked through my hair until he was able to glide the brush through every strand. Then he turned me to face him.

"Much better." He handed me the brush. "It's so pretty this way." He ran his fingers the length of my hair on one side. "So damned pretty."

Was he going to kiss me? Oh, God, please let him kiss me.

For what felt like about three hours but was probably less than a minute, our eyes remained locked on one another's. Then Carey stepped back.

He grabbed his stack of records from the countertop. "I've gotta go," he choked.

As he started for the door, I called out his name. Across the darkened space, he turned.

"Don't be a stranger," I said. "You're a mean old daddy, Carey—but I like you."

He smiled, catching the Joni Mitchell reference. "You know your stuff," he said. Then he was gone.

22

— · —

2004

I slept in on Sunday morning and upon rising, walked into the astonishing kitchen tableau of Caitlin and Austin standing side by side at the gas range, dripping sample beads of pancake batter onto the griddle to ensure it was heated. Giggling, they watched the beads do a sizzling dance.

Brett sat at the table, reading the Sunday *Denver Post*. "Hey, sleepy-head," he said, jumping up to pour me coffee.

"Wow, who *are* these young people in our kitchen?" I asked.

Caitlin scooped batter, dropping it in neat circles on the griddle. "He asked," she said, nodding toward Austin. "And who doesn't like pancakes?"

I met her eye. "That's really nice of you, Cait."

She shrugged. I sipped coffee, thinking that everyone has the ability to surprise you sometimes.

Then, glancing at Stevie's empty bed, I felt my face grow hot. Was Caitlin just trying to make up for letting my dog run away?

Later, Chris took Austin for the afternoon—lunch and a video game arcade were on the agenda. I went to Zoe's, where I finished the shelving paint job and logged Tori Flynn's information into a database on the desktop computer we'd purchased for the store, kept in the back room and used to track everything from expenses to artist portfolios to marketing opportunities.

I arrived home in time to greet my son and my brother. They drove up in Chris's gleaming Chevy Silverado pickup, Austin leaning out the passenger window and waving. The truck had a crew cab, and Austin should have been riding in the back, but presumably Chris didn't know that. I'd make sure to mention it next time he took Austin somewhere.

Austin hopped down from the truck, and we went inside while Chris searched for parking on our narrow, crowded street.

"That is a ridiculous vehicle for city driving," I told him when he showed up on foot ten minutes later.

"It's the 2005 model," Chris said. "Latest thing."

"Where is it, Uncle Chris?" Austin asked. "Did you bring it?"

"Of course." Chris produced a large plastic bag from behind his back. "Show your mom."

Austin opened the bag and pulled out something made of luminous, yellow polyester fabric. Pikachu's lightning bolt-shaped tail and brown stripes appeared along the back. There was also a Pikachu-shaped head covering, with its long ears, wry expression, and round red pouches on the cheeks—used, I knew, to store electricity.

"Isn't it beautiful?" Austin breathed. "Mommy, I can't wait for Halloween."

I fingered the cheap fabric. In homage to my mother, I'd taught myself to sew when my kids were little. I was nowhere near Renee's caliber, or even my mother's, but I enjoyed sewing as a hobby. "I was making Austin's Pikachu costume," I told Chris. "I couldn't find a pattern but Renee offered to help me design one. I have the fabric—velvet, much nicer than this."

"Yeah, Austin told me. But I figured I'd save you the trouble."

"It wasn't trouble." Hands on hips, I faced Chris. "Did you even *think*? Did you use your head? I *wanted* to make it." I felt hot tears in the corners of my eyes. "You've ruined the whole thing!"

"Jesus, Suzanne," Chris said. "It's just a Halloween costume."

"You of *all* people," I shot back, "should understand how important the right costume is."

I had him there. His whole life, Chris had adored Halloween. He still dressed in an ornate costume each year—rented these days—and went to every party and Halloween-related event for which an invitation came his way.

"I'm sorry," he said, his tone authentically contrite.

Austin looked from one of us to the other. "Does this mean I can't wear the costume Uncle Chris bought me?"

His voice was so heavy, his eyes so downcast, I could do nothing but gather him into my arms. "You can wear whatever you want," I told him. "It's *your* costume."

"Oh, good." Austin smiled. "Because I like this one, Mommy. It's just what I wanted."

My tone wobbly, I said, "Did you thank Uncle Chris?"

Eyes shiny with rock-star adoration, Austin said, "Thank you, Uncle Chris."

Chris high-fived him. "No problem, buddy. My pleasure."

Halloween was a week later. Caitlin told us she was headed to a party at Claudia's house but promised not to stay out late. The Friday before, she'd brought home a midterm report card featuring all As. Given her good grades, knowing the party was only a few blocks away and the parents would be there—and Shelton Jr. was likely in Dallas, not Denver—I let her go. She didn't need a costume; in her goth getup, every day was Halloween.

I took Austin around the neighborhood while Brett stayed home handing out candy. The area was hopping—more kids by several-fold than there'd been when I was growing up nearby in the 1970s. It was a crisp, clear evening, perfect for trick-or-treating.

I'd hoped by now Austin would've made a friend or two with whom he could trick-or-treat, but it hadn't happened. With the incidents at school, the calls I was still getting from the principal, it was unsurprising yet disheartening. I'd met with the school psychologist, who gave me several book recommendations. I was making my way through the suggested texts, but thus far, they'd failed to provide an "aha" moment of any sort.

Austin shivered in the cheap Pikachu costume Chris had bought. I carried his jacket but when I offered it to him, he refused to cover his costume. By the time we got home, he was exhausted and freezing.

"I'll run him a bath," Brett offered. "We're almost out of candy, and it's getting late." He blew out the candles in our pumpkins, lined up on the porch railing the way my family had always lined up ours. "You relax, Suzanne."

I went to the kitchen and made a cup of tea. But I felt restless. Climbing the stairs, I caught Brett as he was grabbing a towel from the linen closet.

"I'm going for a walk," I said as he opened the bathroom door. "Okay with you?"

Brett grinned. "Going out for more candy?"

"Mommy, that's not fair." Covered in bubbles, Austin half-rose from the tub. "Not fair—not *fair*. I want to come."

"Sit down, honeypie, or you'll slip," I said. "Everyone's done giving out candy, and they don't give it to adults anyway. I'm just taking a walk."

In my bedroom, I closed my eyes, trying to envision the missing drop-point knife with the purple spacer. I saw it in a dresser drawer—not mine, nor anyone else's in my home—among some nondescript pairs of socks. But I couldn't pinpoint anything else. Still, buoyed by the vision, I attempted to locate Stevie in my mind's eye. But no sense of her materialized.

Blinking, biting my lip, I selected from my knife case a tanto fixed blade with a walnut handle and pumpkin-colored spacer. I'd rehandled the tanto several years ago, following a particularly tortuous visit to Denver, one I'd cut short by two days. Because of the handle's black-and-orange color combination and the knife's angular, dual-planed blade—in Japanese, tanto meant dagger—Brett called it my "Halloween knife."

Slipping the sheathed knife into my coat pocket, I stepped outside. The moon was nearly full and the sky was bright. I thought about Claranna Lewis. Where was she buried? What happened to her husband and daughter?

Who adopted her son?

With everything else going on, there'd been no time to look into it further. I resolved that after Zoe's grand opening, I'd resume my search.

Missing Stevie with an intensity that made my leash-less wrist feel as if a weighted handcuff encircled it, I knew where my feet were carrying me. I was simply following along.

Ahead of me on the sidewalk, I spied another pedestrian. Her height, gait, and clothing were unmistakably Caitlin's. I followed a half-block behind her, detouring from my intended path and turning north on Race Street.

Caitlin had provided the name of the girl hosting the party—Claudia Bates, the girl with whom she'd mentioned going to the movies a few weeks ago—but that was all we knew. I should have pressed for details. Tomorrow, I'd look up the Bateses in the family directory that East had provided. I'd call the parents, introduce myself, ask how the party went.

But why wasn't Caitlin at their house?

I followed for another block, listening to her heavy-booted footfalls on the sidewalk. Watching her open the side gate of a lit-up house and slip inside, I felt my tensed muscles loosen. Maybe she'd just needed some air. I about-faced and made my way toward Cheesman Park.

At the park's entrance, I steeled myself. Would the spirit I wanted to connect with be here? Even if I was that lucky, she wouldn't be the only one. I knew I might sense ghosts I preferred not confronting. Was I willing to risk that, in hopes of feeling my mother's presence?

Yes, I told myself, stepping onto the dirt path. Yes, I was.

Cheesman was abuzz on Halloween night—people in groups on the grass, dog walkers, couples strolling arm-in-arm. In the lighted pavilion, several young guys sat on the steps, drinking beers and strumming guitars. Throughout the park, ghost hunters snapped photos and took notes.

Did they sense what I did? The figure with a bullet hole in his back—I felt the hollowed-out depth of his stare over one shoulder at me. The young man, a boy really, missing an arm and half a leg. Far across the park, I sensed the cocky flip of an unseen firearm. My head throbbed with the knowledge that the gunslinger's final duel would be his opponent's triumph.

I closed my eyes, hoping to convey solace. Your story matters, I wanted them to know. *You* matter.

Then I whispered, "Mom? I'm looking for you. I'm listening for you."

A coldness—colder than the cool night air, colder than anything I'd ever felt in the presence of my mother's ghost, crept beneath my glove and grasped my hand. The feeling wrapped itself around my fingers and yanked me forward. I cried out as I stumbled and fell onto the ground. Reaching into my pocket, I pulled out the tanto.

The guitar strumming stopped. "You okay, lady?" someone called from the pavilion.

At his words, the cold vanished. I stood, resheathing my knife. I pulled off my glove and held my hand to my mouth, warming it with my breath.

"I'm fine," I choked. "Just tripped over a tuft of grass."

"That person behind you scare you, ma'am?"

I whipped my head around. "What person?"

"There was someone behind you," one of the guitar players said. "They wore dark clothes. Took off when you yelled."

I hesitated. "A...person, right? You saw a person?"

The guy laughed. "As opposed to a ghost? Yeah, it was a person."

"Man or woman?" I asked.

"Couldn't tell." He resumed strumming. "They're gone now. But be careful out there, ma'am."

I nodded, then sprinted out of the park. Clenching my knife's handle, I turned around every few seconds to scan the area behind me. Shadows transformed into moving figures. Breezes sounded like footsteps.

Heart pounding, I crossed streets and skittered across corner lots. I'd go home, climb into the safety of my car, and fetch Caitlin—immediately.

Gripping my knife, I ran faster.

23

1979

I went to Zoe's the next two afternoons but on neither day did Carey appear. I couldn't stop thinking I'd done something wrong. Otherwise, he'd have kissed me. He'd have returned, or at least let me know when I'd see him again.

Over dinner on Halloween, I offered to take Chris trick-or-treating—something my mother had always done and something I'd expected Peggy to worm her way into. To my surprise, she agreed to my offer. "Your dad and I will stay here and man the candy station," she said.

Later, in the kitchen, she cornered me. "Suzanne? Can I speak to you?" When I shrugged, she continued. "Tell me what happened to my pumpkin."

I met her eye. "This isn't the suburbs. Stuff happens around here. We've been broken into twice—did you know that?"

Peggy scraped dinner plates into the sink. "Why anyone wants to live here, I'll never understand."

Damn right she won't, Mom-not-Mom said. *She's nothing like us, Suze.*

Behind Peggy, I sensed the kitchen ghosts nodding their agreement. It occurred to me that, other than Mom-not-Mom, these two were the only spirits I'd sensed in our house for months. I used to feel all sorts of spirits in the house—people who'd lived there or visited, presumably—but now it was only the three of them.

While I was pondering that, wondering where the others had gone, Peggy asked, "But why just *my* pumpkin? It seems so...targeted."

"Probably because it was the nicest one," I said. "I'm sure it was just kids fooling around."

Her mouth flattened into a thin line. She ran water over a stack of silverware. "Teens today," she said, shaking her head. "They are monsters. Complete monsters."

"Hey, Peggy," I said. "It's a bummer what happened to your pumpkin but it doesn't have anything to do with me." I stepped toward the door. "Anything else? Because if not, Chris and I are heading out."

Laurie's house was the first one we hit. "Hey, Suzanne, you're looking *good*!" she said, putting an M&Ms packet in Chris's bag. "Nice job on the hair."

"Thanks," I replied. "And thanks again for showing me."

There weren't tons of kids in our neighborhood, but most people gave out candy. Chris's haul grew, his bag bulging like an overgrown squash. Neighbors touched my shoulder. "Miss seeing your mom, honey," they said, and all I could do was nod, mumble my thanks, and make a quick exit. Fortunately, Chris's enthusiasm kept me hopping after him.

We'd been out for forty-five minutes when we reached the Eameses' block. Five candlelit pumpkins lined their porch but otherwise it was dark. "Maybe nobody's home," Chris said.

I encouraged him to try. "Those lit-up pumpkins tell me they're giving out candy."

Chris knocked. From a nearby speaker, witchy, prerecorded laughter floated over us, and the door creaked open. Chris was all set to run for it, but I held his arm. "Let's see what happens."

From the shadowed interior, a robed figure emerged, its face obscured by a hood. A green plastic glove with long, hooked fingernails held a bowl toward Chris. "Take one, if you dare," a voice intoned from inside the hood.

Scott or Carey? I couldn't tell.

As Chris reached tentatively into the bowl, a fake spider on fishing line dropped from above. Chris flinched—then, with resolve, he grabbed a Snickers bar. "Thank you," he said, his voice wobbly.

The spider rose on some sort of automated system. The ghoul pushed his hood back. "Take another one. You're brave, kid."

It was Carey. He held out the bowl to me. "You want a piece?"

"Sure." I selected a Reese's, ignoring the spider as it fell onto my hand. "Somehow, this isn't quite as scary the second time around."

His eyes met mine. "Lots of things aren't as scary the second time around."

Chris tugged my sleeve. "Can we go?"

"You dash over to the next house," I told him. "I'll catch up."

"Speaking of dashing," Carey said as Chris sprinted away. "I'm sorry I dashed off the other day." He leaned against the door jamb. "You going to be around Zoe's another time?"

"Like I told you," I said, doing my best cool-girl impression of Laurie, "I'm there most afternoons."

A group of kids came up the walk. Carey pulled the hood over his head. "Great. I'll see you, Suzanne...sometime."

"Right," I said, stepping away. "Sometime."

"Suzanne! Over here!"

Just before I caught up with Chris, Peggy joined me on the sidewalk. She wore a black wool coat with a narrow green scarf coiled around her shoulders. The scarf's color matched her eyes.

"There you are," she said, breathless. "I thought I'd take over with Chris."

"You don't have to do that," I replied. "We're fine."

She frowned. "Following a little boy trick-or-treating seems more bothersome than pleasurable for a teen girl."

"Well, it's not." Taking Chris's hand, I mounted the steps of the next house. "So please, Peggy—get lost."

To her credit, she did.

24

— • —

2004

Knife in hand, I ran inside my house, bolted the front door, and grabbed my car keys from the hall table. As I was turning to go out back toward the garage, I heard a key scrape into the front door lock.

"You're home!" I wrapped both arms around Caitlin before she stepped fully inside.

"Jesus, calm down." Untangling herself, she cocked her head. "What's your problem?"

"Nothing." I re-bolted the door, peering through the glass onto the darkened street. "I'm just glad you're home. Did you have fun?"

"It was okay." She turned to go upstairs.

"Caitlin." Fingers lingering on the deadbolt, I asked, "Are you sure you closed and locked this door the day Stevie ran off? Are you *sure*?"

"This again." She crossed her arms over her chest. "You either believe me or you don't."

I regarded her. In the past few years, we'd caught her in plenty of bald-faced lies. Was this one of them? Or was she being truthful?

"Anything else?" she asked. "Because if not, I'm going to bed."

I sat on the bench in the hallway, motioning for her to sit beside me. "Tell me again about Alli Powles," I said. "Do you hang out with her? Have you..." My voice shook. "Her sister's boyfriend, that man they're looking for...have you ever..." My eyes darted about. "...met him? Talked to him?"

"What? No!" Caitlin shook her head. "Alli doesn't even go to East. I only met her because she was hanging out with some East kids. I barely know her."

I stared into her indigo eyes—so like my own. But Caitlin's combination of eye color, heart-shaped face, luxurious mane of dark hair, and curvy figure made her gorgeous in a way I hadn't been at her age.

My daughter was beautiful. Desirable. Any boy—any *man*—would see that.

I was still gripping my Halloween tanto. I placed it in her palm. "Keep this," I said. "You can't take it to school, obviously..." Unlike in my day, East now had a zero-tolerance policy for weapons of any kind; the rule was clearly stated in the family handbook. "But everywhere else you go, carry this with you, Caitlin. Just in case."

She studied the knife. "Just in case what?"

"Just in case...anything. Anytime you feel unsafe, take it out."

I closed her fingers around the knife's sheath. "Don't let anyone mess with you, Cait."

That night I tossed from side to side—all these years later I was still a side-sleeper—unable to settle myself. Was Robert Shelton Jr. still around? Had he hovered behind me in the park, followed me through the streets? Had he taken my dog, just to mess with me? Was I—or worse, Caitlin—in danger?

Should I consider halting the opening of Zoe's? If Shelton Jr. wasn't already stalking us, maybe he'd begin to once he figured out who I was. Renee and I had been busting our butts getting as much press coverage for Zoe's as we could. At every opportunity, I talked about how the shop was an homage to my mother, Alexandra Parry, one-time owner of Zoe's Records.

The clock radio's ticks pierced the silent darkness. I nestled closer to Brett. Mom would want me to be brave. She'd want me to follow my dreams, not torment myself about who could be messing with me or my family.

Which might be no one. Yes, I'd sensed ghosts in Cheesman, like when I was a kid. But mostly, they were harmless. They had stories. They wanted to be acknowledged.

That's what *most* of them wanted. But whoever grabbed my hand—that spirit wanted more from me.

I shuddered. I wouldn't go to the park again. And if a living person was chasing me, a living person who could threaten Caitlin—well, I'd just have to be cautious and ensure Caitlin was cautious.

Everything would be fine.

I awoke groggy the next day, but there was nothing I could do except chug extra coffee at home and Diet Coke at Zoe's. We were four days away from opening, and Monday was a frenzy. I paid someone from the babysitting service Brett had used on my birthday an exorbitant amount to pick up Austin from school, bring him home, and stay until dinnertime.

That evening, I called the Bates residence—which checked out as the address where Caitlin had slipped in a side gate. Mrs. Bates was cordial on the phone but said there'd been lots of kids at Claudia's party; she hadn't kept track of who was who.

On Tuesday I had to make time to vote, which took longer than I'd anticipated. There was buzz that Colorado, following the lead of several other states, might soon institute a mail-in ballot system. Unfortunately, we weren't there yet.

Stopping in Wild Oats for groceries, I glanced at the community board and saw a flier tacked up by a college student looking for babysitting work. I copied the number, went home, and called. I was thrilled when the girl, Lucy, said she was available the next afternoon.

I stayed up that night watching the election returns. Brett came home early, for him—around nine—and watched with me. Nationwide, John

Kerry and George Bush were in a virtual tie, but Bush was announced as the winner in Colorado. Eventually, Brett and I headed to bed without knowing who the next president would be, but knowing that we lived in a red state now, albeit by a sliver.

"Fifty-one percent of Coloradans for Bush," Brett said. "It's almost like living in Ohio again."

"But things will change here," I predicted. "When I was growing up, there were hardly any transplants. Now it feels like everyone in Colorado is from somewhere else, and that tends to shift things to the left." I slipped into a short cotton nightgown. "I predict that by 2008, when Caitlin votes in her first election, Colorado will be turning blue."

Unbuttoning his shirt, Brett smiled. "Okay, Ms. Fortune Teller."

I smiled back, pleased that Brett and I were actually conversing, sharing more than a quick hello on the way out the door in the morning or a good-night peck deep into the night, when he usually came home from work. In bed, when he suggested that the hour wasn't all *that* late, I wrapped my legs around his, relishing the sensation of his skin against mine. It had been a long time.

Wednesday was a political letdown, as New Mexico, Iowa, and Ohio called it for Bush, and Kerry conceded. I couldn't give it much thought, though. I was frantic at Zoe's—putting the finishing touches on the displays, making sure every piece was logged into our system, and being interviewed by *Westword*, the local weekly that ran a terrific arts section and agreed, at the last minute, to come to Zoe's, take photos, and talk with me about my vision. It was our biggest promo piece and it would pub the day before grand opening.

After school I picked up Austin, rushed him home, and met Lucy there. She seemed like a capable girl, and I'd called her two references, who both gave glowing reviews. Gratefully, I went back to Zoe's.

Several hours later, returning home in the black night and crossing the back yard from the garage, I saw Lucy peering through the lighted kitchen window at me, then glancing at the wall clock.

"Sorry I'm late," I said, coming inside. "Everything okay? Where's Austin?"

"He's playing on the Wii." She put on her coat.

"Can you come tomorrow?" I asked.

Lucy shrugged. "I suppose."

I'd have preferred more enthusiasm, but at least it was a problem solved.

My relief was short-lived. Lucy called on Thursday to say she'd reconsidered because she didn't think she was "a good fit with Austin."

"Why not?" My hands felt cold. "Did something happen?"

"No, I just...look, I'm sorry, Suzanne," she said. "Thanks anyway, for the opportunity."

When I fetched Austin from school, I asked if he'd had a good time with Lucy.

He scrunched up his face. "Who's Lucy?"

"The girl who babysat you yesterday. Remember?"

"Oh, her. I didn't see her much."

I frowned. Something in his tone—combined with what Lucy had said—caused my heart to race. "Are you *sure* nothing happened when Lucy was there?" I asked, unlocking the car. "Did you...was something upsetting you?"

Austin climbed into the back seat. "She didn't want to play on the Wii with me." He pulled the seat belt out of its holder, then let go, watching it zip back. "I was kinda mad about that."

"Buckle your seat belt, please." I started the car. "What did you do when you got mad?" When he didn't reply, I asked again, "Austin? What did you do?"

"Nothing!" he said. "I just got mad. Just mad, mad, mad."

I glanced at him in the rear-view mirror. "Okay."

Austin kicked the back of my seat. "Why can't Dad watch me some-times, like he did when we lived in California? It was more fun there than here."

FFA-865. *Fun for all.*

The grand opening was scheduled for Friday from five until nine p.m. Renee and I set out drinks, snacks, and a celebratory cake. We invited the artists with consigned pieces to stop by and bring their friends. I'd even emailed Aspen Ferraro, the musician who'd spoken so highly of my mother all those years ago, to ask if she'd come play a song. She sent her apologies, saying she had a gig but would mention Zoe's during her show.

After my experience with Lucy, I had no choice for Friday other than to fetch Austin after his movement program, then set him up in Zoe's back room with a portable DVD player. Over breakfast I'd asked Caitlin to meet us at Zoe's, spend some time celebrating, then take Austin home and give him dinner.

Her eyes remained on her Frosted Flakes. "Can't," she said. "I'm busy."

I set my fork on my plate, next to a half-finished omelet. "Caitlin, I expect you to be there. You can stay a while and be supportive. Then you can take Austin home and heat up a frozen pizza."

Caitlin looked up. "This is such *bullshit.* Why do I have to do every-thing?"

Brett glanced away from pouring coffee into his commuter mug. "Cait, that's not fair," he said. "We ask almost nothing of you. Your mother expects your help."

Caitlin rolled her eyes.

"You know," I told her, "When I was your age, Uncle Chris was my responsibility." An awareness came to me. "At the time, it seemed like a burden, but in retrospect, I don't regret it. In fact, I wish..." Dryness baked my throat. "I wish I'd spent *more* time with him. I wish I'd been less resentful. If I had, maybe some things would have turned out...differently."

Caitlin regarded me. "I'm not sure why you're telling me this." She rose from her seat. "Just remember, Mom—you are not me, and I am not you."

"You can say that again," I shot back. But she was already leaving the room.

Brett and I watched her go. "You'll be there, right?" I asked him. "The whole time?"

"I hope to be," he said. "But you know how things are, Suze."

I stared at him. "Fine."

I took my cold coffee to the sink. My back to Brett, I dumped it out and left the room.

We lucked out with an unseasonably warm day. A group of about twenty-five—consigning artists and their friends, the public, Chris, Austin, Donna, Renee, Evan, me, as well as Mr. Frederick the tailor, retired as I suspected but there to show support—basked in the setting sun outside Zoe's. Standing on the sidewalk, Mr. Frederick, Donna, and I remembered the grand opening of Zoe's Records in 1972.

"Your mom was so excited," Donna said. "Your dad, too. He was the one who cut the ribbon, with these big, corny fake scissors he had. Guess they did the same thing at his car dealerships, so they had the thing sitting around."

Mr. Frederick chuckled. I said, "I remember."

Donna lit a cigarette. "Your mom would be excited for you, too, kiddo." Blowing smoke upwards, she added, "But you don't have a ribbon."

"No, but we have art," Renee said—and with that, to a chorus of cheers, I opened the door and let everyone inside.

While talking with customers and artists, ringing up sales, and periodically checking on Austin, I tried keeping my mind on the success of the launch. This is your baby, Suzanne, I told myself. You made it happen. Enjoy it!

But how could I? Caitlin—and Brett—were nowhere to be seen.

My cell rang at five-thirty. "Things got hung up," Brett said. "I was trying to leave but every time I turned around, somebody wanted something."

"I'd like to say it's okay," I replied. "But it's not."

"I didn't make any promises—remember?"

Sipping white wine from a plastic cup, I put on a smile as a customer approached. "Gotta go, Brett."

"We'll be there in twenty minutes," he said.

I hung up. It was only after I finished chatting with the customer, a woman who wanted to know more about the black-and-white photographs of downtown Denver on the west wall, that I began to wonder who "we" might be. The answer came a half hour later. Rushing in through the propped-open door, Brett was preceded by his coworker, Nicole.

I'd met Nicole a few times in the Bay Area at Brett's work functions. What struck me about her then, and caught me again tonight, was the laser focus of her pale blue eyes. They reminded me of cat's-eye marbles. Nicole held herself in the way some not-too-tall women do, where something about them suggests height even though they're shorter than you. Her dark hair was clipped, Audrey Hepburn-ish, and the look went well with her sharp cheekbones and long white neck. She was, as always, complete business in her attire, although Brett had told me their office's dress code was business casual on Fridays.

"I'm sorry," he gasped.

"We both are," Nicole agreed. "But you know how it goes in tech, Suzanne." She chuckled. "At least, you might *remember* how it goes." Glancing around, she added, "Nothing at the office is ever simple, the way it must be in this cute little place." She touched Brett's arm. "I kept trying to pull this guy away, but one thing after another came up."

My face reddened. Two of our artists—Tori Flynn, the woman who painted those gorgeous abstracts, and Daphne Hesse, a local musician whose CDs we carried and whose second album was currently playing on the stereo—were standing next to me. I knew they'd heard every word.

I wasn't going to let it rattle me. This was *my* moment. Nicole could make little digs; she could do all her supposedly marvelous stuff—but she hadn't done *this*. She didn't own this warm, glowing space full of merry, slightly buzzed creatives and patrons of the arts.

So shut the fuck up, Nicole, I thought, and let me enjoy my moment.

"Drinks and snacks are over there," I told them, waving toward the corner. "Help yourself. Browse around." I stared at Brett. "I hope you find something you like." Before he could reply, I turned my back, facing Tori and Daphne.

"Yikes," said Tori—a pretty, thin-framed woman with a halo of blond hair, slightly streaked white. "We heard the whole thing." She looked at Daphne, who nodded. "You okay, Suzanne?" Tori asked.

I managed a smile. "I'm fine." I raised my plastic cup. "This is a night for celebration!"

We clinked cups. When the CD shifted to the next song on Daphne's album—a funky, soulful tune called "Give Me Your All"—Daphne provided a quick tutorial on the chorus. Before long, Brett and Nicole rejoined us, and we all laughed and sang along.

By six-thirty Austin had hit his limit. He kept coming out from the back room, asking me to change the DVD. I had a whole box for him to choose from but he'd watch only a few minutes of something before requesting something else. He said he was hungry, and he was happy to devour a piece of cake but didn't want the protein-rich, kid-friendly snacks I'd brought specifically for him.

"Where the hell is Caitlin?" I hissed to Brett.

"I'll take him home," Brett said.

"You just got here."

"Suzanne, what else can we do?" He set down his wine.

"Brett, Suzanne," Nicole broke in. "It's unfortunate that your daughter is a no-show, but I have an idea. How about I run Austin to your house and give him dinner for you?"

I regarded her. "That's a kind offer. But we couldn't ask that of you. And I'm sure you have other plans."

"I don't, actually." She clapped her hands together three times—clap, clap, clap.

The sharpness of those claps impaled my eardrums. My hand on my collarbone, I looked down, searching my lilac-colored blouse for blood-red anemones.

"I'm free as a bird tonight!" Nicole went on brightly. "And I'd love to spend time with your sweet boy, Suzanne."

As if on cue, Austin came out for the millionth time. "This is *boring*," he whined. "You promised pizza, Mommy. When can we go home?"

Brett squatted to our son's level. "Austin, this is my friend Nicole. She's going to take you home and heat up the pizza for you."

Confused, Austin looked at me.

"Hey, Austin," Nicole said, bending down next to Brett. "I hear you have a Wii. Do you have *Super Mario*?"

"Sure," Austin said. "It's my favorite."

"Mine, too. What do you say we heat up that pizza and see who's the Mario champ?"

He laughed. "That's easy. It's me, me, me!"

"Oh, yeah? We'll see, hotshot." She reached for his hand.

Again, he looked my way. So did Brett. So did Nicole.

I glanced around my shop. The glowing lights. The music. The artwork on the walls and shelves. The laughter, the chime of the cash register as Renee rang up a purchase. The support of my husband, standing beside me as my fledgling business pecked its way out of its shell.

How much my mother would love this, I thought. If she were here, Alex Parry would soak up every second of this evening.

I looked at Austin. And at Nicole.

Then I nodded.

25

1979

November started out the way October had ended: cold. The temperature didn't rise above forty degrees, and it was windy. At East, you could feel the dreariness. Nobody wanted to be there.

After school I walked to my phone booth. I dropped a dime in the slot and dialed Rosalie's number.

"It's Laurie," I said—shouted, because the baby was crying. "Remember me?"

"I remember. Hang on a sec." A door opened, then closed. The baby's cries were muffled. "Didn't think I'd hear from you again."

"I wanted to make sure you're okay."

"We're okay," Rosalie said. "Rent's due but I have a week before it's late. Phone will probably get cut off soon, though."

"I'm working on getting you that money." A flat-out lie, but she didn't know that.

"I'll believe it when I see it—but thanks."

I slid my backpack off my shoulder, taking out a notebook and pen. "Maybe now you can give me your address. In case the phone gets cut off, so we can stay in touch."

She paused. "It goes against my instincts to give my address to a total stranger. But I guess I don't have much choice. And besides..." She took a breath. "I can't put my finger on why, but I'm beginning to trust you, Laurie."

Well after midnight, gunshots woke me. I waited, breathless. They didn't sound *that* close. Not on our block. Soon, I heard a siren's wail. In my mind's eye, I saw the victim splayed in the middle of Colfax Avenue, blood pooling beneath his body.

I pulled the covers over my head. I *hated* guns.

At dinner the next evening, Peggy brought it up. "Just *two* blocks from here. One man dead." She shook her head. "This is *not* a safe neighborhood, Jimmy."

"Well, who's to say?" he replied. A non-answer if there ever was one.

"We're *all* to say. And you know it." Peggy put her hands together as if in prayer. "A different type of house, in a safe neighborhood, is a wonderful idea. A ranch with a big yard. Perfect for the whole family." Her eyes soft, she added, "For everyone."

Dad set down his fork. "Peggy. We've discussed this."

My eyes narrowed. No way we'd leave this house. It was our mother's home—Chris's and mine. Mom had loved this old whorehouse, with its history, its quirkiness—and its spirits, which Mom hadn't sensed like I did, but she believed me when I told her they were here. Now she was one of them. What would happen to Mom-not-Mom and our other ghosts if we left?

"Well, it doesn't need to be decided right now," Peggy said. "It's just a thought."

"Let's shift subjects." Dad tapped his water glass, smiling at Peggy. "Let's annunciate our announcement. You want to tell them?"

"Sure." She lined up utensils along her plate's rim. "We've set a date for the wedding. March twenty-second." Clap, clap, clap. "Just over four months! Time will fly."

The *twenty-second*. Was she serious? Was my dad? It was March, not February—but still.

Clenching my jaw, I asked Dad, "You sure about that date? The twenty-second?"

He chuckled. "Peggy was campaigning for the fifteenth, but since that's the Ides of March, it seemed a rather deleterious date."

Jesus Christ. My dad's bizarre speech patterns, all the odd stuff he knew, sometimes made me smile. But at times like this, he enraged me. Did the date truly mean *nothing* to him?

"We could look at the eighth," Peggy mused. "The sooner the better, in my view."

Chris wiggled in his seat. "If I have to be in the wedding, can I wear my wizard costume?"

I felt a sharp, stabbing pain in my lower back, and I arched forward, twisting my napkin into a tight ball.

Peggy smiled at Chris. "That might not be appropriate, sweetie, but I'll come up with an outfit you like." She sipped water. "We'll figure out roles for each of you. This is a family celebration."

I stood, throwing my napkin onto my plate. As I began to leave the room, Dad called me back. "Suzanne..."

I turned and stared him down.

"You forgot to clear your place," he said.

I grabbed my plate, silverware, and cup. Taking them to the kitchen, I scraped the unfinished meal Peggy had cooked into the disposal. I ran it, appreciating the din of the grinder destroying meatloaf, potatoes, peas. Nearby, I sensed the kitchen ghosts, felt their apprehension.

On Friday, I headed to Zoe's Records. From a block away I saw Carey, hands in pockets, leaning against the brick wall next to Mr. Frederick's storefront. "Hiya," he said, waving.

"Hi." Pulling the key on its leather cord from around my neck, I unlocked the door.

Inside, I inserted a Blondie tape into the boombox. It started with the sound of a phone ringing as the band broke into "Hanging on the Telephone."

I gestured toward the floor by Zoe's feet. "Have a seat."

Carey and I sat side by side. "I saw Blondie at the Rainbow Music Hall a few months ago," Carey said. "You ever been?"

I shook my head.

"It's kind of a new place, opened about a year ago," he said.

"Yeah. I know."

"They have great acts come through," he went on. "I saw the Boomtown Rats there, first time they ever played 'I Don't Like Mondays' anywhere. Then it became this huge hit in England over the summer. You've heard that song, right?" When I shook my head again, he said, "It's about a school shooting."

"Shootings abound," I replied softly.

He winced. "Sorry. It was rude of me, saying that."

I didn't reply. After a moment, Carey said, "Can I ask you a question, Suzanne?"

"Sure."

"Why are you alone most of the time? Why do you hang out here all by yourself?" He shook his head. "I just don't understand it."

I crisscrossed my legs in the other direction. "I've been coming here for lots of years. It's as much my home as my actual home, you know?"

But he *couldn't* know. Nobody could know except Chris—and he was too little to have the attachment to Zoe's Records that I did.

"When we first moved to Denver, last year," Carey said, "I used to go to Grand Junction nearly every weekend. I'd stay with friends, hang out with the same guys I'd known forever. I started thinking I should move back, because I didn't seem able to make a clean break."

"So what happened?"

He hesitated. "Weather, more than anything. I had my motorcycle, and you can't ride a bike across Colorado in the winter. So I stopped going. I forced myself to make a life here."

"And what exactly *is* your life?" I asked—challenging him the way he'd challenged me. "You work nights, alone. You visit me. You help with your sister. Do you have friends? Do you have..." I fumbled for words, then burst out, "Do you have a girlfriend?"

Carey looked away. "In Grand Junction, I did. But we broke up. Here..."

He trailed off. Blondie began singing "One Way or Another."

Carey stood, stepping toward the checkout counter. My gaze tracked him, and I sensed Zoe's plastic eyes doing the same. "Here," he said, "I didn't date anybody."

"Bummer. Sorry to hear that." I rested my chin on my knees. "I guess it takes a while to find the right one, huh?"

"Sometimes, yes." He sat down again, this time close beside me, our hips touching. My skin, partitioned from Carey's only by the denim of his jeans and mine, felt aflame. I inched toward the heat.

"Suzanne," he said. "I know I'm not supposed to feel this way."

"What way?"

"The way I feel...about you."

I lifted my chin, tilting my head at him.

"You're fifteen, Suzanne. You're too young for me. And yet..."

"And yet...what?" I asked.

Carey put his hands around the back of my head, pulling me close. "Your hair feels soft," he said. "Much better without all that hair spray in it."

Then he kissed me. The kiss was deeper and more satisfying than any I'd ever known. My prior kissing experience consisted of pecks from boys in the neighborhood when I was a kid and Spin the Bottle at middle school parties. This kiss made me feel warm and weightless, as if gravity had vacated the space around me.

"Your lips," he whispered, when we broke apart, "are soft, like your hair."

"My lips are all yours, Carey," I said—not caring that it sounded like a line from some corny romantic movie. "Yours for the taking."

26

2004

As soon as the last guest left Zoe's grand opening, I locked up, then rushed home. Waiting at a red light on Colfax, fingers drumming the steering wheel, I let my mind race to images of—what? An empty house? Nicole running off with my son?

Get a grip, I told myself. I glanced in the rearview mirror, reassured to see Brett's car behind mine.

At home, Nicole was seated on the couch, reading *5280* magazine. "Everything go okay?" Brett asked.

"Perfectly. No hitches. He's sleeping." Nicole stood, reaching for her bag. "Your daughter is here, too—she's up in her room. But I thought it best to wait for you before heading out."

"You're a lifesaver," Brett said. "We can't thank you enough, Nic."

I didn't have time for niceties. I nodded at her, then scurried upstairs. I had to see for myself that my children were here—and safe.

"You put me in a terrible position, accepting Nicole's offer," I told Brett the next morning. "I'd have felt like a total asshole if I'd said no."

He held up his hands. "What are you talking about? It was a win-win. You and I got to enjoy your opening. Austin and Nicole had a great time. She's more than capable, and her offer was generous."

"It would've been better if I'd used the babysitter service," I replied.

"It worked out." He sipped coffee. "I don't know why you're worried about it."

Later, collecting the mail, I opened a blue airmail envelope that was addressed only to me.

Suzanne,

Chris tells me you're establishing a new Zoe's. I understand there will be various versions of artwork for sale. As your father, I must express my unease.

For years, you generated only a modest income, but this was an acceptable alternative because it permitted you to be present for your family. Now you're opening a business that likely will take years to turn a profit, if it ever does, and will amputate your attention from your primary position: caring for your children. This concerns me, Suzanne. Do you realize what a behemoth burden your choices place on Brett?

Additionally, I'm skeptical about your safety. None of us will ever forget what happened at the original Zoe's.

Perhaps it's too late for my opinion. I don't know when the new Zoe's opens. But if it hasn't yet happened, I recommend you reconsider.

I look forward to seeing you in a few weeks.

Love,

Dad

Sinking onto the hallway bench, I read it again. "Who the hell do you think you are?" I said aloud, crumpling the thin page. He wasn't even here, but he thought he could waltz in via airmail and burst my bubble?

I heard Brett in the kitchen, putting dishes into the dishwasher. Was my father right? Did I make things harder on Brett than they needed to be? If so, was that why he found Nicole so easy to be around?

Logically, my anger should be directed at Caitlin. When I confronted her, she had no explanation for her lack of attendance at the Zoe's opening—only that she "forgot."

"I can't see how that's possible," I said. "You knew this was important to me, Cait."

"Look, I'm sorry, okay?" she replied. "This girl...her name is Samantha...she asked me to hang out at her house and I told her yes without remembering about your opening." Her voice low, she said, "I really am sorry, Mom."

I couldn't recall the last time she'd sounded this sincere. I decided to take her word for it.

On Day Two of the new Zoe's, we again enjoyed nearly record high temps. I opened the shop door, letting in sunshine and mild breezes. Business was brisk, particularly in smaller pieces and jewelry, and I closed out the day with a full till, content as a well-fed house cat.

After turning the sign in the window to "Closed," I walked around the store—admiring everything, resetting pieces that customers had moved, and listening to local blues favorite Hazel Miller on the stereo. My thoughts were on Mom, how ecstatic she'd be about what I'd accomplished.

I tried not to let my father's opinion creep into my mind.

On Colfax, I heard an ambulance's wail. I stepped to the window as the ambulance halted across the street and the siren was muted. I watched as paramedics unloaded a stretcher and rushed inside a nearby apartment building. The ambulance's flashing lights reflected red on Zoe's pale walls. My eyes darted, following their luminous pattern.

My father was being ridiculous. He was just another paranoid old guy.

I felt my spine stiffen and my jaw muscles tighten. Breathe, Suzanne, I told myself. Just breathe.

That night I walked over to Donna's. She was at Evan and Renee's house, babysitting her grandson, Jasper, while they went out. Once Jasper was in bed, I told her about my dad's letter.

"Oh, James," she said, shaking her head. "What were you *thinking*?"

"Exactly. What *was* he thinking?" Seated on the family room floor, I picked up a green Duplo block, fitting it into a red one. "You said he was supportive when Mom opened Zoe's Records. Why isn't he supportive of me?"

Donna went to the kitchen and poured two glasses of Bordeaux. "I guess...because of how things turned out." Setting a wineglass on the coffee table beside me, she added, "And because of Chris, of course."

I sipped wine. "What do you mean, because of Chris?"

"It was stressful, that's all. You can't remember, I'm sure." She sat beside me on the floor. "Alex got pregnant with Chris only a few months after opening Zoe's Records. James wanted her to close the shop. Focus on their son—James was certain the baby was a boy. 'A son needs a full-time mother,' he'd tell Alex. 'Not one who's only occasionally present.'"

I thought of Claranna Lewis. Had she been "only occasionally present"?

Donna joined me, fiddling with the Duplos. Before long, a multi-angled house began to take shape. Three-year-old Jasper was just beginning to get the hang of making basic rectangular structures with the oversized Lego blocks. Before he went to bed we'd played with him, but things were simplistic in Jasper's world. It sounds stupid, but Donna and I were enjoying creating something more elaborate.

"So Dad wasn't happy that Mom kept running Zoe's?" I asked.

"That's an understatement. She made it work—remember that sling she used to carry Chris around in? She looked like a peasant who'd wandered into a record store. But Chris adored it, and it allowed Alex to work in relative peace."

I began fashioning a turret on the Duplo house, like the one on my childhood home. "But were they angry with each other? Was Dad resentful? I don't remember them fighting about it."

"Maybe not in front of you. But it was a contentious issue," Donna said. "It was one of the factors leading to their separation. Alex tried for years to make it work, but James never made it easy on her. He didn't lift a finger around your house. It was all on her, almost as if he was punishing her for running Zoe's. For wanting to do something besides raise their son."

I furrowed my brow. What Donna said—that Dad thought Mom should have focused on domesticity—had shades of what he'd pressed upon me in his airmail letter.

Before the Alzheimer's, Grandma Parry had been the most domestic person I knew. Her house was meticulously clean. She organized family gatherings, determining the menu and doing much of the cooking. She doted on her family, especially Dad. Even when he was an adult, they'd talked daily.

Her priorities were not all that different, I realized, from Peggy's.

What about Claranna? What had *she* been like as a wife and mother?

"So he fronted Mom the money to open the store," I said. "Then he got resentful about it, but only because of Chris?"

"Yep." Donna drained her wineglass and went to the kitchen, bringing back the bottle. "When it was just you, he was fine with it. You were older, you were in school. And you're a girl. I guess he figured she'd manage. But when they found out Chris was on the way..."

"It's not like Dad had nothing to do with *that*."

"Oh, James *wanted* Chris. He'd always wanted more children, but she was happy with only you." Donna refilled our glasses. "Jesus, I need a cig, but I'm not allowed to smoke in here." She stuck two Duplos together, adding them to our second story. "Don't get me wrong—Alex adored Chris." Donna's look was faraway. "It's a tragedy that Chris doesn't re-member that."

"It is," I agreed. Then, lower, "I guess most people don't remember things that happened when they were that little." I paused. "Did you ever hear my dad talk about his adoption? Or did Mom ever tell you anything he said about it?"

Donna tilted her head. "What makes you ask?"

Not meeting her eye, I began putting a roof on the turret. "I just wonder if there's more to it than he's ever said."

"Suze." Donna put a hand on mine. "What's going on?"

Feeling her touch, her trust, I took a breath. Then I spilled the whole story.

"Wow." Donna hugged her knees. "What are you going to do?"

I shrugged. "Dad's out of the country for a few more weeks, so I can't ask him. And I'm not sure I want to." I blinked. "I don't know if he'd be honest with me."

Donna's look was thoughtful. "I want to tell you something," she said. "At Alex's funeral, James said something to me that I've never forgotten." She took a breath. "He said he'd do anything in the world to provide a new mother for Chris." She shook her head. "I've never understood that comment. It seemed so insensitive, at his wife's funeral—even for Mr. No Filter. But now, it makes sense."

"And he did exactly that." My voice was raw. "He brought in Peggy."

Donna shuddered. "Ugh, Peggy." She found a window piece and fitted it onto our house. "Did I ever tell you what Alex told me about meeting Peggy, at James's reunion? Or maybe Alex told you at some point...?"

"She didn't."

"James introduced them," Donna said. "Peggy jabbered on about the missionary work she'd been doing, yadda, yadda, yadda. But when James showed Peggy a picture of Chris, your mom said Peggy did this thing..." Donna's tone became more deliberate. "Alex told me that Peggy stroked Chris's cheek in his picture. Your mom told me she couldn't take her eyes off Peggy's index finger stroking that picture. Peggy called Chris, if I'm remembering this right, 'a beautiful, wonderful little boy.' Your mom said she wanted to slap Peggy's hand away from the photo, but she held herself steady."

I emptied my wineglass in one gulp. "That's *so* creepy."

She stood, reaching for my hand. "Come outside with me while I have a smoke."

I looked at my Duplo turret. The top of it was wavering and I bent forward—grabbing the pieces, trying to hold everything in place.

On my way home, the streets were silent. Clouds had rolled in, and the evening felt cold and raw. I turned onto Ninth, then York, passing the Botanic Gardens. Several streetlights were out and the sidewalk was dark. Aching for Stevie, I paused and closed my eyes, trying to feel her. Was she alive? I couldn't get a sense of it, but I had to believe she was. But was she in pain? Was she being harmed, abused? The thought rattled me like a blast of arctic air through leafless trees.

Halting at a crosswalk, checking for traffic, I heard someone behind me. I turned but didn't see anyone. Taking an abrupt right, I hastened my steps. When I stopped, I heard the footsteps again.

I whipped my head around. Patting my pocket, assuring myself of my knife's presence, I turned and planted my feet wide.

"Are you Robert Shelton Junior?" I yelled.

The footsteps went silent.

"Do you have my dog?"

No answer. I slipped my hand into my pocket, clenching my knife. "Stop following me, or you'll regret it." Pulling out and unsheathing the knife, I added, "If you don't believe me, just try me, asshole!"

Gripping the knife handle, blade gleaming in the dim light, I felt a wave of nausea overtake me. I about-faced and began running. I didn't stop until I was inside my house.

Hearing *Saturday Night Live* from the family room, I considered going down. I could curl up with Brett on the sectional. Tell him about my fears. He'd hold me and beg me not to walk around alone at night. He'd tell me that he couldn't bear anything happening to me. I'd put my head on his shoulder. We'd get lost in the humor of Seth Meyers, Tina Fey, and the rest.

Then I remembered the way Nicole's cold eyes warmed when they met my husband's. Suddenly Brett was the last person I wanted to be with.

Upstairs, I got ready for bed and climbed under the covers. I resolved that tomorrow I'd go to the police—questions I didn't want to answer be damned.

I needed to tell the cops I was afraid for myself and my family. I needed to ask for protection.

27

— • —

1979

I floated home that Friday afternoon, ignoring everything around me, including Peggy's insistence that our neighborhood was dangerous, and even the vision of the dead man lying on Colfax. All I could think about were Carey's arms around me, his kisses on my lips, my cheeks, my neck.

Inside the house, Chris and Jeff were playing on the Atari and Peggy was scurrying around, getting dinner on the table. I wasn't sure I'd ever get used to having a full-time cook.

You see, Mom-not-Mom said. *She doesn't belong here, Suzie Blue.*

My mother was right. I couldn't let myself get sidetracked by Carey. Acquiring proof of the connection between Peggy and Bobby was my best possibility for breaking up Dad and his fiancée. To do that, I had to meet Rosalie in person, bringing her the money I'd promised. I had to see if Rosalie could help me uncover the connection.

On my way to the kitchen, I noticed Peggy's purse on the hall table, its zipper open. Something gleamed, and I peered inside. Peggy's small handgun was tucked beside her wallet.

Jesus Christ. My brother and his friend, two six-year-olds, were a few feet away. What was she *thinking*?

I picked up the purse and knocked on the half-open door of Dad's study. "Can I show you something?"

He looked up. "What's going on?"

When I revealed the gun, he shook his head. "I'd prefer Peggy wasn't so paranoid. And you're right that a gun has no place in our home." His eyes took on an unexpected, blazing darkness. "There's no reason for potential peril in a home with children. I'll speak with Peggy immediately." Locking the gun in a desk drawer, he said, "Thank you for telling me, Suzanne."

How gratifying to be heard, for once. "You're welcome," I replied.

On Saturday morning I headed out, bank book in hand. Walking along Colfax, I opened the book and studied the tiny balance. Where did my money go? As always, I'd pissed it away—on fast food, clothes, trinkets.

According to my bank book, I had under forty dollars to my name. There *had* to be more. Perhaps I'd deposited some birthday check or other windfall that I no longer remembered.

No such luck. "You have thirty-nine dollars and seventy-eight cents in here," the teller said.

I winced. "I'll take thirty in cash."

"You need to maintain ten dollars to keep the account open."

"Fine." I dug in my pocket, coming up with some change. "This gets me over forty. Deposit this, then give me back thirty."

I was way short on what Rosalie needed. Would she even talk to me if I didn't bring her the full amount?

You do what you have to, Suzie Blue, Mom-not-Mom said.

At home, no one saw me slip into Dad's study. He was working, and Peggy had come over in the morning to take Chris to the library. I dug into Dad's stash, extracting seventy-five bucks. Before leaving the room, I checked the drawer where Dad had stowed Peggy's gun. It was unlocked and the gun wasn't there. Good. Dad must have told her to take it back to her place and keep it there.

I now had over a hundred dollars. It was the best I could do. Shoving the cash in my pocket, I headed out again, toward the bus stop.

Rosalie lived a few miles west and a short walk north. The garish, orange-carpeted hallways of her building reeked of smoke, cheap perfume, and wet dog. The three-story building had no elevator and no security; I simply walked in and headed upstairs.

I knocked on the door marked 3-C. No one answered.

A young guy, maybe in his twenties, stepped out of 3-B. "You looking for Rosalie?"

"Yeah. I'm...a friend."

"She's usually around but I haven't seen her. I don't think she got kicked out, though."

I sidled closer. "You know her well?"

"I knew Bobby pretty good. Her boyfriend, you know?"

I nodded.

"It's lousy, what happened to him." He sniffled, his expression grim. "Damn fucking pigs. Shoot first, ask questions later."

I wanted to remind him that Bobby had shot an officer before his partner returned fire, that the idiot died because he ran into the street—and that he'd just *murdered* someone, for chrissake. But that wouldn't get me anywhere. Instead, I said, "You were friends?"

"We hung out. Bobby liked to party hard."

It occurred to me that I was likely chatting with a junkie. I gave him a careful look, trying to get a sense of him and decipher signs of addiction—bleary eyes, the shakes, stringy hair like the kids in that movie *Go Ask Alice*. But he looked normal. Medium height, medium build. Bouncing up and down on his toes. His dark, feathered hair and chiseled face made him look like Erik Estrada, the actor who plays Ponch on *CHiPs*. Inwardly, I smiled at the notion that a guy who looked like a TV cop hated cops.

He wiped his nose with the back of his hand. "Bobby was into some bad shit. You don't have to do that crap to party. There's other stuff you can do. You like to party, sweetheart?"

Ignoring his question, I asked, "If you were to party like Bobby did, where would you get the money for it?" I swallowed. "I mean, the question is, did Bobby have a job?"

"He had lots of jobs. So did Rosalie, 'til she got big as a house and had a kid." He laughed. "Holding down jobs wasn't their thing. Me, I got this sweet gig. I work for the sanitation department. Sounds like it sucks, right? But they sure as shit don't fire your ass, long as you show up and get the job done. I offered to try getting Bobby on, but he said he didn't want to deal with other people's shit. But you deal with other people's shit one way or another, you know?"

Jesus, this guy could babble. I nodded. "Sure. But listen. Did Bobby ever mention a lady named Peggy? Peggy Hicks?"

The dude whistled. "Peggy Hicks. That's a name I haven't heard in a long time."

"You know her?" I asked. "How?"

"Peggy was..." He bounced up and down.

"Was what?"

He cocked his head. "Listen, I don't even know who you are. How old are you?"

"I'm twenty," I said. "I just look younger."

"If you're twenty then I'm Santa Claus. You look the same age as my kid sister." His voice softened. "Listen, sis, I don't know who you are or why you're asking these questions. But get lost, okay? You got no business here." He turned toward the staircase. Hand on the newel post, he glanced at me. "Take my advice. Don't come around here anymore."

After Erik Estrada left, I hung around another twenty minutes but Rosalie failed to show. I left her a note.

> Rosalie, it's Laurie. I have your rent money. I didn't want to leave it with no one here. But I'll come back tomorrow. Here's ten dollars if you need cash tonight.

After shoving the note and ten bucks under her door, I headed out.

Riding the bus home, I thought about everything Erik Estrada had said. He knew who Peggy was. That provided further ammunition, along with what I'd found at Peggy's place, that there was a connection.

"Mom?" I kept my voice low. "Can you explain this?"

The bus lurched along Colfax—past the State Capitol with its gleaming rotunda, past the neon signs of bars, restaurants, and strip clubs. Beside dirty sidewalks, staggering drunks, and parked cars. I waited to hear my mother's voice inside my head.

Finally, she said, *Suze, I wish I could. But you have to figure it out.*

After a moment, she added, *Use your instincts, Suzie Blue. Rely on your intuition.*

The next afternoon, I headed back to Rosalie's. She opened the door to my knock. She was holding the baby, who began to wail.

"Who're you?" she asked.

"I'm Laurie. I brought your rent money." I held out an envelope. "As much as I could get, anyway."

Swaying the baby, Rosalie glanced at the envelope. "You didn't tell me you were a little kid," she said, accepting it from my grasp.

It was an ironic statement, because Rosalie didn't look much older than me. I pegged her for eighteen, at most. She had a narrow brow and thick hair pulled into a ponytail. Her sweatshirt was frayed at the collar and she wore no makeup.

"I'm seventeen," I said.

She stared at me, unblinking. Then she opened the door, gesturing for me to come in.

We entered a studio apartment with a kitchenette in one corner and a closet-sized bathroom beside it. A TV sat on a card table beside a metal folding chair. The only other furniture was a double bed and a bassinet. The place smelled of dirty diapers and sour milk.

"Have a seat." Gesturing toward the chair, Rosalie plunked herself onto the bed. She picked up a bottle, sticking it in the baby's mouth.

On the TV was a news clip of an American flag burning outside the U.S. embassy in Tehran. It was Veteran's Day, and we were a week into the hostage crisis. I kept thinking it would be over any day now. How long could a bunch of students hold an entire compound's worth of adults hostage? It seemed absurd, like something from a movie.

I nodded toward the baby. "What's his name?"

Rosalie looked at me as if the question were ridiculous. "Robert Shelton Junior. I call him RJ so he won't get confused with his dad."

Lovely. "You decide what to do?" I asked. "You going back to Texas?"

She fingered the envelope I'd given her. "I wasn't sure how I would, but honestly...I could run out on the rent. I could use this money to take a bus tonight. Is that okay? I'll pay you back, I promise."

Right. Sure she would. Nonetheless, going home seemed like the best thing for her and Robert Shelton Jr. "You have family to go back to?" I asked.

"My parents aren't speaking to me. My aunt might take me in." She blinked.

"Tell me about Bobby," I said. "At camp he was...such a nice kid."

Her eyes lit up. "Yeah? Tell me about it."

Anything to get *her* to talk. "He was good to me and the younger kids. He'd help with our gear. Tie the laces on our shoes. He'd double-knot them so they wouldn't come loose when we went hiking."

She smiled. Warming up, I went on. "He liked arts and crafts. We made God's Eyes, and Bobby's were so pretty, every color of the rainbow. You ever make a God's Eye?"

Rosalie shook her head.

"You use Popsicle sticks and yarn. You make a cross with the sticks and glue them together. When it dries, you wind yarn around it in a pattern. You can hang it on your Christmas tree or in your window."

It was easy to come up with this stuff. Laurie once gave me a God's Eye that she made at camp. It still hung in my bedroom window.

"I guess he stayed like that, huh?" I asked Rosalie. "Always a good guy?" I tried not to choke on my words.

The baby finished his bottle and she burped him, then placed him in the bassinet, popping a pacifier into his mouth. "He was okay. Not super smart. At least, not book smart, you know? Not saying I am, either, but Bobby really struggled. He could barely read."

"What did he do for work?" I asked.

"Odd jobs."

"Like, for who?"

The baby started to cry. Rosalie picked him up and began pacing, lugging him in front of her. "This is the only thing he likes," she told me. "I swear, I'm going to walk off the baby weight going back and forth."

I thought about the sling Mom had carried Chris in when he was a baby. I had no idea where it was or if we even had it anymore. If I'd known, I'd have looked for it and brought it to Rosalie.

"Remember when I asked you if Bobby knew a woman named Peggy Hicks?" I asked. "I wondered if you thought about it more. Peggy was so..." I gritted my teeth. "So nice to us scholarship kids. I wanted to...you know, thank her. If I could find her."

Rosalie hesitated. "You say she donated to the scholarship thing? Are you sure?"

"That's my understanding." I sat up straighter. "I could have it wrong, though."

"Well, it's possible." She stopped pacing. "Listen, Laurie, I don't like to talk bad about anybody, but if you won't stop pestering me, I'll tell you."

My heart pounded. "Tell me what?"

"Peggy used to come around to see Bobby and Milo." She jutted her chin toward the wall. "He lives next door."

"Is he the guy who looks like Ponch, the cop on *CHiPs*? I think I met him in the hallway yesterday."

"Yeah, that's him. Bobby and Milo were friends. Peggy used to meet with them at Milo's place. I saw her a couple times in the hall."

My voice tight, I asked, "What did she meet them for?"

"She was working with them on school stuff," Rosalie said.

It wasn't the answer I'd expected. "School stuff?"

"Yeah. She volunteered in some tutoring program. It was Milo who first talked about getting his GED, and someone told him about this program. Peggy started tutoring Milo, and he introduced Bobby to her. Bobby asked if she'd help him, too. Bobby even asked me if I wanted lessons from her. I said no, though." Her eyes darted around the room.

"Why'd you say no?" I asked.

She hesitated. "Peggy sorta creeped me out. I mean, maybe you're right and she was nice to kids. But I didn't like her much, and I got the feeling she felt the same about me." Rosalie pressed her lips together. "Bobby liked her, though. They got along real good."

"When did you see her last?" I asked.

RJ fussed, and Rosalie resumed walking. "I haven't seen her since Bobby died."

I stood. "Will you go next door with me? I want to talk to Milo again."

"Fat chance of that." Hefting the baby onto her shoulder, she said, "Paramedics were here last night. They took him away."

"Oh, wow." I sank back into the chair.

"Yeah. It was pretty dramatic. A bunch of people in the hallway and in Milo's place. Lots of shouting." She attempted, once again, to lay the baby in the bassinet. "Woke me up in the middle of the damn night, and RJ, too, just when I'd gotten him to sleep. When I stuck my head out the door, they were taking Milo away on a stretcher."

"Do you know what happened?"

RJ wailed. Rosalie picked him up, cradling his head. "My guess is he OD'd. That guy snorts coke like it's sugar."

"Damn." I hunched over, chin cupped in my hands.

Rosalie tilted her head, quite possibly displaying a shred of curiosity for the first time in her life. "Why are you so interested, Laurie? And did you make up that story about Peggy donating money so you and Bobby could go to camp?"

"Of course not. I want to surprise her, that's all."

"Well, I guess it doesn't matter to me. I'll be on a bus to Dallas tonight."

"Good luck to you." Getting up, I held out my hand. Awkwardly—droopy baby curled against her neck—she shook it.

"Good luck to you, too. Finding Peggy, I mean."

"You think Milo will be okay?" I asked. "Do you think he'll be home anytime soon?"

"No idea." Hugging RJ close, she whispered, "I'm *never* letting this kid do drugs."

It had started snowing. On the bus, I stared out the window at the whirling snowflakes. Rosalie had provided a lot of information, but now I was back to square one. I had no idea what to do next.

As we neared my stop, I glanced across Colfax. Standing at the westbound bus stop, stomping snow off his boots, was Carey.

I got off the bus and crossed the street, walking up to him. "Hi."

"Hey!" His smile was wide, much to my relief. I'd been unsure how he'd react after our kissing episode on Friday—but I sure as hell wasn't going to shrink from the opportunity to find out.

"Where're you going?" I asked.

"Work. I have an early shift today. Starts at four." He glanced at his watch. "What about you? Where were you coming from?"

I squinted into the snow, looking west toward the State Capitol. "Nowhere. Just killing time."

Carey touched snowflakes in my hair. "You free tomorrow?"

Definitely. *So* free. "I'm free all day tomorrow," I said. "There's no school, for Veteran's Day."

The light changed and the westbound bus pulled up. "You want to meet at Zoe's?" Carey asked. "I've got to work another early shift but maybe before then...say, around noon?"

"Yes." Oh, yes, yes, *yes*.

"Cool." He stroked my hair, downward toward my ear. Right there on the Colfax sidewalk, he wrapped his arms around me, drawing me in for a kiss.

Then he released me and stepped toward the bus. "See you tomorrow, Suzanne."

28

2004

"Thank you for coming in, Ms. Archer," said the officer at the DPD District 6 precinct. She finished entering data on her computer, then met my eye. "I'll pass this to the detective on the Powles case."

When I'd explained everything and ensured the cops knew about the 1979 connection between the Powles and Shelton families—and how my family was connected, too—I'd been told that yes, they were aware of that and were taking it into consideration as the hunt for Shelton Jr. and Darcy continued.

"And you'll put extra watches on my street and near my business?" I swallowed, my throat dry. "And near East High? I'm concerned for my daughter's safety."

"Well, there's strength in numbers. Make sure your daughter is with other kids as much as possible." The officer shrugged. "I'll put in the request for extra patrols, but we can't be everywhere at once, ma'am."

She stood, leaning over the desk to shake my hand. "We really believe Shelton isn't in Colorado anymore. There are promising leads in Texas." Her hand firm in mine, she asked, "But if it would make you feel safer—have you considered getting another dog?"

During the next few weeks, I fell into a Zoe's routine. In the morning I dropped off Austin at school and went directly to Zoe's, opening at nine. In the afternoons I either locked up briefly or Renee came to relieve me so I could pick up Austin. Sometimes I brought him back with me, setting him up in back with snacks and the DVD player. Or I went home while Renee stayed for the afternoon. Zoe's was closed on Mondays, and Renee frequently spelled me either one weekend day or the other.

I didn't respond to my father's letter. He was in Tokyo now, moving east across the globe, working his way back to Denver. Dad had email but used it infrequently. Chris reported that he and our father talked on the phone every few days. "Mostly about business," Chris said. "But he asks about you, Suzanne."

"Yippee for him," I replied. "Does he want a medal?"

Over our phone connection, I heard Chris sigh. "Suze, give him a chance. I agree he's not the most diplomatic communicator ever. But his heart's in the right place."

Was it? That letter demonstrated zero faith in me. And wasn't that the very definition of *heart*...having faith in other people?

Most annoyingly, my dad could be right about the new Zoe's. After a fruitful launch weekend, business began to slump. We had customers, but we didn't experience the breakout success I'd hoped for. I knew I'd recreated the warm, friendly vibe my mother had at Zoe's Records, the vibe that drew women, especially, to her store. But I was up against competition she hadn't faced. Many artists were taking their wares online, setting up websites with gorgeous photography, selling via mail order. And why shouldn't they? There was little overhead in operating that way.

"We'll see an uptick," Renee assured me. "We just need to keep getting the word out." She smiled. "And the artwork and artists make it worthwhile."

She was right; we just needed to give it time and promotion. And yes, the artwork and consigning artists made it worthwhile. They stopped in to drop off new pieces, pick up payments—and support Zoe's and each other by making purchases, something I particularly appreciated.

I loved hearing their stories. Fatima, a silversmith, was a stay-at-home mom whose husband took over childcare evenings and weekends so she could work on her pieces. Daphne, the singer, was the daughter of a pastor; I laughed aloud as she explained how, as children, she and her siblings had been "sermon fodder" for her mother's pulpit. Kendra, an up-and-coming textile artist, hero-worshiped Renee and couldn't believe she was lucky enough to consign pieces beside those of someone so renowned in the field. Tori, the woman who painted the abstracts, was a microbiologist-turned-artist who'd pivoted her entire lifestyle to pursue a long-held creative dream.

"Once the customers come," Renee said, "they'll be back." She adjusted the spotlight above a set of prints on the west wall. "I mean, who wouldn't?"

Who wouldn't, indeed? It was a dark, dank day, and as I left that afternoon, glancing at the shop's windows, cheery and bright, I wanted to dive back inside. Instead, I headed to pick up Austin.

To my elation, Caitlin developed an interest in extracurriculars. She joined film club, which met weekly to view and discuss a movie, and said she was considering trying out for fencing. I breathed a sigh of relief. She'd just needed time to settle in. Now she'd blossom, stay busy—and, as the police officer said, spend time with other kids, rather than alone.

Besides making sure we were on the same page about schedules, Brett and I stayed out of each other's way. Occasionally he took a Saturday or Sunday off to watch Austin while I worked at Zoe's—but whenever Renee was at the shop and I was home, Brett was in the office. His big project, something called Fides, was set to launch in early January. The pressure on him and Nicole to launch by the scheduled date had, Brett said, ballooned to excessive proportions. Thus the need to work weeknights—and on weekends, too. Or so he said.

One day at Zoe's, I was taking yet another call from Brett about yet another late night. Only two other people were in the shop: a customer waiting to check out and Tori, who'd come in to pick up a commission check. Ending the call, I slammed my flip-phone shut, then smiled as I rang up the customer. After she left, I turned to Tori. "Let me get that check for you."

As I leaned on my mother's counter writing Tori's check, she placed both hands on the wooden surface. "Suzanne, I have to say this."

I looked up.

"I really admire what you've created here." Her eyes scanned the space. "You work so hard. It breaks my heart that you receive so little support from your husband." She lowered her voice. "This is probably TMI, but I just ended a terrible marriage. Zero support. Zero understanding of my dreams." She shook her head. "The icing on the cake? He was cheating on me." Her eyes met mine. "So, I just want you to know—I get it."

I stiffened. Tori was nice enough, but I barely knew her. Her comments felt meddlesome. Still, I knew how dramatic artists could be. It was a price I paid to work with creatives.

"It's temporary," I murmured. "And his reasons are legit."

I had to wonder, though. I'd worked in tech. Even at the call center, I'd witnessed how frantic things became when a release date loomed. But when I remembered the banter Nicole and Brett shared, the looks they exchanged, I had to ask myself: were my husband and this woman he spent so much time with truly just coworkers? Just "friends"?

Amid juggling responsibilities at Zoe's and home, worrying about Stevie, and checking the news daily for updates about the Shelton/Powles case—not to mention forcing myself *not* to let Brett and Nicole occupy my brain space—I hadn't made time to look further into Claranna Lewis. The only thing I'd done was head to Baker, a neighborhood west of Broadway filled with early twentieth-century brick duplexes, as well as Victorians painted a rainbow of colors. Driving down Fox Street, I'd slowed to take in the squat 1950s home at the Lewises' address. It looked out of place. Clearly, it was built after Claranna burned her house to the ground.

One afternoon in mid-November during the first snowfall of the year, I again studied the newspaper articles about the fire. I wished the Lewis children had been identified by name, although it made sense that they weren't, given the circumstances. But if I knew Claranna's daughter's first name, perhaps I could find her.

A long-buried memory muscled into my mind. My mother was pregnant with Chris, talking with eight-year-old me about names for the baby.

"Did I ever tell you that when I was expecting you, Aunt Donna suggested that if you were a girl, we should name you Alexandra?" Mom had asked. When I shook my head, she went on. "I think she was joking, but you should have *seen* Dad's reaction to that innocent little comment. He went on and on about what a burden it would be for you to share my name." She wrapped her arms around me, her spherical belly pressed between us. "I'm happy Dad and I were in agreement, so you could be my Suzie Blue." She'd kissed the top of my head. "You'll always be my Suzie Blue."

I ran for my computer, typing the name into the local phone directory's website. With such an unusual first name—Claranna—she'd either be there or she wouldn't.

There was no Claranna Lewis, but there was a Claranna Newstone with a Denver address and phone number. I tried a few more sites but nothing else came up. Claranna Newstone was the only Claranna in the metro area. I dialed the number, which went to voicemail with an automated greeting. Hanging up without leaving a reply, I scurried upstairs.

"Cait!" I called through her closed door. "I'm going out for thirty minutes. Please go downstairs and watch Austin."

I heard a groan. "Whatevs," she called out.

"Thank you!" After checking in with Austin, playing on the Wii, I headed to the garage.

Claranna lived in a rapidly gentrifying neighborhood called the Highlands by real estate companies but the Northside by everyone else. Skidding on the slick streets, I made my way across town and pulled up in front of her house. Claranna's block featured tiny bungalows interspersed with oversized modern houses—scrapes, they were called, because an older home was scraped off the lot to build a new one. Finding the new homes garish, I felt an immediate kinship with Claranna because she didn't live in one of them.

My breath quickened as I raised my finger to her bungalow's doorbell. If she answered, what would I say?

I almost turned away. Then I remembered knocking on Rosalie's apartment door in 1979. I was brave then—and I could be brave now. But as on that long-ago day, my first visit was fruitless. I rang and waited. Nobody came.

There was no note and ten-dollar bill to be left here. Nonetheless, when I pulled away I felt a measure of success. I'd unearthed a clue, and I'd be back.

29

1979

Dad and Chris were in the library, watching the Broncos play the New England Patriots in a whirl of blinding snow at Mile High Stadium. "Guess who was at the game?" Chris asked me. "Mork from Ork! He was dressed like one of the Broncos cheerleaders."

I smiled. "That's funny, buddy. I'm sorry I missed it."

Stepping into the kitchen, I regarded Peggy. She was leaning over the opened oven, brushing a pork tenderloin with some fancy, herb-infused glaze. Humming to herself.

Then I noticed them. Tacked to the side of our refrigerator by magnet hooks were her potholders, the entire collection.

Honey, Bee Yourself.

My palms began sweating. I wiped them on my jeans. The last thing I wanted to do was lay it all on the table with Peggy—but to get to the bottom of this, what choice did I have?

"Hey, Peggy," I said, opening the fridge and selecting a Tab. "Do you have a minute to talk?"

Her smile was wide—and fake. "Of course, Suzanne." She closed the oven door. "I just need to peel these potatoes."

I took a peeler from the drawer and handed her another one. "I'll help."

Side by side at my mother's kitchen sink, Peggy and I didn't look at each other as I said I had a confession to make. Soggy potato in hand, I told Peggy about going to her apartment. About what I found there and how it led me to Rosalie.

Wrapping up my speech, I turned to face her. Her bogus smile had faded.

"This is serious, Suzanne," she said. "You were trespassing."

"Sure...although your door *was* unlocked."

She pressed her lips together. "Not anymore, it won't be."

"I won't do it again," I said.

"But why?" she asked. "What made you go to my place like that?"

"I guess..." I gazed out the window over the sink at the falling snow. Behind Peggy and me, I felt the kitchen ghosts, their forms reflecting a shadowy pattern on the window. "I was looking for something that might make Dad rethink..."

Peggy waited.

"Rethink being with you." I kept my eyes on the window, concentrating on the ghosts.

Peggy seemed to consider this. "I understand, Suzanne. You and I haven't really had an opportunity to get to know each other, have we?" When I didn't reply, she went on. "In the past few months, your dad and I rushed from being old friends to much more." She reached for another potato. "I made such a mistake when I was young, breaking up with your dad. Thinking I could do better than him. I won't do *that* again."

She laughed—a weird, bitter sound, like she'd swallowed something unsavory. Dumbstruck, I stared at her.

"I'm sorry," she said. "Perhaps that sounded harsh." She added a peeled potato to our growing pile. "Listen, I want you to understand something. I fully comprehend and completely agree that your mother's death was a tragedy. But after it happened, I was only trying to help. I couldn't bring Alex back, but I *could* bring you food."

I kept my eyes on the sink full of potato peelings.

"One thing led to another," Peggy said. "Your dad and I are good company for each other. When things turned romantic, it made me happy, in no small part because it seemed to make *him* happy. And Chris...Chris..."

I pressed peels into the garbage disposal. "I get it about Chris," I said, and the edge I heard in my own voice seemed to thwart whatever she'd planned to say next.

Picking up the peeler, I turned to her. "Tell me about Bobby. How you came to be his tutor. And about him holding up Zoe's." My voice rattled. "Are those things connected? I *have* to know."

She gave me a long look, one I couldn't read. Then she set down her peeler and picked up a knife that was resting on the counter, facing its sharp blade toward my chest. Her eyes were green steel.

Taking two swift steps to my right, I reached for my mother's Santoku from the butcher block holder. But it wasn't there. It was the knife Peggy was holding.

"Dad!" I yelled. "Get in here! I need you!"

He rushed into the kitchen, Chris on his heels. By the time they appeared in the doorway, Peggy had set the knife back on the counter.

Her laughter was light but forced. "Goodness, you're paranoid, Suzanne. I was just going to start chopping potatoes."

I swung my head toward Dad. "She's lying. She pointed a knife at me again. She *threatened* me."

Dad set a hand on Chris's shoulder. "Go back to the library, pal. When the game ends, you can play Atari."

Chris looked at me. I wanted him there—another witness for whatever happened next—but I couldn't risk traumatizing my baby brother.

"Dad's right, bud," I said. "You should go."

After he left, Dad turned to Peggy. "What is going on here?"

"Nothing." Her voice was unnervingly calm. "Suzanne is being theatrical."

"Bullshit!" I said. "Guess what, Dad? Peggy *knew* Bobby Shelton." I shook a finger at her. "She knew Mom's killer."

Dad's face went white. "Peggy?"

Peggy's eyes were hard. "Suzanne only knows that because she was trespassing. She entered my apartment when I wasn't home."

"Yes, and what did I find there?" I planted my feet wide. "Don't try to deflect this, Peggy."

Dad turned his eyes from Peggy to me and back again, as if he couldn't decide what to do. Finally, he put up a hand. "Let's all sit down."

He propelled Peggy to the table. Then he beckoned me. Taking a seat as far from Peggy as I could, I listened while she told Dad about how Bobby and his neighbor had been her tutoring students. Dad sat between Peggy and me, clasped fingers resting on the table. I glanced around the kitchen, but the ghosts were gone.

"I desperately wanted Bobby to succeed," Peggy said. "I'd tutored numerous kids over the years—here in the States, in Delhi, in Bangladesh. With the smaller kids I read picture books. We went over the alphabet, pronunciation, spelling—and eventually, grammar rules. Outside of the U.S., on my missionary trips, I did the same when my students were older and wanted to learn English. It gave them a leg up, no matter their future, if they could read and write English."

"Go on." Dad's voice was neutral.

"In the U.S., with students like Bobby and Milo, it was different. As you know, Jimmy, by the time I returned to Denver, I'd suffered a tragic loss." She turned toward me. "My son was stillborn, Suzanne. Losing a child...it's a terrible, terrible misfortune."

Dad covered Peggy's hand with his. Stone-faced, I said nothing. Sure, that was sad—but if she wanted a reaction from me, she was in for a long wait.

Peggy wiped her eyes. "Afterward, I tried to keep going with my work, but it put a strain on my marriage—my second one, to a fellow missionary. Eventually we divorced and I came back here." She took a breath. "Back home, I knew I couldn't work with the little ones anymore. It was too painful. Every child reminded me of my own lost child." Her look was far away. "My lost child," she whispered.

"Peggy." Dad's voice was hoarse. "I'm sorry." Thickly, he added, "You know how sorry I am."

"Get on with the story," I commanded.

Peggy's mascara was starting to smear. "Older students needed saving, too," she said. "And their age created a distance that I didn't feel with the wee ones. So I began volunteering with an adult literacy program." She folded her hands in her lap. "Milo was my actual student, enrolled in the program. He was clean then. Students in the program had to be."

I frowned. He sure as hell wasn't clean anymore.

"With Bobby, it was…different." Peggy paused.

"Different?" Dad prompted.

"I met him at Milo's," she said. "From the start, Bobby and I connected. I took him to the shooting range a couple of times. He liked to shoot. As you know, Jimmy, so do I. Only for sport, of course." Her eyes gleamed. "Like they taught us girls back in high school."

I maintained my tight posture, eyes on Peggy.

"I knew about Bobby's struggles with addiction. I tried to find him resources to get clean. He was making an effort—truly, he was. I told him improving his literacy skills would help, too." She smiled. "Privately, Milo told me Bobby might be beyond saving. I believe the term he used was 'wasteoid.'"

Coming from Peggy's mouth, the word sounded nonsensical. But I was too angry to do anything besides glare.

"I told Milo that no one is beyond saving." Her look was earnest. "I believe that with my whole heart."

Maybe she did. But it didn't change what happened.

"I worked with both of them, sitting at Milo's kitchen table," Peggy said. "Then one evening Milo told us he could only stay thirty minutes. After Milo left, when we were alone, Bobby told me that his girlfriend, Rosalie, was pregnant."

I frowned. "This would have been…?"

"Probably early February," Peggy said. "Bobby told me Rosalie was due in August. He said they might get married." She gave Dad a pointed look. "I was all for that, as you can imagine."

When Dad didn't reply, Peggy continued. "Then we hit the books." A long moment passed before Peggy resumed. "When we took a break, Bobby searched in Milo's refrigerator for something to offer me. He found a can of Pepsi and poured it into two glasses. While we drank, Bobby and I chatted. He asked me about my day. He was good about that sort of thing. You wouldn't expect it of someone in his situation. You'd think he'd never consider asking someone about their lives." She looked at me.

"You'd think that," I agreed.

"I told him it hadn't been the most exciting day. Just running errands. Then I said…" She paused.

The pause went on so long, Dad prompted, "You said…?"

Peggy seemed to be composing her thoughts. "I told him, 'On my way over here, I stopped into this little record store on East Colfax. It's called Zoe's.' I remember that I blushed. I explained about you, Jimmy, about spending time with you while you and Alex were separated. I admitted that since you'd gotten back together, curiosity got the better of me. 'I *had* to see what Alex's shop was like,' I told Bobby. 'What this woman was like in her real life. At the reunion she'd seemed so glamorous.'"

I remembered how my mother had dolled herself up for Dad's reunion—so different from her ordinary minimalist makeup, flat-soled shoes, and thrift store sweaters. She'd laughed about it—but what the hell, she'd said, it was only one night.

"At the shop, Alex was wearing jeans and a plaid shirt. Hair in a ponytail," Peggy said. "She was counting cash when I came in—she had a big stack of it—but she zipped it into a pouch when we started talking. She sold me a record and we chatted a bit more. She said often she was there by herself—especially when she kept the store open late on Thursday and Friday evenings. Bobby nodded when I said that. 'All alone in her store at night,' he said."

I put a hand to my collarbone. I pictured those blood-red anemones on Mom-not-Mom's chest.

"God help me now, I simply confirmed it. 'All alone, yes,' I said to Bobby." Peggy shook her head. "I don't even know why we were talking about it. The conversation was meaningless chit-chat." Her chin trembled. "Or so I thought."

I stared at her. "So he knew about Zoe's because of you. Did you know he was planning to go there and rob her?"

She shook her head. "Goodness, no. But I did…" She bit her lip. "I told him about Zoe's. About your mother working there alone at night."

I watched her face, trying to read what I saw. Trying to decipher if she was telling the truth. "Why did you have their obituaries and the articles about my mom?" I asked. "Why didn't you have more in Bobby's file? About the tutoring."

"There were some papers in there, reading material he'd been working on. But after what happened, I couldn't go on with that work. I told Milo I'd no longer be able to work with him." Peggy wiped smeared mascara from below her eyes. "When I saw the first article, I was shocked. I felt compelled to keep it. Then…" She trailed off.

"Then what?" Dad asked.

"Then I felt terrible for you. All of you." She curled her hands into one another. "I've suffered enormous guilt about it, even if it was just an…an awful result of my innocent conversation with Bobby." She shook her head again. "I *never* thought he'd do something like that."

I didn't know what to think. I fiddled with my soda can's pop-top, bending it until it broke.

Peggy rose to put on a pot of water for the potatoes. "It's horrible," she said, her back to us. "Both what happened and that I never told you, Jimmy. But I worried what you'd think of me, associating with Bobby." Picking up the Santoku, she began chopping potatoes. "I was only trying to help him. I never thought the repercussions would be so…severe."

"Peggy." Rising, Dad went to her. "You did nothing wrong. You were trying to do right by that boy."

"She threatened Mom," I said. "I have it on tape."

That caught Peggy by surprise. She turned, staring at me.

"Suzanne is being overly dramatic." Dad explained to Peggy about the mix tape. "Go get it, Suze."

While I ran upstairs for the tape, they went into the parlor. Dad called to me from the doorway, and I sat cross-legged on the floor in front of my mother's hi-fi. I sensed the crazy-haired ghost with the hole in her temple squatting on the floor beside me, hitching her finery around her knees.

I inserted the tape and fast forwarded to Peggy's conversation with Mom. The volume knob was set to 2, but the conversation began at more like 10. As Peggy put her hands over her ears, I felt the ghost shrug. Smirking, I fiddled with the volume knob until the sound reverted to a bearable level.

Peggy listened attentively but showed no emotion. When the conversation was over, I pressed Pause.

"That did happen, yes," Peggy said, her voice even. "I had no idea Alex caught it on tape. We were just chatting."

"You threatened her," I repeated. "That was a threat."

"A threat?" Peggy tilted her head. "It was nothing of the sort." She took a step toward me, then seemed to think better of it. She returned to Dad's side but kept her eyes on me. "Please understand, Suzanne. Your dad and I had become friends again, which delighted me. Then he said we wouldn't be seeing each other anymore." She turned to him. "Right, Jimmy?"

"That was Alex's request," Dad replied. "It was a condition of her and me getting back together."

"At that time, that was very raw for me. I was...emotional." Peggy dabbed her eyelids.

"Well," I snapped. "We were all mighty *emotional*, weren't we?" I put a hand on my clavicle. "Still are."

The warm air in the room stifled me, and I struggled to inhale. The ghost leaned toward me—I felt the slightest kiss of her shoulder against mine—then disappeared.

Dad looked from Peggy to me, then back again. If you choose her over me, I thought, I will go get Mom's knife and slit her throat. I swear I will.

A long moment passed before Dad crossed the room and sat on the floor beside me. He put an arm around my shoulder. "Suze," he said. "This is a lot to digest. I'm sorry."

Never before had he spoken so tenderly to me. I turned into his arms. My throat stinging, I let the tears flow as my father tightened his arms around me.

30

2004

The day after going to Claranna's house, I arrived at Zoe's to find a police cruiser parked at the curb. Renee and an officer were inside. "I tried to call you but it went to voicemail," Renee told me. "We've had a break-in."

"Already?" I reached into my purse, wrapping my fingers around my knife's handle. "We've been open less than two weeks."

"I know." Renee shook her head. "No idea why anyone would target us."

"What did they get?"

"A couple of smaller pieces," she said. "And some jewelry and the computer. Good thing Brett installed backup and security software for us. Our data should be okay."

I nodded. "Anything else?"

"All the cash in the till," Renee replied. "Totally my fault there was anything in there. It wasn't much, but last night I neglected to put it in the safe. It appears they tried but failed to get into the safe. I'm sorry, Suzanne."

"It's okay." I touched Renee's shoulder, thinking about my mother, about Bobby Shelton. Such a minuscule amount of money he'd taken when he took her life. "Thank God neither of us was here."

Could Shelton Jr. be responsible? I told the officer about the report I'd filed, and he said he'd look into it. Notepad in hand, he walked around the tiny store. Turned out our back door's lock had been broken. We had a security alarm but it hadn't gone off.

"You're sure you set it last night?" the officer asked.

"Absolutely," Renee said. "I distinctly remember doing it, because I had to go back for a file folder I'd forgotten. It made me scurry to get out in the ninety-second window the system gives us once we've set it."

"Who else knows the code?"

"I think I told my husband once." I laughed lightly. "But I can't imagine he'd burgle his wife's store."

Wouldn't he? It was true that Brett had never been particularly on board with the new Zoe's. The only helpful thing he'd done was install our security and backup software. Perhaps he was trying to jeopardize my business.

Or another possibility—perhaps Brett told Nicole the code, and *she* was trying to jeopardize my business.

Get a hold of yourself, Suzanne, I admonished. Nicole is a grown woman. She has her own priorities. She wouldn't do a thing like that.

I pursed my lips. Being a grown woman with her own priorities, I reminded myself, is not mutually exclusive with jeopardizing another woman's livelihood...or her life.

At home that evening—late, because it was always late when he came home—I confronted Brett.

"That's ridiculous," he said. "Yes, I know the code. Perhaps I said it on the phone to you sometime within Nicole's earshot." He shrugged. "We're together a lot, Nicole and me. That's the nature of my work. Stop being paranoid, Suzanne."

We were in the darkened kitchen, only the dim light over the stove illuminating Brett's face, the stubble on his jaw. He'd gone directly to the kitchen when he got home, pouring himself a scotch. Like my father, back in the day. But Brett did that only occasionally, to wind down after a rough day.

Brett was *not* like my father.

Caitlin came in then. She went to the refrigerator, foraging for a snack.

Brett sipped scotch. "I'm not sure the Colfax neighborhood is safe, Suzanne," he said.

"The 'Colfax neighborhood,' as you put it, is nothing like it used to be," I replied. "It's trendy. It's on its way up." I wasn't sure that would always be the case—neighborhoods change, buildings get torn down and new ones built, businesses come and go. But today, in 2004, East Colfax was on an upswing.

"I'm not convinced." Brett leaned against the counter. "Why don't you move Zoe's somewhere else? Down in the Tech Center there are lots of nice little strip malls. It's safer there, much lower crime rates."

"Oh, for God's sake." I filled a water glass and gulped, facing him. "Do you have any understanding of what I'm trying to accomplish? *Any?*"

"In the suburbs you wouldn't have to worry about break-ins."

The refrigerator door slammed shut. I looked at Caitlin, who ran a hand through one side of her glossy hair, tossing it back. As she did so, the plate of leftover fried rice she was holding in her other hand clattered to the floor.

Brett and I stared at her. "You okay?" I asked.

Her smile was anemic. "I'm fine." On her knees, she scooped rice, cupping it in tense, quivering hands.

I couldn't get it off my mind. Caitlin was a veritable psychology textbook of emotions, but "nervous" was rarely part of her M.O. Could Caitlin have anything to do with the break-in at Zoe's? It seemed absurd, but she *had* witnessed me setting the code.

Tomorrow, I resolved, I'd talk with her about it.

But the next morning she was gone before I even entered the kitchen—unusual for her. Caitlin generally slept until the last possible minute. I'd catch her after school, I decided, leading Austin out the door.

Later, as I drove to Zoe's, my phone rang. It was Renee.

"I feel awful about what happened," she said. "Do you want me to take over this morning? My nanny is here, and I have no other commitments."

"Really?" An idea came to me and I veered onto Park Avenue West, heading toward the Northside. "Thanks, Renee."

"No problem. Take some time off and enjoy yourself, Suzanne."

I rang Claranna Newstone's doorbell. Hanging from the porch eaves was a wind chime; its bells jangling in the light breeze. I took it as a positive sign.

Just as Rosalie had, Claranna answered this second time. She had close-cropped, salt-and-pepper hair and a long, lean build, having outgrown her childhood chubbiness. Her narrow face looked exactly like an older version of her mother's.

"Can I help you?" she asked.

I gave her my name. "I don't even know how to explain this."

Fishing in my purse, I pulled out the newspaper articles and handed them to her. Claranna scanned them. "What does this have to do with me, other than this woman having my same first name?" Handing the articles back, she asked, "Who are you? Why do you have these?"

My eyes, the same indigo as hers, focused on Claranna's. "Can I come in? Can we talk?"

Shaking her head, Claranna closed the door. I was about to ring the doorbell again when she came out with a jacket on. "Sit," she said, motioning to a plastic porch chair.

"Claranna," I said as we faced one another. "Look at the color of my eyes."

She lifted her gaze to mine, then turned away.

"James is my father," I said. "James...your brother."

Claranna shook her head. "I don't have a brother."

I tapped the articles. "Are you saying this isn't your family?"

There was a long pause. Then she said, "I don't know what kind of long-lost family reunion you think you're looking for, but I'm here to tell you it's not going to happen." She hitched herself higher, looming in her chair. "I don't want it to happen. *No one* wants it to happen."

"Does my dad know?" My voice was a whisper. "Does he know how old he was when he was adopted?" I rattled the newspaper printouts. "Does he know about this?"

"I have no idea. Once he went to the home, I never saw him again. I later learned that he was adopted by a wealthy family. Presumably, he received everything anyone could want." She twisted a silver and turquoise ring on her right hand. "It was better for him. Better for everybody."

"But why?" I asked. "Why was it better for him? You were twelve. You could have helped care for him after your mother died."

I was still holding the papers on my lap. Bending forward, fist clenched, Claranna batted them to the porch floor.

I reached into my purse, grasping my knife.

Claranna's laughter was harsh. "What do you have in there? A weapon? Think you can hurt me?" Her face contorted. "I've faced all the hurt one person should for a lifetime, thanks very much." She stood, pointing toward the sidewalk. "I'm done talking to you. Please leave."

A gust blew the wind chimes, twisting them around themselves. Claranna's eyes were wild. "I'm asking you to leave." She cracked her knuckles. "If you return, I assure you I will not be this kind."

31

— · —

1979

That Sunday night Peggy didn't stay for dinner. "I think you all could benefit from a meal without me," she said to Dad.

In the library doorway, she called goodbye to Chris, who glanced up from the TV and waved. She kissed Dad's cheek, then put on her black wool coat and stepped into the blowing snow. She didn't look at me.

Her absence from the dinner table was a relief. But I kept staring at the empty seat, which I still couldn't think of as Peggy's. It would always belong to Mom.

Later, helping Dad do the dishes, I tried to convince him to break up with Peggy. But he said there was no need. "Peggy made an egregious error," he said. "She recognizes that. Isn't her remorse enough?"

It wasn't, but despite my urging, Dad agreed only to one thing: postponing the wedding. "It's too soon," I said. "Give it more time."

"That's a reasonable request," he said. "I'll speak with Peggy about it."

After tossing and turning all night, I awoke at a ridiculously early hour—five o'clock, something I never did, and a complete waste when school was closed for Veterans Day. I read for a while—I was halfway through Joan Didion's *The White Album,* an essay collection about her 1960s experiences—then attempted sleeping again, to no avail.

Despite excessive use of eye makeup, or maybe exacerbated by it, when I arrived at Zoe's to find Carey standing outside, I knew I didn't look my best. I hoped it didn't show. Reaching to unlock the door, I dropped the keys on the ground. "Dammit!" I yelled.

He took my arm as we stepped inside Zoe's. "Everything all right, Suzanne? You seem kind of...edgy."

I stared at him. Maybe I needed to confide in Carey. Tell him about Peggy's connection to Bobby Shelton. Maybe Carey could help. He was, technically, an adult.

But I didn't want to discuss it with him. And if I was honest with myself, the reason was simple: it might distract from what was growing between us. Spending time with Carey was the only positive thing in my life. I wasn't about to jeopardize it.

"I'm fine." I stepped into his arms.

"Jesus, you feel good," he said when we broke apart. "This isn't supposed to feel so good."

Smiling, feeling myself blush, I inserted a cassette in the boombox—Bonnie Raitt's *Sweet Forgiveness*. The bluesy twang of "Runaway" filled the space. Carey and I sank onto the floor, pillows and jackets cushioning us.

Gently, he leaned me back until we were lying side by side. I shivered, the wooden floor chilly even with my down jacket beneath me.

"You cold?" He drew me close.

My heart thudded. Carey wrapped his arms around me, bringing his warm hands together behind me, running them along my arms. His hands wandered the sleeves of my sweater, then below the sweater's hemline, crawling upward. Deftly, he unhooked my bra.

I concentrated on the sizzle of Carey's hands under my sweater, inside the padded bra I'd borrowed from Laurie. Knowing he wouldn't find much there, I worried he'd remove his hand, staring at me as if betrayed. But it appeared Laurie was right. If a guy gets that far, he doesn't care about the particulars as long as it's his skin against yours, his hands on your body.

The opening chords of "Gamblin' Man" came through the boombox's speakers, followed by Bonnie singing. Carey smiled.

"What?" I asked.

"Maybe I'm crazy..." He nodded toward the boombox. "Gambling on you." He rubbed his thumb over the smooth skin of my breast. "Or maybe you're crazy to gamble on me."

"I'm sure it's both," I said.

Carey and I spent that afternoon together, as well as the next two, after school. Then he told me he couldn't see me for a while because he had to work twelve-hour shifts and wouldn't be done until late at night.

"I can maybe come next Tuesday," he said. "But I'm not sure yet about my schedule."

I nodded. "Okay."

"But listen." He pulled a folded piece of torn newsprint from his jacket pocket. "Will you go to this with me?" He tapped the paper. "The one on Wednesday the twenty-eighth?"

I scanned the clipping he handed me. It was an advertisement for several upcoming shows at the Rainbow Music Hall. The Rainbow had opened last January in an old triplex movie theater on the corner of Monaco and Evans. Denver concert promoter Barry Fey had the idea to open an all-ages venue and bring up-and-coming musical artists to Denver.

Mom had been really excited. She said a venue like that was what Denver needed—large but not huge, more capacity than a nightclub but not as big as McNichols Arena or Red Rocks. And it was great, Mom said, that the Rainbow would have all-ages shows, a place for teens to see live music.

My mom had known Barry Fey for a long time—he came to her funeral, even—and she was eager to promote the Rainbow's shows at Zoe's. She went to the inaugural show and later told me the evening was magical.

"The acoustics are amazing," she gushed. "The size makes it feel intimate. It reminded me of the West Village in New York, back in the day. Oh, it's much bigger than those clubs and coffee houses I haunted in my teens—but it had the same vibe." She smiled. "I'll take you to a show there, Suze. Whatever you want."

In July when Rickie Lee Jones had played the Rainbow, I recalled that conversation. I recalled, too, that Mom had said I looked like Rickie Lee Jones. But even if I'd had friends to go to that concert with, I wouldn't have. Not without Mom.

The concert Carey was inviting me to featured someone named Prince. It was no one I'd heard of.

"You sure?" I asked Carey. "I mean...how would we make that work?"

"I've been thinking about it." He stood, pulling me up beside him. "If you told your dad that you were going with a group of kids, one of them my brother, and I was driving everybody—would he let you go?"

I nodded. "Probably. Especially if I said it was a group going. If I said it was just Scott...if it was a date..." I felt my cheeks flush. "...my dad would want to meet the guy I was going with."

"Well, it *is* a date, Suzanne," Carey said. "Just not with Scott. With me."

Silently, we stared at each other. I felt Zoe's eyes on both of us.

"Listen," he said. "On a million levels I know how wrong this is. I get it. You get it." He took my hands. "I've been thinking about this so much. Thinking about *you* so much. I know it's wrong. You're too young, and you're too..." He trailed off, looking away.

"I'm too what?"

He shook his head. "Here's the thing. We can take things at your pace." He released my hands, drawing me toward him. "I'd never ask you to do anything that makes you feel uncomfortable." His gaze was straightforward. "You trust me, right?"

God help me but I did. How could I *not* trust him? He'd paid more attention to me, been kinder to me than anyone else, in all the months since my mother died.

I nodded and he went on. "But we both know your dad's not going to see it that way. No father would." He rubbed the back of his neck. "I don't want to lie to your dad. But what else can we do?"

"No—you're right." I picked up my jacket from the floor. "No way he'd let me go if it was just you and me. It's only a little lie." I smiled. "I mean, I *would* be going with an Eames. And I'd be driven by a responsible adult. Right?"

Carey helped me into my jacket. "It'll be fine. It's going to be great."

"Thanks for asking me," I said. "It means a lot, that you want to do this."

"Do what?"

"Go out with me. Be seen in public with me."

Carey's eyes sparkled. "Why wouldn't I? What guy wouldn't be proud to be seen with you, Suzanne?"

Oh, my God. I was half in love with him at that moment. I leaned in for a final kiss, and he obliged.

That weekend was the school play—*Heaven Can Wait*—and on Friday night, I went with Laurie and a couple of other kids. Carey and I hadn't talked about the play, so I was unsure if he'd be there to see the sets his brother had helped design. I looked for him but didn't see him.

Laurie introduced me to people by saying, "This is my neighbor, Suzanne." I'd have preferred, "This is my friend, Suzanne," but at least she included me. On the way home, she asked how things were at my house, and I said okay.

That was bullshit, but the truth was, Carey's invitation to take me on a date had changed things. Yes, I wanted Peggy out of the picture. But knowing the wedding was postponed indefinitely helped. I didn't have to do anything immediately. Instead, I could savor the opportunity to go out with Carey. I figured I'd ask my dad about the Prince concert over

Thanksgiving weekend. I'd make it sound casual, like Scott and some other kids had invited me at school.

On Tuesday it snowed like crazy. On the radio that morning, they called it "a whopper of a storm," and as people left school that afternoon, everyone wished each other a Happy Thanksgiving—adding disdain about what a waste it was, because we already had the rest of the week off for the holiday.

I plowed through the snow to Zoe's and waited well into the afternoon, but Carey never showed. It was freezing, and snow was piling up. I figured he'd had to work or simply couldn't get to Zoe's through the snow. I hoped he wasn't having second thoughts about our date.

Nothing I could do about it. Waving good-bye to Zoe, I locked up and headed out.

At home, Peggy was all a-twitter about Thanksgiving. Talking about the menu, making a last-minute shopping list, worrying about getting to Safeway through the snow. Not that our Thanksgiving dinner would be much different from any other meal. Senile old Grandma Parry wouldn't come. Aunt Sadie and Uncle Richard and the cousins would be in Vail, like every year. At our house, it would just be the Parrys—and Peggy.

"I wish my mother could be here," Peggy said to Dad over Tuesday night's dinner—a simple one for her, homemade macaroni and cheese. "But it's too risky for her to come out in this weather."

"Why is it risky?" Chris asked.

Peggy smiled at him. "No real reason, sweetie. She's just old."

Chris drained his milk. "Can I be excused?"

After he left, Peggy turned to Dad. "I went to see her today. She's in rough shape—this last stroke exacerbated things. The doctor says she's in danger of another at any time. She's truly living on borrowed time." Peggy blinked. "That was one of the reasons to have the wedding this spring," she said. "I want my mother there, you know?"

Jesus. Could she even *hear* herself?

"Oh, well—*sure*." I broke in. "Wouldn't everyone want their mother at their wedding?" I slammed my empty glass onto the table. "I know *I* would."

I rose, not bothering to clear my things. She was lucky I didn't smash a plate over her head.

32

2004

Driving away from Claranna's house, I gripped the steering wheel, grateful to be safe inside my car. My aunt was one crazy-ass chick. Then again, who almost pulled a knife on who? Maybe I was the crazy one.

At Zoe's, when I told Renee she could head out, she said, "I can stay to keep you company. My schedule is free today."

"That'd be nice. Thanks."

She smiled. "We're partners, right? That's what I'm here for."

Later, there was a call from the principal at Austin's school. "I'm sorry, Suzanne, but you need to pick up Austin immediately. I have him in the office, and I'd like to speak with you." She paused. "I suggest your husband come, too."

"What happened?" I asked. "Is Austin all right?"

"Oh, *Austin* is fine," she said, and I heard the frustration in her voice. "The proverbial question is—what about the other guy?"

Breathe, breathe, breathe, Suzanne. "What does that mean?"

"I apologize for my words and tone," the principal said. "Everything is fine—now. The other child is being tended to. But Suzanne..." Her voice lowered. "We need to talk."

Austin, it turned out, had become enraged when the same kid who'd teased him about carrying Pikachu everywhere made fun of Austin's entire Pokémon obsession. The kid called him a dork. Not because Austin liked Pokémon—lots of kids did—but because, as the principal said, "He *cannot* stop talking about it."

"He talks a lot when he's excited," I said. "Like many kids."

"Indeed," she replied. "But when he's called on it, he needs to learn to control his temper."

"What did he do?"

Her expression stiffened. Reaching into a desk drawer, she pulled out my Halloween knife—the tanto fixed blade I'd given Caitlin. "Do you recognize this?" she asked, placing it on her desk.

My heart pounded. "Yes," I whispered. "He didn't use it...did he?"

"No. But he held it up and threatened the child who called him a name," she said. "The child is, understandably, traumatized. His mother took him home for the rest of the day."

Brett rushed in the door. My throat dry, I told him what had happened.

"How the hell did he get one of your *knives*, Suzanne?" Brett's voice was so loud, the workers in the outer room, which could be seen through the principal's office windows, turned to stare. Austin, seated in the outer room, was unresponsive—a wooden Pinocchio on a bench. His head was down and his arms were wrapped around his knees.

"I'm sorry." I turned to the principal. "I keep the knives locked up. I have no idea where he got that one."

I slipped the tanto into my purse, envisioning scenes in which I demonstrated to Caitlin just how dangerous a knife like this was. Had Austin gone into her bedroom and found it? I doubted it; Austin never went in her room. More likely, she'd left it lying around somewhere.

I gave it to her for protection. How could she have been so careless with it?

"Please use more caution in the future, Suzanne," the principal said. "Many would consider this a mandatory reporting issue. I won't report it this time, because I know you and Brett to be attentive parents. But if something like this happens again, I'll be obligated to report it to the authorities as child neglect."

My cheeks burned. "I'm sorry," I repeated.

"You could lock up every sharp item in our house and we'd still have problems," Brett said. "It's ridiculous. He's out of control." He glared at me. "You have to do something, Suzanne."

"*I* have to do something? He's your child, too!"

"I'm doing plenty. I'm bringing home the bacon. My job provides the health insurance we need in order to address this issue." Nostrils flaring, Brett added, "And you said you'd take care of it!"

"Suzanne. Brett." The principal leaned forward. "I'm sorry this happened. I suggest Austin take a few days off from school, to give him time to settle down and for you as a family to work this out."

"You're suspending him?" I asked.

She held up her hands. "It's unfortunate it came to this, but yes." The principal leaned back in her chair. "Today's Wednesday. Let's have Austin take a reprieve until Monday." She looked at me, then at Brett. "That gives him a good break. I'm sure it will help."

Outside school, Brett took long strides toward his car. Austin's hand in mine, I hurried to catch up.

Brett whirled on me. "This waiting on Children's, waiting for answers—it's an exercise in futility," he said. "Please, Suzanne, find some other resources. Or some way to get him to the top of the list." He unlocked his car. "Surely, you can find someone who can pull some strings for us."

"I'll try." My voice was small.

"Please do." Climbing into the car, he looked up at me. "I'm sorry I snapped at you in there. The pressure on me right now is tremendous. I can't deal with this, on top of everything at work. I need you to fix it,

Suzanne." He started the engine. "And for God's sake, make sure your knives are locked up."

He closed the car door and drove off. Squeezing Austin's hand, I watched him go.

Austin climbed into the back seat of my car. I sat beside him. "What happened, buddy? Where'd you find the knife?"

"In that bin in the TV room—the one blankets and stuff are in."

Jesus. What the hell was *wrong* with Caitlin?

"Why'd you take it?" I asked.

"No reason." His eyes blazed. "Landon is an asshole. Asshole, asshole, *asshole*."

"Oh, bud." I put an arm around him. To my surprise, he shrugged me off—something he rarely did.

I got in the driver's seat. As I started the car, Gerry Rafferty came on the radio, singing "Baker Street"—another popular song from my mother's era.

Baker: the neighborhood where the Lewises once lived. I took it as a sign.

Fox Street was narrow and residential, with almost no traffic. I parked in front of the address that had once been the Lewises'. My phone had a game on it called Hungry Fish, which Austin adored and I let him play occasionally. Handing him the phone and telling him to stay put, I got out and locked the car.

The little 1950s brick home was dark, shades drawn. The day was cloudy, but heat scalded my face and legs. Squatting, I touched the lawn. Flameless, the withered winter grass blazed under my fingers, and I drew them back. I closed my eyes, trying to sense Claranna Lewis's ghost—but as the spirit of someone who'd burned alive, she failed to appear to me.

An elderly woman stepped out of the duplex next door. Hunched back, yellow beanie covering gray hair, floral housedress under a wool coat. "Can I help you, dear?" she called out.

Straightening, I glanced at Austin, who was engrossed in his game, then walked up to her porch. Giving my first name, I said I was a historian working on a book about twentieth-century Denver. She introduced herself as Mrs. Dawson.

"How long have you lived here, Mrs. Dawson?" I asked.

"Decades. I raised a family here." She smiled. "Children *and* grandchildren. All grown and flown now, but they visit. They want to move me into a home, but I'm having none of it. This *is* home."

She was so friendly, I was loath to upset her. But I had to know. "Were you acquainted with the Lewises, who once lived there?" I pointed next door. "Not in that house, of course. I read some articles about the fire."

Mrs. Dawson sank into a nylon lawn chair. It was the only chair on the porch, so I perched on the railing.

"I knew them," she said. "Their house was a little wooden frame structure, single story."

"What were they like?" I asked. "What was Mrs. Lewis like?"

"She was standoffish. Didn't exchange recipes. Didn't invite anyone in for coffee like the rest of us did." Her voice wavered. "She was like people are now, not neighborly. Back then everyone knew everyone. Nowadays people barely say hello."

"It must have been awful to see their house burn."

"It was frightful. One of the worst things I've ever witnessed. I took the children inside until their father arrived—although I was reluctant to have that boy in my house. I didn't like my children associating with him." She shrugged. "But what can you do? I could hardly ignore him and only take in the girl."

I took a deep breath. "What was wrong with the boy? Why didn't you want him in your house?"

She paused. "There was something *off* about him. I can't explain it. But I'll tell you this." She met my eye. "I never believed Claranna started the fire." Mrs. Dawson glanced next door. "That boy started the fire. I'd have put money on it then, and I'd put money on it now."

At home, Brett and I danced delicately around each other. I was unwilling to admit to him that I'd given Caitlin a knife—even if it had been the right thing to do, I told myself: she *needed* protection, whether she realized it or not. Nonetheless, I took responsibility for Austin finding the tanto. Brett, in turn, apologized again for his words, but I still felt hurt by how he'd treated me at school. And I was frustrated by the fact that—of course—Austin's suspension meant *I* had to deal with his days off. I hated myself for relying on DVDs and video games. What a crappy mother, I thought. Crappy business owner and crappy mother, all rolled into a big, Suzanne-sized package.

I made another round of calls—the pediatrician, Children's to check on the wait list, and even some out-of-state clinics, although that would mean figuring out how to manage significant time away from Zoe's *and* how to afford the travel. I had no solution for either of those dilemmas.

What I didn't do was tell Brett about the Lewises, even if an investigation of my family's genetic past might count as "doing something to fix it." I wanted Brett to know I was trying, but I was afraid of what he'd say. Afraid he'd get angry, claim I was wasting my time.

The first time I didn't tell Brett something big—in our early months of dating—it was because I was afraid that if I told him, he'd end things with me. Our relationship was so young then. I didn't want to jeopardize it.

I'd first laid eyes on Brett at a house party in Berkeley, freshman year. He'd been in the bathroom, holding a girl's long hair while she puked into the toilet, when I barged in.

"Oops, sorry," I'd said, backing out—but not before noticing how gently he held that girl's hair. Noticing the leather jacket he wore, how his shoulders filled it out. Noticing the way his eyes, over the girl's head, stared into mine. The rest of the evening, I looked for him but didn't see him.

A week later I ran into him in the student union. "Hey," he said. "I'm sorry about that night. Should've locked the bathroom door."

"I should've knocked." I eyed him. "It was nice of you, helping a girl you'd never met before."

His brow furrowed. "How'd you know I'd never met her before?"

I reddened. I'd only recently begun pretending I didn't sense things, but occasionally I slipped. "Just a feeling. Are you going to ask her out?"

"Nah." He put a hand lightly on my arm. "But can I buy *you* a coffee...um..."

I glanced at his hand on my sleeve. Strong, with firm fingers but a relaxed grip. He wore the same leather jacket he'd had on at the party. Meeting his eye, I said, "I'm Suzanne. And I'd love a cup of coffee."

After that, we were inseparable. When Brett held me in his arms, when we danced, when we made love, I'd think about how lucky I was. Brett's love felt like a protective shell around me—the protection I'd longed for but hadn't felt since losing my mother.

Late one night as we were snuggling in the single bed in my dorm room, I told him how my mother died. I didn't tell him about her ghost—or any ghosts. I didn't tell him I'd been Mom's little seer. I left out other details, too. I said only enough to reinforce Brett's protective shell, but not enough to risk breaking it. Not enough to risk losing him.

Could I lose him now? Thinking about Nicole, I couldn't dismiss the possibility. If I asked too much of Brett, if I was too needy, would he'd walk away from me? From us?

As for Caitlin, my first instinct was to confront her. To yell at her for her carelessness, leaving the tanto lying around. But after giving myself time to calm down, I decided to let it go. Caitlin didn't want the knife. She didn't want anything I had to offer.

Chris called on Monday, when Austin was, thankfully, back at school, with strict orders to "Count to ten anytime you feel mad." Chris said our father would be touching down in Denver that evening.

"He wants everyone at his house for Thanksgiving," Chris said. "He's got a whole thing planned. A catered meal, everything. Made arrangements from halfway across the globe."

"Tough shit," I said. "I have a sixteen-pound turkey defrosting in my refrigerator. You can come over, if you like. So can Dad...if he really wants to."

Chris sighed. "Are you sure you can't come to his place instead? He's going all out."

"He's going all out in his typical clueless way. Did he even think to check with me before he made these plans?"

"He said he tried to reach you. You didn't answer, and you didn't respond to his voicemails."

Chris was right. I'd noticed the intercontinental calls, not from my father's regular cell phone number but clearly from a phone he'd rented for the trip, one that gave him international access. When I saw that number pop up again and again, I'd ignored it. And I'd never listened to the voicemails.

"How about going over to Dad's for dessert?" Chris pleaded. "Just a slice of pie, Suzanne. One slice of pumpkin pie."

My fingers twitched and I pressed them to my chest. "Fine. We'll come in the evening. For a slice of pie."

My dad lived in a five-bedroom Mediterranean-style ranch house on Seventeenth Avenue in the Park Hill neighborhood of Denver. Seventeenth was a parkway with a grassy esplanade and large, stately homes strung along it like necklaces in a jewelry store display case. When we arrived, Chris's enormous pickup truck was in the driveway.

Getting out of the car, I frowned at the white stuccoed, tile-roofed house. Then I reminded myself to keep my emotions in check. This house, unlike some houses, was just a damned house. Just four walls and a roof. Nothing wrong with it.

Nothing at all. I simply didn't like it.

All day, I'd tried to make the holiday fun for Brett and the kids—and I'd enjoyed the Thanksgiving aromas that permeated my house as I cooked turkey and assembled all the trimmings. But I hadn't been able to get what Mrs. Dawson said out of my mind. Whenever I thought about it—and when I thought about seeing Dad later—my throat tightened and my heart raced.

I hadn't seen Dad in two years. Since I'd rarely come to Denver before we moved here, seeing him usually occurred when he'd pay us a visit—often unannounced—in California. He never stayed with us, and honestly, he didn't ask for much. A couple of times taking the kids for some fun, over-the-top activity. A meal or two at my house. It wasn't much, so I'd agreed to it. But I'd never particularly enjoyed these visits. I was always relieved when he left.

Dad and Chris appeared on the steps. Dad opened his arms and I let him hug me. He shook Brett's hand, then moved on to each of the kids. Caitlin, like me, kept their hug brief.

"I have three pies!" Dad said. "And they all look delectable. Come in, come in!"

I hadn't been inside this house in a long time. It felt neglected. While clean—he must have had someone coming in while he was gone—it had a forlorn air. At the risk of being sexist, it felt like the house lacked a woman's touch. No fresh flowers. No crispness to the curtains. Everything felt oversized and dull, like a warehouse long since abandoned.

In the common areas of the house—the cavernous living room and dining room, the family room off the kitchen—there was no longer any furniture from my childhood. Everything had a 1980s feel to it—vertical blinds, floral prints, clear glass tables. There was nothing quirky, nothing out of place.

Dad had a roaring fire going in the family room fireplace. Logs crackled; towering flames licked the flue. I thought about what Mrs. Dawson claimed—that my dad, as a little boy, had started the fire that burned down his modest childhood home. In this behemoth of a house where he now lived, I adjusted the fireplace screen, ensuring it was completely closed. No risk of sparks on the carpet. No risk—here, anyway—of danger to my children.

When we were all seated, the TV tuned to football and pie plates balanced on our laps, Dad said, "Now, I want to hear the aggregate of your activities in Denver. Tell me everything."

He looked at my family when he said it. First Austin, then Caitlin, then Brett. He didn't look at me.

Fine. He had no interest in the new Zoe's. That was his prerogative.

If not for Austin's babbling, the conversation would've been stilted. Brett and Caitlin never got a turn to talk. Eventually Caitlin murmured something about the bathroom, then rose and wandered down the hall.

Once Austin had exhausted himself talking, he asked for more pie. My father went to the kitchen, Austin tagging along.

Chris looked at me. "Anything to say here?"

I shook my head. "Not a thing."

Chris's phone rang. He answered it, then put his hand over it. "Customer—just bought a car yesterday," he whispered to Brett and me. "I wouldn't normally take it on a holiday, but she sounds frantic." He headed down the hallway.

Brett squeezed my hand. "You okay, Suze?"

I tightened my hand in his. "I'm okay. Thanks."

When Chris returned, Dad and Brett were discussing the football game, Austin was playing with the Pokémons he'd brought along, and I was gathering plates to bring to the kitchen.

"Suze," Chris said. "Can I speak to you?"

I followed him down the hall. He ushered me into Dad's office. His desk was the same one he'd had for years, with its usual assortment of items. Ink blotter, date book, ancient desktop computer. A thick, well-worn dictionary to one side.

Seated at a chair in front of the desk was Caitlin. Chris nodded at her. "Tell your mother."

She crossed her arms. "I don't have to take this bullshit. You're not the boss of me, Uncle Chris."

"No, but she is." He jutted his chin toward me. "Tell her."

Caitlin glowered. "It was for a good cause, all right? There's this fundraiser at school. It's to collect money and supplies for a women's shelter." She arched an eyebrow. "I'm sorry. I was just going to take a little. Grandpa has tons of cash. He wouldn't have missed it."

I shook my head. "I don't understand."

"Caught her as I walked in here to take my call," Chris said. "Rifling through desk drawers, her sticky little fingers on a wad of cash." He frowned at her. "So surprised at you, Caitlin."

"You barely know me," she shot back. "So lay off with the avuncular treatment."

He laughed, sounding downright spiteful. "Big word, little girl."

"Stop it, both of you." My head felt woozy. Sitting beside Caitlin, I met her eye. "Tell me what this is about."

"I told you. It's for the fundraiser."

"Caitlin—please," I said.

I remembered the times I'd stolen from Dad. To go out with Laurie, sure. But also for Rosalie. My own personal fundraising project?

"Fine. You don't have to believe me," Caitlin said. "Let's forget this happened."

"That doesn't seem like the best idea," Chris said. "The 'forget it happened' part." He looked at me. "We should tell Dad."

"We should do nothing of the sort." I stood. "Caitlin apologized. The money wasn't taken. Case closed."

Caitlin sighed. Relief? Boredom? I wasn't sure.

"Pie is done," I said. "I did what you asked, Chris—we came over. Come on, Cait." She rose, and I put my hand on her shoulder, steering her toward the door. "I'm taking my family home."

Did I detect a smirk she directed at him, as we left? If so, I told myself I didn't care.

33

1979

We ended up with eighteen inches of snow. The entire weekend, I didn't see anyone besides Peggy, Dad, and Chris.

Peggy's presence created a cavern in our Thanksgiving. We did not raise a glass in Mom's honor. We didn't take a moment to remember the Thanksgivings—and Christmases, birthdays, and other milestones—that we'd celebrated with Mom, back when we'd had no idea their final tally would, in the grand scheme of things, be minuscule.

On Saturday I asked Dad about the Prince concert. "Some kids from school are going," I said, placing the newspaper clipping on his desk. "I know it's a school night but if I have my homework done and I promise not to stay out late, can I go?"

He scanned the paper. "How would you get there?"

"One of the guys who's going, Scott Eames—he said his older brother can drive us."

"How many kids?"

"Like five or six, maybe. Me, Scott, a girl named Kara—she's my biology lab partner—and a couple of other people." I met his eye. "The Rainbow isn't a bar or nightclub. It's all ages. Remember how Mom loved that place?"

He nodded. "I remember."

"So, can I go?"

"Well," he said. "This sounds fun, and it's an acceptable opportunity for you to socialize with classmates. You can go." He handed the clipping back. "Make sure this brother comes to the door when he picks you up. I want to meet the person who'll be driving you."

Carey showed up at Zoe's on Monday, and we made our plans. "I'm nervous about you meeting my dad," I told him. "Do you really think we can pull this off?"

He wrapped his arms around me. "It'll be fine, Suzanne. Trust me."

On Wednesday I flew home from school and rushed through my homework. That evening when Carey knocked, my heart pounded. It *would* be fine, I told myself. Carey said so.

He stood on the doorstep wearing his Levi's jacket, even in the chill of near December. "Hey, there," he said, his voice loud. "You're Suzanne—right?"

I giggled softly. "Yep," I replied, my voice equally strong. "And you must be Carey."

Dad appeared, followed by Chris. I made the introductions.

"I remember you," Chris said. "You were the scary guy giving out candy on Halloween."

"That's right," Carey said. "And you were dressed as a wizard."

He *remembered* my little brother's costume? How sweet was that? My heart beat faster. Calm down, Suzanne, I told myself. Calm the hell down.

"We live a few blocks away," Carey explained to Dad. "Suzanne probably told you she goes to school with my brother, Scott."

Dad nodded. "She did. Where is Scott?"

"Oh..." Carey glanced out the door. "He's at home. I have to run back for him. He forgot to take out the garbage, and our mom said he couldn't go until he did it. I didn't want to be late picking up the other kids, so I said I'd get Suzanne, then swing back for him."

Jesus, I'd had no idea he was such a good liar. Almost as good as me.

"You ready?" Carey asked me.

"Sure." I grabbed my jacket and kissed the top of Chris's head.

"Don't keep the kids out late," Dad said to Carey. "It's a school night."

"Yes, sir. My mom said the same thing."

Carey ushered me to the car—a beat-up Dodge coupe he said belonged to his father, nothing like the shiny new cars from PAG that my dad drove. He'd parked down the street, on the other side. At a stop light outside of our neighborhood, he kissed me. "We did it," he said.

"Yeah, well, you're pretty damned smooth."

"I hate doing stuff like that," he said. "But sometimes..." He pressed his lips to mine again. "It's worth it."

We drove down Colorado Boulevard. Several miles south, we passed the turnoff for Peggy's apartment building. I stared as we went by.

"What's up?" Brake lights ahead of us came on, and Carey slowed.

"What? Oh, nothing." I reached across the seat, fingers grazing his shoulder. "Thanks for this. I'm looking forward to it."

He smiled before accelerating past the other car. "Me, too, babe."

Babe. Without responding, I let the magical word hang in the air between us.

When we reached the corner of Monaco and Evans, the parking lot was crowded and an endless line of people waited outside. "Most of the other shows I've seen here, we got in line early," Carey said. "But I figured with the cold weather, there wouldn't be many people lining up."

I tried, unsuccessfully, to ignore the word he'd used: *we.* Who was this "we" with whom Carey attended other concerts?

"I think we'll be okay," he said. "It's open seating, and we might be toward the back, but there's not a bad seat in the house."

He handed me a ticket, and I studied it. *Rainbow Music Hall and KDKO Presents PRINCE, Wednesday, November 28, 1979, 7:30 p.m.* The ticket price was two dollars and thirty-five cents.

After we'd settled into seats, Carey went to get us Cokes and snacks. When he returned, he ripped open a large pack of M&Ms, holding it out to me. "Watch out for the green ones," he said. "You know what they say, right?"

I grinned. "Yeah. I know what they say."

The hall was warm with teenage synergy. The stage lights went up and the band appeared on stage. But calling the act a "band" was a misnomer. It was this one guy, Prince, with his backup singers and musicians.

Really, though, it was mostly him.

I listened and watched, hypnotized. When Prince—this twenty-one-year-old, mostly unknown musician—appeared on stage dressed in black silk underwear and thigh-high boots, chest bare, his guitar with its leopard-skin strap slung across his body, I knew I was witnessing something that hadn't existed before.

It wasn't just his looks. It was his melodic range, his skill on the guitar. And most of all, his energy as he moved around the stage.

Prince was all talent and raw sexuality. There was no other way to put it.

"That was 'Soft and Wet,'" he said into the mic as he wrapped up the first song.

I felt heat between my legs. Carey squeezed my hand.

The hall began to reek of pot. "You want a toke?" Carey asked. "I have some."

I shook my head. I'd been high a few times, with Laurie. But it wasn't what I wanted for this night. I didn't want to chance losing the memory of how it felt to be at the Rainbow—in that crowd, with that music. With my skin alive, my body warm, and Carey's hand in mine.

In total, Prince's set was seven songs, ninety minutes—short, yet magical. The time he spent on stage flew by, but in some ways, it felt like a lifetime had passed when he finished with "I Wanna Be Your Lover"—and Carey and I, among throngs of hopped up, chattering teens and young adults, stepped outside into the bitterly cold night.

Maybe, I thought, it wasn't that *time* had passed. Instead, maybe *we* had changed.

At a minimum—*I* had changed.

Before that night I'd been to a few concerts, but none compared with seeing Prince. Carey, six years my senior, presumably had attended many other shows. I didn't know what artists he'd seen and what emotions they'd brought up in him. I didn't know if a show ever made him feel the way Prince's performance made me feel.

Like a sexual being. Like I was partly a woman, partly an animal. And only a tiny part of me was still a girl.

Carey started the car's engine, then rubbed his hands together before reaching toward my face, touching my cheek. "Too cold?"

"No. Your hand feels good."

He kissed me, long and deep. My heart thudded. I love you, I love you, I thought.

Carey leaned me back so we were reclined on the vinyl bench seat of the Dodge. "Jesus, you're so sexy," he said. I could feel him pressed against me—every part of him, chest and torso and legs.

And what was between them. I arched toward him.

Sharp tapping on the driver's side window caused us both to sit up. A security guard stood outside the car. Carey rolled down the window. "We were letting the car warm up, sir."

The guard peered inside, then drew his head back. "Car seems warm to me. Move it along. We're trying to clear people out."

Carey shifted into drive, gripping the gearshift on the steering wheel column. I leaned back in my seat, away from him. The guard waved us on and we joined the line of cars headed for the exit.

Rolling up his window, Carey turned toward me. "Come over here."

I scooted across the seat to him. He put his right arm around me. Steering with his left elbow, he took my left hand in his and pressed it into his crotch. Then he put his hand back on the steering wheel and looked me in the eye.

I didn't remove my hand. I didn't do anything with it. It just rested there.

But let the record show, I did not remove my hand.

All around us, through the closed windows of the car, we could hear the muffled sounds of horns and kids calling to one another. Carey spoke quietly. "This is up to you," he said. "I can take you home, Suzanne...if that's what you want."

I squeezed gently, feeling the vibration through his jeans, reacting to my touch.

"We don't have to go home yet," I whispered. With my other hand I reached inside my sweater and pulled out the leather cord that was always around my neck. I fingered Zoe's keyring. "There's somewhere we can go instead."

34

—·—

2004

The Friday and Saturday following Thanksgiving, I forced Caitlin to watch Austin for the morning so I could work. Brett said he could take over in the afternoon, but the Fides project had some looming Monday deadline, and Nicole's schedule was such that they needed to work together in the morning both days over the holiday weekend.

Was that all there was to it? Or were there other reasons Brett wanted to be with Nicole?

"I thought only retail was crazy busy on Thanksgiving weekend," I said.

"Also techy people with less than six weeks to get a major release out the door." Brett grabbed a banana and his commuter mug. "Surely you haven't been out of tech so long that you've forgotten that, Suze." He brushed a lock of hair from my face. "I'll take Sunday off, okay? We can do something as a family."

"Can't," I said. "Retail."

Unsurprisingly, Caitlin grumbled about having to watch Austin. She tolerated Friday but that night asked if she could sleep in the next morning and let Austin manage himself until Brett got home.

"You know that's impossible," I replied. "You know how he is."

She crossed her arms. "I am so damned *sick* of how he is. Sick of everything revolving around his needs."

Me, too, I wanted to say. Instead, I told her, "I'm sorry his needs are so immense." Tentatively, I placed a hand on her shoulder.

She shook me off. "What do I have to do get some attention toward *me*?" She threw her arms wide. "I mean, how drastic should I go, Mom?"

Before I could respond, she whirled and left the room.

All day, I couldn't stop thinking about Caitlin. It didn't help—or maybe it did, in its way—that things were busy at the store, finally. The holiday shopping season began in earnest, and the ad campaign we'd put together seemed to be paying off. I crossed my fingers that the uptick in sales was a trend, not a fluke.

When I got home, Brett was already there; I could hear him and Austin downstairs playing on the Wii. I went upstairs and knocked on Caitlin's door. When she didn't answer, I opened it. Finding the room empty, I frowned.

I phoned her but it went to voicemail. After leaving a terse message that I wanted her home for dinner, I sat in the living room to wait. When she finally stepped inside, I called out, "Come in here, please, Cait."

She appeared in the living room doorway, glaring at me.

"Where were you?" I asked.

"We went to a movie. Then we were hanging out."

"You and who?"

"Just me and this guy."

"A guy?" I sat up. "Are you dating him?"

She shrugged. "I guess so."

"What's his name?" I asked. "Does he go to East?"

She hesitated, then said, "Yeah, he goes to East. And no, I'm not telling you anything else." She turned, clomping up the stairs.

I followed, opening her door. She was curled up on her bed, pulling headphones over her head. She took them off when I came in.

"Sorry for barging in," I said. "No, wait—I'm not sorry. If you're dating someone, Caitlin, you need to bring him around to meet us."

She narrowed her eyes. "Did *you* bring home every guy you went out with? Truth, Mom."

I squirmed. "Things are different now. This is a house rule."

She laughed. "Since when?"

"Since five minutes ago, when you told me you have a boyfriend."

"Jesus. I shouldn't have said anything." She gave me a pointed look. "Would you leave, please? I'd like to change before dinner."

I held up my hands. "I do *not* know what to do with you."

"Leave me alone," she said. "That's all I ask."

"This morning you said we don't pay you any attention."

"You don't pay me the right kind of attention," she said. "You only notice me when you want something. Or when you're trying to catch me doing something *you* consider wrong."

The attempted theft at my dad's house hung between us. That *was* wrong, I told myself. Even if she had a good excuse—and who knew if she'd made up the story about the fundraiser?—stealing wasn't the way to go about raising money.

I said, "If you worked for me, Cait, I'd pay you. You want to earn money for the fundraiser, or anything else, you could work at Zoe's."

Something crossed her face then. Her eyes darted away and she hunched her knees, forming her body into a ball. I recalled her discomfort when Brett and I discussed the break-in at the shop. I sat beside her on the bed, and she scooted toward the wall.

"Did you break into Zoe's?" I asked. "Tell me the truth, Caitlin."

"Why the hell would you say that? Why would you accuse me of that?" She pointed a finger at me. "Whenever there's a screwup of any kind, you blame me."

"Just tell me if you did it."

She looked out her darkened window.

"Caitlin." I maneuvered myself so I could see her face.

Tears sprang to her eyes. I reached forward, setting my hand on the bed. Not touching her—just getting closer. I thought about my mother's touch. How I'd longed for it, at Caitlin's age. How I longed for it now, at age forty.

"Be honest," I said. "What happened?"

Caitlin wiped the tears streaming down her cheeks. "I told some kids the code, okay? I didn't think they'd do anything with it." She faced away from me. "I actually don't think they *did* do anything with it. When I asked them about it after the break-in, they said they'd told some other people...who might have told some other people." Her shoulders lifted into a shrug. "And so on."

"Caitlin. Why would you tell *anyone*?"

She looked at her knees. "Because I wanted them to like me. I thought..." She scrunched down on the bed. "I don't know what I thought."

I attempted to keep my voice gentle. "Was this before or after the boyfriend came into the picture?"

She didn't lift her head. "He has nothing to do with it."

"Okay." I rubbed my cheeks. "But I expressly forbid you from seeing a boy we haven't met. If you want to continue seeing him, you need to bring him home to meet us."

She shrugged again. "Fine. I'll break up with him. I don't like him that much anyway."

My eyes narrowed and I gritted my teeth. "You know what? You're grounded."

She laughed. "For what?"

"For everything," I stood. "For trying to steal from Grandpa. For telling your friends the code at Zoe's. For *not* telling us you have a boyfriend." My mind replayed the disastrous scene in the principal's office. "For letting Austin get to the knife I gave you."

"He found it?" She sat up. "I'm so sorry, Mom. I misplaced it, and I felt terrible." Her chin trembled. "Oh, my God. I'm so, *so* sorry."

I'd anticipated anger, a few choice words thrown my way. The last thing I'd expected was an apology. Still, when I tried reaching for her, she recoiled.

"I'm sorry about the knife," she repeated. "But can I be alone now, please?"

I paused, unsure what else to say, what to do. Then I nodded and left the room.

In the darkened living room, I sat on the couch, arms wrapped around my knees. Why did I have so much trouble understanding my own daughter? Who *was* this girl?

My mind went to that long-ago night at Zoe's, the night of the Prince concert. Recalling that time, my emotions hurled like pinballs against the recesses of my mind. I felt regret, yes—for being naïve. And rage at Carey, certainly, for taking advantage of his power over me.

Beyond that, I also felt sorrow for the girl I was. The fifteen-year-old who would never get back what she gave away so easily.

My whole life, there'd been sadness in knowing that if my mother had been alive, it's unlikely—nearly impossible—that night would have happened the way it did. In a different world, one in which my mother didn't die, maybe I *would* have gone to the Prince concert with goofy Scott Eames and some other kids from school. Maybe Carey would have simply been the older brother who gave us a ride.

Perhaps I would have, at some point, dated Scott. Maybe my first sexual experience would have been with Scott, not Carey. Some fumbling episode in Scott's bedroom or mine, neither of us having the slightest idea what we were doing other than giggling, exploring, and hoping we wouldn't get caught.

Certainly, had my mother been alive, the repercussions of that night—which went far beyond losing my virginity—would never have occurred.

35

1979

After the Prince concert, after what followed at Zoe's—afterward, Carey and I lay together wrapped in a blanket he'd brought inside, pulled from the trunk of his dad's car.

"You okay?" He frowned. "I didn't hurt you, did I?"

"No," I said. "It didn't hurt. Not much, anyway."

He tightened his arms around me. "Look, Suzanne. That was beautiful. You're beautiful. In my eyes, you're beautiful."

Waiting for him to continue, I glanced toward Zoe. She seemed to be waiting, too.

"But I can't make any promises," Carey said. "I don't know what happens...when people like you and me get together." He took a breath, then added, "You know?"

I *didn't* know. Was this his way of saying it would never happen again? I wasn't going to let go that easily, but desperation would make things worse. *Play it cool*, I imagined Laurie advising me.

"I don't need promises, Carey." I kissed him. "All I need is to know that this, right here, is perfect."

He buried his face against my neck. "I feel so close to you right now. I wish I never had to take you home."

"I'd love nothing more than that—to stay with you." My mouth tightened. "And to *never* have to go home."

He raised his head, taking my chin in his hand and turning my face toward his. "Suzanne. Is everything all right...at home?"

I didn't reply. Beneath the blanket, I clenched one hand in the other.

"Suzanne, if anything is going on, I can help. You can trust me."

I stared at his gorgeous face. The way his eyes held mine in the darkness, illuminated only by the streetlights on Colfax.

I'd permitted Carey inside my body. If that didn't imply trust, what did?

And so, in a rush, I explained everything I wanted him to know. I didn't tell him about Mom-not-Mom or any other spirits. I did not reveal how Laurie taught me to fix myself up. But I told Carey about Dad and Peggy. I told him what I'd learned about Peggy since then.

He sat up, pulling me next to him. "I have to tell you something. I think I saw Peggy here a few times." He grimaced. "She and Alex...there was definite animosity between them. Alex tried to be gracious, but you could tell Peggy got under her skin."

My hands felt as if I'd plunged them into ice water. "What did Peggy say to my mom?"

"It was as if she were...I don't know, making fun of Alex. She'd say things like, 'Well, this place is quite the little hovel. What a shame Jimmy's money paid for it.'" Carey looked at me. "Jimmy...is that your dad?"

"Yeah. No one calls him that except Peggy." I wrapped my arms around my knees. "Do you think you could you identify her?"

"Absolutely."

I began pulling on my clothes. "I need to go home and come up with a plan." Hooking my bra, I said, "If I tell my dad all this, will you back me up?"

Carey hesitated. "If you tell your dad all this, how will you explain why we came to talk about it?" He stood, zipping his jeans. "How will you explain...us?"

"No idea," I said. "But I'll think of something."

At home, I composed a list:

<u>What We Know About Peggy</u>
- Tutored Bobby Shelton—Mom's murderer

- Told Shelton about Zoe's

- Told Shelton that Mom was in the shop alone on Thurs and Fri nights & had cash in the store

- Knew the above because she went to Zoe's multiple times

- Is on tape saying she didn't think Dad should get back together with Mom

- Was witnessed by a Zoe's customer harassing Mom multiple times

- In front of the witness, called Zoe's a "hovel" and said it was a shame Dad's money paid for it

I pondered the final two points. When Dad asked for details, what would I say?

The next evening, I showed my list to him. Seated at his desk, he scanned the page.

"Suze," Dad said. "We've had enough of this. Respectfully, I direct you to cease and desist."

"I am *not* ceasing and desisting." I tapped the paper. "There's a witness. There's more than what was on the tape."

He eyed me. "Who is this witness?"

I squirmed. "It's Carey. The guy who drove us to the concert last night. Turns out he knew Zoe's. He saw Peggy there, talking to Mom. He said…" My hands balled into fists. "Well, it's there on the page."

"I fail to understand how this arose during concert conversation." Dad crossed his arms. "You got home rather late. Where did you go after the show?"

"Nowhere." I looked away.

"Suze."

I forced myself to look directly at him. Eye contact, like my mother taught me.

Exactly, Suzie Blue.

"Just to hang out at Scott and Carey's house," I said.

He handed the paper back to me. "I'd like to meet Scott. And their parents."

"Um, actually, it wasn't their house. It was someone else's."

He regarded me. "Suzanne, were you drinking? Or smoking grass?"

I almost laughed. "We don't call it grass. We call it pot or weed. And no, I wasn't smoking pot or drinking."

Dad leaned back in his chair. "All of this is decidedly dubious."

"It's not the least bit dubious."

He stood. "Must we do this again? Have a conversation with Peggy?"

I nodded.

Peggy was seated at the kitchen table, a calendar in front of her. "I've been looking at dates, Jimmy," she said when we walked in. "It gets difficult as we get into traditional wedding season. Things are booked up." She laughed lightly. "I've *been* a June bride. I don't need to do that again. If we don't reserve something for early spring, we might have to wait until fall."

"Peggy." Dad poured scotch, then sat beside her. "Please recall that we're not setting a date. Not now."

"Oh, I know that! I'm just throwing ideas out there."

I crossed the kitchen, standing in front of her. "We have something to show you." I handed her the list.

After scanning it, she met Dad's eyes. "Jimmy," she whispered.

"You are not obliged to offer an extended explanation," he told her. "I just want to know—is this true? *Were* you harassing Alex?"

Her laughter was high-pitched. "I'd hardly describe it that way."

"My witness would," I said. "He heard how you talked to her."

"Peggy, what was the situation? What did you do?" Dad put a hand on hers. "And did it, somehow, lead to Alex's death?"

Her eyes were stony. "That was an accident. It was *not* meant to happen that way."

My knees buckled. I reached for the table, gripping the edge.

Dad removed his hand from hers. "What way?"

Peggy rose, crossing the kitchen. She stood at the sink, her back to us.

Finally, she turned. "Here's the God's honest truth, Jimmy. I did *not* tell Bobby to shoot her. I would never have instructed anyone to do such a thing."

My throat tightened. I longed for the kitchen ghosts, but they were absent.

Dad's eyes widened. "What *did* you instruct him to do?" he asked.

Peggy tapped her fingernails on the counter. "I told him to scare her, all right? I said go there and shake her up a bit." Her lips were flat. "I just wanted to rattle her. She was so damn smug, Jimmy."

Bitch, Mom-not-Mom said. *What an absolute bitch!*

"She had it all," Peggy railed. "She had you, Jimmy. She had Christopher. And she got to keep her daughter. She got to keep the daughter she had with you." Peggy glanced at me, then looked back at Dad. "*I* didn't get to keep *my* daughter. *Our* daughter."

Dad stood. "She wasn't my baby, Peggy. Last summer, you stated unequivocally that she wasn't mine."

"Dad?" I said. "What the hell is she talking about?"

Her eyes narrow, Peggy looked at me. "Every day, I'm forced to see Alex all over again, through this girl. Every day, I'm reminded of what I was denied." She wiped tears from her cheeks. "That is my penance. That's my penance for getting Bobby to do what he did."

"Peggy." Dad's voice was hoarse. "How *did* you get him to do what he did?"

She didn't say anything.

"Peggy, how?" Dad pressed.

"I paid him!" Peggy cried. "I gave him fifty dollars to give Alex a good fright. That's *all*." Her chin trembled. "I never thought it would turn out the way it did."

"Why the hell not?" I screamed. "He was a junkie!"

Peggy's shoulders shook. "He was trying to get clean," she whispered.

I marched across the room and slapped her face. Putting a palm to her cheek, she gave me an icy stare.

"Suzanne," Dad said. "Please go. I'll handle this."

"We need to call the cops." I reached for the kitchen phone. "She's an accessory to a crime."

"We'll do nothing hasty." Dad took the receiver from my hand and hung it up.

My ears were pounding, my pulse racing. I lunged for the phone. "Jesus Christ, Dad—we need to *do* something!"

Dad took me by both elbows. "Go upstairs and stay there."

"No!" I whipped my head around, staring at Peggy's white face.

"*Yes*, Suzanne," Dad said.

He dragged me across the room. The phone cord stretched until I was forced to let the receiver go. I heard the dial tone, like a warning siren, as my father pulled me from the room.

Upstairs, Dad said, "Stay here. I'll return momentarily." He pressed me into a seated position on my bed. "Don't move."

After he left, I sprang up—just as Mom-not-Mom appeared.

"Did you know?" I whispered. "Did you know Peggy paid Shelton to go to Zoe's?"

"No," she said. "I figured she had an agenda, a scheme of some sort. But I had no idea it was so heinous."

"What's this about a baby?" I asked.

"Dad told me after I met her at the reunion," Mom said. "Peggy got pregnant during their freshman year of college, after they broke up. They saw each other over Christmas break, but your dad said..."

"That the baby wasn't his," I finished. "Did she give it up for adoption?"

"She did."

I sank onto the floor in my circular space. Hunched over, I let heaving sobs escape my throat. Mom-not-Mom's feathery touch floated onto my back.

"I wish I could change things," she said. "I wish I could..." She trailed off.

I looked up. "Wish you could what?"

"I don't know," she choked. "Not keep Zoe's open late. Or I wish I'd left your dad, let Peggy have him. Who cares? It cost me you and Chris." Her voice quivered. "It cost me everything."

I half-rose. "I'll tell the police. I can call them from the phone in your bedroom. Peggy should be in jail."

"That wouldn't change anything," Mom-not-Mom said. "It wouldn't give me my life back."

I dropped back onto the floor next to her. "But it would be justice."

"Suzie Blue, don't go against your dad. Wait and see what he does. Chris needs you. If you and Dad have a rift..."

"A rift? A *rift*? He wants to *marry* the woman who's responsible for your death."

"He won't marry her now," Mom-not-Mom said. "I guarantee it."

Soon afterward, I heard Dad knock on my door. As he opened it, Mom-not-Mom vanished.

He lowered his lanky frame onto the floor next to me. "Peggy is gone," he said, slumping against the wall. "I told her our relationship is over." He met my eye. "And I am truly, truly sorry, Suzanne."

I flexed my twitching fingers. "She should go to jail." A vision of Peggy in an orange jumpsuit filled my head.

"She knows she made an appalling error," Dad said. "She'll live with that for the remainder of her life."

"It's not fair." I thrust my fist into the face of a teddy bear, crushing its insipid smile. "She wanted it all, no matter the cost."

Dad stared at the bear in my lap. "I don't believe it's that basic, Suze. I think she considered her actions—after Mom was gone, I mean—to be honorable. She abhors the notion of Chris growing up motherless. Especially after..."

I threw down the bear and hugged a pillow to my chest. "She had a baby in college, huh?"

Dad nodded. "She wanted to wed, but we were so young, and we weren't even together anymore. I believed the baby wasn't mine. It couldn't be. We only saw each other once over winter break...we sneaked into the clock tower at East. It was a simple shenanigan, nothing more."

I nodded. The clock tower was still an infamous make-out spot.

Dad's face reddened. "But we didn't...well, we mostly didn't..."

I waved my hand. "Spare me the details. So she decided to give the baby up for adoption?"

"I encouraged that, especially because of my excellent experience as an adoptee. Peggy's child, too, deserved a stable home." He blinked. "Peggy stayed with distant relatives during the pregnancy. After the baby was born, the relatives adopted her. They stipulated that Peggy have no further contact with the child." He looked at me. "That's how it was done back then. It's right, really. It's confusing for a child to have two families." He fiddled with his collar. "When I was a child, I never wanted two families."

"So Peggy never saw her daughter again?"

Dad shook his head. "Last summer, she told me that the child, as far as she knew, had grown up well. She said after all this time, she could admit the baby wasn't mine. She claimed the situation was water under the bridge. Meanwhile, Chris needed a mother. And so..."

"And so nothing," I said. "That's not enough reason to marry someone."

"You are correct." He looked at the twinkling lights on my ceiling, then back at me. "Tomorrow, I'll have my assistant research nanny services. Chris will *not* become your responsibility." Dad shifted closer to me. "It's preferable that we tell Chris none of this, Suzanne. We need only say that Peggy left and won't return. Your brother, at age six..." He bit his lip. "At age six, a boy needs no additional anguish."

"What if Chris wants more of an explanation?"

"We'll ensure that he doesn't. I'll find the right person to care for Chris. If I have to search the city high and low, I'll find that individual. Someone compassionate and capable." He grimaced. "But someone who does *not* want to marry me."

Dad stood. Taking my hand, he pulled me up next to him. "You're becoming so tall," he said hoarsely. "Each passing day, you resemble your mother more."

I withdrew my hand from his.

"Suzanne," he said. "I completely comprehend that it will take time to repair our relationship. But can we try?"

I considered what Mom-not-Mom had said—that a rift between Dad and me would further damage Chris.

"I don't know," I replied. "You're right. I need time."

36

2004

The following Tuesday, during a late morning lull at Zoe's, I locked up and headed to Claranna's house. After what I'd learned from Mrs. Dawson, I *had* to try again.

"I told you not to come back," Claranna said, opening the door a crack.

"Please talk with me," I said. "I visited your old neighbor, Mrs. Dawson."

Claranna began shutting the door. I put my hand on it. "I know what it's like to lose a mother," I said. "Mine died when I was fourteen."

"I'm sorry to hear that," Claranna said, through two inches of opened door. "Did she, by chance, burn down the house and try to kill you and your brother?"

My mouth went dry. "No."

"Then we have nothing to discuss."

Desperately, I said, "Mrs. Dawson told me some things...about James..."

I kept my eyes on Claranna's. After a moment, she widened the opening. "What did she tell you about James?"

I explained what Mrs. Dawson had said about James being "off"—and her suspicion that he lit the fire. "Claranna, I need to know if what she said is true. It's for my son. He's—" My fingers felt cold. "He's only nine, and he has behavioral problems. And I worry..."

She stared at me for a moment, then opened the door and motioned me inside.

Claranna didn't invite me to sit. Standing by the front door, I shuffled my feet and clasped my hands in front of me. Claranna's arms were crossed over her chest.

"What's this about your son?" she asked.

I lifted both hands. "He's quirky. And challenging. We're trying to get him help, but at the same time I wonder if there's a genetic component. That's what started me researching my dad's past."

"Does James know you're doing this?"

"He has no idea. I won't tell him if you don't want me to."

She paused. "Here's the truth. My mother was in and out of a mental ward for half a decade. She did crazy stuff. Spending the day canning, then smashing all the jars on the kitchen floor, leaving it for me to clean up. Ripping my father's photo into shreds when he forgot to bring home a book she'd asked him to pick up at the library." Claranna bit her lip. "Hitting me when she was mad. Hitting James."

"Why didn't your father stop her?" I whispered.

"I think he was scared of her. She was a force." Claranna looked toward the ceiling, then back at me. "Before they married, she'd been in college—the first female in her family to work toward a post-high school degree. Instead of finishing, she married and had me. She'd hoped to go back eventually, but then she had James. I was little but I remember her talking about her education—a lot." Claranna pressed her lips together. "Her slide happened after James was born."

"Why?"

"James was a handful," Claranna said. "Impulsive, naughty. Talked nonstop. We never knew what he was going to say or do next."

"Did he ever receive a diagnosis of any kind?"

She shook her head. "The doctor said James would outgrow his peculiarities. He said Mother was schizophrenic, and it came from having James." She sat in an armchair, motioning me toward the couch. "Back then, they used the term schizophrenia for pretty much all mental health conditions. Now they'd probably say she had postpartum depression that never really went away. She had good days, sometimes. But the day of the fire...that wasn't a good day."

"So she *did* light the fire," I said, sighing with relief. "Not James."

Claranna took a long breath. "She tossed kerosene all over the furniture and walls. She said the words I told the police she said. She lit a match." Claranna's indigo eyes stared into mine. "Then she handed the match to James and he threw it onto the couch."

My mouth fell open. "Why would she do that?"

"I think she was toying with him. She wanted validation, I think, for her own actions."

"But he was only six!"

"He was only six. And I wasn't going to let him die that way. I took him and ran outside." Claranna closed her eyes, then opened them. "Afterward, my father swore me to secrecy. He claimed that James would be better off if he had no memory of what happened. He said if James went to another family or even grew up in an orphanage, he'd soon forget." She rose from her chair. "And that turned out to be true. Over the years, I saw James's picture in the society pages. Débutante balls. Charity fundraisers." She shrugged. "Money solves everything, right?"

"My grandmother really loved him," I said. "She died from Alzheimer's, but before that, she doted on him."

"Was he an only child?"

"They had a biological daughter, a few years older. My aunt died a couple of years ago." I took a breath. "My dad was—is—quirky. But not dangerous." I recalled the raging fire in Dad's fireplace on Thanksgiving. "Probably."

"Well, he got what he needed when he was still young," Claranna said. "And that's what I suggest for your son, too. Get him all the help you can."

"Can I see you again?" I asked. "Would you like to see James?"

She shook her head. "I have my own life. There's no place for him—or you—in it."

"Can I leave my number? In case you change your mind?"

Claranna regarded me. "Listen," she said. "I'm going to say this once and only once. I've given you more information—and more of my time—than most people in my position would." She squared her shoulders. "I owe you nothing. I owe James nothing. He might have been the one who was given up, but I think we can agree that he didn't exactly suffer, did he?"

"I—" Words escaped me. I shut my mouth.

"I want you to leave now." Claranna pointed at the door. "Get out of my house. Don't come back."

Claranna had been clear: she wouldn't give me anything else. Whenever we finally got in at Children's Hospital for Austin's eval, I'd let the clinician know there might be a history of mental illness on Dad's side, but because he was adopted, we knew nothing beyond that.

As it turned out, when I listened to the messages on my voicemail later that day, there was one from Children's. "We're calling to let you know that your child, Austin Archer, has reached the top of the list for an evaluation. Please call to schedule an appointment."

Relief showered over me. I scheduled the appointment, then called Brett at work to give him the good news. "Finally, we'll get answers," I said.

"That's great, honey," he replied.

"Can you come home for dinner tonight? To celebrate?"

"I wish I could. But we're so close here. If we let up on the momentum, we're screwed." Without missing a beat, he said, "I'm sorry, Suzanne. Another time."

What was I—a pestering, doddering old friend that he had to continually brush off? "Fine," I said. "I've got to go."

Austin's appointment was on Thursday. I had to take the entire day off, but Zoe's was slow—slower than we'd hoped to be during prime holiday shopping season. "It'll pick up," Renee assured me. "The ad runs again this week in *Westword* and the *Denver Daily News*. The weekend will be busy."

"I hope so." But I couldn't help worrying. Most of our seed money was Renee's, but if the shop failed, it was on me.

Mid-morning, I took Austin to Children's. It wasn't far from Zoe's or from home. They were building a new campus in the suburb of Aurora, but for now the hospital and its outpatient facilities were in the main medical area of town, north of Colfax and west of City Park.

In the waiting room, Austin was wiggly and asked numerous questions. "What will they do? What will they ask me? Why do they want to talk to me?" I answered as clearly as I could—attempting to convey the information he needed without frightening him.

"Austin Archer?" someone said from the doorway to the treatment area.

I got up. "Here we are."

Then I froze—gripping Austin's hand as the clinician crossed the waiting room to us.

She was probably in her forties. She had a good figure and impeccably coiffed auburn hair, cut in a perfect Dorothy Hamill haircut.

Her green eyes met mine. "I'm Dr. Patricia Morris," she said, holding out her hand. "I'll be conducting Austin's evaluation today."

I stared at that hand without taking it. Stared at the manicured fingernails.

Looking up, I met her eye. I tried to be cerebral. She didn't *really* look like Peggy. Just the same haircut and color, same green eyes. Same perfect nails. But her face was shaped differently. She had fuller lips and less pronounced cheekbones. She was, certainly, several inches shorter than Peggy.

She was not, I told myself, Peggy. She was Dr. Patricia Morris of The Children's Hospital. She was qualified to evaluate my son. She would provide Brett and me with answers.

To do so, she'd want to know everything about us. There would be endless questions for Austin and for me.

Then I'd be asked to leave the room. She would be alone with my son, likely for several hours.

Again my eyes traveled to her long fingers. I imagined them holding a knife. Imagined them holding a gun.

Behind us, an elevator dinged, echoing in the hallway. Grasping Austin's hand, I turned on my heels and practically ran for the open elevator door. "I'm sorry," I called as we stepped on. "We have to go."

37

1979

On Friday morning Dad told me he'd pick up Chris from school. He said he hoped to have a nanny in place by Monday. I had to give him credit for acting fast, even if I did still believe Peggy should be turned in to the police.

That afternoon at Zoe's, I waited ninety minutes and was about to give up and go home when Carey stepped inside. I was listening to Chaka Khan singing "I'm Every Woman." It was her first hit single without the band Rufus. Mom had loved the song, said Chaka Khan had an auspicious solo career ahead of her.

Carey nodded toward the boombox. "No Prince?"

"I don't think we carried his albums."

"He's not well known." Carey stepped closer. "But I'll bet that changes if he keeps playing shows like the other night." He jutted his chin toward the floor. "You wanna sit?"

I felt Zoe's eyes on us as we sat side by side on the floor, listening to the music. "What did you decide to do?" Carey asked. "About that Peggy lady."

When I told him what happened, he whistled. "Do you think she'll really stay away from your family?"

"I hope so." My eyes narrowed. "If she goes near my baby brother, I'll kill her."

"Suzanne." Carey patted my shoulder. It felt like something a friend or older brother would do. "No one your age should have to go through everything you've been through."

"Yeah, well…" I closed my eyes, then opened them. "Let's talk about something else." I glanced at the underside of Zoe's guitar. "You ever play?"

"A little, in high school. What guy doesn't want to be a rock and roll star? I saw myself as Keith Richards." He grinned. "But I wasn't very good. I like music, though. That's why I started coming here. It's how I got to know Alex."

I sat up straighter. "How come I never met you here?"

"What?" Carey leaned away from me.

I frowned. "You were never around Zoe's when I was. After school."

Carey didn't reply. I waited.

Finally, he said, "Alex told me her daughter worked with her after school. And that her young son was usually here, too." He took a breath. "The truth is, I didn't want to meet either of you."

"Why not?"

"Because if I had…I'd have had to face the fact that…"

He made a choking noise, as if something was caught in his throat. I prodded, "That what?"

"That Alex…had a life…" He shook his head. "We shouldn't talk about this."

The Zoe's space, always chilly these days, suddenly felt like the inside of a freezer. "That she had a life what?" I asked.

"Seriously, Suzanne. Drop it."

"No." I heard the harshness in my voice. "That she had a life—*what*?"

"That didn't include me." His voice was barely above a whisper.

I couldn't help smiling. For the first time, Carey—not me—seemed like a kid. Like someone who had to prove he was old enough to hang out with an adult. "So you had a crush on my *mom*?" I asked.

He didn't respond. My smile grew wider. "Come on. It wasn't some sort of Dustin Hoffman, Mrs. Robinson type of thing, was it? My mom loved *The Graduate*, by the way."

As soon as I said it, I knew. My smile faded.

"Yeah," Carey confirmed. "It was pretty much exactly that type of thing."

I shifted across the floor.

"Suzanne." He reached for me.

I pulled away. "Don't you fucking *touch* me!"

"That's why I said to drop it." He held up his hands.

"Screw that." I crossed my arms over my chest.

"It was only a few times. Honest to God."

"It shouldn't have been *any* times!" I pointed to the spot where fewer than forty-eight hours earlier, Carey and I had been naked together. "It was right here, wasn't it? What does that make me—a nostalgia lay? Your consolation prize because my mother is *dead*?"

"Oh, God, Suzanne. No." He stood, facing me. "It's not like that at all. Yes, I think you're beautiful because you remind me of her. You *are* beautiful because you're like her. You're like her on the outside—and on the inside, too. You're as warm as her, as generous, as smart..."

"Stop!" I whirled away. "I am not warm. I'm not generous. And I sure as hell don't feel very smart right now."

"Look, I'm sorry, okay?"

He took a step toward me. I held up my hand.

"Okay," he said. "I'll go. But Suzanne...I really did care about Alex. And I really, truly care about you."

"You *care* about me?" I cried. "You care—what? If my heart only hurts a little, or if it's shattered?"

He gave me a helpless look. "You said you were okay with no promises. Remember?"

"I remember a hell of a lot more than you." I pointed toward the door. "Get out."

He didn't look at me as he crossed the darkened space of Zoe's and walked out.

Chaka Khan sang on.

At home in my room, lying on my bed, I let the tears flow. "Mom?" I said aloud. "Why didn't you tell me?" I wiped my eyes. "And why didn't I see it for myself, before it was too late?"

I gave myself over to thinking about Mom and Carey. Not the act—I couldn't go there—just the idea of them. I pictured them sharing conversations, learning about each other. Did Carey connect with Mom in ways he couldn't connect with me? She'd been an adult, after all—and I knew that in many ways, Carey saw me as a child.

As for Mom, did she confide in Carey? Did she tell him things she'd never told me?

I felt Mom-not-Mom appear beside me. Behind her, the lights in my circular space glowed through her body. "You want me to apologize," she said.

"That'd be nice." Sharply, I asked, "Are we able to talk about this? Or are you going to disappear because it's not about *Peggy*?" The bitterness in my mouth stung, like eating something raw and unflavored.

"I don't know," she replied. After a moment, she added, "But I think it's important that we *try* talking about it, Suze."

I flipped over, facing the wall.

"Suzie Blue," Mom-not-Mom said. "I'm sorry about Carey. If I could have, I'd have prevented your involvement with him." She paused. "But I can't apologize for *me* being involved with Carey."

"Why not?"

"Because things like that happen when people reach the stage of life I was in. Especially people of my generation," she said. "Especially people like *me* of my generation."

"What does that mean?"

"Just that there's so much I missed out on," she said. "I could have gone to Woodstock. I could have danced barefoot with flowers in my hair during the Summer of Love. Could have dropped acid and partied all night. Instead I was up all night with my child when she spiked a fever. Instead of dancing barefoot in the rain, I was insisting you put on boots before I walked you to school."

I bit my lip. "Did you kick Dad out so you could be with Carey?"

"No. I met him after your dad moved out."

I turned. "Did you ever tell Dad?"

"No need to. What happened between Carey and me was…brief." I sensed the shadowy outline of a lifted hand, a single twinkling light piercing it. "Listen, Suze—Carey is too old for you, and he was too young for me. He made mistakes with both of us, especially you. But I don't think any of it was malicious."

"Somehow, that doesn't help."

"I'm sure it doesn't. I'm so sorry, Suze."

I wanted to be furious with her—but I couldn't be. I knew that if I tried to hug her, it would be like hugging air. Still, I reached forward, staring at my hand passing through the anemones on her chest.

Deep in the night, Chris entered my room. It had been months since he'd done that. His sleeping bag was still on my floor, shoved against the baseboards in my circular space.

"What's up, buddy?" I whispered as he crawled under my covers.

"I don't want to be alone," Chris said. "Our house feels lonely since Peggy left."

I wrapped my arms around him. "It'll be okay."

In the moonlight, his blue eyes glistened. "Why did she go away? She told me she loved me but she couldn't come to our house anymore. Why'd she *do* that?"

I ran my hand across his hair. "Sometimes people leave when we least expect them to. And there's nothing we can do...except carry on."

Chris burrowed his face into my neck. His skin against mine made the longing for my mother's touch almost intolerable.

Feeling his hot little tears on my neck, I blinked back my own. Knowing that while Chris and I didn't share the same loss, his sorrow and mine, like separate injuries on the same body, were equally unbearable.

38

2004

On Friday afternoon at Zoe's, my phone rang. It was Renee, and she was frantic.

"Donna's been in an accident," she said. "A hit-and-run while she was out walking."

I gripped the phone. "Is she all right?"

"I don't know." Renee's voice shook. "They took her to Rose Medical. I'm heading there as soon as possible, but I have to wait for my nanny—it's her day off. She's across town and it could take a while. And Evan is away on business." She took a breath. "Will you go, Suzanne? I'll meet you there when I can."

"Of course." I hung up and grabbed my purse. I turned the "Closed" sign in the window, set the alarm, and locked up.

On the way, I called Chris and recruited him to pick up Austin from school. When he heard what had happened, he said he'd keep Austin as long as I needed. Since Thanksgiving, Chris and I had been restrained with each other, and he seemed to welcome an opportunity to get past that.

I turned on the car radio. Chrissie Hynde's voice filled the car—"Brass in Pocket," the Pretenders' first hit, from December 1979.

"Brass in Pocket" was about feeling confident in yourself no matter what others thought. It had been years since I'd heard this song. And there'd been a time in my life when I couldn't listen to it at all, because of the memory it invoked.

I gripped the steering wheel. Perhaps, I decided, abruptly switching off the radio—perhaps that time was occurring still.

In the emergency room, when I told the admissions nurse that I was family—close enough, I figured—I learned Donna was in surgery. "The surgeon will have more information later," the nurse said.

"Any idea what happened?" I asked.

He read something on his computer screen. "A hit-and-run on Eighth Avenue near Cheesman Park."

I nodded. "She lives around there. Any witnesses?"

"Several people saw the accident," he said. "They assisted Ms. Tomlinson and called 911, but I don't think anyone got a license plate. The police would know more, ma'am." He wrote a number on a piece of paper and handed it to me. "You can request a report."

We'd had no precipitation lately—the streets were dry—so it was probably someone driving too fast. Eighth was a wide, one-way street, and people treated it like a freeway. Unsurprising that a jerk who'd go too fast would also flee the scene.

When Renee arrived, we sat side by side in the waiting room. "I can't believe this happened," Renee said. "She always uses the crosswalk. Always makes sure before she crosses that no asshole is driving too fast, ignoring the crosswalk."

"But they *do* drive too fast," I said. "And they *are* assholes."

An hour later, the surgeon appeared. "No internal injuries," he said. "But she's heavily bruised and has a broken arm, which we've set. Her hip is also broken, and I put in temporary screws. They'll hold as long as she doesn't move much. She'll need a full replacement at a later date. It will be a long road of rehabilitation, but it would've been much worse if her head hit the pavement."

"Can we see her?" Renee asked.

"She's groggy and likely won't know you're here, but go ahead."

I was alone for dinner. Caitlin had gone to the mall with girlfriends—too weary to fight with her and still rattled by her sincere apology about the misplaced knife, I'd failed to enforce her grounding for more than a few days. I called her to check in, and she said she'd be home by nine. Then I called Chris, who told me that he and Austin were eating burgers and he'd bring him home afterward.

As for Brett, he was with Nicole. I could think of it no other way than that they were *together*.

I took the refurbished Santoku with the honey-brown handle, the one I'd completed back in September, from the locked knife cabinet on the kitchen wall. Chopping vegetables, I admired the knife handle under the bright kitchen lights. Such a pretty color. The exact color of my mother's hair.

I made a stir fry, heated leftover rice, and poured myself a glass of wine. I ran upstairs for my current read—*The Kite Runner* by debut author Khaled Hosseini—and sat at the kitchen table with my dinner and book. It was an excellent novel, but I couldn't keep my mind on it.

The surgeon had been right; Donna hadn't known Renee and I were there. We sat with her for a while, then Renee said I should go. After promising to return the next morning before opening Zoe's, I'd headed out.

I was washing dishes when the front door burst open. "Take your shoes off!" I called, hearing Austin clomp down the hall. In the kitchen doorway, he wriggled out of his tennies. Chris came up behind him. I smiled at both of them. "Did you have fun?"

"We had awesome fun." Austin's eyes widened. "Did you know that Uncle Chris lives on the twenty-eighth floor?"

"I did," I replied. "But you're the first in the family to see his place, Austin. Lucky you!"

"I've been meaning to have you all over," Chris said. "We'll have to figure out a time."

"Sure," I said. "Thanks for taking him tonight. You're a lifesaver."

"How's Donna?"

"Stable." I stood. "Would you like a glass of wine? Or a beer?"

"I'll take a beer."

I grabbed one from the fridge and poured milk for Austin. No doubt he'd had soda at Chris's place.

"Uncle Chris's apartment is so cool," Austin said, sitting between Chris and me at the kitchen table.

"I'll bet." I sipped wine. "And the view is the best part, right?"

Austin shook his head. "No, the best part is the gun. Uncle Chris let me hold it and everything."

I set down my glass. "The what?"

"Gun," Austin repeated. "I guess it's a pistol. Right, Uncle Chris?"

"A revolver," Chris clarified. "Remember, that means the bullets are loaded into chambers in a revolving cylinder. A pistol uses a magazine to hold ammunition."

Chugging milk, Austin nodded. "Now I remember you said that."

Mouth open, I listened to this exchange. "What the hell is he talking about?" I asked Chris.

He turned to me. "Don't worry. It wasn't loaded. And it's an antique. A Remington from the eighteen-nineties. Dad bought it for me...a birthday present, a few years ago." He shrugged. "Austin wanted to hold it."

"Austin." My voice was low. "Put your cup in the dishwasher, then go play on the Wii."

He glanced at the clock on the microwave. "The rule is no Wii after eight o'clock."

Chris chuckled. "Don't look a gift horse in the mouth, pal."

Splashing milk everywhere, Austin set his cup right-side up in the dishwasher's top rack. "I don't know what that means, Uncle Chris, but I'm gonna go play Wii before Mommy changes her mind."

Chris laughed again. "That's exactly what it means. Go."

"What the actual fuck is going on?" I asked Chris after Austin left.

"He wanted to hold it. No bullets. No possibility of injury or accident. What's the problem?"

I finished my wine and poured another glass. "The problem, Christopher, is that your mother was *shot to death*. Or have you forgotten?" I took a long sip of wine. "I cannot believe you own a firearm. Or firearms. How many do you have?"

"Four," he replied. "The other three are for protection. They're stored safely. No worries."

I shook my head. "You're out of your mind."

He snorted. "You should talk. Which of us is the Knife Lady?"

I met his eye. "You clearly need a lesson in the difference between killing with a knife and killing with a gun."

He held up a hand. "Spare me, Suze."

"No." I slammed a fist into the table. "Do you know how much energy it takes to kill a human being? With a knife, every ounce of that energy has to come from the person wielding the weapon. With a gun, the energy is all in the bullet. With a knife—unless you're damn good at slicing and dicing arteries, *and* you're lucky enough that your victim doesn't raise an arm to defend themself—you've got several minutes of solid work ahead of you. And you better be damn strong and damn accurate." My mouth tightened. "But a gun? Seconds, Chris. Seconds!"

"You just proved my point." Chris crossed his arms. "Dad told me he always wanted Mom to learn to shoot. He thought she should keep a gun at Zoe's, but she refused."

"Guns are used for harm more often than good." My throat tightened. "Take suicide, for instance. How many gun-related suicides are there every year? Thousands, Chris."

"Committed by mentally unstable people. They shouldn't have guns anyway."

Instinctively, I reached down to stroke Stevie's ears—then felt again the pain of her absence. My fingers traveled to the back of my head, twining in my hair. I gave it a sharp pull to keep myself from thinking about blood spatters, about police.

"You truly think you could use a gun for protection?" I asked Chris. "How often does that work, anyway?"

"More often than you'd think. We've had holdups at the dealerships."

"And you went all Clint Eastwood on the thieves? Waved your gun around? Made the day?"

"No." He pursed his lips. "You're overreacting, as usual."

"And you're under-reacting." I gave him a steely look. "Thank you for taking Austin today. But please know, Chris—that was the last time it will ever happen."

He stared at me. Then he rose and, without another word, stalked down the hall. I heard him calling goodbye to Austin. Seconds later, my front door slammed so hard the entire house shook.

39

1979

I stepped off the front porch into a brisk Saturday afternoon. Dad had made arrangements for Chris to spend the night at Jeff's and had taken him there on his way to work. "I surmised that you could use space and time for yourself," Dad said to me before they left.

I'd nodded. Even if Dad was wrong about Peggy—she belonged in jail, and nothing would convince me otherwise—I felt gratified that my father was making an effort.

With nowhere to be, I walked west on Colfax, away from Zoe's. My eyes smarted when I thought about Mom and Carey, but I was angrier at him than her. How could I stay mad at someone who'd lost her life like Mom did?

In the distance, the mountains glistened, snow-covered from last week's storm. Fleetwood Mac's "Landslide"—a song my mother had loved—began playing in my head.

I recalled what she'd said about the choices she'd made. Maybe those choices were the reason for Zoe. Not Zoe's, but *Zoe*. When Mom dressed up that mannequin and gave her a guitar, was she creating an alter ego? Was Zoe the consolation prize Mom gave herself for everything she'd never had the opportunity to do? Follow bands around the country, hitching rides in some stoner's VW bus. Dance in flowing dresses like Stevie Nicks. Sleep with beautiful, romantic men—artists and musicians, the kind of men who must have filled my mother's daydreams.

But Mom's choices set her on a different path. Would she have made the same choices if she'd known she'd get fewer than forty years on this planet?

When I reached the State Capitol, I headed south, wandering down to Thirteenth before turning back east. At the corner of Thirteenth and Washington, I stopped. Wax Trax was there, another indie record store. I nearly walked away—then I stepped toward the door. I couldn't avoid record stores for the rest of my life.

Wax Trax was owned by two guys whose names I couldn't remember. The year before, they'd bought the store from its original owners. "Good guys, music lovers," Mom had said. "They'll do well."

Just weeks before Bobby Shelton killed Mom at Zoe's Records, Wax Trax had its own tragedy: a car crashed into their building. One of their workers had been pinned under the car but survived. When my mother mentioned it, she'd said, "Somehow, I feel much safer in cozy little Zoe's."

The walls of Wax Trax were covered in posters. Every inch of space contained bins full of albums. The music radiating from the speakers—lots of bass, lyrics that seemed to be shouted rather than sung—was louder than it was ever played in Zoe's.

I got it: different clientele. The majority of customers in Wax Trax were young guys. I recognized some kids from school, one or two of whom nodded at me.

I shuffled through a bin. Wax Trax carried lots of cutting-edge music. Underground, progressive, and something new called punk. I'd heard Laurie mention it. Many punk bands, it seemed, were from England.

"Can I help you find something?"

A guy stood nearby—not quite middle-aged and not quite bald, but getting there. He wore khakis and a blue button-down. He looked like he could've been a teacher at East.

"Just browsing," I said—loudly, over the music.

"Suit yourself." He turned away, then faced me. "Maybe I shouldn't say this, but you're the spitting image of a woman I used to know. Another record store owner."

I felt a knot in my belly. "Alex Parry, right? She was my mom."

He whistled. "Wow, kid. I'm sorry. What's your name?"

"Suzanne."

"I remember Alex had a couple of kids." He stepped closer, leaning in so we didn't have to shout. "Look, is there some record you want? On the house."

I shuffled my feet. "I'm not sure you have music I'd like. My mom and I had similar musical tastes."

"Alex had good taste," he said. "And she knew what her customers wanted. They loved her—with good reason. So did the artists whose work she promoted." He put a hand on the nearest bin. "But you know what? I'll bet we could find some common musical ground, Suzanne Parry."

In the end, he gave me a single by The Pretenders. I'd heard a few songs off their debut album, due out in early 1980. But I hadn't heard this one, though he told me it had released as a single a few weeks ago.

"It's called 'Brass in Pocket,'" I read off the label.

"It's about having balls," the guy said, then added quickly, "Sorry. It's about being gutsy. Knowing who you are." He shifted into a wider stance. "My prediction? The Pretenders are a bit pop for most of our customers, but I think they're gonna make it big. They're crossing musical genres—rock, punk, pop, new wave." He smiled. "And they're fronted by a woman—Chrissie Hynde. Your mom would have appreciated that."

I blinked. "She would've."

He placed a hand on my shoulder. "Stop in anytime, Suzanne. You're always welcome here."

"Brass in Pocket" tucked under my arm, I turned onto our street. I was thinking about the owner of Wax Trax, how kind he'd been. And about how even Dad had taken my feelings into consideration today. Maybe everything would be okay after all.

I noticed the porch swing chains first—briskly swaying, too fast to be caused by the mild afternoon breeze. Moving, instead, as if someone were on the swing.

Stepping onto the porch, I saw her lying there. One foot on the concrete floor, pushing back and forth, rocking herself in the swing like a baby.

Sitting up, Peggy met my eye, then darted her gaze sideways. "Suzanne. You're here."

"Get off our porch," I said. "Dad told you not to come back."

She placed her feet side by side on the floor. "I came to see you. I knew you'd be alone."

"How the hell did you know that?"

"Chris told me he was spending the day and sleeping over at Jeff's."

I narrowed my eyes. "*Chris* told you? When?"

"At school," she said. "I talked to him yesterday on the playground." She held up both hands. "I had to see him, Suzanne. I *had* to."

"You're crazy. Get the hell out of here."

"Sweet boy," she murmured. "Sweet Christopher."

I gripped my record—wishing it was a weapon, something I could use to defend myself. Crazily, my mind darted to Laurie's bat upstairs in my room, useless to me now. "Go away, or I'm calling the police."

Peggy patted the swing. "Talk to me for a minute." Her face took on a flushed, reddish tone. "A minute of your time, Suzanne."

I took a single step toward her, then crossed my arms. Pretenders 45 pressed to my chest, I stared her down.

"I want to apologize," she said. "I'm just asking for forgiveness."

I felt my jaw tighten. "Why? Whether I forgive you or not, my mother is still dead, Peggy."

She lowered her head into her hands. After a moment, she looked up. "Mine, too," she said. "My mother died last night."

I blinked. "What do you want me to say? That I'm sorry for your loss? Fine. I'm sorry for your loss."

"I've lost everything. Everyone. I lost my baby girl." Tears streamed down her cheeks. "I wasn't allowed to keep her, did you know that? I *wanted* to. I waited out my pregnancy, staying with my father's second cousin. When the baby was born, I said I'd changed my mind. The cousin said—" Peggy swallowed. "She said I'd have to pay her back for everything. My living and travel expenses, doctor's bills, hospital bill. I couldn't keep the baby unless I paid." She shook her head. "I didn't have that kind of money. Neither did my mother. So I signed the papers. They stipulated that I never see my daughter again." She wiped away tears. "For years, I wrote to her. But she never wrote back. Likely she wasn't permitted to see my letters."

"That's sad," I conceded. "But it has nothing to do with me or my family."

"It has everything to do with you. When I met you...and when I met Alex..." She clasped her hands together. "It wasn't fair, Suzanne."

"Fuck you," I said. "Don't talk to me about *fair*. My mother is dead because of you, Peggy."

"And all I want is forgiveness."

"Forget it!" I screamed. "What you did is unforgivable."

On the sidewalk, a man passed, walking a dog. Hearing my raised voice, he looked up.

"This woman is trespassing," I yelled. "Will you call the police for me?"

Behind Peggy's head, I saw Laurie step onto her porch. "Call the police," I repeated to the man. Then I shouted, "Or you do it, Laurie! Call the cops!" I pointed at Peggy. "And when they get here, I'm telling them everything."

She stared at me. Slowly, she breathed in and out. Once, twice, three times.

"No need for that," she said.

She reached into her purse and pulled out her gun, pointing it at me. I screamed, scrambling toward the other side of the porch. I covered my chest with "Brass in Pocket," as if it were a shield.

Mommy, Mommy, I thought—I'm going to die!

No, you're not, Suzie Blue.

Cowering, I looked up. On the swing opposite me, Peggy was alone. There was no one else there. No one except Peggy, aiming her gun at me.

Then—abruptly, as if forced by an invisible hand—Peggy turned the gun away from me and inserted it into her mouth.

It went off. Just once, a single shot. I screamed again, ducking my head.

When I looked up, Peggy was splayed on our rattling porch swing, arms and legs dangling.

And the back half of her head was gone.

40

2004

They're everywhere.

At seventeen I left home, trying to forge a new life where they couldn't follow me. But I couldn't make them go away. I told myself that if I sensed one but did not acknowledge the bullet holes, eventually the sensing would cease. Over time, I would stop feeling the ghosts of people killed with a gun.

They are the only spirits I sense. There are so many ways to die, and so many people who die before their time. But ever since my mother's death, only those who die via gunshot present themselves to me.

There's no explanation for it. No reason why I'd know there was a man in an empty seat on the BART with a marble-sized bullet hole perfectly centered on his forehead. Or I'd feel a woman moving through a grocery store parking lot in Mountain View, anemones like my mother's blazoned across her chest. Or that an awful, unforgettable day would occur, a day when I sensed the presence of a toddler, tears streaming down her face—accidentally shot, I knew, by her sibling.

It was only after Peggy's death that I made the connection. Afterward—every day since—I've expected her. Expected to be haunted by her half-blown-off head, her curvaceous figure that my dad found so appealing. Her hands, those perfect fingernails that used to reach out and stroke my baby brother's cheek.

Constantly, I look over my shoulder. I got a dog because I needed a steadfast, living being beside me day and night. I always carry a knife—knowing it won't matter, won't help if Peggy appears—nonetheless reassured by the knowledge of it in my purse, the feel of it in my hand.

To this day, I cannot fathom Peggy's intentions. Was she going to kill me, then herself? Or did she think she could kill me, then escape? And somehow, in her unhinged mind, did Peggy believe that without me in the picture she could reclaim Dad and Chris?

Whatever her plans, something changed the course of Peggy's actions. Some force.

Was it my mother? I have no idea.

Learning that Chris owned firearms surprised me, but perhaps it shouldn't have. I knew so little about my brother. The days when I'd been his protector passed long ago.

After Peggy killed herself on our porch—after the police arrived, while I sat in Laurie's living room, sandwiched between her mother and a white-faced Laurie, after my dad got home, after the questioning—long after all that, when it was only Dad, me, and the spirits in my mother's house, he sat me down in the library. The room was lit by a single lamp, and in the corner I sensed the kitchen ghosts. For the first time ever, Mom-not-Mom joined them.

"I'm sorry you went through that." Dad took my hand. "Suzanne, I find myself at a loss for words other than 'I'm sorry.'"

My hand, in his, was limp.

"*Sorry* changes nothing," he went on. "I understand that. Nonetheless, I'm certain of this: your brother is never to know. Losing a mother figure so soon after your mom died—and learning it happened in such a macabre manner—would devastate someone his age." Dad squeezed my hand. "I can't eliminate your pain, Suze. But together, we can spare Christopher."

"He's right, Suzie Blue," I heard Mom-not-Mom say. "Chris is never to know."

I felt the other spirits nodding. Mom-not-Mom's words, her presence, the others' affirmation—these convinced me to acquiesce.

Later, through the halfhearted attempts at therapy that Dad put me in (I never told the therapists a thing), through his meeting and marrying a woman named Linda—my stepmother, a perfectly nice, nearing-retirement fifth-grade teacher with her own adult children—through all that, I revealed none of this to Chris. I never told him our house was haunted and one of the spirits was our mother.

And I never told him what happened to Peggy. Her death wasn't sensationalized; perhaps it would've been if the connection between her and Bobby Shelton was common knowledge, but few people knew about that. Dad and me. Carey. Laurie, if she remembered. Rosalie, who'd likely skipped town. Milo, if he was alive and if he'd known what Peggy asked of Bobby—which, given how evasive Milo had been, perhaps he had.

Peggy's death, while gruesome, was nothing more than a blip on Denver's radar the first weekend in December 1979. Still, for anyone capable of conducting basic research, Peggy's obituary likely could be unearthed. I don't know what it said—if it mentioned suicide, mentioned my family. I've never looked it up.

Throughout the years, I've asked myself why I never told Chris what happened. When he was little, I wanted to protect him, as our mother requested. So I maintained the fiction that Dad composed for Chris. Mom was killed in a random hold-up at her store. Peggy, for reasons of her own, broke ties with our family and was never heard from again.

Only once did I come close to telling Chris the truth. It was shortly after Austin was born, and Chris was visiting, one of the few times he came to California. My brother was, surprisingly, great with the baby. I remember being in the nursery at dusk one evening, Chris in the rocker and Austin, in a rare period of calm, sleeping in his uncle's arms. They looked so sweet together, and in that moment, I felt closer to my brother than I had in years. I wouldn't have broken the spell, but throughout the rest of Chris's three-day visit, I considered it.

But by the time I dropped him at the airport, I'd changed my mind. Why risk reopening Chris's wounds?

That is the fiber of information. Once you know something, you can never *un-know* it. And once you know something, you must determine what to do with what you've learned. I didn't want to put Chris through that. All these years later, I still wanted to spare my baby brother.

I kept Zoe's regular hours that weekend, spending most of my free time at Donna's bedside. She was on painkillers and mostly slept while I held her hand.

Reading the incident report gave me pause. Two eyewitnesses claimed the driver had come out of nowhere and drove onto the side-walk to hit Donna. The driver was going unbelievably fast for a residential street, and nobody caught a license plate.

Why would someone veer onto the sidewalk? Was it targeted? Were they after Donna specifically?

Was it Shelton Jr.? What if he'd figured out Donna's connection with my family? Was this some sort of twisted revenge for the way his father died?

It was a relief to begin a fresh week. I was uncertain what to do about Austin's evaluation. I'd looked up Dr. Morris online but found no personal information about her. When I called Children's to apologize and ask for another eval appointment—preferably with another provider—I was told that with the wait list so long, they'd try to get us in when they could, but there were no guarantees of when, nor could they guarantee which doctor would do the evaluation.

Admitting to Brett that I'd run out of the waiting room at Children's invoked his frustration, if not downright fury—especially because when he asked why, I had no answer. His exasperation was understandable, yet I couldn't help feeling I'd done the right thing.

On Tuesday, while I was rearranging a display of local musicians' CDs, trying to bring some of the less-recognized artists' work to the forefront, Chris walked in. He hadn't been to Zoe's since our grand opening, the magical evening that was less than five weeks prior but felt like months ago.

"Looks good in here, Suze," he said. "You've done a great job with the displays."

I faced him. "It would be a better job if we weren't in the red."

He didn't respond. I got the sense that Chris, like Dad, found my endeavor frivolous. Uncomfortably, I had to wonder if they were right.

"Do you have a minute to talk?" he asked.

Nodding, I walked to the counter. I glanced at the corner where Chris had hung out when we were kids. Mom had set up a play area for him with blocks, trucks, and other toys. Customers' kids had played there, too. I'd considered doing something similar, but with so much fragile stock—the glassware and pottery items we carried were sheer perfection—it seemed risky. Now that area contained a display of mosaics—mirrors, picture frames, vases.

I jutted my chin toward the corner. "Remember playing there when you were small?"

"Sort of." He shrugged. "I was so little, Suzanne. You seem to forget that."

"I don't forget it." From below the counter, I retrieved a bottle of glass cleaner and a paper towel. I began polishing a mirrored tray on the counter.

"I came to apologize," Chris said. "I'm sorry about letting Austin hold my gun. It's in a display case in my living room, but I can put it away when he comes over."

I regarded him. "The damage is done, Chris. He won't forget about it." Since Friday night, Austin had brought up the gun repeatedly, until I finally snapped and said I'd heard all I ever wanted to hear about Uncle Chris's antique revolver.

"I still don't understand what's the big deal," Chris said. "This is the world we live in, Suzanne. There are guns. There's violence. Austin sees it every day in video games."

"Not the ones I let him play."

"Well, he's going to get older, and he'll want to play others. You can't control him forever."

"I can control him for as long as I can control him, though." I continued polishing the mirror, although it sparkled in the reflection of a nearby lamp.

Chris's mouth tightened into a thin line. "We'll have to agree to disagree about this one."

A customer came in. I welcomed her, asking if she needed help finding anything. "Just browsing," she said.

"Any questions, feel free to ask." Lowering my voice, I turned back to Chris. "Thank you for the apology. Austin is still not allowed in your apartment. I don't know about you taking him other places. I worry, Chris."

"No shocker there," he said. "You've always worried. But you worry about the wrong things."

I felt my eyebrows knit together. "What does that mean?"

He leaned on the counter. "Look, I'm no psychologist. I'm not a parent. But Austin seems to be a regular kid. A bit hyper but basically not so different from other kids." Before I could reply, he said, "It's Caitlin who's messed up."

I took a breath. "How, exactly, in your unprofessional, non-parental view, is Caitlin messed up?"

"She's a thief. She was trying to steal money from Dad." He pressed his fingers onto the counter. "Do you truly believe that's the first time she's stolen anything? Do you believe that bullshit story about a fundraiser?"

"I'm dealing with her," I said.

"You are *not* dealing with her," he countered. "Until you make her confess to Dad what she did, you most certainly are not dealing with her."

"And what good would that do?" I shot back—my voice a hiss, hoping the customer would continue ignoring us. "Caitlin didn't take the money. There's no reason for Dad to know."

"Honesty is the best policy, Suzanne. Dad has always said that."

"Oh, for God's sake!" I slammed the glass cleaner bottle onto the counter, the sound reverberating throughout the store. The woman looked up, waved one hand, and scurried out.

As the customer left, Daphne—the singer with the gorgeous, soulful voice—walked in, joined by Tori, the artist who did abstracts. Since meeting at Zoe's grand opening, Tori and Daphne had become friends. Today they'd invited me to join them for lunch.

I made the introductions, then said to the artists, "Just give me a minute."

"Take your time, Suzanne," Daphne said. "We'll just browse." Side by side, they turned to examine the displays.

My voice low, I said, "Chris, I think we're done here. There's nothing more to say."

"I don't want us to fight, Suze. So before I go, please tell me: what's got you so riled up? Especially when it comes to Dad. I don't get it." He shrugged. "Dad's just Dad. He does the best job he can."

I felt my face flush. "You always defend him. But he's far from perfect, Christopher. And he is far, far from honest."

"What the hell does *that* mean?"

"Dad's got his secrets."

"Like what?" Chris asked. "Dad is as honorable as the day is long. And I'm tired, Suzanne—so tired—of you maligning him."

That made me furious. "He never told you about Peggy!" I blurted. "And he wouldn't let me tell you, either."

Daphne and Tori pretended not to hear.

Chris held up his hands. "What the hell are you talking about? What didn't you and Dad tell me about her? About...Peggy?"

Saying her name, he enveloped his voice in softness. Although he must have some memories of Mom, and although our stepmother, Linda, had always treated Chris lovingly, I could tell by the way Chris spoke that he'd never forgotten Peggy.

He talked of Peggy with more affection than he did Linda. Than he did our own mother.

"Peggy was responsible for Mom's death," I snarled. "She paid a man fifty dollars—*fifty* lousy dollars, Chris—to come here, stand where you are on the other side of this counter, and threaten Mom." I pressed my fingers against my chest. "Things got out of hand...and you know the rest."

"Oh, my God." Chris stumbled back from the counter. His face was white.

"There's more." I planted my feet wide. "After Peggy confessed, Dad told her to never come around again. But she came to our house and sat on our porch swing and asked for my forgiveness." My voice pitched upward. "And when I wouldn't grant it, she took out a little pistol she carried around—oh, excuse me, perhaps it was a *revolver*, I didn't really know the difference until you schooled me the other night—and she blew her head off. Right in front of me."

Chris gaped at me.

"I was fifteen years old." I pressed my lips together. "Talk about being a messed-up teenager. I was the very definition of one." I put the glass cleaner away and stuffed the paper towel in the trash. "But *you* were spared, Chris. You were spared."

"Jesus, Suze," Chris whispered. "I can't believe this."

I fixed him with an icy stare. "Well, you should, because it's the truth. And if you don't believe it, perhaps you should go talk to our honest, honorable father."

41

—·—

1979 - 1980

That Saturday night, after Peggy's body was hauled away, sheet covering her blown-off head, the police questioned Dad and me. We answered them honestly, giving as much information as we could. We told the cops about Peggy's connection to Bobby Shelton. They may have had some questions for Rosalie—if she was still around—and for Milo if he was able to answer them. But the detective said with Shelton and Peggy both dead, there was no one to charge with these crimes.

To everyone else, Peggy's suicide was simply that: a self-inflicted gunshot wound by a woman who'd hidden her mental instability. Her engagement off and her mother suddenly passing, she ended her life. To anyone who asked, this was the explanation Dad and I gave.

Jeff's family kept Chris for another two days. After that, the nanny my father hired, a grandmotherly woman named Marilyn, began fetching Chris from school every afternoon, bringing him home, and starting supper. Our meals took on the casserole-like deportment they'd had after my mother died—Marilyn was a decent cook but it wasn't her job to produce gourmet meals. After a while, I told her I'd handle dinner a few nights a week. While I didn't turn into a gourmet cook, either, I did become a regular consultant of Mom's weathered copy of *The Joy of Cooking*. Dad didn't say anything; he just made a weekly trip to Safeway for everything on the grocery list I handed him.

I stopped spending time at Zoe's. One Sunday afternoon while Dad and Chris were watching the Broncos, I went to the shop and cleared out my assortment of stowed items—the pillows, the writing implements, the flashlights and batteries—throwing everything in the dumpster out back. I assembled a collection of favorite cassettes to bring home. Before locking up, I nodded an apology to Zoe. She stared back, unblinking but sympathetic.

At home, I tossed the cassettes into the bin in my room. The mix tape my mother had made me was buried underneath the haul. I didn't listen to it again.

Mom-not-Mom ceased coming around. I'd hoped for her continued presence, but she completely disappeared—and this, I knew, was outside her control. I ached for her with a longing that kept me awake at night as I listened to Chris's quiet, even breathing from his sleeping bag on my floor. Our other ghosts were still around; they hung out in my mother's kitchen, sometimes flicking the overhead light or a stove burner on or off. I didn't know what they wanted; I never could figure it out. Eventually, I decided they just wanted to be in the house. I didn't blame them. My mother's house was a comfort, one of the only comforts remaining.

My father and I rarely spoke. When he looked at me, I tried to read what I saw in his eyes. Was it pity? Perhaps—but I couldn't help noticing the way his jaw reflexively clenched when I entered a room. He never touched me.

Our only bond was Chris. By silent assent, Dad and I shared a goal of ensuring that Chris's needs were met. Otherwise we felt less like a family and more like strangers who, by some unfortunate twist of fate, happened to occupy the same household.

Christmas was grim. Dad acquired a tree, which we set up in the library and decorated with our collection of family ornaments. No doubt with help from his assistant, Dad purchased and wrapped piles of presents for Chris and me. Alone in my room, I listened on repeat to John Lennon singing "Happy XMas (War is Over)." I tried telling myself that someday I'd feel happy again, like John and Yoko and the kids in that song.

A spark of brightness arrived on the twenty-seventh, when Dad took me to the airport and I boarded a plane for San Francisco. I'd stay with Donna through the New Year. Evan was making the reverse trip, visiting his dad, Vern, in Colorado. I'd have Evan's room for nine whole days.

Eighteen months earlier, the summer before Mom died, Donna had dumped Vern and moved, along with Evan, to San Francisco. Until Mom's death, she and Donna had talked on the phone several times a week, with Donna updating Mom on her half-hippie, half-lavish lifestyle. Living in a converted loft that she shared with a gay couple. Working on the curatorial team of the San Francisco Museum of Modern Art. Sending Evan to a language immersion school where the lessons were partially in English and partially in Spanish, French, or Mandarin. For reasons unclear to Mom (and by extension, me), Evan was on the Mandarin track.

"It will lift your mood, being here," Donna said to me in mid-December over the phone. "It'll feel like a million miles from Denver. We'll check out the museums and browse City Lights Bookstore. We'll stroll the Wharf and Golden Gate Park. Maybe take in a concert. My roommates are planning an awesome New Year's Eve party. You'll love them, Suze—they're the best two guys on the planet. They'll make sure you have a good—" She paused, laughing lightly. "A good, yet age appropriate, time."

I couldn't wait to get away. As Donna had predicted, it did lift my mood. In San Francisco, I could pretend nothing and no one else existed. No one except Donna and her roommates, Billy and Gordy—both of them feisty, beautiful men. Their laughter rang through the apartment at all hours. The sounds of their lovemaking were unavoidable as I lay next door, tucked into Evan's single bed, eschewing the fan that Donna said she turned on in Evan's room, facing away from him on chilly nights—creating white noise to, Donna claimed, "drown out the sounds of the city."

Closing my eyes and shutting out the ten-year-old-boy accouterments, I could pretend this was *my* room. I could pretend that I, not Evan, lived with Donna, Billy, and Gordy. Pretend this was my life.

The first Saturday in January 1980—five weeks after Peggy's death, just over seven weeks before the first anniversary of Mom's death—Dad picked me up at the airport. As we pulled into our garage, he said, "Before you witness it in person, I'm compelled to tell you something." Idling the car in the opened garage, he went on, "You'll see boxes in the house. Moving boxes."

"What are you talking about?"

He had, he explained, put out feelers to sell the house. He'd done this even before I left for San Francisco. But my absence, he said, only confirmed it was the right decision.

"Chris cried every night," Dad said. "He'd wander into your room, find it vacant, and enter mine. He refused to sleep alone. He barely ate. He took no delectation in his Christmas toys. He was infinitely inconsolable."

After a few days, Dad sent Chris to stay with his sister, Sadie. Unpleasant as a monkfish and more concerned with status than kindness, Aunt Sadie was not a family favorite—not of mine, not of my mother's when she was alive, and not, I was pretty sure, even of Dad's. I could only imagine the bribing Dad had to do to make it happen. But he'd already used up too many favors with Jeff's parents.

"Sadie took him up to Vail. He's learning to ski. Sadie reports that he's enjoying himself." Dad glanced at me. "I comprehend that you're crestfallen about this. But it had to be done, Suzanne. There's too much desolation here. Too many melancholic memories." He gripped the steering wheel. "I received an immediate offer on the house. It's a lowball offer; nonetheless, I took it. Homes around here are worth little, other than for the sentimental value some longtime residents have."

"Like me." I wrapped one hand around the other, the whiteness of my knuckles shining in the darkened garage. "I'm a longtime resident. Did you forget that?"

"I bought a delightful ranch house," he said. "It's on Seventeenth Avenue in Park Hill. You'll still go to East. Nothing will change."

I gaped at him. "*Nothing* will change? What the hell, Dad?"

Scrambling out of the car, I strode across the yard, up the steps, and inside. The half-packed boxes I passed in the kitchen, hallway, and library rattled as if they contained something alive. The ghosts didn't want us to leave any more than I did.

My room, at least, was intact. Flinging myself onto the bed, I gave way to the choking sobs that clogged my throat and threatened to strangle me—if not directly, not physically, then inside my heart.

42

— · —

2004

Over lunch, Daphne and Tori were sympathetic about the conversation they'd overheard me having with Chris. "That's a hell of a story, Suzanne," Daphne said. "I knew about the holdup and your mom's passing, but not those details. I'm so sorry." She shuddered. "That woman you talked about—Peggy? Wow."

Tori, mid-sip of her Diet Peach Snapple, nodded over the bottle's rim. Pulling a hand through her wispy hair, she looked out the plate-glass window.

I bit into my tuna-on-rye, forcing myself to swallow. "It was an awful, awful time. But it's in the past." I put on a bright smile. "It doesn't have anything to do with today."

That wasn't entirely true, but there was no need to discuss it further with them. I admired Tori and Daphne. The blue headband with silver threading that Daphne wore caught sunlight through the windows, as did the array of rings on her fingers. She wore cat's-eye glasses that might look nerdy on someone else but were funky on Daphne. As for Tori, from her ears hung huge, beaded earrings in a colorful chevron pattern; a matching necklace nestled between her breasts. Both women wore jeans, high-heeled boots, and fitted tops. They had that hip, city-girl cool—the type of persona I wished came naturally to me.

Maybe their hipness would rub off on me. Maybe they'd become my friends.

Finishing my sandwich, cupping my hands under my chin, I said, "Tell me about your latest projects, both of you. I want to hear every detail."

After a week in the hospital, Donna was released. Renee and Evan hired an attendant and moved Donna to a first-floor suite in their house, into which they'd installed a rented hospital bed.

On Thursday, Renee called to say that Donna was feeling gloomy about her confinement. "Would you visit her?" Renee asked. "It'll cheer her up."

"Of course. Anything she needs, anything you need—I'm there." We hung up after I assured her I'd come see Donna after fetching Austin from school.

That afternoon, I drove to the Cheesman mansion. It was cloudy and windy, and I blasted heat in the car. While Austin prattled on about Pokémon, I took a circuitous route—west on Colfax, then turning south. When Supertramp came on the radio with "Take the Long Way Home," I smiled.

Then my smile transformed into a frown. It wasn't the long way home. It was an intentional detour. One I'd been putting off but now felt compelled to take.

In the nearly four months we'd been living in Denver, I'd purposefully avoided my childhood street. I hadn't wanted to see it. Hadn't wanted to feel the nausea that I knew would overtake me as the familiar address came into view. I knew what I'd find there—and what I wouldn't.

Some years ago—the same brief trip to Denver after which I'd gone home and made the Halloween tanto knife that I'd attempted giving to Caitlin—I'd driven down this street. Neither Dad nor Chris had prepared me for what to expect.

My mother's wonderful, rambling old whorehouse was gone.

After my father sold the house, it changed hands several times. Sometime in the late 1990s, a developer bought it, demolished it, and built a fourplex apartment building. It had a nondescript stucco exterior, something between gray and beige. It featured a flat roof and no porch, just concrete steps to a shared entryway. The building stood like an oversized cardboard box against the street. A row of single-car garages was crammed into what had once been our back yard.

Next door, Laurie's family's bungalow was still there, though they'd long ago sold it. A few years after high school, Laurie had moved to Las Vegas. We exchanged holiday cards and occasional emails. She worked for the City of Las Vegas's tourism department, was divorced, and had a couple of teenagers. Her mom was in a retirement community near her. Bruce still lived in Denver and worked as a grocery store manager.

Approaching the address that had once been ours, I slowed down. For years, Mom had talked about petitioning the city to get historical designation for the house. There was proof of its whorehouse status—there'd once been an infamous raid at the house, during which several prominent local politicians were arrested. It was, I knew, the occasion when the maid was killed—caught in the crossfire as some of the prostitutes attempted fleeing. I had no idea when the wild-haired woman died, nor who placed that single bullet hole in her temple.

The grim, horrific raid made the front page of the newspaper. The article featured a group photo of the arrest, complete with menacing cops and the house's distraught madame. Mom had a framed copy in the hallway. She'd adored showing it to guests. "Such history," she'd say. I still had that framed article—had, in fact, hung it in the hallway of my own vintage Denver home.

Mom had often mentioned the historical designation to Dad and me. If the house had such a designation, future owners could make city-approved modifications, but no one would be able to tear the house down.

"I don't expect we'll ever leave," Mom said. "But just in case, we should try to get the designation."

Dad murmured assent but never said anything else about it. Mom had looked up the information and discovered there were numerous steps involved in the historical designation appeal. Getting it done always fell through the cracks, never rising to the top of my mother's long to-do list.

An irritable honk sounded from a car behind us. Austin paused his Pokémon soliloquy to ask, "Why are we stopped here, Mommy?"

I hadn't realized I'd idled in the middle of the street. Putting my foot on the accelerator, I pulled away. I didn't look back.

43

1980 - 1982

My new room never felt like my room. It was large and bright, with southern exposure through high windows facing the back yard and in-ground pool. When my father asked what color I wanted for my bedroom walls, I said I didn't care.

Several days later I came home to find my room had been painted a soft, cool green. There were new, coordinating spring-green bedding items and bath linens for the adjacent bathroom, which I had entirely to myself.

"Do you like it?" Dad asked from the doorway. "I'm hardly a dexterous designer, but my assistant knew just what a fifteen-year-old girl would like."

"It's fine," I said. "Thank you."

He clasped the door frame with both hands. "Settle in. Acquaint yourself with your new surroundings, Suze."

I didn't know what to make of him. Sometimes I got the sense that my very existence made him uncomfortable. Other times he seemed to want to mend fences. Both notions unnerved me, and I avoided him whenever possible.

On the first anniversary of Mom's death, Dad asked Chris and me to share remembrances of her. I didn't know what to say. There was so much, but where to begin?

Chris said he remembered that Mommy had long hair and never yelled at him. "Peggy didn't yell, either," he added. "Jeff's mom yells at him and his brothers all the time. But neither of my mothers yelled."

I felt a stinging in my throat, as if a wasp had made its way inside.

Chris looked at our father. "Daddy, will you tell me again why Peggy went away?"

Dad patted Chris's shoulder. "Sometimes people do, that's all." He took a long drink of scotch.

"Can we get back to talking about Mom?" I asked.

"Of course, Suzanne." Dad smiled woodenly at me, then at Chris. "Mom was smitten with both of you."

I didn't need him to tell me this. I excused myself and headed to my room.

In my darkened doorway, lit only by the moon, my eyes met hers—Zoe's. By then, Dad had closed up Zoe's Records. I don't know what happened to the remaining stock; I never asked. But he brought Zoe home. "I thought you might want her," he'd said to me.

I'd nodded, picked her up, and dragged her to my bedroom. I set up Zoe in a corner, straightening her guitar and clothing. She took up residence with me—a silent, all-knowing roommate and companion.

Mom-not-Mom never came around the ranch house. She no longer commented inside my head. When I thought back on our discussions, I wondered how much she'd actually said—and how much I'd embellished. There were phrases that I distinctly recalled my mother's ghost saying: *I need you to fix it. Listen to the tape. I'm sorry about Carey.* But our long conversations, all her words that I heard inside my head—did those things truly happen? Or did I only imagine what I thought she'd say? Was that simply how I processed my grief?

I went to Cheesman, trying to conjure her among the half-buried dead. I walked from East to our old house, peering in the windows when I was sure no one was home, hoping to catch a glimpse of Mom-not-Mom or the other ghosts. But the house was different—new paint, refurbished hardwood floors, a remodeled kitchen—and looking in as an outsider, I sensed none of its former occupants.

As for Peggy, I never stopped looking over my shoulder. Surely, someday she would find me. Would it be this week, or next? A month from now? A year, a decade? I lacked the clairvoyant skills to determine a date, a location, any specifics. I only knew it would happen.

By spring, I was spending as much time away from home as possible. Laurie continued hanging out with me, even inviting me to do stuff with her and other people. When I asked why, she said, "You grew up, Suzanne. I *want* to hang with you. Lots of people do."

Some kids at East knew about my mother, and perhaps a few knew about Peggy. But these events didn't define me. That spring I submitted several articles to the school newspaper, and in the ensuing years of high school, I continued to write. My focus was on kids who were making inroads artistically. I reviewed the shows of East kids who'd formed rock bands. I wrote features about students who created stunning paintings and photography. I interviewed the stars of school plays—including Don Cheadle, a fellow member of the Denver East High class of 1982.

As I talked with kids about their passions, I remembered what Carey had said to me: that I'd find my place. I wouldn't have expected to find it among, as I'd once called them, the "artsy kids." But helping them showcase their talent was surprisingly fulfilling.

Dad began dating Linda the summer before my junior year, and they married ten months later. Linda didn't try to mother me, which I appreciated. But she did a fine job mothering Chris. We still had Marilyn part-time, but Linda ran our household. She and I never argued, but we weren't close. We were like coworkers who got along but each had her role in the organization—hers more vital than mine.

Chris changed schools when we moved. At his new school, he made plenty of friends; our house rang with their shouts and laughter after school and on weekends. The sprawling ranch house with the rec room in the basement and pool in the back yard became a neighborhood hangout for kids Chris's age. For so many reasons, I missed our old house, but I couldn't deny that our new environment was better for Chris. In the ranch house, he never came into my room at night. Never cried. He was just a happy, well-adjusted little boy.

Occasionally I invited kids from East over to sun and swim. But others had houses and pools as nice as ours—and I tried to stay away from home as much as possible. I lifeguarded at a city pool over summer breaks, and during the school year I volunteered at the Park Hill branch library, doing story time for little kids.

I dated, but never anyone serious. No one would label me a slut; nonetheless, I wasn't above sleeping with a guy after we'd been going out a couple of months. On the night when my first post-Carey boyfriend asked if I was a virgin, I said yes. It was easier than explaining.

I never saw Carey again. Scott Eames was around, showing up in my classes here and there, and our paths intersected in the arts world. But we never dated and weren't really friends. Once, I overheard him say his brother lived in Grand Junction, so Carey must have moved back. I believe I caught a glimpse of Carey at East's commencement exercises in 1982—but it was an enormous crowd, so I'm not sure.

Second semester sophomore year, not long after Dad sold my mother's house, I took industrial arts as my elective. Our first project was a set of bookends. We used the bandsaw to shape two pieces of pine for each bookend, sanded and stained them, then affixed brass screws with finish washers to hold the pieces together. While satisfied with my completed bookends, I also found the project hackneyed. When the class moved on to welding a plant stand, I asked the industrial arts teacher, Mr. Smith, about more advanced woodworking projects.

"What do you have in mind, Suzanne?" he asked.

"A knife handle," I told him. "Preferably one that I could attach to a functional knife."

"Hmm." Mr. Smith rubbed a hand along his beard. "I think we could work something out."

I still had to make the plant stand, but he let me come in after school to work one-on-one with him. He showed me how to make a Finnish carving knife called a puukko; his maternal grandfather had been Finnish and taught Mr. Smith the art. It involved using metal pins to hold the puukko blade between two pieces of wood, or scales, outlining the handle shape, then cutting the scales on the bandsaw. Afterward I re-inserted the blade, glued the handle pieces together, and sanded them smooth.

I was thrilled with the result. My handle was hickory, and while my sawing and sanding skills were rudimentary, I'd given the handle a pleasant shape, with a grip that felt comfortable in my hand. The blade was sharp but not long, less than four inches.

"Traditionally, puukko handles were carved by hand," Mr. Smith told me. "Making puukkos is a centuries-old Finnish tradition." He placed a hand on the sander. "No such thing as power tools back then. You had to fashion your puukko manually."

"What do people use them for?" I asked.

"Hunting, sometimes, or working in the kitchen or anywhere around food. People often take them hiking and camping. It's a versatile little knife."

I eyed him. "Could you defend yourself with it?"

"You could...but it'd get messy, since a traditional puukko has no finger guard." He took the belt off the sander and hung it on the rack with others of various grits. "Personally, I'd only do that if I had no alternative."

I stowed my knife in the sheath he'd given me. "Got it. Thanks for showing me."

Mr. Smith smiled. "Anytime. I love seeing students take an interest in traditional arts."

"I'd like to set up a workshop in that humongous garage," I told Dad, showing him my puukko. "I'd like to start making knives like this as a hobby."

He frowned. "With what possible purpose, Suzanne?"

"Because it's cool. It's a basic utility knife. Check it out." I put my knife in his hand.

"This is exceptional," he said, turning it over. "I'm impressed."

"Thank you."

"But a knifemaking hobby sounds hazardous."

"It's not," I said. "My teacher taught me all the safety protocols. And the tools are pretty basic—they're just expensive. I can get supplies at Rockler Woodworking, down on Colorado Boulevard."

"It seems like an improper pastime for a young girl."

"Tough," I told him. "I'm doing it. It's just a matter of who pays for it—you or me."

Dad sighed but acquiesced. Was he driven by guilt? If so, I didn't care. By then, I figured he owed me plenty.

By high school graduation, I'd made handles for more than thirty knives—not just puukkos but also kitchen knives, hunting knives, and yes, knives with finger guards, appropriate for self-defense. Occasionally—and only after careful vetting of the customer—I sold a handmade knife. At school, I developed an underground reputation as someone who might supply you with a well-made knife. Other than those I sold and the kitchen knives, which I contributed to our household—Linda and Marilyn both raved about them—I stored my knives in a locked box in my room, where Chris had no access to them.

I always kept a drop-point or tanto on me. There was comfort in knowing my sheathed knife was there, either in my purse or a pocket—ready and available, should the need arise.

In June 1982, a week after graduation, I moved to San Francisco. Evan was on a European tour with Vern and Vern's girlfriend, and Donna invited me to stay in Evan's room. I'd already been accepted at Berkeley, so spending the summer before college with Donna was a no-brainer.

I packed two large suitcases and promised Zoe I'd be back for her, someday when I lived somewhere with more space. Dad, Linda, and Chris took me to the airport, and I hugged all of them goodbye. My arms lingered around Chris—my now nine-year-old brother, nearly as tall as me.

Then I boarded the plane. Sinking back in my seat, I closed my eyes and felt the 737 lift off. As it left Colorado soil, I had the sensation not just of flight but of deliverance. I was grateful for the plane's straightforward expeditiousness. Traveling in this manner made it impossible to look back.

44

2004

At Renee's house, she suggested Austin go upstairs to play with Jasper. I hesitated, unsure about Austin's behavior around a younger boy, then decided a short visit would be okay. "I hope he's not any trouble," I said to Renee.

"I'm sure they'll be fine." Renee was cooking, something I assumed she rarely did. She and Evan had a chef, a housekeeper, and a gardener—none of them the same person—so I was surprised to see her being domestic. "Go see Donna. She's down the hall, third door on the left."

Donna was lying on her right side under a fleece blanket, broken left arm resting on a pillow. Her face was as gray as the bleak day outside, and her usually dancing eyes were cloudy. Even with a window cracked open, the room stank of cigarette smoke.

"This sucks," she said when I walked in.

"It does." I sat beside her bed. "What's the latest?"

"Lying around this God-awful hospital bed. Watching daytime TV. Having the nurse help me to the john. She's pleasant, but ugh...I hate it." She grabbed her cigarettes from the nightstand. "At least they're letting me smoke. I think Evan feels kinda responsible, although he shouldn't. Not his fault I was in the wrong place at the wrong time." She pressed a button and the back of the bed lifted slightly.

"Will they do surgery?" I asked.

Awkwardly, her arm heavy in the cast, Donna lit up. "Eventually, yes. But not until my arm is fully healed and I have some strength back." She blew smoke toward the window. "I'd rather get it over with, but the doctor says I have to be a—" She air-quoted. "…'patient patient.'"

I didn't smile; it was a sucky way to put it. Still, I said, "He's right."

She scowled. "I know, but I hate that feeling—like I have zero control."

I laughed. "Who's the one who told me to let go and trust in the process?"

"Touché." She smoothed the blanket across her middle. "I'm glad you're here, Suze."

"Me, too." I gave her a long look. "How do you think you got hit?"

"No idea. That car came so fast, I never saw it. Apparently, no one else did, either." She exhaled. "At least, not enough to identify the car or driver."

I shook my head. "People are awful. Can I get you anything?"

"Refill my water, please."

From a pitcher on the nightstand, I filled her cup, exchanging it for her mostly smoked cigarette, which I ground out in an ashtray.

"Wanna hear something weird?" When I nodded, she said, "Your dad visited me."

I rubbed my brow. "I'm sorry, did you say my *dad* visited you? *My* dad?"

"Your dad." She sipped water through a straw. "Not sure how he heard about my accident, but he knew. Told me he came because he's an experienced cheerer-upper. I guess he meant all the time he spent at Linda's bedside."

Two years ago Linda died of breast cancer, after years of treatment—long years in which Dad cared for her. I felt a lump in my throat. Linda and I hadn't been close, but she was a good person. And she'd meant a lot to Chris and Dad.

Donna stretched her neck from side to side. "James and I had good chat. He told me all about his trip."

"Did you tell him what I said about researching his past?"

"Of course not. You told me that in confidence." Her eyes searched mine. "But maybe *you* should."

"I can't. I promised I wouldn't." I explained about meeting Claranna Newstone.

"Wow." Donna took my hand. "That's a lot to hold, honey."

I nodded. "I've been thinking about knowledge—the idea of it. Knowledge is power, sure, but the hardest part isn't figuring something out." I took a shaky breath. "The hardest part is figuring out what to *do* with the knowledge, once you have it."

Renee appeared in the doorway, holding Jasper. His cheek was red—and her face was white.

"Everything all right?" I asked her.

Her voice was tense. "Actually, it's not. Can you come upstairs, please?"

"He hit me!" Jasper cried, tears streaming down his face. "Austin hit me! And he break-ed my train layout."

Yellow plastic GeoTrax train tracks were scattered across Jasper's bedroom floor. A large station was on its side. Upside down on the carpeting, a bright green engine continued to chug, its skyward-facing wheels moving uselessly.

Austin's eyes had a wild look. "I *told* him how to set it up," Austin said. "But he wanted to do it his way, but his way is wrong, wrong, *wrong*!"

I put a hand on his head. "You can't hit people when you disagree with them, Austin. You have to compromise."

He ducked away from me. "I hate compromising! I hate that fucking word!"

All three of us stared at him. Renee gave Jasper a squeeze. "Let's have a snack, boys."

We set them up in the family room with individual small bowls of cheddar goldfish. Renee tuned the TV to Nickelodeon. I checked on Donna, who was asleep, then returned to the kitchen.

"I'm sorry," I said to Renee, my voice low. Across the space of the open floor plan, I glanced at Austin, seated on the opposite end of the big sectional from Jasper.

Renee was silent. She heated oil in a pan, dropping in chopped onions and garlic. Then she turned to me. "Suzanne, I know how hard Austin's behavior is on him—and on you."

"I..." Bowing my head, I looked at my hands.

"Listen, I want to tell you something. I don't tell many people."

I looked up.

"I had a sister," Renee said. "And she was a lot like Austin." She stirred the pan's ingredients. "This was before there was much understanding of kids' behavioral health. They were expected to fit the mold, and if they didn't, there was little compassion and few resources. Especially for poor families like mine was back then, before my mom's career took off."

I sank onto a stool, watching her cook.

Renee turned to me. "What happened at Children's must have been difficult for you."

I looked away. Renee had covered for me that day at Zoe's, and when she asked the following morning how things went, I told her I'd gotten a weird vibe from the doctor and left before the appointment began.

"I know it wasn't what you'd hoped for. But please don't give up." Renee paused. "My parents...after a while, they just gave up. My dad started drinking, then he left us. My mom threw her energy into her work." She bit her lip. "My sister got knocked around...by life. She had a hard, short life."

My throat felt dry. "What happened to her?"

"She hung herself." Renee's chin trembled. "She was twenty."

"Oh, Renee. I'm so sorry." I thought about the babies she'd lost. About her sister's death, her mother's. Her father's abandonment. And now she was dealing with Donna's accident, too.

She added carrots to the pan and stirred. I watched her lovely hands—so skilled with the needle, so good at everything. It would be easy to think she had it all, never had to deal with loss or grief or disappointment.

Before I could talk myself out of it, I said, "Renee, what had happened at Children's was frustrating, but I own it. I screwed up." I leaned forward. "Here's the thing. You and Evan know every influential person in this town." I took a breath, then asked, "Can you help me? Do you know anyone who could help me get Austin in again? Soon?"

I reached out, putting my hand on hers. "I'd be indebted," I said.

On the way home, I veered into Cheesman Park. It wasn't the most direct route, but I steered through the entrance as if on autopilot. The park was opaque, lit only by a few dim streetlights and the glowing pavilion.

As I approached, my eyes widened. The pavilion and lawn were awash with ghosts. I'd never sensed this many—not when I was a kid, not this past Halloween when I went to Cheesman hoping to feel my mother's presence. Tonight, they appeared to me with more clarity than ever before. I didn't just sense them; I saw them: hobbling on half-missing limbs, dancing in pairs, raising single arms skyward because they only had one to raise. Each one featured a bullet hole somewhere in its body.

Hitting the brakes, I glanced at Austin. He was looking out the window, but his expression was impassive. I knew he wasn't experiencing what I was.

Peering at the pavilion, I spied something else. There were people there—two of them, one male and one female. They huddled close together on the steps.

I tried to discern the living beings through the chaos of the ghosts. Was that her black trench coat? Her dark veil of hair, wind whipping it around her shoulders?

What was glinting in his hand?

Rapidly, I dialed Renee's number. "Can I run Austin back to you?" I pleaded. "Just for a few minutes."

"What's going on?" she asked. "You sound panicked, Suzanne."

"I'll explain later. Please, can I bring him?"

"Of course."

Hanging up, I turned off my headlights and reversed to the park's entrance, then made a beeline for Renee's house. After delivering Austin safely to Renee, I drove back and parked in shrouded darkness. Knife in hand, shielding my face from the wind, I crept across the snow-encrusted grass. "Excuse me," I whispered, elbowing my way through the ghosts. More than once I landed on the frosted, slippery grass.

My eyes darted around and behind me. Peggy was here—I was sure of it. And now I knew why I'd been drawn to the park. I had to get Caitlin out of here before Peggy found either of us.

The pavilion faced west, with piney groves surrounding it on the other three sides. I inched through the southern grove, stepping around the pavilion's perimeter until I was close enough to make out the male's profile.

He looked so much like his father, I'd have recognized him anywhere. He was holding a gun, showing it to Caitlin, who reached for it.

I sprinted into a thicket, out of earshot, and dialed Caitlin's number. To my relief, she picked up.

Attempting to convey urgency but not panic, I said, "Caitlin, please come home right away. There's an emergency."

"I'm kinda busy." Irritation permeated her tone.

The ghosts closed in and I could barely see Caitlin and RJ. "Please, Cait," I said. "I need you right now."

"What is this emergency?" she asked.

A wild lie came to me. "Dad had an accident. He's all right, but he needs me—and I need you to watch Austin."

"Hold on a sec." I heard the muffled words, then she was back. "Okay, I'll be there in ten minutes."

"Thank you, honeypie." Hanging up, I sighed with relief. She'd believed me.

Caitlin and RJ remained on the steps. "Please go," I pleaded—my voice a whisper, hoping she'd mentally catch the message. She fondled the gun, then returned it to him. He wrapped his arms around her, the gun clutched in his hand, pressed to her back. Then he kissed her—*kissed* her! All around, spirits danced—and bile rose in my throat.

Then the ghosts closed in. My daughter and this man with a vendetta against my family were obscured from view. Would he shoot her? Or would Peggy find me?

I wanted Shelton Jr. caught, and I'd been counting on the cops having the element of surprise—*after* Caitlin was safe. After she and I were away from him, and from Peggy. But it was too late. I could no longer simply hope for things to play out as I wished them to.

Wishing wouldn't keep my child safe. I stepped forward, out of hiding.

45

2004

I ran toward the pavilion, calling Caitlin's name and simultaneously dialing 911. Breathless, I told them that Robert Shelton Jr. was in Cheesman Park with another young woman, this one a minor. Leaving the line open, I sprinted toward the pavilion.

As I did so, I felt a cold, thin hand reaching for mine, but I yanked out of its grasp. "Get the hell away from me, Peggy!" I yelled. I whipped my arm around, swinging my knife across her blurred face, toward the blown-off back of her head.

Through the plethora of spirits, I heard Caitlin's voice. "What the *fuck*, Mom?"

"Caitlin, come here now! Come here to me."

Peggy remained on my tail. I turned to slash her again, my knife traveling through the bitter energy that made her what she was.

Shelton Jr. stood. He raised his gun, looked wildly around, and aimed toward me. I hit the ground but heard no gunshots. I raised my head in time to see Shelton Jr. jump off the pavilion steps and dash toward the north entrance of the park.

I clutched my phone. "He's headed toward Twelfth Avenue," I told the 911 operator. "Please have someone get him—*now*."

Attempting to rise from the icy ground, I felt Peggy on top of me. Adrenaline coursing through my body, I threw her off, scrambled to my feet, and ran toward my child.

Reaching Caitlin, I heard a siren in the distance. As I wrapped my arms around her, I felt Peggy's fingers grip my shoulders. How was it possible, I wondered, that a spirit could manifest such a tight grasp?

Only fury could do that. Fury and a thirst for revenge.

But I was alive and she was not. I was unafraid. I shook myself and my daughter so violently, Peggy toppled backward. She never was as strong as she believed herself to be.

In the car driving home, Caitlin was fierce as a wildcat. "You are an awful person," she said. "You have zero respect for anyone else. Not me, not anyone I hang out with." Her voice rose. "RJ is innocent. Darcy wanted to leave and he helped her get away. She's in New York now. Or LA or somewhere—I don't remember what he said. But she's fine, and I was fine—and *you* are a first-class *bitch*!"

"Caitlin," I said. "I know you don't understand. But you were in danger."

"You're damn right I don't understand." She pressed her face to the window.

At home, she stormed to her room. But as I listened to the violent shatter of her door slamming, I didn't care. Shelton Jr. was detained. Caitlin might be furious—but she was safe.

I felt victorious. I'd confronted Peggy—and beat her. She might appear again; I knew this and even anticipated its likelihood. But preventing RJ from harming Caitlin was worth every risk I had to take.

That night when Brett finally got home, I told him I'd caught Caitlin in the park with the man suspected of abducting Darcy Powles. I omitted mention of Shelton Jr.'s connection with my family. I couldn't go there. What if Brett didn't react? What if he didn't care?

Appalled and scared for Caitlin, Brett said he'd make time in his schedule to tag-team with me driving her to and from school. This further incited her, but Brett and I dug in our heels.

"Total *bullshit*," she said. "For how long?"

"Until winter break," I replied. "And maybe afterward. We'll see."

"I hate you!" she said. "I really, truly hate you, Mom—you know that?"

My stomach, accustomed to flip-flopping when Caitlin screamed at me, felt relaxed. Without replying, I turned away.

46

2004

The ease with which we received a new appointment at Children's—with Renee's help—made me both uncomfortable and grateful. I knew there were other kids who needed this as much as Austin did. At the same time, I didn't want Austin to suffer because of my screw-up. Not when I had a way to fix it.

I worried that again we'd be assigned to Dr. Morris, but I wasn't going to jeopardize the appointment by requesting someone else. Besides, Brett had promised to meet us at Children's. As Austin and I sat in the waiting room, my gaze oscillated between the elevator doors and my watch.

Where was Brett? He'd goddamn *promised*.

There was no sign of him when Patricia Morris called our names. Seeing her again, her similarity to Peggy, startled me as much as last time. Taking Austin's hand, I walked over on wobbly legs.

"Good to see you both," Dr. Morris said. "Let's go inside and talk." She bent toward Austin. "Would you like a juice box, Austin? We can grab one on the way." When he nodded, she said, "Which do you like best? Grape or apple?"

"Orange," Austin said.

"Yes," she replied smoothly. "Orange is fantastic. But sometimes we only have two choices. So if you *had* to make a choice—grape or apple—which would it be?"

He stopped walking, putting a finger against his chin. "I guess...apple?"

She nodded. "Apple it is."

I took one last look at the closed elevator doors. Then we stepped inside.

"Things got hung up," Brett said on the phone. "I'm sorry."

"You're always fucking sorry! I'm sick of it, Brett!"

I was driving with my phone pressed between my shoulder and ear. I hadn't spoken much with Austin about the appointment, although after I'd been dismissed and he spent some time alone with Dr. Morris, he'd returned to the waiting room chatting with her about—what else?—Pokémon. Now he was huddled on the back seat, and when I glanced in the rearview mirror, his eyes were huge in the darkness.

"What do you want me to do?" Brett asked. "Quit my job? Is that what you're asking, Suzanne?"

"No." I swerved, avoiding a delivery van. "I'm asking you to keep your goddamn promises. I'm asking you to care about your family."

As much, I thought, as you care about Nicole.

Because no matter how hard I tried to convince myself that Brett's unreliability was entirely about work, I didn't believe it. I'd known women like Nicole before. I knew how such women operated. I knew how they schemed.

Austin saw Dr. Morris twice. Children's Hospital employed a two-day evaluation because doing the entire eval in a single day was exhausting for most kids. "One thing we emphasize with families is how tired kids are," Dr. Morris told me before she took Austin—without me—into the clinical area for his second appointment. "It's not the same as 'adult tired,' where we're overwhelmed with responsibilities. Kids, especially the kids we see here, get tired because they work so hard to hold it together." She tucked a strand of auburn hair behind her ear. "They really do try—until they reach a breaking point. Our job is to minimize that by identifying triggers and helping kids learn how to handle the times when the break inevitably comes."

I stared at Dr. Morris's manicured nails, feeling my own fingertips prickling as if I'd touched a cactus. But I only nodded. "We could all use some help there, I guess," I said.

Dr. Morris smiled, revealing a row of straight, perfect teeth. "Indeed. We all have our breaking point." Her eyes, meeting mine, seemed to suddenly darken. "The question is, how does a person handle it?"

Everything felt close, stifling. I couldn't sleep, had to force myself to eat.

I called the police to get a report on Shelton Jr. but was only told that he'd been questioned and released. "We can't disclose any other information, ma'am," said the officer on the line.

My heart thudded. "Can I get a restraining order against him?"

"You can request one." The officer gave me information about who to contact.

I took care of it, but still I was nervous. That weekend, I implored Brett to stay home with the kids while I worked at Zoe's. To his credit, he agreed—but I suspected it was mainly because he felt guilty about missing Austin's appointment.

Was that *all* he felt guilty about?

Mid-morning the next Thursday, the mail carrier arrived at Zoe's with a box of office supplies I'd ordered, as well as a stack of bills. On the bottom of the stack, I spied a plain white, stamped envelope.

A printed address label identified the recipient as me, care of Zoe's. The postmark was in our neighborhood, and there was no return address or name. I slit the envelope open. Unfolding the single sheet of paper, I scanned the note, which was laser-printed in large type.

Suzanne Archer,

You are in danger and you know who from. Why are you letting her get away with this?

You managed to get your daughter out of harm's way—for now. As for your son, it's hard to say.

Be smart and keep your children locked up at home. Cross your fingers for their safety.

As for your dog, she's alive—but barely.

Suzanne, I think you know what needs to be done.

- A Friend

I pressed my fingers to my collarbone, rolling the skin over my bones. What the hell *was* this?

Who sent it?

Could it be Shelton Jr.? Was he feeling remorseful? He was the only one who knew what had happened with Caitlin at the park, unless she'd told her so-called friends. And even if she did, would a high schooler write a note like this?

I locked up and drove to the police precinct, handing them the note and asking them to check it for fingerprints. "It will take a few hours," said the officer—the same one who'd taken my report several weeks earlier. "We'll call you if we find a match." Her smile was kind. "It's likely just a prank, Ms. Archer. But we'll do what we can."

"I appreciate it." But when they called that afternoon, they said the prints didn't match Shelton Jr.'s or anyone else's in their database.

Maybe the police were right. Maybe it *was* a prank. Still, I'd keep my kids under lock and key; I'd keep them safe.

And my heart surged at the idea that Stevie might be alive. That there might be a way I could rescue her.

That night after Austin was asleep, I hesitated only a moment before knocking on Caitlin's door.

"What do *you* want?" she asked when I opened the door. She was at her desk, leaning over a thick piece of scarlet paper. In her hand was a lightweight craft knife.

I sidled closer. "What are you doing?"

Caitlin put her hands over the paper. "Paper cutting. A way to make designs by cutting them into paper." She looked up at me, her eyes hooded. "We were doing it in art class and I thought it was kind of cool, so I asked the art teacher if I could borrow some supplies."

Recalling my industrial arts teacher showing me how to make a knife handle all those years ago, I smiled. Then I remembered something else. "I commission works at Zoe's by an artist who does paper cutting," I said. "A woman named Evangeline Moyers. She creates the most beautiful, intricate portraits and designs. You should come by and see them."

Caitlin didn't respond. I told her Austin was sleeping and I needed to run a quick errand. "It goes without saying that you are not to leave this house, right?" I asked.

She glared at me but nodded. I left her room, then checked every door and window to ensure they were locked. I grabbed a jacket and headed out.

I hated leaving the kids, but I saw no choice. I *had* to know.

It was bitterly cold. In the garage, I switched on my knife sharpener, pulled the tanto from its sheath, and inserted the blade between the grinding wheels. I listened to the wheels' hypnotic hum as I ran the gleaming blade between them. When I was satisfied, I turned off the sharpener, resheathed the knife, and climbed into my car.

The lot at Brett's office park in the Tech Center was dark, only a few cars in it, scattered lights on in his building. Brett's Audi was parked beside a black Mitsubishi. I backed into a spot at the rear of the lot, under a cottonwood tree. Looking up through branches that were leafless and skeletal, I stared at the crystalline sky, bright with tiny stars.

The building door opened and I snapped my head forward, watching. They came out together, walking close, heads bent toward one another's. That could simply be from the cold, I told myself. When it's cold outside, we instinctively move toward familiar figures.

Familiar figures—such as people we're sleeping with.

Nicole drove off in the Mitsubishi, with Brett following her. I kept my distance behind them. A few miles later, Nicole continued driving west while Brett took the I-25 North on-ramp.

So he *wasn't* following her to her place. He was going home. I told myself I should do the same—but I continued driving west.

Two miles. Three. Nicole turned into a condo complex and pulled into a covered parking space.

I backed into a guest space across the lot. Under her car's dome light, Nicole reached toward the passenger seat, gathering her things. My eye caught the whiteness of her long, slender neck.

Knife clenched in my hand, I jolted to a mental image of what could be. How quickly I could step behind her. How swiftly I could run the blade across her throat. It takes a lot of effort, I'd told Chris. But would it—really? In conversation with my brother, I'd been talking about a face-to-face attack. With a rear approach, with the element of surprise—*would* it take that much effort?

No. No, it would not.

Stop, Suzanne, I told myself. It's madness to even *think* about it.

Yes, it was madness—but it would end things once and for all. It would ensure that Nicole could never destroy my family, the way Peggy had destroyed my mother's family.

Nicole got out of her car, slinging her bag over one shoulder. I opened my car door and crept out.

Honeypie, I heard in my head. *Don't do it.*

I gripped the knife—its handle smooth, the orange spacer bright, the blade gleaming.

Suzie Blue, Mom-not-Mom said. *Turn around. Now!*

47

2004

I expected Peggy.

Expected to sense her half-gone head, her curvy figure. Spectral but unmistakably *her*—just as she'd been in Cheesman. But when I whirled around, I saw instead a slight, darkly dressed, and very human figure. The person vanished behind a stand of juniper bushes. I heard a car engine start, then tires screeching.

"Suzanne?" Nicole called across the parking lot. "Is that you?"

I sheathed my knife, slipping it into my pocket as she approached. She touched my shoulder. "You're shaking. What happened?"

It seemed Nicole hadn't seen the figure. I composed my thoughts. "I'm sorry to have startled you. I was looking for Brett. Austin has a fever and Brett's not answering his phone, so I told Caitlin to watch Austin, and I ran down to your office. I saw you both driving away, and I thought I saw Brett following you here."

"Poor Suzanne. What a night. Brett went home as soon as we left the office. He should be there now." Nicole's hand was still on my shoulder. "Do you want to come inside? Can I make you some tea?"

I considered. She wouldn't invite me in if she had Stevie, would she?

"I should get home," I said. "But could I trouble you for a glass of water first?"

Driving home, I watched my rearview mirror. What the hell was going *on*?

While Nicole poured me water, I'd asked to use the bathroom. On my way there, I did a quick search of her place. No Stevie. No signs of a dog.

If it wasn't Nicole who'd been following me all those times, was it Dr. Morris? Was the doctor Peggy's daughter? They looked enough alike, and she was the right age. Did she also write the note? Had I been set up?

And was she the person who'd jumped into the bushes, then run off?

"You stopped me, Mom," I said aloud. "You saved me."

Of course, she replied. *You're my baby.*

Blinking, pinching my lips together, I said, "Just like you saved me when Peggy died." I swallowed. "Mom? Did you make Peggy kill herself?"

There was a long pause. Then she said, *Peggy was going to kill herself no matter what. You have to believe that, Suze.*

"I do believe it." Turning onto the highway, I asked, "Is Dr. Morris following me? And if it's her, what does she want?"

I don't know. You need to find answers to these questions yourself. And for God's sake, watch your back.

"I just wanted to talk with Nicole." It seemed important to say this aloud. "That's all."

Was it? It didn't look that way.

I didn't respond.

Suzie Blue, Mom-not-Mom said, *think carefully about who you truly need to talk to. And who you can trust.*

He was in the kitchen. Locking the door behind me, I turned to face him.

"Caitlin told me you were running an errand." Brett glanced at my empty hands. "Did we run out of milk again?"

"Are you…" I gulped. "Are you and Nicole having an affair?"

"Suzanne." His face paled. "Why would you think that?"

I pursed my lips. "Why *wouldn't* I think that? You're with her all the time."

He reached forward, trying to take my hand. I pulled away.

"Suze," he said. "Nicole and I are *not* having an affair. I don't want Nicole—or anyone but you." His smile was wry. "And even if I did, Nicole wouldn't want *me*. She's engaged."

My mouth fell open. "She is?"

"Yeah. Her fiancé lives in Cupertino but he's making plans to move here soon." Brett's eyes brightened. "Nicole loves her career—and damn, she's brilliant at it. She has no intention of giving it up, but she's looking forward to marriage and kids, too." He smiled. "I mean, you saw her with Austin. She'll be a great mom."

I furrowed my brow. "Why have you never mentioned this?"

"I didn't know Nicole's romantic life was of interest to you." He tilted his head. "What's going on, babe?"

I thought about what Mom-not-Mom had said: that I should think about who I truly needed to talk to. She was right. The person I needed to talk to was right here.

But not because I needed him to come clean about some invented liaison. Rather, it was because Nicole was not Peggy. And Brett wasn't my dad.

He was Brett. He was the sweet college boy who'd comforted a drunk girl, a stranger, with no intentions beyond that. He was the guy everyone called on when they needed a helping hand. He was the guy *I'd* relied on, too—for years. For half my life, and then some.

"Brett." I swallowed. "Would you...hold me?"

He pulled me into his arms. I leaned my head against his neck and took slow, calming breaths.

"Okay," I said. "Let's sit down."

He brought me a glass of water, and as I sipped, I thought about all the things Brett didn't know. Like my sense that someone had been tailing me since we moved to Denver. Or about Chris's and my fight. My suspicion that Donna's accident wasn't an accident. The secrets I'd unearthed about my father's past.

Especially, Brett didn't know about Shelton Jr.'s connection with my family.

Explaining all of it meant I needed to go back to the beginning. So that's where I started: by confessing the reason I'd run out of Children's the first time.

I told Brett what I'd never told him before. About Peggy. About Mom-not-Mom and the other ghosts. I even told him about Carey. I told him every detail about the fall of 1979.

I talked and talked. And he listened. When I'd said all I had to say, he pulled me out of my seat, wrapping his arms around me.

"Can you forgive me for keeping all of this from you?" I whispered. "I was so scared, Brett—so scared I'd lose you if you…knew who I really am."

"Suze." He raised my chin, meeting my eye. "I know who you are. I've always known who you are."

"Did you know *this* about me?" I swallowed. "If I'd told you when we met that my mom called me her 'little seer,' would you have backed off? Never gone out with me again?"

He kissed me. "There was always something special about you. Something other girls didn't have. I knew it…and I loved it." He tapped my heart. "I knew—I *know*—who you are here. That's what counts."

I buried my head against his neck again. "Do you believe me?"

"Of course I believe you."

My voice muffled against his skin, I said, "I should have gone in the first time at Children's."

Brett tightened his arms around me. "I should have been there. Once Fides launches, I'll have a talk with upper management. We need more people on the team. We need work-life balance. If they refuse, I'll look for a different job."

I lifted my head. "You'd do that?"

"Absolutely."

I inhaled his familiar scent—coffee, leather, after-shave. "What do we do now?"

"I don't know," Brett said. "But I *do* know your fears are valid, Suze. Something's going on, and we need to figure out what." He ran his hands up and down my back. "Have you told the cops? Not about the ghosts—we know how *that* would go. But everything else...?"

"I've talked with the cops several times. They're not doing anything."

"But that was *before* you verified that someone is actually following you. You're not making it up." He was still, his eyes on mine. "You really think it's Austin's doctor? That she might have Stevie?"

"It's so irrational." I shook my head. "So wacky. Why would she jeopardize her career that way?"

"No idea," he said. "But if she's dangerous, the cops should have a talk with her."

Brett called the police, and an officer arrived. Not wanting to wake the kids, we ushered him quietly into the living room, where he took my report. I told him everything—omitting mention of ghosts and also leaving out the reason I'd been following Nicole. Instead, I provided the same excuse I'd given Nicole in her parking lot.

"I think I have everything I need," the officer said. "I'll file this, but I have to be honest, ma'am. There's really nothing here that implicates Dr. Morris in any way."

I nodded. "I understand that."

"You can try filing a restraining order against her. But since there was no imminent threat—and, significantly, you can't clearly identify her as the person following you—a restraining order might not go through."

I squeezed Brett's hand. "What do you suggest I do, officer?"

"We'll look into these developments." He capped his pen. "We let Shelton go because he gave us an address in LA where he says Darcy Powles is.

He provided contact information for himself, too. Very cooperative kid, to be honest. LAPD is following up, but we'll try to get Shelton back in, see what else he knows." He stood. "In the meantime, keep your doors locked. Be on the alert." His expression was kind. "We'll get to the bottom of it, Mrs. Archer."

48

— · —

2004

As I unlocked the deadbolt at Zoe's the next morning, implying welcome to anyone who walked in off the street, my hand trembled. I considered turning out the lights, scribbling a note saying, "Closed Indefinitely," posting it in the window—and running home to hide.

But no. This was my business. It might take time to see the results I craved from this venture—but I needed it, my consigning artists needed it, and I had to believe the public wanted it. I had to keep going.

Throughout the day, Brett phoned to check on me. I told him I was hanging in there. I had a decent showing of customers, including, late in the afternoon, someone who purchased one of my knives. The steady stream of customers was comforting. I didn't want to be alone in the store.

It was Friday and Austin had his after-school movement program until five. Just past four-thirty, the sun completed its descent behind the mountains. I turned off most of the display lights, leaving only one to guide my way when I exited through the back.

As I approached the front door to turn the deadbolt, a woman appeared. She was there so suddenly—one moment no one was outside, in the next a face loomed in the door's darkened windowpane—that I drew back, jerking my hand from the brass lock as if it were in a hot forge.

She pushed open the door. When I realized it was Tori Flynn, I sighed with relief.

Tori put a hand on my arm. "You look as if someone's been chasing you, Suzanne."

"I'm fine," I said. "It's just been a hectic day."

"Well, that's good, right? I'm glad business is brisk." She smiled. "I came by to show you more pieces."

Fishing in her portfolio, Tori laid several paintings on the checkout counter. She beckoned me. "What do you think?"

Standing beside her in the half-lit space, I studied the designs. Like all Tori's work, they featured vibrant paintings that looked like abstracts until you figured out what they represented.

But there was something different about these. As the images came into focus, I frowned. Instead of clock towers and dancers, in these paintings I saw images that twisted knots in my stomach.

A hunched, crying woman.

A snarling rat.

The retreating figure of a young girl—looking over her shoulder, eyes large with fear.

And in the final image, a gun. It was a pistol; I could make out its magazine and grip. Handless, it was aimed at a female figure who knelt on the ground, hands folded as if praying for mercy.

When I looked up, Tori was holding my favorite knife—the missing drop-point with the plum spacer. Her eyes, usually so warm, were blazing.

"Couldn't do it after all, huh?" she said.

I pressed a hand to my collarbone. "What?"

She tucked my knife into her bag. "You should have killed her, Suzanne. You had the chance and you blew it."

I stepped back. "It was *you*. What were you doing there?"

"I was watching out for you." Tori attempted touching my hand, but I recoiled. Her eyes narrowed. "You don't believe that?"

"Not for a second." I went behind the counter, which felt sheltering—until I remembered that my mother had died in this exact spot. I moved in front of it. Pushing aside Tori's artwork, setting a hand on the surface to steady myself, I asked, "Tori, what the hell is going on? Are you the one who's been following me?"

She rolled her eyes. "Jesus, Suzanne, how dumb are you? Of *course* I'm the one who's been following you."

I held up my hands. "But why? What do you want?"

Tori looked away. I stared at her. The shape of her face, the tilt of her nose and chin.

Viewing her profile in the low light, I saw it. I saw who she was.

"*You're* Peggy's daughter," I said slowly. "*You* were the baby she gave away."

Blinking back tears, Tori faced me. "I didn't know I was adopted until my adoptive mother died. I never felt like I belonged, but I couldn't figure out why. I didn't—" She choked on her words. "I didn't understand myself. I don't think my parents understood me, either. Pop died when I was in college. Ma and I never really got along." She swallowed. "After she died last summer, I went through her papers. And I found them. Dozens of letters from Peggy Hicks to me—her baby girl. Starting when I was born, ending just after Thanksgiving 1979. The last letter Peggy wrote me talked about her engagement to James Parry, a widowed father of two—and her high school boyfriend. She talked about the big, modern ranch house she hoped they'd buy. And her most cherished wish...that *I* could live with all of you someday."

Tears streamed down Tori's face. "Ma never told me about Peggy. Or about my father." She gave me a steely look. "*Your* father."

I shook my head. "You look nothing like him. And he said the baby wasn't his. Peggy said so, too."

"Not to me, she didn't. Not in those letters." Tori strode across the room. "I came to Denver to find out what happened, why her letters abruptly stopped coming. When I discovered Peggy's death notice, found the tiny article about her suicide—just a few newsprint inches, Suzanne, nothing like the miles of editorial space covering *your* mother's death—I had to confront him." She stepped toward me. "Then I learned James was out of the country. So I did some more digging—and I found you. I figured out a way to infiltrate your life." Her laughter was brassy. "It wasn't difficult."

I trembled. "Did you take Stevie? Did you steal my dog?"

"Of course I took your stupid, pain-in-the-ass dog."

"Is she alive?" I whispered.

"Jesus, you're pathetic," Tori sneered. "You really do care more about that dog than about your kids, don't you?" She shook her head. "You almost lost your own goddamn *daughter*—if not for sheer luck of you being in the right place at the right time and busting RJ. But you *still* care more about the dog."

My stomach clenched. "Did you get Shelton to get involved with Caitlin? How?"

"Easy. I found RJ when he came to Denver for his grandfather's funeral—*and* to extract a little revenge of his own on the Powles family." Indulgently, she smiled. "Kindred souls, I guess, RJ and me. So I befriended him. God knows the poor kid needed a friend." Her expression became almost maternal. "I was the only one he told that he'd killed that girl—an impulsive thing to reveal, but I think he needed to get it off his chest."

I felt the color drain from my face. "Darcy is dead?" I whispered. "But...the cops think she's in LA. That's what he told them."

"Well, he sent them on a wild goose chase, then." I gripped the counter as Tori went on, "After he confessed to me that he'd killed her, I agreed to take him in...as long as he did a little work for me in return. I knew he could do something I couldn't: seduce a lonely, vulnerable girl while simultaneously scaring the shit out of her mother."

My hands shook. "Where is he now?"

She shrugged. "Texas, probably. Although if he's smart, he's crossed into Mexico. It might be dangerous as hell across the border, but it's safer for him there than here."

I glanced at the paintings on the counter. "Did you even *do* this artwork, Tori?" I thought about the "friend" she'd made at Zoe's. "And is Daphne involved in all this?"

Tori wrinkled her nose. "No and no. Daphne's nothing. She was just a safeguard so you wouldn't get suspicious." She waved her hand at the paintings. "As for my 'work'—well, you can find anything on the internet, Suzanne." She lifted her shoulders, almost coyly. "Provided you have the money for it, which I did. I really do have a rich shithead of an ex—I didn't make *that* up—and in our divorce settlement, I took him to the cleaners." She waved her hand at the paintings. "Money made it easy to get this shit commissioned. And easy to transform myself into the cool, hip, not to mention *good* girl I needed to be for this charade. Like the good girl *you* are." Her tone was bitter. "*Such good girls. You*—and your goddamn mother, too."

"Don't you dare—" I shook a finger at her. "Don't you dare talk about my mother that way."

"Oh, she was such a saint, right? Saint Alex." Her laughter was sharp. "Saint Alex, who stole my father from my mother."

"She did not steal him," I protested. "They met years after Peggy and Dad broke up."

"Doesn't matter," Tori said. "Because of Alex, Peggy was denied the family she dreamed of. First when she was nineteen, and again two decades later. But *Alex* was never denied. *Alex* got everything she wanted." She snickered. "Well, she got what she deserved, in the end."

Slowly, Tori's hand went into her bag. "You're just like her," she said. "You think everything will always fall into place for you. Because it always does, right?" She took a step toward me. "Well, it's time to pay up, Suzanne Parry Archer."

I saw the nickel-plated gleam of the little pistol, shining in the single spotlight still turned on. Dashing forward, I knocked it from Tori's hand. It scuttled across the hardwood floor, landing under a raised display case.

Tori hadn't expected my blow. We both went to the floor, diving for the gun. I was taller and heavier, but Tori was fast. She whipped away from me, grabbing the pistol and rising to her feet. She stood above me, gun pointed at my chest.

"Drop it." I pulled out a pocketknife, wishing I'd had the foresight to keep my tanto close by. "Drop it now, or—"

"Or what? You'll somehow get up, come at me full frontal attack, and see how many jabs you can take with that pathetic little knife in an attempt to disarm me? And while you're making that noble effort, why wouldn't I shoot you?" Tori's lip curled. "Too bad you don't have the element of surprise you had on Nicole. And too bad you didn't take that opportunity when you had it, Suzanne. If you had, we'd be having a nice little heart-to-heart now. We'd be trying to figure out how to keep you from going to prison." Her eyes were cold and flat. "Instead—"

"Instead, you'll drop it right now," a voice behind her said.

A knife came up, pressed around Tori's throat.

49

— · —

2004

She'd come in so silently, I didn't hear her—and neither did Tori. I *still* hadn't gotten around to installing a bell. Thank God for that.

I hadn't heard her, but I'd seen her, and from my position on the floor I had the presence of mind not to betray her by darting my eyes in her direction. Instead I'd kept them fixed on Tori as she spoke her hateful words.

While Tori talked, Caitlin had slipped noiselessly—how she did it in those combat boots, I'll never know—toward the display case of my knives, which I'd left open after one was purchased. Selecting a particularly deadly looking clip-point, Caitlin had stepped behind Tori and pressed the blade to her neck.

"Drop it," Caitlin repeated.

The gun clattered to the floor. I scrambled to my feet, grabbed the gun and my phone, and dialed 911.

After the cops hauled Tori away and took statements from Caitlin and me, she and I sank onto the floor together. Side by side, we leaned against my mother's checkout counter.

"You were supposed to be at film club until five-fifteen." My voice was barely above a whisper. "I was picking you up."

"Yeah…I didn't feel like staying today."

"But why did you come here? I thought you hated Zoe's."

Caitlin looked around. "I wanted to see the artwork by that woman you told me about. The one who does paper cutting."

My arm felt weak as I lifted it to point across the space. "I have some of Evangeline's pieces hanging up, and a bin with others." My hand dropped to my lap. "Where did you learn to wield a knife like that?"

"Come on, Mom." She grimaced. "Don't you think I've picked up a few things along the way that *you* didn't specifically teach me?"

I thought about what Tori had called her—a lonely, vulnerable girl. "Caitlin," I said. "I wish…"

I closed my mouth. I didn't know how to go on.

She looked at me. "You wish what?"

"Are you lonely, Cait?" I shook my head. "I thought you were settling in. You've joined clubs. You go to movies. You went to a Halloween party."

She stared at her knees. "Yeah, no. I went out that night—but not to a party."

"I saw you…"

Caitlin raised her head, nostrils flaring. "You were *following* me?"

"Not on purpose. But I saw you turn into a yard, go through the back gate."

She blinked. "I was spying. I was watching the party…from the outside."

"Oh, Caitlin." I put an arm around her. "What about the clubs?"

She looked down, then back at me. "I lied about those. I figured you'd get off my case if I said I was doing stuff at school." Her lips twitched. "Although fencing *does* sound kinda cool."

"It does." I paused. "And going to the mall? And the shirt you borrowed?"

"I didn't *borrow* it." Her eyes darted to the side. "I just figured you'd leave me alone if I said that."

I stroked her hair, thinking about her wandering the streets alone. Thinking about Tori's artwork, the scared eyes of a girl. "How did you get involved with RJ?"

Caitlin huddled into herself. "He was hanging around school one day after final bell. We got to talking. He was nice to me when..." She looked away. "...when nobody else was."

In my mind's eye, I saw Carey—here in Zoe's, as he'd been all those years ago. Carey, who was misguided but not malicious. Perhaps I'd been luckier than I could've fathomed back then.

I thought about how I'd wanted Caitlin to be more like me—a quiet girl who loved music and hanging out with her mother—and yet also *not* like me, a popular girl who always had something fun to do. But Caitlin was neither of those people. She was entirely her own self. And she was more badass than I'd realized.

"I'm sorry." I bit my lip. "You have a mom who's supposed to be looking out for you, and..." I looked at my hands. "I haven't done a very good job of that."

Caitlin didn't reply. She stood, stepping behind the counter. Rising, I joined her.

"Your mother died here, didn't she?" Caitlin said. "Here in Zoe's."

I stared at her. "How did you know that? Did you read the articles from when I opened the shop?"

She shook her head. "I just had a feeling. What happened to her, Mom?"

I looked down. "What happened was...Alex Parry lived a full life. Everything she did, she did intentionally. She made sure her life was meaningful."

"But what *happened*?"

"Cait." I placed both palms flat on the counter. "I'm making you a promise: someday, I *will* talk with you about this." My eyes meeting hers, I said, "I'll tell you everything. But for now, all you need to know about your grandmother is that she made sure the people she loved knew it." I took a single step closer to my daughter. "Every day, she let me know I was loved."

Caitlin waited.

"I want you to know you're loved, too," I went on. "You are very, very loved." I closed my eyes, then opened them. "I love you, honeypie. You're my everything."

Brett came in then. He drew us both into his arms.

"My girls," he breathed. "My beautiful, wonderful girls." He pressed his cheek against Caitlin's, then against mine. "I'm beyond grateful that you're both safe."

"Austin's okay?" I asked him.

"Yes, I called school. They're waiting with him in the office until we can pick him up."

My throat dry, I asked, "And Stevie? Did the cops tell you anything?"

"They found her in Tori's apartment," Brett said. "She's at the Denver Animal Shelter, being treated by a vet."

Relief flooded through me as Brett entwined Caitlin's left and my right fingers into his strong, warm, hands. "Come, my ladies," he said. "Let's get Austin. Then let's go get our dog."

50

2004

Tori was charged with a Class 5 felony for threatening another with a deadly weapon, a Class 4 felony for being an accessory after the fact to murder, and a Class 1 misdemeanor for animal abuse. If convicted, she'd serve up to ten years in prison, although her sentence could be mitigated because she led the authorities to Robert Shelton Jr. They found him at Rosalie's apartment in Dallas, apprehended him, and extradited him to Colorado. He was being held without bond, awaiting trial for the strangulation death of Darcy Powles, whose body he confessed to dumping in a remote section of the South Platte River. When I heard that, I sobbed, thinking about that innocent girl—and all innocent girls, and what can so easily happen to them.

Both Tori and Shelton Jr. were questioned about Donna's hit-and-run, but both denied involvement. Tori tried telling the judge that I'd threatened Nicole but since there was zero evidence of that, he dismissed her words. She was released on bond and we had a restraining order against her. Nonetheless, I was watching my back wherever I went.

When the cops found Stevie, she was dehydrated, malnourished, and astonishingly thin—but alive. The vet said she'd recover with plenty of love and gentle care, although she might never be as robust as before her ordeal.

I loved on her every second I could. And when I wasn't loving on Stevie, I was loving on my kids.

Three days later, Austin's evaluation results came in. Dr. Morris asked Brett and me to meet her in person to discuss them. I hated the idea of facing her, afraid of what she'd think if she knew about my accusations against her. Had the cops been in touch with her? I could only hope they hadn't.

Dr. Morris gave no indication that they had. She smiled warmly, shook our hands, and handed us a stack of paper-clipped pages. "You can look at those in detail later, but first I want to say that Austin is a delightful child. He's smart, creative, and funny. And I can tell by the way he talks about both of you that he knows he's well-loved."

Brett and I exchanged smiles, waiting for her to go on.

"As you've been told, Austin doesn't meet the criteria for an autism diagnosis. He does have ADHD, as has been diagnosed, as well as moderate anxiety."

Brett and I nodded. None of this was news.

The doctor looked from one of us to the other. "But there's something else I suspect. Have either of you heard of Smith-Lemli-Opitz Syndrome?"

I shook my head. "That's a mouthful."

"Generally, it's abbreviated SLOS." She pronounced it to rhyme with *gloss*. "It's a developmental disorder that manifests behaviorally in similar ways to autism. Physical characteristics vary, but in most affected children it's obvious because of those characteristics—often a small nose and jaw, large ears, narrow forehead, and slight stature. None of which Austin has, except being small for his age." She paused. "Some affected individuals, however, have only mild physical traits. For such patients, a SLOS diagnosis often isn't made until a child is older." She looked at me. "Does Austin have webbed second and third toes? Did he ever have an extra digit?"

"No extra digit," I said. "But he does have the webbed toes."

She nodded. "Virtually everyone with SLOS has that trait. I'm surprised no one ever mentioned it."

Dr. Morris explained that many people with SLOS have severe cases, but some are mild. First identified in 1964, SLOS is a rare genetic condition in which both parents have to carry a certain gene—and even if they do, their chance of having a child with the condition is only one in four. When it does manifest, fetal development is affected, which leads to complications after birth.

"So it's genetic but it comes from both sides?" I asked.

"That's exactly right," Dr. Morris said.

I thought about my hunch that whatever was going on with Austin, my dad had the same condition. Did my father have webbed second and third toes? I had no idea. I'd lived with Dad for seventeen years, but I couldn't remember an occasion when I'd closely examined his toes.

In any case, it didn't matter. That realization came to me swiftly, like sunlight breaking through during a storm that had been forecast to last all day. The important thing wasn't where Austin's condition came from. The important thing was that we now had knowledge we could work with.

As if reading my thoughts, Brett asked, "So what do we do?"

"I suggest that all of you undergo genetic testing," Dr. Morris said. "Doing so will provide a definitive diagnosis of SLOS, if that's what it is." She glanced at some papers on her desk. "From a behavioral health standpoint, I highly recommend therapy. We can work to identify Austin's triggers and help him manage stressful situations." She clasped her hands together. "We're talking about lifelong learning. Ideally, all of you will learn to celebrate his strengths and manage his challenges."

Dr. Morris looked at Brett, then at me. "Typically at this point, I'd pass the patient to a different provider. For the most part, I do evaluations. But I feel Austin connected remarkably well with me. I can make space for him in my caseload, if you'd like."

Brett turned to me. I kept my eyes on his but I could feel the doctor looking at me, too. I recalled how terrified I'd been upon meeting Dr. Morris, seeing her physical resemblance to Peggy. How even now, seeing her each week would likely bring Peggy to mind.

But Dr. Morris and Austin *had* connected. Their work together had a high probability of success.

Besides, Austin was not Christopher. And despite their resemblance, Patricia Morris wasn't the daughter of Peggy Hicks. That was Tori.

I'd been unable to see it. Instead, my intuition, which I'd always so heavily relied upon, had been overpowered by fear.

No more. Squeezing Brett's hand, I faced Dr. Morris. "That sounds like an excellent plan," I said. "Thank you."

Puzzle pieces were falling into place. But there were conversations yet to be had.

"Chris," I said when my brother answered the phone. "Can I see you?"

We met at a coffee shop on South Broadway. "I'm sorry for what you and Caitlin went through," he said before I opened my mouth. "Thank God you're both all right."

"Thanks. I'm here to apologize, too." I stirred cream into my coffee. "When I told you about Peggy, I wanted to hurt you. That was wrong, and I'm sorry."

He nodded. "And I'm sorry Dad made you carry such burdens all these years."

"You were so little. We wanted to spare you." I looked away, then back at him.

"I don't know, Suze." His face tightened. "I'll be honest...when you said I was 'spared,' that stung. I put on a good show. But..." He adjusted his tie, then dropped one hand onto the table. "Despite all you've been through, the truth is that I envy you, Suze."

I thought about how Chris lived alone in his fancy apartment. How he bought himself expensive toys, did whatever he wanted to do. How he dated but didn't let anyone get close.

I put my hand on his. "I'm listening."

"I could never figure it out," he said. "But there was always something missing. I didn't know what it was until you moved here. I might have felt an inkling of it when your kids were little, but I saw all of you so rarely. Here, though, when I saw you with your kids, especially with Austin..." He blinked. "Linda was great. But what...who...was missing, my whole life...was Mom." His voice cracking, he added, "And I didn't even know it."

Tightening my hand around his, I thought about his pain. And about Tori, who'd said pretty much the same thing about her unknown, absent mother. And about Dad—who never said it but who must have felt the void of his missing mother.

A woman doesn't have to give birth to a child to love and nurture that child. Linda and Grandma Parry were both proof of that. And giving birth doesn't guarantee a woman *can* love and nurture a child. Claranna Lewis was proof of *that*.

Still, for most people, biology pulls tightly on the heart's leash.

"Dad tried to make everything great for me," Chris said. "Trips. Toys and electronics. Tickets to sporting events. Anything I wanted. Even..." He swallowed hard. "Even trying to acquire a replacement mother for me."

"I think Dad really loved Linda," I said. "They were together a long time. And he was so devoted to her at the end."

"I'm not talking about Linda," Chris replied.

My throat constricted. I set down the muffin I'd been about to bite into.

Chris took the lid off his black coffee, blowing on it. "I don't remember Peggy being as...unstable...as you say." Steam rose from his cup. "I only remember her being kind to me. So attentive, so affectionate."

"That's the thing. She was." I glanced out the window at the chilly December day. "But she'd lost Dad when they were young, made a mistake breaking up with him. Then she lost her children, one after the other. Finally, she knew her mother was dying." I sipped coffee. "Suddenly, there *you* were—this adorable reimagining of Dad, this 'what could have been' child." I heard the bitterness in my laugh. "*I* certainly wasn't that child—I was too much like Mom. But you...it's easy to see how she made the leap. Easy to see why she became obsessed with you. Why she wanted you—at any cost."

I felt a breeze then, though the coffee shop's door was closed. Was it Peggy? I closed my eyes, expecting to sense her gruesome head poking around a corner or her gaze on me from among the line of customers at the counter. But she was absent. Maybe, I thought, opening my eyes, Peggy wouldn't come around again. Maybe when I'd shown her in Cheesman that I wasn't afraid, I discovered a way to keep her from me—forever.

Or maybe it was something else. All those years ago, Peggy had told me she wanted forgiveness. I'd never forgive her, but considering how close I came in Nicole's parking lot to making a deadly mistake—how I'd let fear drive me—maybe I could understand how Peggy's obsession led her to making such irrational, heinous decisions.

"I wish..." Chris paused. "I know I was too little to understand back then. But I wish there'd been a way for me to...share your pain. Make it easier on you."

"Chris." I bit my lip. "You and I were just kids. We didn't know how to talk about what happened." I reached forward, taking his hand again. "But we can be here for each other now. It's not too late."

I rose, and so did Chris. Taking him in my arms, amid the clinking china and churning espresso machines, I listened to his heartbeat. I felt his small self and my—despite all I had to carry in those days—not much bigger self.

Closing my eyes, I embraced the warmth of my brother, the truth of him.

I let myself feel comforted. And hoped that I, in turn, could comfort him.

51

— · —

2004

On Christmas Eve, Brett, the kids, and I drove downtown to Chris's high-rise apartment building. We walked into his penthouse to find a beautifully decorated tree—no doubt the woman of the hour, whoever she was, had helped Chris, though no such woman was in attendance. He never cooked or baked, but he'd acquired a dining room table full of fancy appetizers and gorgeously piped sugar cookies, the latter of which both kids dove for.

As I filled a plate with apps, I glanced around. There was plenty of tasteful artwork on the walls, including a wooden sculpture on a lighted shelf, a piece Chris had bought on opening night at Zoe's, made by an artist named Sharon Lee. There were also several vases filled with holiday themed bouquets—a nice touch.

But there wasn't a gun in sight.

Face covered in frosting, Austin glanced at a bare spot on the wall. "Uncle Chris," he said. "Where's the gun?"

Chris used a napkin to gently wipe frosting from Austin's chin. "Locked away, bud. Sorry."

"But I wanted to show it to Dad."

"Not tonight, okay? Let's focus on the food and..." Chris nodded toward the tree. "There might be a few things under there for you."

As Austin dove for the presents under the tree, Brett stepped to the west wall of the living room, which consisted entirely of windows and a sliding glass door to the balcony. I watched him take in the million-dollar view.

"Incredible," Brett said. "This is some place, Chris."

Grinning, my brother jabbed his thumb to the right. "The unit next door is vacant, if you want to be my neighbor."

My father, who was decked out in a comically patterned sweater—neon green and red checkerboard—turned to me. "Can I speak with you, Suze? Alone?"

I nodded, setting my plate on a side table and following him to Chris's study.

Dad closed the door behind us. He seated himself on the leather sofa and patted it. "Come here. I have to tell you something. Several somethings."

I perched beside him. "I'm listening."

"While Tori was being held, I visited her," Dad said. "I told her I was willing to take a DNA test to prove or disprove my paternity." He cleared his throat. "She admitted she's already tested both my DNA and yours. When I asked her how that was accomplished, she said she'd worked in microbiology and still had friends in the industry who'd helped her out." He sipped his scotch. "She said someday we'll all be able to spit into a vial, send it off, and smoke out a slew of long-lost relatives." He paused, as if considering it. "The technology isn't yet there but if you have connections..." He shifted toward me. "When I asked how she acquired your DNA and mine, she refused to explain. Just said she had methods."

I nodded. Likely Tori had acquired my DNA from Zoe's; I left plenty of empty Diet Coke cans lying around. And now that I knew how stealthily she got around, it wouldn't surprise me to learn she'd broken into Dad's house and stolen something of his to have tested.

"She tested our DNA," I said. "And...?"

Dad rattled the ice in his glass. "She's not related to us. I am not her father. She said she was stunned, because Peggy's letters—a good number of them—indicated I was." He twirled the glass in his hand. "I suspect Peggy was a conflicted communicator. A conflicted character, overall. Perhaps Peggy didn't know who the baby's father was. In those days, not knowing something like that was regarded as incredibly immoral."

I shook my head. "I don't understand why Tori was so angry, when you're not at fault."

Dad shifted upright. "Tori and I talked at length. I'm by no means excusing her, but when she confronted you, she was at the end of her rope. She'd seen this search as validation of her very being. And when the information eluded her, especially after she'd been so sure, she became embittered. It fueled her fury."

"All these secrets," I murmured. "It's sad. It seems things would have turned out differently without so many secrets." I thought about my own secrets, how long I'd tucked them inside. "If the relative who raised Tori had told her about Peggy, allowed Tori and Peggy to have a relationship, think how that would've changed things for both of them."

"Perhaps." Dad glanced down. "But perhaps some secrets are best kept that way."

I studied his profile. I wanted so badly to tell him I'd found his long-lost sister. Facilitate a reconciliation. But it wasn't my place to release that caged bird of knowledge into the world. Claranna could do that, if she wanted to. As for Dad, if he wanted to know, he'd have searched himself.

Holding up his glass, Dad turned to me. I clinked my glass against his.

"To denouement," he said. "And the inevitable inception that ensues."

I sipped. "To both of those."

He leaned back on the overstuffed sofa. "This time of year inevitably leads to introspection, doesn't it? It leaves lingering thoughts of reflection and regret." He stared into his glass. "Benjamin Disraeli, the British states-man, once said, 'Youth is a blunder, manhood a struggle, and old age a regret.' But I believe all three—blunders, struggles, and regrets—can occur at any age."

I gazed at the carpet. "You got that right."

"Do you have regrets, Suzanne?" Dad asked.

"Sure." I paused, then looked up at him. "I guess...I was pretty mean to you for a lot of years, wasn't I?" I swallowed the lump in my throat. "I was so mad at you for selling Mom's house."

"I know you were. I wish I could've made a divergent decision, but to me it felt like the only option."

I nodded. Neither of us had quite apologized, but maybe we came close.

Dad took a drink. "I look back and think, had I made different choices, might circumstances have turned out differently?" He furrowed his brow. "Yes, they *might* have...but perhaps what was meant to occur did."

I wasn't sure I agreed, but I let it go. Something I'd learned was that trying to change other people, wishing they were someone else, was an exercise in futility. As true as that was for Austin, for Caitlin, it was also true for Dad.

"Suzanne," Dad said. "I do have one overwhelming, overarching regret."

When he didn't continue, I prompted, "And that is...?"

He took a breath. "It's that your mother likely died without..." His voice broke. "...without knowing how deeply I loved her."

"Dad." I didn't know what to say.

He met my eye. "Alex was the love of my life. I loved Linda, of course; she was the perfect partner for my later years. When Peggy and I were kids, I loved her in that worshiping way kids love one another. And after losing Alex so suddenly, so savagely, I couldn't imagine being alone. Peggy prevented that—for a while." He blinked again. "But I've never loved anyone the way I loved Alex. I should have shown it more. I should've showered Alex with affection. Should've declared my devotion daily." Dad put a hand on mine. "There was no one like Alex...with the exception of you."

On my other side, I felt a gentle touch on my shoulder. "Thank you for saying that," I told Dad. "It means the world to me."

To *us*, I thought—Mom and me both. Her light touch brushed across my hair, as if in agreement.

"I've been thinking," Dad said. "Zoe is still in your old room at my house. Would you enjoy having her for the store? I could…" He paused. "I could deliver her. If you'd like to meet me at Zoe's, we could install her."

I stared at him. "I thought you didn't approve of the new Zoe's."

He fiddled with the hem of his ridiculous sweater. "I've given it considerable contemplation. It's clear how much the store means to you. And your mom would be euphoric over your accomplishment." He raised his eyebrows. "So would you like to have Zoe?"

"I'd love that. Thank you."

He stood, and I joined him. "Let's rendezvous with our relatives," Dad said.

Everyone was gathered near the floor-to-ceiling windows, watching the sun set behind the snow-capped Rockies. Dad shuffled next to me. Our sides lightly pressed together, he spoke quietly. "Your mom would cherish this moment, Suze. I wish she was here."

On my opposite side, through the silk of my blouse, I felt her touch. "She *is* here," I said softly.

Dad didn't answer, but he looked at me and smiled. I went on, "And it's good to be here with you, too, Dad."

It *was* good. Still, as the sky darkened, I could have sworn I saw someone outside on the balcony. Long, light hair; dark clothing. A footfall, a silent creep toward the vacant unit to the right. Three steps until the figure disappeared from view.

I put a hand to my collarbone.

One, two, three.

Author's Note & Acknowledgements

Friends, this one has been a long haul.

The themes of *Anyone But Her*—grief, knowledge, intuition—are likely apparent. For me, this novel is also about persistence. The version in your hands is unlike the first, second, third, or even fourth full draft I wrote. Each complete rewrite contributed to making *Anyone But Her* into the story it was always meant to be. For my readers who have patiently waited (years!) for a new novel, I hope you feel it's worth the wait.

My heartfelt gratitude to early readers Sara Alan, Jillian Cantor, Leslie Lindsay, Amy Meyerson, Kate Moretti, Holly Robinson, Mark Stevens, and Sonja Yoerg. Shana Kelly has the sharpest editorial eye in the business, and I'm thankful for her friendship and insight. Thanks to all those in the traditional publishing world who championed my previous titles. Much appreciation to my agent, Jill Marsal, for facilitating an audiobook deal for *Anyone But Her*, bringing the novel to an ever-widening audience.

I'm nearly as passionate about research as I am about writing—and as always, I relished a deep dive into books, photographs, newspaper articles, field trips, and especially the many conversations that bring a story to life. Mediums Ali Sweeney and Diane Mayer heightened my understanding about clairvoyance. Todd Yokley provided a fascinating look at the process of refurbishing and rehandling old knives. Gratitude to Marni Goldman for helping me experience SLOS through a parent's eyes. The Facebook group Rainbow Music Hall (yes, there is such a group) shared memories" of concerts in that venue, including Prince's November 1979 show. Many thanks to Marcia Goldstein and the Denver Architecture Foundation for an insider's look at Denver East High and its rich history. East High alums Michel Brossmer, Judy Cardenas, Heidi Elliott, Jennifer Jones, Tommy Kaui Nahulu, Diane Mahoney, and Tracy Wohlgenant graciously shared high school memories. To all the East community, my apologies for fictionalizing teachers, students, and certain details as necessary for the storyline. Additional poetic license and unintentional errors anywhere in the book are entirely mine.

I'm grateful for my writing communities, particularly Lighthouse Writers Workshop and Sisters in Crime-Colorado. Thank you to the *Denver Noir* crew, especially Twanna LaTrice Hill and Mathangi Subramanian, as well as writer pals Jennifer Kincheloe and Maura Weiler, for their support. Much gratitude to Amy Rivers and Helen Starbuck for sharing knowledge about indie publishing.

Evil stepmothers are abundant in literature, making me particularly grateful for my kind, generous stepmother, Sandra Theunick. Thank you to Jane, Dennis, and Charlie for being the best trio a mom could ask for, with special thanks to Dennis for the creation of supporting graphics. So much love for my husband, Sammy, who never doubted I could do it. Many thanks to Mary Elliott, Sue Fisher, and Mary Hauser for love, loyalty, and the ability to refrain from asking too often, "So, any news on the book?"

Finally—but nowhere near last in my heart—thank you to the readers, book clubs, booksellers, librarians, members of the media, podcasters, friends, neighbors, and all who read books, recommend books, write reviews, and support the writing community. I believe I speak for authors everywhere when I say we couldn't do it without you—and you are the reason we keep going.

Questions for Discussion

1. The novel opens with a visit from the ghost of Suzanne's mother, Alex, warning Suzanne about her father's new girlfriend, Peggy. Alex later expresses regret for tasking Suzanne with investigating Peggy; nonetheless, her request places a heavy burden on her grieving child. Do you feel Alex's actions were unavoidable? Are they justified?

2. Do you believe in ghosts or spirits? Have you experienced clairvoyance, visits from deceased loved ones, or other incidents from a realm beyond our physical world? If so, how did you react?

3. When considering whether to partner with Renee and open the new Zoe's, Suzanne recalls, "My mother used to say that what we feared most was what we most needed to confront. I knew what I feared now: trying something new and having it turn into a sinking ship." Describe a time when you confronted something you feared. How did things turn out? How did you later feel about the experience?

4. Adolescence is a crucial time in most people's lives, but when it's coupled with grief or other emotional upheaval, the impact can last a lifetime. What challenging circumstances from your adolescence stand out to you? How have these circumstances affected who you are today?

5. Compare Suzanne's relationship with her mother, Alex, to that with her daughter, Caitlin. Do you think Suzanne's expectations of Caitlin are too high? How does Suzanne's own adolescence affect her ability to mother a teen girl?

6. Raising a neurodivergent child poses both rewards and challenges, but it's not uncommon for parents of neurodivergent children to feel doubt about their parenting abilities. In what ways does Suzanne try to compensate for her insecurities about raising Austin? What do you think she learns via the experiences of pursuing her family's genetic history and receiving Austin's eventual diagnosis?

7. Discuss Suzanne and Brett's marriage. How does their relationship change over the course of the novel?

8. Suzanne says to Donna that "...the hardest part isn't figuring something out. The hardest part is figuring out what to *do* with the knowledge, once you have it." Describe a time when you were unsure what steps to take regarding something you discovered. What did you decide to do about the information you'd gleaned?

9. How do you feel about Peggy? About her daughter? In what ways do they create their own circumstances, and in what ways does fate deal them an unfair blow?

10. Do you believe things happen for a reason, or do we have control over the events of our lives? What experiences, people, and principles have shaped your views on this issue?

ABOUT THE AUTHOR

Cynthia Swanson writes psychological suspense, often using historical settings. Cynthia's debut novel, *The Bookseller*, was a *New York Times* bestseller, an Indie Next selection, and the winner of the WILLA Literary Award for Historical Fiction. *The Bookseller* has been translated into eighteen languages. Cynthia's second novel, *The Glass Forest*, was a *USA Today* bestseller and has been translated into seven languages. Cynthia is the editor of the Colorado Book Award winning anthology *Denver Noir*, part of Akashic Books' celebrated *Noir* series. Cynthia lives with her family in Denver. Find Cynthia online at www.cynthiaswansonauthor.com and follow her on Instagram (cynswanauthor), Facebook (Cynthia Swanson Author), Bluesky (cynswanauthor), and Substack (The What If Journal).

A Note to Readers

Thank you for reading *Anyone But Her*. I'm honored that you chose to spend your valuable time discovering Suzanne's story.

If you enjoyed this book, please consider leaving a review. Find review links at www.cynthiaswansonauthor.com/anyone-but-her, or you can scan here:

I also hope you'll stay in touch by signing up for my newsletter, *The What If Journal*—my home for sharing reflections, happenings, and possibilities.

Sign up at www.cynthiaswansonauthor.com/the-what-if-journal or scan here:

— Cynthia
S